ALMOST IMMORTAL

A TALE OF TWO BROTHERS

A Novel
by
Stan Hill

RED OAK PRESS
White Bear Lake, Minnesota

Almost Immortal
A Tale of Two Brothers

Copyright   1996 by Stan Hill

For information address Stan Hill, President, Red Oak Press, P.O. Box 10614, White Bear Lake, Minnesota 55110-0614.

Printed in United States of America
99 98 97 96   10 9 8 7 6 5 4 3 2 1

Cover Design and Art: Steve Harmon
Editor: Douglas C. Benson
Copy Editor: Doris H. Hill
Printer: Bethany Fellowship
Photo: Back Cover: Lark Gilmer

J. Stanley Hill 1914-
        Almost Immortal

1. Fiction   2. Geography, East-Central Minnesota

ISBN 0-9640439-2-0

Another Book by Stan Hill: *Confessions of an 80-Year-Old Boy*

To Doris

"They never fail who die in a great cause."

--*Lord Byron*

"In this world it is not what we take up, but what we give up, that makes us rich."

--*Henry Ward Beecher*

"Public confidence in the integrity of the Government is indispensable to faith in democracy; and when we lose faith in the system, we have lost faith in everything we fight and spend for."

--*Adlai E. Stevenson*

"The American wage earner and the American housewife are a lot better economists than most economists care to admit. They know that a government big enough to give you everything you want is a government big enough to take from you everything you have."

--*Gerald R. Ford*

Table of Contents

Almost Immortal

Acknowledgements

I would like to extend my appreciation to my editor, Doug Benson; my compositor, Erin Dwyer; my copy editor, Doris Hill; and my artist, Steve Harmon. All of these dedicated people have contributed their expertise to make *Almost Immortal* a quality book.

Stan Hill

Preface

   This book was born of my deep conviction that the kind of life a person leads, and the level of happiness and fulfillment achieved, is very heavily dependent on her or his beliefs, values and outlook on life, Of course, people with strong, positive beliefs are all subject to the vagaries of fortune; but, they are not spoiled by good fortune, nor are they disillusioned or defeated by bad fortune. Dramatic examples of the latter statement are the survivors of the holocaust, many of whom went on to live triumphantly and victoriously. In the story that follows, the twins' parents have markedly different values. The mother has exceptionally good values and beliefs; she is loving, lovable, honest, generous and accepting--a giver. The father, on the other hand, has equally bad values and beliefs; he is greedy, grasping, bigoted, selfish, deceitful and strong in his beliefs that his approach to life is the only way to survive and "succeed"--a taker. One twin is strongly attached to his mother and accepts her beliefs and values with a whole heart. The other admires his father and tries to be like him.

   In the book I purposely chose identical twin brothers who become the good twin and the bad twin. I did this to make my illustration more dramatic. Most people believe that identical twins live the same kind of lives, a belief born of both their own observations and the striking similarities noted by professional researchers. They include examples of identical twins separated at birth and raised by different parents. I agree that, since both twins have identical genomes (collection of genes) they will certainly look alike, have identical general intelligence, both be right brained, left brained or ambi-brained, and so on, to the extent that genes shape our lives. For example, one identical twin can't be a brilliant brain surgeon while the other doesn't have enough learning skills to do other than the most menial work. But I still believe identical twins can live totally different lives.

As you read this book, I hope you will agree that I am faithful to my own beliefs, as just stated.

I must add that any opinions our hero expresses concerning taxes or other business matters are only his personal opinions. The reader must not construe them as advice on which he or she can rely.

Stan Hill
December, 1996

Chapter One
The Accident

Timothy John Hamilton sat by himself during breakfast at Kula Lodge, one-third of the way down the steep, winding road that leads from the top of Haleakala, the famous 10,000-foot volcano to the distant shore of Maui's north coast. The other 12 bikers sat at nearby tables, laughing and chatting, already exhilarated by the first part of this exciting ride on which they would coast almost all of the snaking roads 38-mile path to the sea.

When Tim had taken this breath-taking ride three years ago, his usually exuberant personality had responded similarly to the adventure and the fantastic scenery. This time the experience did nothing to pull him out of his emotional funk. He had plenty of reasons to feel low. His mother and father had been killed two weeks ago in an auto accident. Then last night he had had a dreadful nightmare in which he watched helplessly as his beloved identical twin brother fell over the rail of a cruise ship in the dark. He didn't know whether it was suicide or an accident, but he was certain that his brother was dead.

On top of those emotional burdens, Tim also was struggling with the worst dilemma of his life. As Senior Vice President of the Cornerstone National Life Insurance Company, he was responsible for the $12 billion dollars that over four million policyholders had trustfully placed in Cornerstone's care. His mission was to earn for them the highest rate of return consistent with the safety of their investment. The higher the risk, the greater the return, and vice versa. He had plenty of sharp managers to do the actual buying and selling of securities. His job, with the advice and consent of the Cornerstone directors who sat on the Investment Committee, was to determine where to draw the line, to decide how great a degree of risk was appropriate.

In the last few years he had seen his peers in other good life insurance companies take far more risk than he felt was prudent. Jack Fredericks, Cornerstone's marketing vice present was putting tremendous pressure on him to follow their lead. Jack's many challenges were always the same: "Tim, when are you going to have the courage to go after these higher yield securities? Your old fashioned investment ideas are making it impossible for my sales people to compete!" At first it seemed like the kidding of a long-time friend, but each time Jack approached Tim he seemed more serious. The last time he sounded grim. Then came the call from John Stuart Symington, Cornerstone's board chairman, president and CEO: "Tim you should know that Jack has asked me to put the issue of investment strategy on next Monday morning's Management Committee agenda. He considers it such a serious matter, I've also called a special meeting of the Investment Committee at noon that same day. Of course, I would expect you to be present at both meetings, and I know you will come well prepared to support your position. Good luck!"

The events of those meetings three days ago were as vivid in his mind as if they had just taken place: At the Management Committee meeting Jack was concise, eloquent and persuasive in stating his case: "Good morning ladies and gentlemen! Cornerstone faces a serious problem: We are losing sales because our products are priced too high. I don't blame the actuaries, they have to price the products on the basis of Cornerstone's mortality, expense and investment performance. Thanks to Fred Johnson, one of our actuaries, I have this chart to show how we compare on these three vital numbers with a dozen well-managed, prestigious companies with whom we must compete. You can see that our mortality rates are in line and our expenses are on the low side, thanks to our outstanding managers. It is our investment performance that has gotten us into trouble. It is a full 175 basis points lower than the **average** of our competitors. Folks, that's 210 *million* dollars *less* than we should be earning, *every year!* I've always had the greatest respect for my good friend, Tim Hamilton, and I still do; but our investment policies are no longer what they should be in the world of the 90's. We must have more aggressive investment policy to survive in this modern age. We have already lost over 20 of our *best* sales people to companies with more aggressive investment strategies. Unless we do something shortly, Cornerstone will no longer remain the great company it has become. We will be faced with downsizing, lay-offs at *all* levels and in *all* departments."

Looking around the table, Tim could see that Jack's presentation had hit its target. The listeners' facial expressions had evolved from interest, to concern, to worry, to outright fear. Jack was a master salesman: he had hit these people at their three most vulnerable points: their prestige, their pocketbooks, and their fervent desire to avoid laying off their employees. None had questions or comments. They just sat glumly. Tim felt overwhelmed. He had lost the battle even before he had a chance to make his rebuttal. He was alerted by John Symington's question: "Tim, do you wish to state your position?"

Tim delivered his rebuttal, but it lacked the fire and passion of Jack's: "As you all know, investment yields are inversely related to risk. These companies with the apparently better performances are investing significant, even major, portions of their assets in what we call "junk bonds" which are bonds of lower quality than the lowest acceptable investment quality. They are also buying large quantities of poorer grade mortgages: shopping centers that are poorly located, lack managements with good track records, or have other elements that make them unsatisfactory for our portfolio. Our four million policyholders have placed their trust in us. That, my friends, is a sacred trust, which we must never violate. I'm convinced that these companies with the exceptionally good-looking investment performance will run into serious trouble, and we won't have to wait many years to see it happen."

This time several of the vice-presidents had a question: "Can all of these good companies be wrong?" It was more a statement of their opinion than a question; but Tim felt obligated to reply: "I can understand how you feel; but the fundamentals of investing have not changed. My peers in these other companies have caved in to the same kind of pressure I feel today; and my conscience and, hopefully, good judgement won't let me do that."

Then President Symington had said, "This is a very serious decision I must make. I would like advice from all of you. Please call my secretary before noon today and give her your answer to this vital question: Should Cornerstone adopt a more aggressive investment policy?"

The Investment Committee meeting had been virtually a replay of the morning's devastating ordeal. Jack Frederick had changed only the last sentence of his statement: "We will see Cornerstone's prestigious position diminish until none of us can feel the pride that we do today." Again he had hit his mark. Only J. Frederick Thompson, president of the city's leading investment management firm supported Tim. After President Symington had adjourned the meeting he had asked Tim to come to his office. His statement to Tim had been compassionate but quite clear: "Tim, in all my years in this job this is the most difficult position I have ever been in. I understand your feelings and I respect your judgement as an investment officer. You have played a significant role in making Cornerstone the great company it is today, and I'm very grateful to you for that. But, as you know, we have moved into a new era where competition for people's investment dollar is nothing short of fierce. You know that I've taken advice from many people who are as loyal to Cornerstone as you and I are. Despite my great admiration, respect and even affection for you, I am forced to tell you this: Unless you can adopt a more aggressive investment strategy, I'll be forced to replace you with someone who can. I'll have my secretary reserve a large suite for you and Becky at the beautiful Maui Hill resort in Kihei. Please be Cornerstone's guest there for a week to relax and take time to think carefully about your position. May I wish you the best."

Tim and Becky had left for Maui the next day. The Maui Hill resort was just as lovely as they had expected. They had a large three-bedroom unit overlooking the ocean. That spectacular view was framed in impeccably manicured, rolling green lawns punctuated with stately royal palm trees, tropical gardens and patches of darker green ground cover. Immediately below them was a large, spotless swimming pool, and not too far away were two immaculate tennis courts. The interior of their spacious suite was no less elegant. Tasteful tapestries and paintings adorned the walls of the large rooms. The living area housed an expansive glass table at its inner end. Beyond this stretched a sectional davenport that seemed to extend forever. The deep-pile carpet almost caressed one's feet. A large-screen, remote-control TV, two inviting easy chairs, an elegant coffee table and the usual array of end tables completed the inviting scene.

But neither of them had been able to enjoy the luxury. Becky's beautiful and usually radiant face had been clouded with worry and concern. Tim had appeared gloomy and depressed. There was no evidence of his usual bright countenance and cheery smile. He had already shared those traumatic meetings and Symington's ultimatum with Becky. The dreadful conversation with president Symington had run through his mind a hundred times, and he had been unable to resolve this crucial dilemma. Dismal silence had replaced their usual lively conversation. After a day of this dispirited and oppressive silence, Becky had recalled Tim's utter delight in his previous bike ride down Haleakala, and had suggested he do it again. And so here he was. As he sat brooding at his table, a dreadful foreboding began to rise in him. He sensed himself as the victim of a horrible accident, but he could get no clear idea of how or when this would happen. Such premonitions had always come true in the past, so he took this one very seriously. The most logical outcome would be an accident on the bike. He was an experienced, careful rider; it could be an equipment failure. He rose rapidly from the table and hurried to the parking lot where he found the group leader.

Butch Nakasone had lived all his 21 years in a poor section of Kahului, within sight of Maui's main airport. At age 15 the thrill of surfing had lured him away from school, and he had never gone back. His father, a janitor at the airport, had literally kicked him out of the house at age 16 for being an incorrigible beach bum. He had moved into a small, dilapidated shanty with Badger, a surfing buddy who had been leading bike tours down Haleakala for over seven years, a long time for tour leaders. Badger had persuaded Butch to sign on as an apprentice tour leader with Rider Bob's, the originator of these famous trips. Badger had vouched for him and taught him the tricks of the trade, such as how to sit sideways on the saddle with both feet on the left side of the frame so you could see your riders behind you and the road ahead without getting neck cramps. Badger also passed along enough corny humor and history of the volcano to keep the passengers amused and interested as the van labored its way up the mountain towing a trailer full of the bikes with the specially reinforced drum brakes. And he also taught Butch the spiel that imparted the simple safety rules (stay in line, don't get ahead of the leader, stop on the shoulder when the leader raises his hand) and put the fear of God into them as to what would happen if they broke these rules. After five years with Rider Bob's, Butch had moved to the company he now worked for, because they paid 50 cents an hour more.

While the riders were breakfasting, Butch had been relaxing with a coke and a smoke in the parking lot. His tall, thin frame was draped on the fence and his long, black, glossy hair that framed his tanned, chiseled features was pulled carelessly into a ponytail. His faded shirt and well-worn jeans attested to many hours of service in the sun. As he saw Tim approach, he flicked his third cigarette over the wall (smoking on the job was a company no-no). Tim opened the conversation: "Butch, I wish you'd check the brakes on my bike; its that one over there with the blue frame." Butch slowly unwound himself from the fence, carelessly ambled over to the blue bike, and mounted it with the continuous, smooth motion that bespeaks many, many hours on bikes. He got up speed quickly, then skillfully squeezed both brake handles with just enough pressure on each to come to an astonishingly rapid stop without skidding a tire on the pavement. After repeating this operation several times, he parked the bike and reported to Tim: Mister, you got the best brakes in the bunch."

A couple of other riders, who had finished their breakfasts early and had come out for a smoke, observed the brake testing maneuver with more than casual interest. As Butch resumed his position on the fence, Tim wondered silently: If the brakes are OK, what else can go wrong? An errant auto driver? Not likely with their van and its big CAUTION! ABSOLUTELY NO PASSING! sign following behind the bikers. When a few cars accumulated behind the van, the van driver would radio the leader to stop his riders on the shoulder and let the cars pass. This procedure was done often enough so that the motorists would not become impatient and try to pass the riders on the narrow, winding roads. Tim thought about riding down the mountain in the van, but the van could be rear-ended by a truck and knocked over the side of the mountain. Or it could lose its brakes and go hurtling down the mountain on its own. He resolved to stay with the bike and do his best to enjoy the rest of the ride.

Shortly after the bikers had resumed their ride down the mountain they approached a relatively long, straight, steep stretch of road. They had been rolling along at 20 to 25 miles an hour, slowing only for the hairpin turns. Now Butch increased his speed to over 30 mph on this steep straightaway and the bikers followed suit. Tim had barely gotten his bike up to the new speed when it happened: He heard something snap and felt the brake handle give way in his right hand. The cable that controlled the rear wheel brake had broken! As an experienced biker he knew what applying full pressure to only the front brake would do: As the brake locked the rest of the bicycle to the front wheel, all the weight of the bicycle and the rider would be transferred to the front tire, giving it greatly increased traction. The result is a spectacular forward spin that pitches the rider head first over the handlebars as the bicycle rotates around the front wheel. Tim knew that the result was nearly always serious injury and occasionally death.

Tim applied as much pressure to the front brake as he felt he dared; but he could no longer control his speed.

As Tim pulled ahead of the other riders, Butch screamed at him to slow down and get back in line. Tim was too busy trying to think of ways to slow down to even reply. He tried dragging his feet, but the rough pavement quickly tore the soles off his shoes. He thought of turning quickly and putting the bike into a skid; but, at over 30 miles an hour, going out of control on the narrow, rock-strewn shoulders of the road didn't seem to offer a solution.

In designing this road the engineers had faced many challenges. The switchback that Tim was approaching all too rapidly was one of the toughest. Following the contour of the mountain would have required them to construct a turn that would be much too dangerous and sharp. So instead, they blasted a somewhat gentler turn into the mountain, but in doing so , they left a vertical wall of rock at least 20 feet high on the outside of the turn. As Tim hurtled toward this menacing wall with frighteningly increasing speed, he tried to set up a race driver's turn: As he approached the sharp right turn, he steered as close to the left edge of the road as he dared, then started his right turn early, thus increasing the radius of his turn and reducing the centrifugal force. But even this skillful maneuver wasn't adequate. As he tried to make the turn, his bike went into a wild skid that laid both bike and rider flat on the rock-strewn shoulder. The small, sharp stones tore away both clothes and flesh until a large rock flipped both bike and rider. Tim was aware of his body flying briefly through the air before it splattered against the rock wall. In an instant of colossal trauma he could hear and feel bones breaking, sense the tremendous wrenching of his internal organs, and hear an incredibly loud, cracking bang as the rock wall stopped his head, and his helmet and glasses disintegrated. He had never felt such excruciating pain before. And then, merciful unconsciousness swept over him.

Tim became aware of his spirit leaving his mangled body, seemingly through the top of his head. As it rose to a height of perhaps 15 feet, he could see his prostrate and bleeding body on the rocks below. Beside it was a tangled mass of rubber, chain, handle bars and blue-painted chrom-aly that, just seconds before, had been his bicycle. Butch was already bending over the bloody body, talking frantically into his radio as the other riders dismounted and formed a concerned and curious semi-circle around him. One of the riders turned white-faced and sat down with his head between his knees. Another went to the edge of the cliff and parted company with his breakfast. Two looked away with tears streaming down their faces as three others pulled out clean handkerchiefs and knelt over the body, attempting to stop the most profuse bleeding. Tim continued to watch as the state patrol's large station wagon arrived and screeched to a stop; a nattily uniformed man and woman jumped out, each with a first-aid bag in hand. The officers who patrolled this mountain road were specially trained and equipped to do double duty as paramedics, since the nearest ambulance base was well beyond the 30-minute time limit within which state law required such service to be available. As they bent over Tim's mangled body, they quickly, but carefully and skillfully applied pressure bandages to the three sites that were bleeding profusely, and put splints on both legs. Then they ran back to their wagon onto which they slowly and tenderly eased Tim's body. Before they sped off for the hospital, one officer used his radio briefly while the woman spoke to Butch and the bikers, gesturing for them to remain where they were. In just a few minutes Tim saw another patrol car arrive. Two officers stepped out, each with notebook and pen in hand, and began interviewing Butch and the riders. The two riders who had observed the brake-testing scene in the parking lot seemed particularly agitated and had much to say to the interviewing officer. When they had finished the interviews, the officers put all of the pieces of what had been a bicycle into their wagon and drove down the mountain.

And then the scene dissolved into the oblivion of total darkness.

Chapter Two
The Near-Death Experience

Tim felt as if he were being rapidly propelled through a long, dark tunnel as he felt and heard the wind rushing past him. All he could see was a tiny pin-point of light ahead of him. As the point of light grew larger, he recognized that he was approaching the end of the tunnel. Moments later he emerged into a lovelier scene than he ever could have imagined. An indescribably beautiful landscape lay ahead of him, all bathed in a brilliant yellow-golden light, which despite its brilliance, produced no glare. Instead, it seemed remarkably soothing as he was enveloped in it.

As he drifted slowly along he could see numerous small groups of people, their faces wreathed in love and serenity. None seemed to be talking; but the nods of understanding made it plain that they were communicating in some way. Then he saw a lonely-looking figure standing by himself. As Tim drifted closer, he recognized his beloved identical twin brother, Tom. When he saw Tim, Tom's countenance brightened and broke into a wide grin. Tim felt, rather than heard him say, "I knew you'd come, old buddy; I've been so damn bored and lonely since I've been here. The others ignore me, as if I weren't here. God, I'm so happy and relieved that you've come. How in the devil did you get here?"
Tim replied, "Doin' the Haleakala bike ride again. My brakes failed and I hit the rock wall on a hairpin turn. Now, how'd you get here?"

Tom looked thoughtful for a long moment before responding: "It's a long story that starts when we were kids." Tom's life began to flash before him, and Tim could sense his thoughts: When we were about six, I snuck off to the playground alone just as it was getting dark. I fell off the swing and broke my leg. I yelled and yelled for help, but I couldn't make anybody hear. You and Mom finally came to my rescue. You must've sensed I was at the playground. Nobody else knew where I was. God, was I ever glad to see you. I was so lonely and scared--that was worse than the pain in my leg.

"When we were a little older, I loved to play cards with you; but you didn't like to play because I always won. I would just read your mind and tell what your cards were. And then you'd cry and get mad and yell that I didn't play fair. That was even more fun. Even so, you always stuck up for me when I got in trouble at school. Then, on the way home you'd bawl me out. I'd use my ESP whenever I could to take advantage of the other kids. Dad always told us, `You gotta look out for number one; if you don't, nobody else will'. And he was always saying to us, `Remember the Golden Rule: do others before they do you.' Then he'd chuckle. Mom would try to get him to stop, but he never did. I was nine when I started playing poker with the kids out in our tool shed. I always won the same way I won when you and I played. I had more spending money than any of you. I could buy cigarettes for the others. It made me feel like a man.

"I remember the day Mom caught us playing poker in the tool shed. She made all the other kids go home and then hauled me into the house and told me in no uncertain terms what she thought of that kind of activity. Then she told me she still loved me and hoped and prayed I wouldn't do it again. Mom didn't seem to understand the real world like Dad did. I learned an important lesson that day: Don't get caught. We moved our game over to the old barn back of Freddie Murphy's house. His folks didn't care, so nobody came to bother us there.

"We were both good at sports in high school. We sure had a lot of fun together. I was a great defensive back. The coach loved me because I could sense what the other team was going to do. We were undefeated two years in a row. The third year we lost one game when I was home sick. I got the Most Valuable Player award all three years and I was always captain of the team. You didn't think it was fair to use your ESP that way, and bawled me out for doing it--you said it was cheating. I hated you for that. You were like Mom; you didn't have the street smarts that Dad taught me. He was so right; I was the most popular guy in class. The fellows all looked up to me, and I could have any chick I wanted. Dad used to brag about me. He would tell everybody that I was the really smart one.

"We were seniors in college when we met the Keating twins. Vicky and I hit it off right away. I liked her because she loved a good time, and she was easy. She liked me because I always had more money to spend than the other guys. I won most of it playing poker in the frat house. I had trouble, though: It got so the other guys didn't want me in the game; I nearly always took their money.

"When we finished college and moved back home, I went right to work for the biggest brokerage house in town. I had no trouble getting clients. Word quickly got around town that I had an incredible ability to pick winners. You knew how I did it, but no one else did. You'd tell me you didn't think it was right, but I'd tell you there was nothing illegal about it. You'd just shrug your shoulders and look troubled. Making money was easy as shootin' fish in a barrel. Every morning before I got out of bed I would shut my eyes and imagine that I was looking at the stock tables in the next day's paper. I would memorize the names of half a dozen that had done well. I kept a pencil and paper on the night stand and would write them down right away. Before long I was doing so well that the manager gave me a private office and a personal assistant. The other guys spent long hours every day calling prospects; but I never had to do that after the first few months. New clients would call *me*. I'd chat with them a little; then my assistant would do all the paper work. Pretty soon she could place the orders from my notes. I did an awful lot of buying and selling, sometimes selling in the afternoon stocks I had bought that morning. The clients never objected, and why should they--they were making money hand over fist. The manager had a little problem with what I was doing until he realized how much money I was making for the firm; the commissions were huge. It wasn't long before I was able to do a lot of trading for my own account. It grew beyond my wildest dreams.

"You were like the others; you had to work for your money. You used to tell me about your job at Cornerstone. It sure sounded dull to me, but you seemed happy; I never quite understood it. You said you enjoyed using your training to study the fundamentals. I was never very good at that stuff. The company made us attend seminars on it, but I would just register in, sit in the back row and never come back after the first break. The instructor didn't care; he collected his fee whether I was there or not. I spent the time on more important things, like playing golf with customers. The other brokers were envious when I got away with breaking the house rules, but they didn't say much. Oh, once in a while one of those losers would challenge my work habits, but I'd tell him to buzz off and come back when he was making as much money as I was.

"Then we moved out and got our own apartment. Mom missed us, but Dad didn't seem to. You saw Mom twice a week and seemed to enjoy visiting her, but I didn't; it was boring. Mom was proud of us both, but she was puzzled about how I made so much money. I never told her, because I knew I'd get a lecture. She never did understand the business world like Dad did. He and I golfed every week. He would tell me proudly about how he had gotten the best end of his latest deal, and he'd chuckle over how much money I made. He knew I was living the life of Riley, but never asked how I did it.

"I would take Mom to a fancy restaurant once in awhile and buy her a nice present, but we never seemed to have much to talk about. When she asked me about my life, I'd clam up, and we'd finish our dinner in silence. About the only thing we could talk about was the weather and the upcoming wedding. Mom sure looked forward to that double wedding. She liked both Becky and Vicky, but she and Becky seemed to really hit it off. That was a big wedding. Mom had a ton of friends there. Dad invited his cronies from the club. He bragged to them about how much money I was making. We really got a big spread in the paper -- twins marrying twins. I got several prospects out of it.

"I quit my job and started my own business shortly after the wedding. You were surprised because I had been doing so well. The fact is, the stock exchange compliance inspectors started sniffing around, my manager was getting nervous and I decided that absence of body was better than presence of mind. Besides, for some time I had resented the big cut the firm took from my trading commissions. If I opened my own office, I could take home *all* the commissions. The expenses were peanuts compared to what I was making. What's more, I could trade for my own account without anyone asking questions. That's when I started making the really big money.

""You made a big fuss when I started doing drugs; you were scared I'd get hooked. I almost did; but the drugs really sharpened my ESP so I could make even more money. That was more important than feeling high. I was into a lot of different drugs. If I stayed on one too long, its effect would start to wear off and I'd have to use more to get the same effect. But then people would start asking me what was wrong. Two guys got suspicious and left me for another broker.

"Things began to go bad between me and Vicky. She knew about the drugs and started to get on my case. And she fussed about other things. She was always complaining that I didn't spend enough time with her and the kids. That only made me mad, and I'd spend even more time away from home. I told her I was spending the time at the office, which was partly true. I always hired good-looking secretaries who liked a good time. Things really got nasty at home when I started staying out all night. Vicky accused me of ruining our marriage. I told her that *she* had ruined it by being such a nag and that she was no fun any more. The stuff really hit the fan when I told her what an ingrate she was: I had given her a beautiful home, all the money she could spend, and she had a much better lifestyle than she had before we were married. She told me the kids didn't really have a father and that she no longer had a husband. That's when I moved out and got my own apartment. You tried to tell me I wasn't exactly the model father and husband. but then you had Mom's Victorian standards. I really enjoyed my new freedom. I didn't have to make excuses to anyone or explain my whereabouts. When my secretary began to think she owned me, I fired her and found one who was even more fun.

"It was about then I made another trip to the Amazon. The drugs I'd been using were no longer doing the job, and I was losing my ESP. I was desperate. Remember our vacation trip to the upper tributaries of the Amazon, where we found that remote tribe of natives with the interesting pastime? They made a strong tea out of a local vine. The biologist who was with us called the vine *banisteria carpi* and said it was supposed to have some amazing psychedelic properties. I tried a little of the tea and wow! What a kick! And it really boosted my ESP. On my return trip I found an exporter who would do anything if there was enough money in it. I promised him plenty to procure this vine and smuggle it to me. I kept him honest by advancing him only enough to cover his expenses. His big payoff came when I received a shipment.

"I lost a lot of money after I came back. It took that first shipment forever to arrive. My clients kept throwing money at me and wanting to see the quick results they were used to. They forced me into making some bad buys. I had to cover the losses with my own money or my clients would drop me. They were used to getting the big bucks. But then things turned around. That vine worked wonders. My precognition was better than ever. I became richer than either of us had ever dreamed of. But you still worried about me. I was worth a cool thirty million before I got sick.

"It was right after you threw that whee of a party for my big five-oh. I started feeling lousy a little after midnight and wondered if you had fed me some bad booze. I felt even worse the next morning. I went to doctor after doctor; but they couldn't figure out what was wrong with me. I didn't bother to tell them about the vine; since I'd never felt any side effects from it. Apparently the traces of *banisteria carpi* weren't recognized by any of the labs to which the doctors submitted my blood, urine and stool samples. I was so miserable I couldn't work. I thought I was going to die. I was plenty scared by then. I couldn't keep anything down. I looked like death warmed over.

"You took me to see some hotshot Ph. D. you knew; he wasn't even a doctor, you said he was a brilliant toxicologist. He had taken an Amazon vacation trip like ours and was familiar with *banisteria carpi.* While he was there he made careful notes on the symptoms of the long-time users, and, just before he flew home, he took blood and urine samples from them. He recognized my symptoms and started giving me the third degree. I was still drinking the tea. because it made me feel better, and it was the one thing that would stay down. I had never told anyone but you that I was on the vine. He asked me if I had ever been to the upper Amazon. I even denied that; I was afraid I would get in trouble with the law. You finally squealed on me, and then your friend confirmed his suspicions by checking my blood and urine samples. He warned me that I'd die if I didn't stop using the vine completely. He gave me a terrible-tasting 'antiemetic' to help me keep food down. You and your friend talked hard and fast to me for a long time. I still wasn't ready to give it up because it would ruin my business. You said I already had more than enough money to retire on, but making money was the only pleasure I had left in life. You guys gave me the old highwayman's challenge: Yer money or yer life', and finally you persuaded me that I couldn't make any more money until I got my health back--my business was going down hill because I couldn't take care of it. I was able to get a good offer for my client list from my former brokerage. Those poor, dumb brokerage people; they couldn't keep a lot of those clients, because they couldn't make the kind of money for them that I did. They never did recover the money they paid me. It wasn't my fault that they didn't know how to make the big bucks.

"You helped me transfer my stock holdings into a balanced portfolio. You said I had enough investment income to live very, very well--close to half a million a year before taxes, but it wasn't nearly what I'd been used to. You took my client calls until I got better, which I did gradually. I was furious when you told them I had lost faith in my ability to pick the winners. You just ignored my anger and said I had fulfilled the dream of many men: to retire at 50 and enjoy life with no financial worries. But how the hell was I supposed to enjoy life? Vicky had divorced me. My kids wouldn't have anything to do with me; the last time I can remember seeing any of them was when they needed money, the damned ingrates! I had given them everything they wanted when they were younger. You said they missed a father's love. How *could* I love them? They acted like spoiled brats! I was still giving them money, but only after making their life miserable. That's the only pleasure I could get out of the process. You said I still had friends down at the club. Some friends! Not one of them ever came to see me when I was sick. The only guy who'd even talk to me was Joe Devins. He was a bachelor about my age. When I got well enough to go down to the club, Joe and I spent our time complaining to each other about our aches and pains, and griping about the sad state of things in general. That was no fun, but I couldn't think of anything else to do. I was so bored.

"So I started traveling a lot. A coupl'a times around the world. Big deal; when you've seen one country in Asia, you've seen 'em all. Same with Europe. Africa and South America were depressing, and we couldn't go to Russia or Siberia during the cold war. You

said I should find the real joy, satisfaction and fulfillment that comes from giving some of my money away.
What a ridiculous idea! Like Dad used to say, `What was
the point of giving my money to other people? Let them
earn it the hard way, like I did.

"Then I leased out my big house on Lake
Minnetonka, went to Naples, Florida, and bought that
huge ocean-front condo on the Gulf. Playing golf every
day was boring, and besides, the pro had a hard time
finding people who would play with me. I tried deep-sea
fishing, but all I got was seasick. After that I bought a
big yacht. I couldn't find anybody to help me sail it, so
I hired a crew and invited people to go with me. But
they'd just stick to themselves, and I felt like a paid
captain. Once I asked a couple of girls to stay aboard.
They didn't want to at first; but the sight of some good
old American greenbacks changed their mind. Did we
have fun? Not a chance! Ever since I was so sick I had
a hard time getting it up. The girls got disgusted and
went ashore. Finally I tried taking cruises on large cruise
ships, but the novelty soon wore off. The casinos were
dull compared to the stock market--that's the world's
most exciting game; and when you've seen one stage
show, you've seen 'em all. The only women I found
interesting didn't want any part of me. It's pretty bad
when the most exciting thing you can find to do is to
watch the ship's wake. I looked at some books, but I
couldn't seem to concentrate long enough to get very far
into them. I never was much of a reader, you know.

"And that brings me to how I got here. I was on
yet another cruise, this time from Honolulu to Sydney.
The days were long and monotonous and the nights were
even worse. I kept thinking, is this all there is to life?
What had I struggled so hard for these last 30 years?
What's it all about, anyway? I developed more aches and

pains than the ship's doctors could fix. All they could suggest is `a thorough physical check-up when you go home'. Go home? To what? I asked myself `How many years of this misery must I endure? Is there no solution?' It seemed like I was sleeping less and less every night. One particularly wakeful night, about 2:00 A.M., 500 miles from the nearest land, I put on my robe and slippers and went out on the private veranda of my class AAA penthouse stateroom. I was fascinated by the rhythmic roll of the ship's bow wave 110 feet below, and became almost hypnotized by it. Ah, what a simple solution! I climbed as high as I could on the rail, leaned out as far out as I could, and lost my balance . . . I was sucked under the hull, got spun around in every direction, and then BANG: a terrible blow on the head--probably clobbered by one of the ship's screws. After a journey through a dark, windy tunnel I arrived here. Gee, Tim, I'm so glad you came to keep me company. No one else does. . ."

After Tom had finished this telepathic reminiscence, Tim's own life began to spin before him.

"We must have been about six when you fell off the playground swing. I had just finished helping Mom with the dishes. I loved being with her. She was always so loving and full of fun; she made doing the dishes into a game. I had just snuggled into her lap as she sat in the big chair in the living room to read a book together. Then I had this vision: I could see you lying under a swing crying and writhing in pain. I yelled, `Mommie, Tommie's hurt! We've got to help him!' She had a hard time believing me, but I gave her no peace until she agreed to get in the car and drive us to the school playground. And there you were, screaming your head off and writhing in pain. When we were a little older, you always nagged me to play cards with you; but I didn't like to play because you always won. And then I'd cry because you weren't playing fair and you'd make fun of me and call me a sissy. But I still loved you and always stuck up for you when you got in trouble at school, which happened a lot. You would use your ESP whenever you could to take advantage of the other kids. It always bothered me when Dad talked about looking out for number one and told us his version of the Golden Rule. I knew it was wrong at that time, but I didn't dare open my mouth or he'd blast me.

"I was very good at finding things that had been lost, and was called on frequently as more people heard about me. I got a real bang out of the joy and the delight of the owners. It was special fun to help Mom find things around the house.

"When we met the Keating twins during our senior year in college, it was love at first sight for Becky and me. We used to have wonderful talks about life and love and what God was like.

"After I got my MBA in finance I went right to work for Cornerstone. I enjoyed the work right from the start. My first job was a death claims examiner. I always enjoyed sending those checks. Some widows wrote to me and told me how much the money meant to them. I felt sorry for most of them; they didn't really know how to invest it properly, and I wasn't allowed to advise them. So I asked for a transfer to the Investment Department. Before I left the Claims Department, though, I had an unforgettable experience. One night I had an extremely vivid dream, in which I saw a death claim report on a holder of a large policy. I could see clearly the name of the deceased, the date of death and the cause of death: a plane crash three days later! The next morning I rushed to work and consulted the computer's alphabetic index of policyholders. Sure enough, there was such a policyholder! I called the policyholder and suggested that he take a different flight. The man laughed and said, `No way, this is nonsense!' So I called the airlines operations office and suggested they cancel the flight. They laughed, too, and hung up on me. So later that day I called the man's wife and told her to urge her husband to take a different flight. She took me seriously and, terribly agitated, gave her husband no peace until he finally did change his flight plans. The husband finally agreed, but he also called the president of Cornerstone and complained loudly about the crazy young claims examiner who had meddled in his personal affairs and upset his wife. I got bawled out by the claims manager who told me, if I ever pulled a stunt like that again I'd be fired. Three days later came news of the terrible plane crash. The policyholder again called the Cornerstone president, but this time he thanked him profusely for having an alert young employee who saved his life. The president called me and the claims manager to his office and expressed his gratitude for saving the policyholder's life (and the company's $500,000!)., his apologies, and his curiosity about how I knew. I could only say, `I just knew.'

"My first job in the Investment Department was to pick the closing prices out of the morning paper and run the daily values of our variable accounts on a desk calculator. That's all done with a PC and a modem now, using one of the subscription services. They provide both the data and the program. But long before we had PC's I had moved up the corporate ladder. By the time the novelty wore off one job, I got promoted to a higher level. My next job was as a junior trader, dickering with the brokers and giving them buy and sell orders that the traders wanted filled, and filing the confirms. I wasn't on that job too long either before I became Assistant Vice

President and worked directly for one of the portfolio managers. We called them PM's. My PM would tell me what industries he wanted to build on, and I used my investment research training to analyze the fundamentals and make recommendations to him. I was really putting my education to work.

"Then we moved out and got our own apartment. Mom missed us, but Dad didn't seem to. I visited Mom twice a week and loved talking to her about our lives and how we felt about people. I always left with a warm feeling and a resolve to be someone she could be proud of. She was proud of us both, but I didn't have the heart to tell her how you made so much money. She would have been heart-broken."

Just then Tim saw their mother in a small group of women a short distance to the right and started drifting toward her. At about the same time Tom saw their father alone on the left and headed for him.

Chapter Three
The Great Commission

When Tim's mother, Laura Hamilton, spotted him, she left the group and drifted to meet him.

"Mother!," Tim exclaimed, "You're more beautiful than ever! You look positively radiant! I'm so glad to see you!"

"Tim! What a marvelously pleasant surprise! Dad and I left earth so unexpectedly, we didn't have a chance to say good-bye to you and Tom. But how did you get here?"

Tim told her about the bicycle accident. Then, in loving, silent communication, they reviewed their lives together.

"You were always such a good boy. Reading to you was, I think, the greatest joy of my life."

"Mine too, I have such fond memories of those hours. You also taught me such wonderful values. I owe so much of my success to you."

"You always used those strange ESP powers in such helpful ways. I remember, when you were 10, Mrs. Gardner lost her purse with all that money in it and you told her where to look for it. She was so overjoyed; she gave you a big hug and a twenty-dollar bill."

"Yes. It didn't seem right for me to take her money, but she insisted. I got more pleasure out of seeing her so relieved. She really didn't have a lot of money."

Then, a couple of years later, the Bigelows lost that cute little springer spaniel. Their kids loved that dog so, they were broken-hearted. You volunteered to go in the car and help them look for it. You kept telling Mr. Bigelow where to turn, and pretty soon they spotted their dog."

"He didn't want to follow my directions at first; but I was pretty insistent. After we found Spot, he took us all to the Dairy Queen for sundaes. He kept asking me how I knew where to turn. All I could say was, `I just knew.' I've never seen three such happy kids, and that made me incredibly happy. It was a real high."

"You developed quite a reputation for helping people find things. You would come home whistling and singing, a very happy boy."

"You taught me very early in life that real happiness comes from serving and helping others. Lots of people, including my own brother Tom, spend their whole lives looking for happiness without ever discovering that you can't buy happiness and fulfillment--it's a by-product of the good things we do."

"I wish Tom could have used his ESP to do the kind of things you did."

"Unfortunately, Tom never learned the intense feelings of satisfaction that come from helping others. When I told him about warning our policyholder, he asked me why I didn't call the airline president. I had thought of that, but I didn't think it would do any good. He wouldn't have believed me."

After a long, happy exchange Tim's mother's face suddenly fell as she said, sadly, "I'm so sorry, Tim; you can't stay. You have a long life ahead of you on earth, and you have a lot of good to do. Goodbye for now. I'll be waiting for you to come back."

Tim barely had time to say goodbye before he felt himself being pulled back into his body.

Chapter Four
Liability

Tony Bachinelli, the owner and president of Biking Adventures, sat at the cheap metal desk that was placed corner-wise in a shabby office. Of medium build, he wore his black hair slicked straight back with too much hair oil. His small eyes were framed by olive skin, made even darker by the Hawaiian sun. He wore a deep frown as he faced two men across the desk.

Frank Myasaki, claim adjuster for the company that carried Tony's liability insurance, spoke first, "Tony, this doesn't look good. I've read the police report. It says that two other riders heard Mr. Hamilton complain about his brakes to the tour leader at the breakfast stop. The tour leader assured him there was nothing wrong with the brakes. The police lab had taken apart what was left of the bike and found a frayed rear brake cable. The lab also reported that the bike showed other signs of wear and should have been taken out of service long before, that it was in an unsafe condition considering the demands made of it on that Haleakala ride."

"But," Tony protested, "Hamilton signed our standard contract that's supposed to relieve us of all liability for accidents."

It was Charles Richard's turn to speak. He was the attorney that Tony had retained when he bought Biking Adventures: "Tony that contract won't protect us from a claim if we're found negligent, and such a finding is almost a certainty in the light of the police report. It's a miracle that Hamilton survived. I bribed a nurse to tell me about his condition. I lost count of the number of bones she said were broken. And it took major surgery to put his internal organs back where they belong. He'll be out of commission for months, and no one knows what his handicaps will *be, if* he recovers. The jury will award a settlement in the millions, probably well in excess of your $2 million coverage. They'll give Hamilton everything you've got and then some. I wish you had taken the $10 million I recommended. I would advise both you and the insurance company to offer a quick settlement."

Glancing out the window, Tony responded, "I told Nakasone to get his ass in here just as soon as he finished his morning tour. Here he comes now."

Butch Nakasone, the leader of the ill-fated tour, barged into the office looking belligerent and angry. He dropped his rangy body insolently on the corner of the president's desk, and his anger rose to an even higher level as Tony accosted him: "A hell of a mess you've gotten us into. How come you didn't give Hamilton a better bike when he asked about the brakes? You always carry a couple in reserve."

The blood rose rapidly in the leader's neck as he turned, put both hands on the desk, leaned over and stuck his face close to Tony's and replied angrily, "Listen up, asshole. Hamilton already had the best of the crummy lot. I warned ya when I came here those f---ing junk heaps ya call bikes would get you in trouble. I've had two bikes break down before this. Yer just lucky some dude wasn't killed on them. I'm goin' back to where I worked before. They've got decent bikes, and I don't have to take this kinda shit. I'll stop back next Tuesday to pick up my check from Mabel. It better be ready and have the bonus in it you promised me, or I know several people who'd like to know more about your sleazy operation. Now you can take your f---ing business and shove it up your ass."

As Butch strode out he slammed the door so violently that a picture fell off the wall, and one of the door panels splintered. The three men sat silently and glumly for a long time, immersed in their unhappy thoughts. Finally Frank rose slowly from his chair. As he turned to leave, he said quietly, "I'll talk to my company about an early and generous settlement."

Chapter Five
The Long Road Back

A s Becky Hamilton saw her husband's eyes flicker open, she leaned over his bed in Maui County Hospital, kissed him gently on the cheek, and began to cry as she exclaimed, "Oh Tim, you're going to make it! Do you realize you've been in a coma for almost two weeks?"

"Hi!" he said weakly, then groaned, "O-o-o-oh." Every part of his body was flooded with intense pain, pain like he had never felt before. He couldn't move. He was in a body cast up to his waist, his left arm was casted from wrist to shoulder, and his head was swathed in thick bandages. He continued to groan with every breath. A nurse came in quickly after Becky pressed the call button. "Is he coming out of it?" she asked.

"Yes, but he seems to be in a lot of pain."

"We can take care of that." The nurse went to a machine that had been standing in the corner, wheeled it over to the bed, plugged it into one of the many wall sockets, and quickly inserted a small needle in Tim's right arm, not too far from the IV feeding tube. As she placed something that looked like a call button in his hand, she asked, "Tim, can you hear me?"

Tom nodded slightly.

"I'm Susan, your daytime nurse. When you feel pain, press the button in your right hand and you will receive a shot of morphine. You can press it as often as you feel the need. Don't worry, you won't overdose. In fact, you'll get less morphine than if I gave you shots, but you'll pass out before you can get too much. You'll get it when you feel the need and have much less pain. Do you understand all that?"

Tim nodded again as he pressed the button. The machine acknowledged his request with a quiet beep.

"Good, now if you need anything else, you or Becky can press the call button. It's the larger button lying near your right hip. We're glad to see you made it."

"So am I!," Becky exclaimed emphatically. As she watched Tim, she couldn't tell whether he was sleeping or unconscious, but he had quit groaning and seemed more comfortable.

An hour or so later Becky recognized Dr. Bedell as he entered the room.

"Good morning Becky. I hear that your vigil has been rewarded."

"Yes, thank God."

As he approached Tim's bed, he said cheerily,

"Good morning, Tim. Welcome back to the real world. Can you hear me?"

Tim nodded weakly as he opened his eyes. "Yes."

"I'm Charles Bedell. I'm an internist and I've been assigned as your attending physician during your stay here. I also happen to be chief of staff. I've a great deal to tell you. Do you think, you're ready to hear it?"

"Yes."

"Good. You've been attended by a team of doctors: an orthopedic surgeon, a neuro-surgeon, a neurologist, a cardio-vascular surgeon, a plastic surgeon, a general surgeon, several residents, and another internist with whom I consult. You're something of a celebrity because none of us has ever seen another human being as badly injured as you were who still survived. Congratulations! You have an iron constitution. Your good living habits have really paid off."

Tim nodded to express his understanding.

"Now, I'd like to tell you about what we've got planned for your immediate future. Since you've regained consciousness, you can have regular food as soon as those bandages come off your face. I'll ask the plastic surgeon to do that as soon as he can. Your right arm is in amazingly good shape, so you can probably feed yourself, but I'd like Becky or a nurse to be in attendance when you do." Bedell continued, "From everything we can see you should make a normal recovery, except for minor problems. Because of the severe trauma to your brain, you will have some difficulty in speaking for several weeks, but the speech therapist will visit you regularly until you're speaking normally again. In three to four weeks all of these casts should come off and you'll be able to start physical therapy. By then you'll have lost so much muscle tone, your limbs will feel virtually useless. The PT will be the hardest, most painful work you've ever done, and it will be a long road back. With your persistence and full cooperation, you should regain full function in both legs and your left arm; but it may take as long as two years. In a couple of months you should be able to fly back to Minneapolis and resume your PT, and you can get whatever medical attention you might need there."

Becky, who had been listening with rapt attention,exclaimed: "Oh, Dr. Bedell, that's such good news! I've been terribly worried. Tim had such an active life; I didn't see how he could ever endure being crippled or permanently disabled. His full recovery will be my main mission until he is back to normal."

As Bedell prepared to leave, he put his arm around her and said, "God bless you, Becky. I'm sure you've been a very important part of Tim's life; but you'll be much more important during his convalescence. Don't be surprised if you feel yourself married to a stranger."

Becky wondered what he meant, but decided not to ask questions.

A few days later the plastic surgeon carefully removed Tim's bandages. As he placed a large hand mirror in Tim's right hand and nodded in approval, he spoke: "Your face was incredibly torn, lacerated and bruised. We had to use skin from other parts of your body to do a restoration. You'll look like a stranger at first, but your features will gradually resume a more familiar appearance. You'll never look quite the same as before, however."

Tim nodded his understanding and then shook his head sadly. His face felt numb and stiff, particularly around the mouth, and he wondered what eating would be like. Even the effort of holding the mirror had taxed him and moving his body slightly had brought on another flood of pain. He laid the mirror down and pressed the morphine button . . .

That noon the nurse cranked up the head of the bed until Tim began to feel pain. As she pulled a bed table in front of him and an assistant appeared in the doorway with a tray, the nurse motioned her to put the tray on the bed table and said, "Congratulations, Tim, you're about to eat your first meal in your new world. Enjoy!"

Tim took one bite of the dry chicken sandwich and had trouble chewing and swallowing it. The pureed applesauce and the Jello tasted good. He ate all of it, drank most of his milk in small sips, then indicated with a motion of his right hand that he was through.

Three weeks later, after a medical imaging technician had taken pictures, the orthopedic surgeon came in and announced that the casts would come off the following week and that Tim could use his limbs as much as he felt like it. Tim looked forward to that day with great anticipation and wondered why the nurse cautioned him not to try standing until she was there to help him. When the cast came off he looked at the pale white flesh in shock, but was still eager to get out of bed. As he put weight on his legs he quickly found out what the nurse's caution had meant: Pain, weakness and nausea swept over him, and he was glad the nurse was there to help him back into bed. "Tomorrow will better," she assured him, "and each day we'll do a little more. You'll be going to PT in just a few days."

He had looked forward eagerly to starting PT; but as he headed for his first session he began to wonder why. As the nurse wheeled him down the corridor to the PT, he felt light-headed. He didn't know whether it was from excitement or weakness. As they came to the PT room, an athletic-looking young woman met them at the door and said, "Good morning, Tim. "I'm Mary Kammer, your physical therapist. I look forward to helping you regain your athletic ability. We can help you in many ways, but most of your progress will be the result of your own determination, willpower and persistence. At first, every movement will be painful; but as you persist, you will get stronger and feel less pain. Our goal is to help you regain full strength, full function, and full range of motion." She helped Tim onto a padded table and started him on some gentle exercises. Every muscle in his body seemed weak and the pain was agonizing. In less than five minutes he was exhausted. His left arm seemed to be the biggest challenge; he could barely move his upper arm. Mary explained the problem: "Your shoulder was immobile for so long that it's frozen. With heat, ultrasound and massage we can help to loosen it up; but the most important therapy is exercise."

When he moved his arm as much as he could, Mary gently moved it just a little further. "O-w-w," Tim cried. The pain was so excruciating that all he could think of was getting back to bed and having the nurse reconnect the morphine through the shunt that now resided in his left arm. The nurse helped him back into bed. "Some days will be better than others", she assured him. "Every patient who has been immobile as long as you have feels the same way on his first day. But, if you do as much as you can every day, things will improve and you can look forward to a good recovery."

Tim nodded his understanding and fell into a sound sleep. When he awoke, a strange man was standing in the doorway of his room. "Good morning, Mr. Hamilton, I am Frank Myasaki, a claim adjuster for the company that insures Biking Adventures. We're truly sorry about your accident and want to do everything we can to help you. My company is known for its generosity and consideration. We're sure you will have many expenses. Biking Adventures admits no liability for the accident, but it's my privilege to offer you half a million dollars in full settlement of any claim you might present."

Tim groaned and shook his head as he tried to speak: "Please go away...too early...don't know how I'll be. . ."

"I'm sorry, I'll come back in a few weeks."

When Myasaki came back, he was accompanied by another man. "Good morning, Mr. Hamilton. This is Charles Richards, attorney for Biking Adventures. How are you feeling?"

"Better, thank you; but it's still too early to talk about a claim settlement."

Charles Richards ignored Tim's comment as he spoke, "Mr. Hamilton, I've discussed this matter with Mr. Bachinelli, the president of Biking Adventures and with Butch Nakasone, your tour leader on that fateful day. I have also studied the police report carefully. The police didn't witness the accident, nor were they present when you discussed the condition of your bicycle with Nakasone, who assured you and us that you had the best of equipment. I'm thoroughly satisfied that Biking Adventures is in no way liable for your accident; but we want to lean over backwards to help you. I have here a check payable to you for one million dollars and a release form for you to sign. I suggest that you sign it before Mr. Bachinelli changes his mind."

Again Tim shook his head: "Gentlemen, I've no idea what kind of recovery I'll make, what financial losses I'll incur, or how I will be able to make a living. Thank you for your consideration. I'll be in touch with you when I know the answer to these questions. Thank you for coming to see me."

Chapter Six
Coming Home

Almost four months after the cycling accident Dr. Bedell was just finishing his weekly examination of Tim. The kindly doctor had an especially radiant expression this morning as he announced,

"Well, Tim, this is the day you've been eagerly waiting for. It's time for you to go home and get on with your life. You've worked hard and made wonderful progress, better frankly, than any of us dared to hope for. In a couple of weeks you'll be able to throw away that cane."

Tim's face became equally radiant,

"That's wonderful news, doctor. What about the physical therapy?"

"By all means continue it at home, you don't have full range of motion in your left shoulder yet, and that left leg is not back to normal. Check in with your own doctor and he'll refer you for more therapy. It's really none of my business, but I hope you sue Biking Adventures for all they're worth. They've put you through tremendous pain and suffering."

Tim looked thoughtful, but he did not respond immediately. Then he smiled and said,

"Thank you, doctor; you've been wonderful and so have all of the staff. I intend to write a letter of commendation to your board of directors."

"Thank you, Tim. You've been an exemplary patient. Good bye and God speed in resuming your life."

As they shook hands vigorously there seemed to be an excessive amount of moisture in four eyes.

It was still early in the morning when Tim called Becky in the nearby motel room that had become her second home.

"Oh, Tim, that's ma-a-arvelous news. I'll start packing. What else can I do for you?"

"If you would get us plane reservations and arrange for the kids to meet us that would be great. I've a lot of thank you's and good byes to say here, and some telephone calls to make."

As Tim dressed, he thought of all the things he wanted to do before he left Maui: get the full name and address of the president of Biking adventures, ask the police department for a copy of their report, get the name and address of the hospital board chair, ask Dr. Bedell for a transcript of his initial findings, and call Cornerstone's agent in Honolulu. The agent had called him frequently and had actually flown over to see him twice.

Tim was not at all prepared for the scene that greeted him as he walked slowly and stiffly with the help of his cane into the gate area of the Minneapolis-St. Paul air terminal. A large arch of purple balloons held up big letters that spelled WELCOME HOME TIM. One end of the arch was anchored by their handsome, six-foot, 20-year-old son, Peter; the other by their radiant-faced, attractive 16-year old daughter, Tiffany. Underneath the letters stood none other than John Stuart Symington, president of Cornerstone, flanked by several other company officers, his personal secretary, and many other friends from the office, church, country club and other contexts. Strangers looked curiously to see if they could recognize the celebrity who deserved such a lavish and enthusiastic welcome.

As they spotted Tim and Becky, the group broke into a loud, spontaneous cheer and shouts of "Welcome

Home." Tim and Tiffany embraced in a long hug, as she murmured, "Oh, Daddy, I'm so glad you're home."The handshake with Peter was warm and enthusiastic as they clapped each other on the back. Tim acknowledged each greeting with tears and a warm smile. He didn't speak for fear he would break down completely. Peter announced, "I'll meet you folks at door five" before he disappeared down the concourse. Tim managed a repeated "Thank you for coming out" as he shook hands all around and acknowledged the many warm greetings. Becky and Tiffany were already beckoning him toward the electric cart that was waiting to take them the next step of the journey home.

As they drove to their home in Edina, an upper-class suburb west of Minneapolis, Becky and Tiffany chatted excitedly. Peter concentrated on his driving and Tim was grateful for the opportunity to rest in silence. But as they got nearer to their home, he came alive with excitement. He loved the neighborhood streets, heavily lined with beautiful, large oak and basswood trees, the luxuriant green lawns that bordered the large, attractive homes and the general atmosphere of peace and tranquility on this calm, sunny July day. His excitement increased as they entered the large northern colonial house with its spacious, well-furnished rooms. He entered the living room, headed for his favorite easy chair, and dropped gratefully into it, exhausted from all of the effort and excitement of coming home.

That evening as Tim was beginning to think about retiring, Tiffany brought him a cup of hot chocolate and a vanilla wafer, his favorite snacks.

"Daddy, I'd like to hear more about what you saw and thought during your near-death experience that Mom told us about."

Becky interceded, "Dad's too tired tonight, Tiff, why don't you wait until another time."

"But I'm really not that tired", Tim protested, "I'd just as soon answer Tiff's questions now. Peter, you're welcome to join us."

Becky shrugged resignedly, "I've heard this story before. I'm going upstairs to unpack."

Tiffany pulled a chair up close where she could hold her father's hand. She sat listening in utter fascination as Tim began his strange story. Peter sat farther away; his body English effectively expressed his skepticism as the story unfolded. It took Tim the better part of an hour to tell his story. Encouraged by Tiffany's eagerness, he had told her everything he could remember. All the while, Peter was shaking his head in disbelief. He was the first to speak when his father had finished,

"Gee, Dad, you sure had a weird nightmare," he said as he stood up, stretched and left the room.

"You know, Daddy, when Mom told me about your near-death experience, I asked Miss Pratt, our librarian, for a book on the subject. She called them NDE's and told me there had been a lot of controversy about them. She found me what she said was the most scientific book on the subject. I read it from cover to cover, thinking 'Wow, did my own dad really go through all of this?' And now I know you went through all four phases, as the book calls them."

"Yeah, I sure did. And I'm so glad you understand what happened to me. You're the only one in the family who does. Maybe you can help your mother. I'm afraid she's pretty bewildered and upset by the whole thing. Perhaps you could get that book again and let her read it."

"I'll be glad to do that, Dad. I have a question, though."

"Go ahead."

"The book said most people feel much more religious after their NDE. I've always felt you were a very good person. Do you feel any different?"

"Yes and no. The experience didn't change my religious beliefs; and I've felt for a long time that doing good for other people was the greatest source of human happiness; but the experience with Grandma has left me with an even stronger sense of mission. My problem is, I don't know exactly what that mission is."

"Wow!" was all she could say. Both had tears in their eyes as they embraced long and lovingly and bid each other sweet dreams.

The next morning, immediately after breakfast, Tim was on the telephone making appointments, first with president Symington, then with his doctor and his personal attorney and finally with a driving instructor. He and Becky had argued about whether he was able to drive a car, and had finally agreed that this was the best way to resolve it.

The doctor congratulated Tim on his miraculous recovery and referred him to a physical center to strengthen his left leg further and help him regain full range of motion in his left shoulder. The driving instructor cautioned Tim to stay a full two seconds behind the car ahead of him and, while he was waiting to make a left turn off a two-way street, not to turn his wheels until the opposing traffic had cleared. Then he congratulated Tim on being a better driver than most of his students and wished him many hours of accident-free driving.

The attorney reviewed the police reports, hospital records and other papers Tim had brought, heard his story about the settlements offered, shook his head as he removed his reading glasses and said indignantly,

"They're guilty as hell; I'd sue the bastards for ten million bucks. In addition to your humongous medical expenses and Becky's meals and lodging, plus your loss of earning power, they've put you through incredible pain and suffering. Most people would sue for more than that."

"I doubt if they have that much insurance, and I've no desire to put Bachinelli out of business", Tim replied.

"Maybe so, but we need to rattle their cage and make them offer a more generous settlement than they have done so far. I'll draw up the complaint and call you when I have it ready for your approval."

"All right, but don't be too tough on them," said Tim as he rose to leave.

Chapter Seven
The Decision at Cornerstone

John Stuart Symington was especially cordial as he greeted Tim in his reception area, ushered him into his spacious office and invited Tim to sit on the luxurious settee which, along with two overstuffed easy chairs, bordered a large glass-topped coffee table across the room from the huge mahogany desk as he spoke,

"Tim, it's great to see you making such wonderful progress. We were all so shocked and saddened by the news of your terrible accident. Congratulations on working through what must have been a very painful rehab program on your marvelous recovery. I hear that you have regained almost all of your normal functions, but I still think you should sue that bike company within an inch of their lives."

"Thanks, John. The rehabilitation wasn't easy; but, all the support from my family, friends and community helped me get through it. It's good to be back in circulation, although sometimes I feel almost like a visitor."

"We've missed you in many ways, Tim. Your staff has carried on well; but the more progressive companies are continuing to eat our lunch. I'm getting incredible pressure from our marketing people to adopt a more aggressive investment policy. They've given me a list of almost a hundred life insurance companies that have successfully adopted more liberal investment policies, are earning a much higher rate of return, and prospering dramatically from their bold approach. These are not fly-by-night companies, Tim. There are many blue chips in that list, and they're the ones that are giving us such a hard time. I think they're right, Tim, and so does almost all of the investment committee. Can *all* of these able people be wrong? Think about it." Tim shook his head sadly as he spoke,

"John, you've no idea how many hours I've spent doing just that. Apart from rehab, that was my principal activity in the hospital: many hours by myself and many in discussion with Becky. This is, by far the toughest decision I've ever faced." Tim didn't think it was wise to tell John, or anyone else, about his nightmarish dream in which he had so vividly seen Cornerstone, along with other good companies, in deep financial trouble because of their liberalized investment policies.

"How does Becky feel about it?"

"She is quite distressed at the very thought of my leaving Cornerstone, but she says it has to be my decision."

"Would you like a few more days to think about it?" Again, Tim shook his had sadly,

"Thanks, John, but I really don't see how it's going to make any difference. Nothing has really changed since I left for Maui. If anything, you and the others have become even more convinced of the need for a change I cannot, in good conscience, make. As you know, I believe the course these other companies are taking involves much more risk than we have any right to take with the money our policyholders have entrusted to us In many cases, I'm sure it represents a major portion of their assets."

"Then, that is your final word?"

"Yes."

It was Symington's turn to shake his head sadly,

"Tim, this is the toughest thing I've had to do. We shall really miss you. You've been a wonderful asset to

Cornerstone for all of these years. But, if you can't see your way clear to follow the new policies of the Investment Committee, you leave me no choice but to ask for your resignation; of course, we'll offer you a very generous separation package."

"What would that be?"

"We would put you on terminal leave with pay until the first of the month following your 55th birthday, at which time you will be eligible for early retirement. We would also offer you a consulting contract with a retainer as follows: full pay for the first year, half pay for the second year, then monthly payments sufficient, together with your early retirement pension, to equal the total pension you would have received, had you stayed and retired at age 65. Under that contract you would have to make yourself available to Cornerstone as a consultant; but we wouldn't expect to use much, if any, of your time. We would make a modest office available to you with a telephone and a PC, and you could use the services of the secretarial pool."

"How much of the payments would be fixed dollar and how much would be variable?"

"As you know, our pension plan provides for one-half the total income to be paid as an annuity that varies each month in accordance with the market value of the stock fund from which they are paid. Because the consulting retainer will be about equal to your pension, we could allow you to take all of your pension payments as a variable annuity, if you wish."

"What about my stock options?"

"They would be fully vested and could be exercised any time during your terminal leave."

Tim sat for what seemed a long time in silent thought and contemplation. Finally he spoke,

"If you'll have the papers drawn up and mailed to my house, I'd like a couple of days to review them with my personal attorney. And could you include a draft of the press release, please."

"We can certainly do that."

Both men rose and shook hands soberly before Tim left the office. He drove home slowly. He didn't relish the prospect of telling his family what had happened. Becky met him at the door. She had understood the significance of his visit with Symington.

"Are you going to stay on with Cornerstone?"

Tim shook his head silently. Becky burst into copious tears.

"Oh Tim! Cornerstone has been such a great part of our lives. I feel a dreadful sense of loss, as if our world were falling apart: all of the wonderful trips we've had, the parties, my many friends. I can't bear the thought of losing all that. And what will we do for money?"

She continued to sob uncontrollably as Tim tried to keep his own composure and to comfort her:

"Our new life style will be much more flexible. We can travel as much as we want. I plan to be very active in the community, and that will lead to a very active social life. I'm sure your friends at Cornerstone will continue to include you in their luncheons."

"Where will the money come from?"

"Cornerstone has offered me a very generous consulting contract, which is really a way of doubling my pension. We'll get a large settlement from the accident insurance company, and I plan to exercise all of my stock options. All that money, wisely invested, will give us about as much take-home money as we had before."

Becky continued to weep, while Tim continued to expound on his plans for the future:

"We have that one large bedroom that we never use. I'd like to convert that to an office and start an investment consulting office."

"What would you do for a secretary?"

"You're very good on the telephone, and you will continue, I'm sure, to do a great job of handling our personal finances, pay the bills, balance the check books, et cetera. Voice mail will take our calls when we're gone. In fact, many of my business friends were already asking to be put on my voice mail, even though my secretary was very good at taking messages. I've been handling more and more of my correspondence by e-mail, Internet and FAX. I'm already pretty good at running a PC, and I enjoy it."

Becky had quit crying except for an occasional quick sob, but she still looked very despondent as she shook her head slowly and spoke,

"I just feel as if we were jumping off a cliff and don't know where or how we'll land--as if we're losing a lot that can't be replaced."

"You're right in a way: our lives won't be the same. In fact, they'll be different in many ways: I see a bright, exciting world of new adventures, new experiences and new opportunities to do fulfilling things that will lead us to greater happiness than we can even dream of. And I hope, with all my heart, that you'll soon come to see it the same way." She began to cry again as Tim kissed her and left the room.

The visit to Tim's personal attorney served a double purpose which became quickly evident after their warm exchange of greetings:

"Tim, I've drawn up the complaint against Biking Adventures and I've reviewed the contract that Cornerstone has offered you. Let's take the easy one first. This complaint is short and to the point: it accuses them of gross negligence in failing to maintain their equipment properly thereby exposing their customers to undisclosed, serious hazards and risks of death or serious injury, such as you suffered. It asks for a million dollars to cover medical and temporary lodging expenses, five million for loss of earning capacity, four million for pain and suffering and loss of services, and half a million in legal expenses."

"I don't think they have that much in insurance and assets put together."

"That's all right; we need to shake them up a bit to make them offer a more generous settlement than they have done up until now."

"Well, you're the expert in these matters, and everyone seems to think they should pay heavily. Let's go ahead and see what they have to say. Now, what do you think of the Cornerstone contract?"

"It's pretty good, but it needs a couple of things spelled out for your protection."

"Such as ...?"

"You agree not to work for a competitor of Cornerstone for two years. It should be expressly understood that this in no way restricts you from making yourself available as an independent consultant, which I believe you intend to do."

"That's right; what else did you see?"

"You agree to make yourself available to Cornerstone as a consultant at all reasonable times. It should be spelled out that that provision in no way restricts your ability to travel, or the amount of time you spend away from Minneapolis."

"That seems important, too. Anything else?"

"Just one thing: I don't think the provisions in your stock option agreement for exercise upon termination of employment were made to fit your situation. I think this agreement should expressly amend those agreements to state a specific date on which your exercise rights expire. I would suggest two months after this agreement is signed."

"Thanks very much, Harry; I'll see to all of these things."

Chapter Eight
Financial Planning

After getting his separation agreement modified and signed, agreeing on the wording of a press release and picking a date for his retirement party, Tim made the rounds of his friends' offices to tell them the news. He used the key expression from the press release: He was "taking early retirement to pursue other business interests." They were all saddened by the news, but very few were surprised or fooled. News of the donnybrook at the management committee and investment committee meetings had thoroughly permeated Cornerstone's management circles. The more outspoken had confidently predicted Tim's departure. Many expressed an interest in having lunch, to which Tim responded, "That would be nice." But he took it no further unless a friend sought a specific date.

He went back to his office, put his personal effects and files in a box and instructed his secretary to consult his successor regarding the remaining files. He was interrupted numerous times by friends stopping in to express their regrets and best wishes. He realized he would have to retreat to the privacy of his home to get started on the job that was uppermost in his mind: his personal financial planning. He had gone over in his mind the strategies, decisions and rough numbers a hundred times, it seemed. But now it was time to play "what if" on his PC, using the real facts to obtain the highest income consistent with safety--just as he had been doing for years for Cornerstone.

Becky came home and found him deeply engrossed, huddled over his PC at the small desk in the bedroom which was to become his office. She half asked, half exclaimed,

"Don't you feel ashamed of having to work in such cramped quarters, after having such a nice big office at Cornerstone?"

The question shocked him like a stream of ice water, as he suddenly realized how much the trappings of his position at Cornerstone had meant to Becky. He felt inadequate to deal with the real meaning of her question at the moment, so he replied brightly,

"No, Hon. I've wanted a combination den and library for a long time, and this room will be quite adequate for the purpose. Peter wants to be out on his own, and he is planning to move in a couple of weeks. I suspect he'll welcome a gift of this bedroom furniture. We'll put bookshelves, paneling and modest office furniture in this room. I'll also need a separate telephone line, a laser printer, and a good FAX machine that will double as a copier."

He had a hard time concentrating on the job at hand: the real thrust of Becky's question continued to haunt him: how could he help her adjust to their new life style? To him it was an exciting quest. To her it seemed to offer only losses and problems. He wished he could call his psychologist friend. Charlie Becker; but Charlie was out of town for a few days. So, back to the numbers for now. Slowly, the numbers began to appear on the screen as he consulted his papers and notes and pressed the keys:

ESTIMATED MONTHLY INCOME

PENSION	8,440
CONSULTING RETAINER	7,500
TAX-FREE BOND INTEREST*	20,000
TOTAL MONTHLY INCOME	35,940
INCOME TAX (ESTIMATE)	6,500
NET MONTHLY INCOME AFTER TAXES	29,440
NET ANNUAL INCOME AFTER TAXES	353,280

* (BONDS BOUGHT WITH BIKING ADVENTURES SETTLEMENT)

Tim couldn't believe his numbers: over a third of a million dollars a year in after-tax income; that was more than they had now! And he had purposely excluded income from two other sources: his Cornerstone stock options and his personal investments. Cornerstone had been generous with stock options for its senior officers, and their stock had done marvelously well. By the time he exercised all of his options, his holdings in Cornerstone stock would be worth over five million dollars. His financial future was too heavily dependent on Cornerstone. He must diversify these holdings. Selling most of his Cornerstone stock would create a tremendous tax liability. He could avoid the tax liability by putting the Cornerstone stock into a charitable trust and letting the trustee sell the stock. He would receive the income from the trust, but that income would all be taxable. More importantly, he would lose his options for the future use of the principal.

Then he had over two million dollars in other personal investments. He had always re-invested the income from these investments, and had always thought of this money as opportunity capital to pursue whatever business interests might intrigue him after his retirement from Cornerstone. How would it be used now? Was this money going to be needed to pursue his mother's mission? What was that mission? What kind of money would it take?

Once he put the numbers down, the decisions seemed easier than he had expected; perhaps all the thinking in the car had paid off. He had elected to take his pension as a straight life income: a gutsy decision since he would lose close to a million if he died soon. But he felt that he would live a long time (his mother's influence again?), and Becky would be more than amply provided for from his other assets. The settlement with Biking Adventures was still pending; but it seemed quite likely they would settle for the full amount of their insurance: two million dollars. The decision to put it into municipal bonds was a no-brainer, considering his high tax bracket. A simple calculation showed him that, if he went the charitable trust route, the present value of the future income taxes would be greater than the capital gain tax he would pay now; so he would sell the Cornerstone stock. What to buy with the proceeds from the sale was a decision to be made as the stock was sold, and that lay in the future.

As Tim looked at the computer screen, he couldn't believe his good fortune: more income than they ever had, a very respectable personal estate, and his entire life free to devote to whatever purposes seemed best. What were those purposes? How would he determine them? Despite their vagueness, the future prospects created in him a tremendous sense of excitement and strange feeling of exhilaration. But right now, he had several immediate things to take care of: make a date with the carpenter to plan his office remodeling, shop for office furniture and equipment, talk to Peter about his interest in the bedroom furniture. Most importantly, he wanted to set up a date with Becky for dinner and dancing at their favorite club and see if that would raise her spirits.

Chapter Nine
Estrangement

The evening wasn't anything like Tim had hoped for; in fact, it was a disaster. They had barely finished ordering and were just starting their cocktails when Becky burst into tears,

"Oh Tim, I don't know what to do; my whole world is coming apart!"

"What's the matter, Hon?"

"Everything's the matter. It's worse than the twilight zone."

"Tell me the worst part first."

"It's you and my feelings toward you. You don't seem at all like the man I knew before we went to Hawaii. It's as if the Tim I knew had left and I'm living with a stranger. I find myself wishing you would leave some day and the old Tim I knew and loved so much would come back."

"Is it because my face is different?"

"No, it isn't that. It's awfully hard to describe."

"Why don't you try."

"I'm afraid of hurting your feelings."

"Don't worry about that; I still love you, and it hurts much more not knowing what it is that makes you so sad."

She sobbed quietly for a few minutes. There were only a few people in the dining room, and Tim had asked for a table in a secluded corner where they could talk by themselves. The maitre d' had not only obliged him but had been careful not to seat anyone else in that end of the dining room. Tim finally broke the silence,

"Go ahead, try."

"I think it has something to do with that terrible nightmare you had while you were in a coma, where you thought you were talking to Tom and your mother."

"That was more than a dream, dear."

"I know you think so, and that bothers me even more: that an intelligent man like you would fall for that NDE nonsense."

""Did Tiff get you that book that describes NDE's so well?"

"Yes, but I just couldn't make myself read much of it. I'd read a few pages and find myself thinking, 'How can anybody be gullible enough to believe this stuff?' I even showed it to Dr. Bannister. She feels the same as I do."

"Other people have the same difficulty . They feel as if their loved ones have been changed by the experience, and they have a hard time relating to them."

"That's what the book said, but that doesn't make it any easier, particularly with the way you and Tiffany carry on."

"How's that?"

"Oh, it's sickening! You act like a couple of lovebirds. She sits at your feet with her head in your lap. You hold hands and talk endlessly about that silly dream. I find myself hating you both."

"She's the only one who understands and accepts what happened to me. Is it so terrible that we talk about it?"

"She spends much more time with you than she does with me, her own mother! When I try to talk to her, I feel as if I were talking to the 'other woman.' It's a terrible feeling!"

"Is there anything else troubling you?"

"Plenty; but you don't want to hear it all."

"Try me."

"I've talked to Mother . . ."

"What did she have to say?"

"It gets worse . . ."

"Go ahead. I can take it."

"She...she thinks that accident knocked you cuckoo. No sane man would take that wild dream seriously. Nor would any man in his right mind give up that wonderful job you had with no real future in mind. Men in their mid-fifties aren't that employable. She thinks you need to see a psychiatrist and work with him until you get your head screwed on straight. She hopes you'll come to your senses before Cornerstone fills your job."

"Did you tell her how happy I am with my decision to leave Cornerstone?"

"Yes, and she says that just proves that you've gone out of your mind."

"Do you agree with her?"

She was silent for several long minutes before she said quietly,

"Yes."

It was Tim's turn to be silent. He was only beginning to realize the depths of the problems in his marriage. There surely weren't going to be any easy answers. Yes, he did need help; but not the kind his mother-in-law had in mind. Finally he spoke,

"Do you remember my old friend, Charlie Becker? He's out of town right now; but we'll get together next Monday."

"But Charlie's only a psychologist. Do you think he can really help you?"

Again, he pondered before he spoke. He had often quoted Mark Twain: "Honesty is the best policy; I've tried both ways." But he knew it wouldn't help to tell Becky why he had really called Charlie. He decided he could ask Charlie how both of them could be helped.

After all, they both had problems, didn't they? Finally, he chose his words carefully,

"I hope so. He's a very wise man and certainly has helped a lot of people deal with their problems. He'll be a good place to start."

Becky sat in silent misery. She looked to be on the point of tears again, but all that came out was occasional short, convulsive sobs as they ate their dinner in silence. Finally Tim spoke,

"Come on, Hon; we came here to enjoy ourselves. The band is playing our kind of music. May I have this dance?"

He had risen and moved to her side of the table. As she took his outstretched hand and rose slowly, a faint smile played across her face momentarily, but quickly disappeared. Instead of the lively partner he was used to holding in his arms, Tim felt as if he were dancing with a Zombie. They had made only two or three rounds of the dance floor before Becky spoke,

"Tim, I just don't feel like dancing. Let's go home."

It was earlier than their usual bedtime; but Becky announced that she felt very tired and was going to bed early. Tim tried to read but found his thoughts returning to their conversation at the club. He put the earphones in his keyboard and turned it on. It was an expensive, versatile instrument, using the latest digital CD techniques. He had pre-recorded, on a solid-state card, the harmony and rhythm patterns for much of his favorite music. He could then use both hands on the keyboard and play piano while his three-piece combo accompanied him. Or he could split the keyboard into different instruments. His favorite was to leave the lower half of the keyboard as a piano and turn the upper half into vibes. He selected two of his favorite songs and began to play. He not only enjoyed the music, but it reminded him of the wonderful evenings he and Becky had spent together on the dance floor.

Finally Tim turned off the keyboard and went to bed. Sleep usually came quickly, but not tonight. His thoughts kept returning to the devastating evening and the enormous task that lay ahead of him. He could hear Becky sobbing quietly in her bed. Perhaps playing the keyboard was one way to help her realize that he was the same guy with whom she had enjoyed such happiness. .

The week-end seemed to drag on interminably. Becky rebuffed all of Tim's suggestions of things they might do with a sad shake of her head and a quiet "I just don't feel up to it." After Tim had made a number of suggestions, she burst into tears and fled up the stairway. In an hour or so she came down, lugging a large suitcase, and exclaimed,

"I just can't stand it here any longer! I feel like a total stranger in this house. Nothing's the same as it was. If I stay here another minute, I'll go out of my mind. I've called Mother and she's invited me to try living with her until you come to your senses."

He tried to hug her, but she merely headed determinedly for the garage door.

Ten o'clock Monday morning found Tim sitting in a comfortable, overstuffed chair in Charlie Becker's office. After brief greetings and a discussion of Charlie's vacation, Tim announced,

"Charlie, problems like I never dreamed of have developed in our marriage"

"Tell me about them."

It took Tim almost an hour to recount all of the events that had occurred since their return from Maui. Charlie listened intently, nodding occasionally to indicate his understanding. After Tim finished Charlie sat quietly for a few minutes before he asked,

"Do you still love her?"

"Oh yes, and it pains me deeply to see her so distressed. What hurts even more is that I can't seem to help her understand where I'm coming from."

"Does it bother you that she thinks you're crazy?"

"Of course it does! But perhaps not in the way you think."

"What do you mean?"

Charlie's secretary had brought them fresh coffee. Tim sipped his coffee thoughtfully before he answered,

"In the first place, I don't think I am; but mostly I see her belief that I've lost my mind as an eloquent expression of her failure to see what I see developing in my life."

"What *do* you see?"

"I see my life so far as a sort of prelude to a long and fulfilling future."

"Doing what?"

"Using my talents, my skills, and my money to help individuals and organizations that are trying to make this world a better place to live in."

"Have you tried to look at this through Becky's eyes?"

"Yes, at first I thought she was just feeling the loss of status, perks and activities she had enjoyed as the wife of one of Cornerstone's senior officers. After our dinner at the club, I realize it's much more than that."

"Like what?"

Tim sipped some more coffee, before he said,

"Charlie, I think I need help articulating it."

"All right, Tim, let me try. After 23 years of an almost idyllic marriage to the ideal husband who's at the peak of an outstanding business career, Becky finds herself living with a guy who has slammed his head into a rock, knocked some of his marbles loose, thrown his great career to the winds and wants to spend the rest of his life trying to save the world--the classic messianic complex of the insane. If that isn't bad enough, she's been replaced as your confidant and soul-mate by your 16-year-old daughter. To top it off, she has no earthly idea of where to begin to fix things, and is deathly afraid that they can't *be* fixed. In short you've destroyed her life."

Tim sat in shocked silence and tears filled his eyes.

"Tim, old buddy, I'm sorry to have been so rough on you; but unless you can see the problem as she sees it, you have little hope of contributing to the solution."

"Has anyone else had a similar problem?"

"Oh yes, it's the most common, and the most difficult, problem that people face after a near-death experience : the inability of loved ones to deal with the new person."

"Am I really that different from the person I was before Maui?"

"Much more so than you realize. It's most apparent to the people who are closest to you and with whom you share your innermost thoughts. Becky really does feel as if you're a stranger. Her problem is exacerbated by the sudden loss of the familiar and enjoyable Cornerstone milieu, and by being replaced by her own daughter. That latter generates unspeakable feelings in her about both of you; she hates herself for having those feelings, but they still persist--the classic reverse Oedipus complex."

"Is there any hope of a solution?"

"Oh yes, but it will be slow and painful. As is often the case, there's no easy answer. It will take incredible effort, patience, love and understanding; but you're capable of supplying all of those elements."

"Where do I begin?"

"Start with a blank sheet of paper. Draw a line down the middle so as to make two columns. In the left column write all of the activities and personal qualities you can think of that have made Becky feel glad she married you. In the right column, but down the newer thoughts, ideas and experiences you've had since your accident. When you're with Becky, speak only of those things in the left column. You'll be tempted to talk of the things in the right column since they're uppermost in your mind."

"It sounds so deceitful."

"No, you're just helping Becky hang on to those things most likely to reassure her that the old Tim hasn't really left her; instead of hitting her across the face with a wet mackerel regarding the dramatic changes that have occurred in your life. It's like the old southern preacher prayed, Lord, Lord, if I *must* bathe the disciples feet, help me not to make the water too hot.'"

"Won't she ever be able to accept my new ideas? Won't we be able to talk frankly and comfortably like we always have?"

"Yes, but it will take time--probably six months to a year, depending how effective you are in pursuing your purpose. Let me assure you, Tim, the changes I see in you are all for the better. You've always been a good person; but I share your mother's beliefs that you will go on to be a great person and accomplish much good in this world."

Tim's eyes grew moist again; then the tears ran down his face as he fumbled for a handkerchief. When he regained his composure sufficiently to speak, he said,

"Thank God for you and Tiffany! At least there are two people in this world who still believe in me."

"Becky will be number three; just help her, continue to love her and give her some time."

They embraced warmly and Tim took his leave without further conversation.

Chapter Ten
Board Memberships

WHEN Tim returned home, his first thought was to phone Becky. He couldn't believe his ears when the computer voice said, "That number has been temporarily disconnected." He thought, "I must've dialed wrong," as he re-tried the number very carefully; but he got nothing but the same computer voice with the same message. His bewilderment didn't last long: As he put the phone in its cradle, the front doorbell rang, announcing a courier with an envelope addressed to him in Becky's handwriting. The note it contained was brief:

Dearest Tim,
Mother and I have left for an extended trip
in Europe. I hope Charlie Becker was
helpful and that you'll make a rapid recov-
ery. I would love to have the old Tim back.
Love and kisses . . .
Becky

The questions raced through Tim's mind: Was this good news or bad news? Was it the end of their marriage? How could he ever convince Becky that the old Tim had never left? (Or *had* the old Tim left?) How could he convince her of anything when she was so far away? Was he going to be able to follow Charlie's advice? How long would Becky be gone?

The telephone interrupted his thoughts,

"Hello?"

"Hello, Tim, this is Rankin Smith, I met you at a Minikahda Club party several months ago."

"Yes, I remember you."

"I'm calling in my capacity as board chair of Abbott-Northwestern Hospital. Scott Wilson, the president, and I would like you to be our guest for lunch at the Minneapolis Club, to discuss your possible interest in coming on our board of trustees. Would you be free next Thursday noon, by any chance?"

Abbott-Northwestern Hospital! Rated as one of the ten best hospitals in the United States, what a privilege and an experience it would be to serve on their board! Tim could hardly contain his excitement as he spoke,

"Yes, what time and where shall we meet?"

"How about 11:45 on the first floor?"

"Fine, I'll be there."

As the most prestigious downtown club, the Minneapolis Club was rich in tradition and steeped in elegance, the large parlor on the first floor was tastefully furnished with comfortable, upholstered chairs and settees done in a deep red leather that set off the rich, dark woodwork. A writing table and comfortable chair graced one wall, and a large table in the center contained plenty of copies of both local and national dailies as well as copies of the current news, business and financial magazines. Potted palms, lemon trees and other greenery, heavy drapes, rich tapestries, and ornate oriental carpets completed the setting of luxurious comfort. The subdued atmosphere gave a first impression of a library. In reality it was a convenient place for members and their guests to await one another's arrival. Older members seemed immersed in their reading or quiet conversation while younger members or guests were peeking surreptitiously over their papers to see whom they might recognize among the club's prestigious clientele. Tim had been a member here for several years and had used the club occasionally to take an out-of-town guest to lunch. It seemed like such a pleasant place to relax, but he had never felt he had the time to do that when he was at Cornerstone. Would he actually use the club more often in his new status? He was five minutes early as he picked up a copy of the *Wall Street Journal* and took a seat from which he could see anyone who entered the room.

Tim's hosts were prompt. After brief greetings and introductions they escorted him to their reserved table in the main dining room. This club had maintained the old tradition in which the host filled out the luncheon order by entering number codes from the menu as the guests expressed their preferences. As soon as the waiter had picked up their order, Rankin Smith, the chairman turned to Scott Wilson and said,

"Scott, why don't you tell Mr. Hamilton about our hospital and what we expect of our board members."

Wilson obliged; and, as he spoke, he handed Tim a packet of materials which he smilingly referred to as "your homework." The president interrupted his presentation when their food arrived, and the conversation turned to small talk while they ate. When they had finished eating, Wilson completed his presentation, answered a couple of questions Tim asked, and ended with an invitation to Tim to tour the hospital. When the time for the tour had been set, Wilson handed Tim a plastic card and said,

"This card will raise the arm that otherwise bars entry to the reserved parking area. One of our staff will greet you at the entrance to the ramp's elevator lobby. The tour will take about two hours and will end in my office's reception area. I will try to answer any questions that others haven't answered to your satisfaction. Please feel free to ask them what you'd like to know."

Smith added,

"Tim, I want to thank you for coming and showing your interest in membership on our board. If it's convenient for you, I'll call you the day after your tour and determine the level of your interest."

The meeting ended with cordial handshakes and thank you's all around. As Tim drove home he reflected on the meeting: They certainly did things in style--or had he received special red carpet treatment? But why would that be? Would there be invitations from other organizations? Would they all seem this attractive?

As a hard-working executive at Cornerstone, Tim had not served on very many boards. Now that he had the time, this sounded like a great way to be of service to his community. He was eager to read his "homework." Tiffany greeted him excitedly at the door,

"Oh Daddy, the workmen have finished in your new office, the furniture was delivered just a few minutes ago. The telephone installer is doing his thing now. The place looks great! And you're going to be so close by. I love it!"

Tim's excitement grew as he took the stairs two at a time. It looked even better than he had pictured it in his mind. He was torn between starting to arrange his books on the shelves and putting things in the desk drawers on the one hand, or getting started on reading the material that Wilson had given him. He decided to work on arranging the office until dinner time and start on the reading after dinner. Tiffany had already moved his PC onto the corner of his new desk and had set up the keyboard, monitor and FAX machine on the credenza, which joined the desk at right angles. He took time to dial into CompuServe and look at the market, including the principal indexes and the individual stocks on his watch list. Cornerstone was continuing its modest rising trend, with only occasional small setbacks. But he was vaguely troubled. He knew he must diversify his holdings; was there more to his concern than that? His staff was already yielding to the pressures for higher returns. He couldn't blame them for that--they needed to keep their jobs--the message had been very clear. Were they taking too many risks in their eagerness to please management? They were in a tough spot. He was more sure that his decision to leave Cornerstone was the right one, even though it had exacerbated his problems at home. His reveries were interrupted by the call that dinner was ready.

Mrs. Schatz, a stout lady in her late fifties, had done her usual good job of preparing a tasty, wholesome dinner. She had been with them since Becky had had her long bout with gallstones and an infected gall bladder; and had become part of the family. She was certainly a blessing now, with Becky gone. His thoughts turned to Becky. Where was she tonight? Were she and her mother enjoying themselves? When would he hear from her? How long would she be gone? Did she miss him as much as he missed her? Was he going to be able to win her back? Tiffany interrupted his thoughts,

"Daddy, you don't look very happy. Are you mad at me for plugging in your computer and your FAX machine?"

"Oh no, Tiff. You were a jewel to do that; and they're just where I wanted them. Thanks a heap for doing it. I'm sorry to be such poor company at dinner. I'm worried about Mother, and I guess it showed."

"I guess she's plenty upset with you for quitting your job. You told me they wanted you do things that weren't right. I'm proud of you for following your heart. I don't know if I'd have the courage to do that. But she thinks it was foolish--or worse."

"What does 'worse' mean?"

"I...I...I don't know if I should say it, it might upset you."

"Try me ..."

Tiffany seemed to be trying to find the right words; but then she just blurted,

"She thinks ... she thinks ... you've gone crazy."

"Don't worry, sweetheart, she told me. Now what do *you* think?"

This time there was no hesitation as her eyes shone and she exclaimed fervently,

"Before this last trip to Hawaii, I thought I had the finest Dad in the world; but now you're like...like wow! I think it's so cool that you're going to devote your life to doing good. Dads don't come any better than that--it's really awesome!"

They had finished dinner. Tiffany looked at her watch and jumped up as she exclaimed,

"Oh, I've got to run, Daddy, or I'll be late to meet Jennifer. We're going to the library to work on our history project, then we'll stop at the Dairy Queen. I'll be home on time, don't worry."

As she reached for the doorknob, Tim called out,

"Tiffany!"

"Yeah, Daddy?"

"I love you, sweetheart."

She ran back and gave him a resounding smooch on the cheek,

"Love ya, too, Daddy."

And she was gone.

Tim sat silently for a long time, eyes moist, immersed in his thoughts. How lucky he was to have someone who shared not only his love, but who understood what he had been through and what was happening to him. How wonderful it would be if Becky could acquire the same understanding. Charlie Becker was encouraging, but could he, Tim, really make it happen? He must follow Charlie's advice: Make a list of all the things that hadn't changed and concentrate his thoughts and actions on them. Would that really do the job? He didn't know, but he had no better ideas, and he did trust

Charlie. He'd give it a good try. But not tonight. He was due for a little time on the keyboard before he turned in.

There were a number of things Tim wanted to do the next day: finish arranging his bookshelves, try his new, higher speed modem on CompuServe, install the new Windows version of CIM (CompuServe Information Manager), plan to do some research on diversifying his Cornerstone stock holdings. He also wanted to design stationery, an announcement and business cards for his investment counseling business and order them from the printer. These things should certainly have his business telephone and FAX numbers on them; but what *was* his business number? He had the new line, but that was for the computer and the FAX machine. A third line? That seemed excessive. He had heard about a service that might do the trick: For a few bucks a month--much less than the cost of another phone line--he could get another number that would ring differently. Then he could answer "Hamilton and Associates." It was called custom dialing. But then Becky and Tiffany used the telephone a lot. Would his clients get too many busy signals?

He came up with a solution that he thought was worth trying. Tiffany had a 17th birthday coming up shortly. He would give her her own personal telephone number with one stipulation: during business hours she must limit her calls to 3 minutes. He hoped she would like the arrangement. When some one dialed their regular number, the phone would ring in the normal manner and Becky would answer it if she were home. If they dialed the number for Hamilton and Associates, the phone would ring in bursts of two short rings and who- ever answered it would say "Hamilton and Associates." If they dialed Tiffany's number the phone would ring in bursts of three short rings and Tiffany would answer it. He would also order the new "voice mail" service, so that someone could leave a message whenever the phone was in use or when no one answered it.

There was another intriguing question. A friend had told Tim that anyone in the world could send him an "e-mail" (a message that he could read or print from his computer whenever he dialed into CompuServe).They needed to know only his Internet "address", which was internet:72317.1208@compuserve.com (where 72317, 1208 was his CompuServe account number). Not too many firms had such an address on their stationery or business cards yet. He decided to ask a friend who used Prodigy to send him a test message. If it worked, he would put it on all of the items he was having printed. It would show that he was modern, and it might be a source of prospects. In any event it would be fun, and that was part of the object of his new business. Then he must prepare a mailing list of people who should receive a copy of his announcement. That would be time-consuming, but very important.

A few days later the morning's mail included a picture postcard from Vienna--from Becky! The message was prosaic: She and her mother were both well and were having a great time. This was the fourth city they had toured. Two things stood out in his mind as he read the card: her failure to mention where they were going or when they'd be home, and the last line: "Hope you're getting better. All my love. Becky." A light turned on in his mind. His consulting business could be the key to persuading Becky that he hadn't really lost his marbles. He would go after business, hammer and tongs. They didn't need more income; but if he made good money, it should show Becky that his head wasn't in the clouds and that his feet still touched the ground. His thoughts were interrupted by the ringing of the telephone. It was Rankin Smith, the Abbott-Northwestern board chair, calling to ask Tim if he had any further questions about the prospective board membership?

"Just one." replied Tim, "Will I have occasion to use my investment management experience on behalf of the hospital?"

"Oh yes," was the reply. "We have a large endowment fund, reserve funds for various purposes, and numerous designated funds. All told, these funds run well into nine figures. As you know, we are part of Allina, the big health conglomerate; and all these funds are currently invested in their common fund, which has done very well. But our board is saying that we should at least look at the alternatives every couple of years or so. You would be the ideal person to head a task force that could guide our staff through this process. Of course, your well-known business acumen will be of great value to the hospital."

Tim was silent for a few moments before he said, "I would like to accept your invitation."

"That's wonderful! You'll receive further information from the president's office: a date for the new board members' orientation, a list of meeting dates and times, options for committee assignments, and so on. We look forward to seeing you again soon."

"As do I" Said Tim, and the conversation terminated with the usual good-byes.

The following week he had a call from the board chair of the Minnesota Orchestra. The pattern was quite similar to the Abbott-Northwestern protocol: a lunch date with the chair and the president, material to read, a tour of the facilities, a follow-up call for questions and acceptance. This board also offered Tim opportunities to use his investment skills as well as his general business acumen. The Orchestra had an international reputation and was highly ranked. He agreed to serve on this board also.

Within the next several weeks Tim received five additional invitations: Fairview-Southdale Hospital systems (declined because of potential conflict of interest), the Walker Art Center (accepted), Macalester College (a liberal arts college in St. Paul, very heavily endowed by the *Reader's Digest* Wallace family) (accepted), the Minneapolis Foundation (accepted) and the St. Paul Chamber Orchestra (declined because of potential conflict of interest). He decided not to consider any additional requests until he saw how his time schedule worked out. He was sure his mother had had many more things in mind, but this seemed like a good start.

He had received four additional post cards from Becky: from Paris, Berlin, Rome and London. Each of them was worded a little differently, but they had a common theme: a hope that he was feeling better. She had called him from Edinburgh to tell him she still loved him very much, how much she missed him and how anxious she was to see him. Her mother had more places she wanted to see, but Becky thought they would be home soon. After all, they'd been gone for seven weeks. Tim felt good about the call, and it strengthened his resolve to win back Becky's confidence in him. That must be his most urgent priority.

Chapter Eleven
Personal Counseling

When Tim answered the phone, he heard the familiar voice of Jim Barker, Vice President and Controller of Cornerstone. After a few pleasantries, Jim came quickly to the point, "Tim, I'm concerned about my son, Ernie. He's 25 and just can't seem to make up his mind what he wants to do with his life. I've always respected your judgement and wisdom in these matters. Would it be imposing on your time to ask you to spend an hour or so with him?"

"I'd be glad to do it, Jim."

"That's wonderful! What would be a good time for you?"

"How about 7:30 tomorrow evening? If he could come over to the house, we'd have a quiet place to talk. Tell Ernie I've invited him. If that time isn't convenient, ask him to call me and we'll pick one that is."

"Thanks a heap, Tim. I want to do something nice for you."

"You're more than welcome, Jim, but I haven't done anything yet."

After Tim had hung up the phone he had mixed feelings. He was flattered by Jim's request and he felt strangely exhilarated; but he also saw a major irony: he was still trying to sort out his own future. Furthermore he had never done any career counseling. His own kids didn't know yet what they were going to do with their lives, although, of course they were younger. Was he really wise in his approach to his own children? He had leaned over backward not to put pressure on them; but many successful people had credited the strong influence of a parent. Could he really help Ernie? He would go to the library in the morning and do some reading on career counseling.

Right now, however, he had to do some work for his first client. This friend-of-a-friend had called Tim even before he had mailed his announcements. He was a gentleman in his sixties who had inherited seven million dollars from a maiden aunt and didn't trust himself to do the right thing with it. He seemed quite confident in Tim's ability to advise him (thank goodness for admiring friends!), and he seemed equally comfortable with Tim's fee basis: a tenth of one percent of the total asset value, payable each quarter in advance. If anything, this was on the low side; but it did not include any custodial services. This account alone would bring him $28,000 a year. He figured he could handle ten of these accounts at a time and still stay within the thousand hours a year he had chosen as the optimum number of hours he wanted to spend in the consulting business. This would be a half-time job and still leave the other half of a work week for community service. As he acquired more clients and Becky saw the income rising to a level near what he had enjoyed at Cornerstone, he hoped that Becky would be persuaded that he was a long way from having lost his marbles. He had completed his list of things that he felt had not changed in his life, and it was long compared to the list of things that had changed. He would be very careful to follow Charlie's instructions: in all of his contacts with Becky he would emphasize the thoughts and actions in that first list and avoid the second list as much as he could.

He spent three hours the next morning at the library, reading books on counseling in anticipation of his meeting with Ernie Barker. He found them interesting and could relate to much of what he read as being common sense. But he acquired a lot of new insights and made copious notes concerning them.

That afternoon, while he was working on his first client's investment portfolio, he answered the phone to hear a well-modulated woman's voice that he didn't recognize. Since it rang in the conventional way, it must be a personal call, so he answered,

"Good afternoon, this is Hamilton's."

"Hello, Mr. Timothy Hamilton?"

"Yes?"

"This is Cynthia Braden. You don't know me, but my father, Fred Braden, knows you well and thinks the world of you. I'm having serious difficulties in my marriage and he thinks you could help me."

"Well, Cynthia, that's very flattering; but I have no skills as a marriage counselor. What makes him think I could help you?"

"My father says you're a very wise man and that you've made a great success of your own life, including your own marriage. I do hope you feel you can take the time to talk to me."

Little does she know about my present situation, Tim thought; nevertheless it bolstered his courage to hear that his old friend thought highly enough of him to entrust him with his daughter's problems.

"I'll be delighted. Would you like to meet me for lunch at the Minneapolis Club tomorrow?"

"That would be marvelous. What time and where shall we meet?"

"I'll be in the reading room at 11:45. That's the first room to your right as you come in the front entrance."

"Yes, I know. I'll be there; and thank you so much."

As they said their good-byes and Tim hung up the phone, he felt excitement sweeping over him. Questions raced through his mind: What were her problems? Would he really be able to help her? What could he do for her that her own father couldn't do? What had he learned at the library that would be helpful in this interview? What was she like? Would she be as charming as she sounded on the telephone? How would Becky feel about it? He tried to concentrate on the preliminary report that he was preparing for his client, but his thoughts kept returning to the telephone conversation. He found himself keenly anticipating tomorrow's lunch date. Was this high level of anticipation a warning sign? He kept telling himself that this was just another form of community service, but the sense of excitement just wouldn't go away.

As he answered the door that evening to welcome Ernie Barker for his career counseling interview, he mentally reviewed all of the new things he had learned at the library.

"Welcome, Ernie, I'm delighted to see you."

Ernie grasped Tim's outstretched hand with a certain limpness that conveyed a feeling of uncertainty, as he said,

"Mr. Hamilton?"

"Yes, Ernie. Come on into the living room and have a seat in that soft chair over there. Would you like a soda? I have several kinds."

"Yes, thank you! A Classic Coke sounds good."

"That sounds good to me, too. I'll be back in a minute. Make yourself comfortable in the meantime."

He had remembered his first lesson: Make your client feel as comfortable as possible. Give him something to do with his hands. If possible, show approval of his actions. As Tim returned with the drinks and seated himself where he and Ernie could be face to face (but not so close as to embarrass his client or make him feel uncomfortable), he said,

"Well Ernie, we're here to see if I can help you figure out what to do with your life, or at least what the next few steps are. Is that your understanding?"

"Yes sir."

"I'd like our conversation to be as informal as possible, and I assume you would too. You don't have to call me sir. And, if you feel like calling me Tim, I'd be very comfortable with that. Now tell me about your life so far, and don't leave out anything you think might help us to achieve our goal."

"OK, I'll try."

As Ernie told his story, Tim listened intently, eyes intent on Ernie's face, nodding occasionally to show his understanding, and interrupting only with an occasional uh-huh to show further interest and understanding. It took Ernie almost an hour to tell his story. (Tim thought Becky would never believe that he was silent that long. She didn't consider him to be a very good listener. She was probably right, he thought, but he was learning fast.)

Ernie described a happy childhood in a home where the parents loved each other and showed their love for him (although they never spoke of it). It was only recently that he appreciated that what he thought as a teen-ager to be stern limits and the required accountability for his actions was really showing him love. He told about his schooling; he'd been an A student in elementary school, a B student in high school and a 2.4 (C+) GPA while earning a college degree in liberal arts. It was Tim's turn to talk.

"Were your high school grades higher in some subjects than others?"

"Yes, I got A's in history and social studies and C's and B's in math, physics, chemistry and biology."

"What do you think accounts for this interesting pattern in your grades."

Tim was still trying to practice what he had learned at the library: You want to draw your client out, but you don't want to put him on the defensive by asking questions that sounded judgmental. Ernie thought about it a few minutes before he replied,

"Gee, I really hadn't thought about it this way before. I started goofing off shortly after I got into high school."

Tim's quizzical glance encourage Ernie to go on,

"You see, it was about then that my mom began urging me to be a doctor. Not long afterward my dad starting urging me to go into a business of some sort."

"So you were getting mixed messages from them."

"Yeah, and the closer I got to finishing college, the more it tore me up. I loved them both and I didn't know who to please."

"Did you ever think of pleasing yourself?"

"You mean doing what *I* really *want* to do?"

"That's exactly what I mean. What would you really like to do?"

"I guess I haven't given it much thought; I wasn't sure I had a say in the matter."

"Ernie, you're an adult now; and every adult has a God given right to choose what he wants to do with his life."

After a long pause, Ernie said, "You're giving me a whole new perspective on choices I didn't even know I had, Mr. Hamilton. I'm going to have to think about this for a while."

"Take as long as you need," Tim replied. "But make it your number one priority and don't waste any time. The sooner you make up your mind and get a track to run on, the happier both you and your folks will be."

"Gosh, that makes a lot of sense; but where do I begin?

"Have you ever taken an interest test or a preference test?

"I took some kind of test at the U. I think it was called the Minnesota multi..."

Tim supplied the missing words.

"Multi-phasic Personality test."

"Yeah, that's it."

"That's different. That one is supposed to determine what kind of a person you are. Can you think of any others?"

Ernie thought a few moments before he said,

"Yeah, I think it was called the Briggs-Meyers or Meyers-Briggs; something like that."

"That's a personality test also. Do the names Strong or Kuder ring a bell with you?"

"Nope."

"They're the kind of test I'm talking about. They help to determine what kind of career people have the same interests as you do. I'd suggest you contact Central Counseling at the University. They can give you these tests as a part of a complete career counseling work-up. It's not too expensive, in fact, it may even be free to graduates of the U. But now tell me some things you've done that really turned you on."

"Like what?"

"Jobs you've worked at, volunteer activities, church projects, whatever."

Ernie was silent for a while, then his face brightened up as he spoke,

"Gee, I think the most fun I ever had was being a counselor at a boys camp. I did that for two summers. I had a ball!"

"What else?"

"I was a volunteer at the Special Olympics one year. That gave me a real high. Golly, I was in the clouds for days afterwards just thinking about those wonderful kids: how hard they tried to do things they never thought they could do. I'll never forget the look on their faces when they made it. Wow!"

"Anything else?"

As Ernie hesitated, he looked happier than he had all evening, and then he said,

"Oh yeah. A group of us young people from church spent part of a summer as volunteers at Camp Courage. That was a blast!"

Then his face fell as he added,

"But none of these were real jobs, like being a doctor or a lawyer or a business man."

"Ernie, One of our greatest God-given gifts is the opportunity to do work that really makes us happy and fulfilled. It's sad that most people don't realize that. So they choose their careers for the wrong reasons."

"Like what?"

"To make a lot of money, for security, to please someone they love, particularly their mothers, sometimes their fathers."

Ernie looked as if someone had suddenly raised a window shade and he was looking out at a beautiful vista.

"Mr. Hamilton, are you really saying I can work at something that really turns me on without feeling guilty or inadequate because I don't make as much money as some of my friends ?"

"I know young people that I would hesitate to say this to, but I know your folks and I know what kind of values you've acquired from them. So I feel safe in saying to you: follow your heart! Go for it!"

"But aren't my folks going to be really upset with me?"

"Keep them posted on what you're doing to find the right career for you. Tell them what you learn at Central Counseling. Go over the report with them. Then call me and we'll get together and talk about what to do next."

"Gee, Mr. Hamilton, you've opened up a whole new world for me! How can I ever thank you?"

"You have already."

"Yeah, I said thanks; but I mean how can I repay you?"

"You've done that already, too"

Tim went on to respond to the puzzled expression on Ernie's face,

"You see, Ernie, I, too think we've accomplished something; so I feel the same high that you felt after those experiences you were telling me about. That's something we all need, regardless of our age: the happiness and fulfillment that comes from feeling we've helped someone. The only way I could feel more rewarded is to see you become a happy and fulfilled man; and I believe that you're going to make that happen."

As they said their good-byes Tim wished he had a camera to catch a picture of the young radiant face that Ernie carried away with him. Tim sat down and reflected on the two hours he had spent with Ernie. The interview took twice as long as he had expected; but he felt certain that it had been time well spent. It seemed incredible that an intelligent young man with such good parents and a fine education could have so little self-understanding. It seemed equally incredible that loving parents and a loving child could communicate so poorly. He thought about his own life in his late teens and early twenties. He certainly had gotten mixed messages from his parents. Why didn't he experience Ernie's problem? He had always had good communications with his mother and had accepted her values with a whole heart. On the other hand, he loved his father *despite* his father's values, which he never could accept. So he really hadn't experienced the kind of tension that poor Ernie had felt. His next thought was more disturbing: Had he really done as much good as he thought he had? Was Ernie's problem really that simple, or had he missed something significant and jumped too quickly to a diagnosis and a solution? He decided that only time would tell. All in all, he

felt quite satisfied with his first attempt at career counseling.

The sound of a key in the front door interrupted
his reveries. Who could it be? Tiffany had spent the
evening in her room. Was it Peter, or *could it be Becky?*
He rushed to the door.

Chapter Twelve
The Surprise

I t *was* Becky! They fell into each other's arms and murmured in chorus,

"Oh Darling! I've missed you so!"

Tim set her bags at the bottom of the stairway, flopped down on the left end of the sofa, a position in which he had spent many intimate hours with her) and said,

"The bags can wait; come and tell me all about yourself."

She took her cue, sat down close to him, swung her feet up on the sofa, and rested her head, half on his right shoulder, the other half up against his cheek before she exclaimed,

"Oh Tim darling, do you realize it's been seven weeks to the day since Mother and I left for Europe. I think it was about day two that I started missing you; and not a day passed since then that I haven't wondered how you were and what you were doing. Mother and I had a good time, in a way; but every day I I thought how much more fun it would be if Tim were here. I sent you a card from every place we stopped; and I kept a diary, which you can read later. But now I'm anxious to know what's new here."

"Peter and his apartment mate are settled in their new digs. They seem to be getting on well and are both happy with their new feeling of independence. He seems like a nice guy, congenial, too. I think it will be good for both of them to be on their own without moms to pick up after them. In fact, I established a strict understanding with Peter about that."

"What do you mean?"

"They have laundry facilities in the building, and he is not to bring home dirty laundry."

"And how are things going with Tiff?" Becky asked somewhat tentatively.

"Tiffany is busy with her schoolwork and happy with her friends. She is delighted with the new telephone arrangement, and especially since she has her very own number."

"I thought we had agreed that we wouldn't put in a separate line for her! She'll spend entirely too much time on it."

"Darling, I've kept that agreement". Tim told her about custom ringing and about the deal he'd made with Tiffany to limit her calls to three minutes in the daytime, and a reasonable length in the evening. He also told her how well it seemed to be working and that Tiffany had lived up to her end of the agreement; then he added,

"The kids have both missed you."

"Do you think they understood why I left home? I wrote Peter, and I knew you would share your note with Tiffany."

"Yes, I think they both understand; and I assured them both that it was only a matter of time until we'd pick up where we left off."

He didn't think it was necessary to tell her about the long hours of delightfully intimate conversations he'd had with Tiffany, about both his marriage and his mission for the future. That was all material in the right-hand column.

"Oh Tim, you're such a darling; but do you really think we can? I've been so worried about you. Was Charlie Becker able to help you?"

Bless her heart, Tim thought, she's trying to be tactful. What she's really wondering is whether I'm still crazy. He decided a good dose of optimism would help them both at this point.

"Oh yes, Charlie was helpful beyond my fondest hopes. He gave me a verbal shock treatment and a dose of reality that helped me see my problems very clearly."

"Anything else?"

"Yeah! He gave me a very clear track to run on; and I think you'll be delighted with what's happened in seven weeks."

"You're going back to Cornerstone!"

This was the moment he knew he was going to face, and he had prepared very carefully for it. He had rehearsed over and over the very words he would use,

"Darling, there is something very important that you must understand very clearly, and I'll explain it to you the best way I know how. My decision to leave Cornerstone was really made before we went to Hawaii."

"Then why did we go to Hawaii?"

He was ready for this one, too,

"I was hoping against hope that *they* would see the trap that they were falling into. I even wrote Symington a long letter pointing out that to take huge risks with the policyholders' money would be breaking faith with the trust our policyholders had put in us. But I knew then that, if they didn't change their minds, it would be impossible for me to continue at Cornerstone. I just couldn't stay in my former position and act against my own judgement, I hope fervently that you can understand that."

"I understand how you feel about it, but I still have a question."

"What's that?"

"How can all of those smart men at Cornerstone be wrong? I know the old saying: They're all out of step but Johnny. Are they all out of step but Tim? I hope my question doesn't upset you."

"Heavens no, Darling! I'm just delighted that we can have such a frank talk about this subject, Think of it this way: The life insurance industry has fallen ill to a strange disease. It's become so extremely competitive that each company looks in feverish desperation for ways to make its products more attractive than those of the other companies. A logical way to do that is to increase the return on their investments. Well, you just can't get higher returns without taking greater risks that you will lose the principal. If--or when-- that happens, it will destroy the policyholders' faith in their insurance company--if not the whole life insurance industry, and that faith is what has made our business the great bulwark of the financial world."

"Tim, when you believe something so passionately, you really become eloquent. If you ever decide to run for office, I'll sure vote for you. I just hope you're right."

"Well, thank you, I think. Unfortunately, I sincerely hope I'm wrong."

"Why in the world would you want to be wrong?"

"Part of my job is--or was--to keep close tabs on how other life insurance companies invest their money. I had able assistants who did elaborate research on that subject. I was shocked at their most recent study, which showed that almost 100 of the 1800 US companies in our business are doing exactly what Cornerstone is planning to do."

"Taking too much risk."

"Exactly, and the worst of it is that they're not all small, fly-by-night companies. Some of the largest, most respected companies in our business are among them. Some of them are bound to go down in flames."

"You mean they'll go bankrupt."

"That's a possibility. Hopefully ways will be found to rescue them; but before the rescue plans are in place, there will be countless policyholders worried literally sick about their life savings, there will be front page headlines and oodles of bad press that will give our industry a shiner that no beefsteak can relieve."

"That's incredibly frightening. When do you think it will happen?"

"It's hard to say. My best guess is you'll see the first casualty within two years. There'll be some domino effect, as word gets around about other companies with similarly risky portfolios. If policyholders lose faith in their company, they quickly cash in their policies. This can start a run on the company, which even a relatively strong company can't withstand because only a small portion of its assets are that liquid."

"It's all so incredible, I'm still confused."

"Well, darling, only time will tell; but I want you to be assured of two things."

"What are they?"

"One is my everlasting love for you."

"And you know that you have mine. What's the other?"

"That my accident in Hawaii had absolutely nothing to do, directly or indirectly, with my decision to leave Cornerstone."

"Yes, Tim. I now understand that and believe it with a whole heart."

"Good! I'm bursting to tell you the exciting things that have happened in my life in the last seven weeks. I think you'll find them both interesting and reassuring. But you must be tired after your trip, so I'll try to contain myself until breakfast time. Come on, I'll take your bags upstairs now."

When they had reached the top of the stairs, she asked softly,

"Tim?"

"Yes darling?"

"Would you share our bed with me tonight?"

"Oh honey! I've been so afraid this day would never come again!"

During his long convalescence he had not been able to fulfill his role as a husband; and, by the time he had felt his strength returning, Becky had felt estranged from him. As he prepared for bed, he felt all the excitement and strength of a bridegroom welling up in him. As they fell into each other's arms he could hardly contain himself. Yes, this *was* like the old times...

Tim awoke in the morning exuberant, excited and eager to get on with his conversation with Becky. He was tempted to wake her but thought better of it; she needed the sleep, poor darling. It had been a strenuous night after her long day of travel. He slipped quietly down stairs, started the coffee, fetched the paper, and tried to concentrate on the morning news, but his efforts were futile. He was filled with an enormous sense of happiness, satisfaction and exhilaration as he reviewed every moment from when he had heard the key in the door until he fell asleep spent and exhausted some time in the wee hours of the morning. Every moment had exceeded his fondest hopes and expectations. He was over the first big hurdle: Becky was satisfied that his decision to leave Cornerstone, right or wrong, was at least made rationally. And certainly last night showed more eloquently than any words that she no longer felt she was with a stranger. But he must remind himself that his task had only begun: He still must convince her, and keep her convinced, that his thoughts and actions were those of the same rational, sane businessman to whom she had been married for years.

His heart jumped when he heard her steps on the stairs and saw her approaching the kitchen doorway. She had put on an enticing negligee, carefully combed her hair--and even added a touch of lipstick. They embraced tightly as he exclaimed softly in her ear,

"Oh darling! You look positively radiant and ravishing!"

"I *feel* radiant!" she responded brightly, ignoring the ravishing part.

Tim flipped a folded napkin onto his arm, stood stiffly at attention and gave his best imitation of the haughty manner and accent of a waiter in a posh restaurant,

"Bon jour, madame. Welcome a l'chateau de Hamilton. Our light breakfast de jour includes juice de l'orange, toast avec cinnamon, and cafe au lait."
When he completed his little speech, he leaned over her, unfolded her napkin with a flourish. placed it in her lap and gave her a resounding kiss on the cheek. The whole performance, particularly his fractured French and futile efforts to make Hamilton and cinnamon sound French, always sent both of them into gales of hearty laughter. When she regained her composure, she responded in mock indignation,

"Merci, but polite waiters in high-class restaurants don't kiss the guests!"

This had been a ritual he had come up with many years before, when he felt that their spirits needed to be raised, or that any tension had developed. He used it sparingly so that it didn't go stale, but it was near the top of his list in the left hand column, which he had totally committed to memory. It probably wasn't necessary this morning, but he felt that it was very important to have the conversation get off on the right foot. When he had served them both, he sat down across from her, and she laid down the paper. Tim smiled as he spoke.

"Darling, I have so much to tell you. I hope you don't mind if I start while we're eating."

"Of course not, Tim. I'm eager to hear it."

He told her first about the investment consulting business he had started and showed her copies of his stationery, business cards and announcement. He told her about the three clients he had already, the two appointments he had scheduled with prospective clients, and the three leads he had just gotten yesterday and hadn't had time to follow up. Annual fees from the first three would total almost $100,000. He could handle a total of ten clients with estimated annual fees of almost $300,000 and still have time to do the other things he wanted to do.

"Like what?" she asked.

He told about the five boards he had agreed to join.

"They all seem to feel that I can make a real difference, particularly by using my investment management skills to make sure that their funds are invested optimally. It makes me feel very good."

"That's impressive. It makes me so proud of you."

"Thank you, and there are other values stemming from these connections."

"Such as?"

"Many of these board members are movers and shakers in the community. Just getting to know them better is a positive experience. What's more, they are great sources of clients for my new business. Three of the people I'm already talking to came from these board members."

"Wow, that sounds great!"

"That's not all. Some of the social occasions to which we'll be invited put Cornerstone's affairs to shame; and we'll have a lot of new friends."

"You've been a busy guy."

"Yeah, and there's more. I've sort of backed into the career counseling business."

Because she seemed so interested, he told in detail about how the interview with Ernie came about, his careful preparation for it, and the highlights of the exchange.

"How wonderful that you could help poor Ernie. Let's make sure we don't do that to Peter and Tiffany. Will there be others?"

So far the morning had developed far better than he had envisioned. But now he became more irresolute. Why had he left this one to the last? He soon found out. As he told Becky about his upcoming lunch date, he could see her stiffen as she asked,

"How did this woman happen to call you?"

Tim told Becky about the recommendation from the woman's father. She was not reassured, and the questioning continued,

"What does she look like?"

"I've never laid eyes on her. She's probably as homely as the ace of spades."

"What are her motives?"

"She said she needed help concerning her divorce. I can only assume that she meant what she said, at least until I know her better."

"Did she know I had gone to Europe?"

"I honestly don't know, but I doubt it. Her father and I don't travel in the same social circles."

"Well, be careful. Don't touch her except for a brief handshake. Be sure to stay in public areas where there are witnesses, and watch for any sign of other motives."

"I didn't know you were the suspicious type. I'm really surprised. After all, you must know that I just couldn't *imagine* a more satisfying relationship than the one you and I have."

"I know that Tim, and I do trust you; but I just don't trust that woman. Charge it up to a woman's instinct, or a sixth sense or whatever; but smart women seem to understand the potential danger in these situations better than smart men, even the wise ones like you.

And you are quite a catch, with all your money, your marvelous personality and your good looks and your social graces. You've got it all, and I plan to keep you all for myself."

Tim looked at his watch and exclaimed,

"My goodness, we've spent over two hours at the breakfast table. I have some things to do at my desk before I keep my date with this--temptress?"

As they stood up and embraced warmly, she tried to think of a quick retort, but none came to her. She gave him a wry smile and said,

"Don't forget to get dressed."

As he tried to work at his desk, he felt the same excitement he had felt when Cynthia had called. Was Becky right? It certainly wasn't fair to pre-judge this woman when he hadn't even met her. But what was this strange excitement? He had dealt with many other women and never felt that way. Was it something in her voice that conveyed a subliminal message? Did it have to do with Becky's having been gone so long when Cynthia called? "This is nonsense! Get hold of your self!", he muttered gruffly, half aloud. He forced himself to turn on his desk-top computer and click on the organizer in which he recorded all frequently used telephone numbers and his dates. He brought up the screen showing three prospective clients and dialed the first number.

The prospect answered the phone, recognized his name from their mutual friend's recommendation, and eagerly accepted Tim's invitation to the Minneapolis Club to discuss the possibility of a client relationship. Ditto for the second call. Two for two, Tim thought. Could he make it three for three? Not quite: The third call was answered by voice mail. Tim identified himself, named the mutual friend from whom he had gotten the prospect's name, offered the lunch invitation, suggested three possible dates, and asked the caller to respond to his business phone number. He ended by suggesting that, if the caller got voice mail or someone besides Tim, he could merely leave the date of his choice and his business number on voice mail, or with whoever answered the phone. If he were home, he would answer personally. If not, Becky would answer "Hamilton and Associates", and proceed in the manner of a highly skilled administrative assistant, which she had been before Peter came along to absorb her attention. Tiffany felt a little rebuffed at being instructed not to answer the business ring. When Tim sensed this, he suggested that Becky train her, including modulating her voice, and let him know when she felt Tiffany was ready. Both women enthusiastically agreed to the arrangement.

After completing the third call, Tim checked his voice mail and made notes of the names and numbers left by two callers. One was another young man looking for career counseling. The other was a woman who didn't identify the purpose of her call. Tim first decided to wait until after lunch to return the calls, but then couldn't restrain his curiosity about the second call. He called the woman's number and got her recording machine. He acknowledged her call and said he would try her again later in the day. Tim dressed quickly and kissed Becky good bye. To her mild kidding that he was dressed better than he usually did for lunch, he merely responded,

"Am I?"

He arrived at the club ten minutes early, which was unusual for him. He picked up a copy of the Wall Street Journal and tried to read the news briefs. He found his excitement and his frequent glances at the doorway too distracting however; so he put the paper down and just watched the doorway. At exactly 11:45 an indefinable, but perceptible, change took place in the room. A vision of feminine loveliness had appeared in the doorway, and at least a dozen pairs of male eyes focused on the vision Some pretended to continue reading, but almost all managed to cast brief, furtive glances in the direction of the doorway while trying not to stare. A couple of pairs of eyes stared without pretense. Dressed in plain black, which contrasted dramatically with flawless, ivory-white skin, the tall woman carried herself dramatically, with the air of a model. Her high cheek bones accentuated turquoise eyes that were framed with perfectly arched eyebrows and long, dark lashes. The makeup looked professional, but it was soft and subtle, giving no hint of the hard look often seen in professional models. Her long, dark-brown hair had a radiant sheen that seemed natural. It was held in place tastefully by a simple but elegant clasp. She stood calmly in the doorway, eyes slowly surveying the room. Could this vision be Cynthia Braden?

Chapter Thirteen
Temptation

Tim had previously experienced the difficulty of two strangers trying to identify each other, and had used a solution that seemed to work well in the past. He walked slowly up to the woman and said,

"Good morning! May I help you locate someone?" The vision smiled as she said,

"Why yes, thank you. I'm looking for Mr. Timothy Hamilton. Are you, by any chance, he?"

"Guilty as charged!", Tim joked.

As he escorted Cynthia toward the elevator, he imagined the remaining eleven pairs of eyeballs turning green; and he struggled to keep the intense excitement he felt from overwhelming him. He pointed to the dining room as he said,

"You were certainly punctual."

Her response was simple and matter-of-fact:

"I dislike it when people keep me waiting, and I try not to do it to others."

"That's very considerate", Tim said as the maitre d' seated them at the choice table that Tim had specifically reserved. He thought the maitre d' used a special flourish as he seated Cynthia and placed the napkin in her lap. Tim continued,

"Let's order now. Then we can start talking."

Tim wrote down his own order while he waited for her to peruse the menu and decide. When he had handed the order to the waiting attendant, he opened the conversation,

"You told me on the phone that you were having some troubles in your marriage. Why don't you start from the beginning and tell me everything that you think bears on your problems and the possible solutions."

She began,

"I have wonderful parents. I reached my full five feet eleven inches before my senior year in high school, and was ashamed to be so much taller than the other girls in my class. But my mother taught me to be proud of my height and carry it with dignity and poise. I had a doting father who might have spoiled me rotten if Mother hadn't kept in check. He obviously admired me and made me feel feminine; but he never went any further than the frequent affectionate fatherly hugs. I respected him for that and was grateful for his restraint, because I knew girls in my class who had been molested by their fathers. One was even raped. I knew how it had torn them up mentally and left scars on their psyche that some of them would carry forever. They both taught me to respect myself and my body and to save my body for my husband. I was popular in high school, but I didn't have too many dates. Many of the boys seemed intimidated by my height. Most of them respected my values; and only two of them came on strong sexually. I told them firmly that, if that's what they were looking for, we had nothing in common. I made them take me home immediately and told them not to call again, and that was that."

Tim was nodding in understanding and silent approval when they were interrupted by the delivery of their orders. He found that her frank openness heightened his excitement, if possible; and he kept reminding himself wryly with the thought: "Come on, Tim! You're here to counsel this woman, not to admire her!"

As they began eating, he urged her to continue, which she did:

"During Christmas vacation one of the big downtown department stores ran a modeling contest for high school senior girls. Some of my friends and I entered the contest as a lark, and I was really quite surprised when I won. The store offered to send me to modeling school if I would agree to model clothes for them at their fashion shows, which were held in the evening so they wouldn't interfere with classes, and so husbands and daughters could attend with their wives. They would pre-pay my tuition; and I would earn so many credits against the tuition for each show I did. They had enough models that I didn't have to do more shows than I wanted to. I had to make only two commitments. One was to show up for the dates I did commit to, or give them as much notice as possible in an emergency. The other was to pay the balance of my tuition if I opted out before I had enough credits. I would receive $50 for each show, and that would increase by $10 a year up to $100 a show as I gained additional experience. That seemed like good money to a schoolgirl back in the seventies; but it seems almost laughable compared to what I make today. A show takes about two hours including preparation and cleanup."

Tim couldn't resist interrupting,

"Sounds like a good deal to me."

"I thought so, too; but my folks were dubious. They told me they weren't impressed with the life of a professional model and didn't want me to become one. I made a solemn promise to them, that I wouldn't let it interfere with my plans to finish college and get good grades. I assured them I would be open with them about my experiences, and would be willing to discuss the advisability of my continuing any time they wanted to. All I asked of them was to continue to trust me, judge me only by my own experiences and pay the balance of my tuition if I opted out early. They were impressed by my mature, realistic approach, and they gave their consent after only a few more questions."

"I'm impressed, too, with the way you handled it. But surely there were other experiences in your life besides modeling."

"Yes, I'll come to them; but I want to tell you more about my modeling because it has had such a profound and positive impact on my life. I quickly learned that show bosses were different. They weren't employed by the store, but by the designer whose clothes we were featured in a show. Some were bossy and rude and upset the girls. Others were pleasant and supportive. Their way of getting the results they wanted reminded me of a cheer leading captain. I learned how to find out who the show boss would be. I didn't want to do all the shows anyway, so I would sign up for the shows with good bosses. That was a very important lesson. I'm in such demand today that I can pick my own assignments."

Tim couldn't resist interjecting, "I can see why."

"Thank you. So I've learned how to stay in control in a profession that ruined many girls by making them slaves to the profession. I think it can be as damaging to a woman's self esteem as prostitution. That's what gives the profession such a bad name."

"But you seem to retain the freshness of youth, despite over two decades in the profession. How do you do it?"

"Thank you. The main factors are what I've told you. Most girls become slaves to the profession and lose their self-esteem. In their efforts to please the bosses they use too much makeup, and do other foolish things. In short, they prostitute themselves, some times literally."

"So how has this affected your marriage?"

"I'll explain. I met my husband, Fred Lambert, at a sorority dance when we were juniors at the University. He was the Big Man on Campus: star football player, class president, president of his fraternity, homecoming king, a good dancer and conversationalist, well mannered and popular with the girls and fellows alike. Everyone liked Freddie Lambert. He swept me off my feet, both figuratively, and literally on the dance floor. I brought Freddie home, and he charmed the socks of my folks. Freddie was also a good student, and we had many wonderful talks about many aspects of life and love. He seemed like an ideal mate. He proposed that we become engaged and plan to be married as soon after graduation as he found a good job. He was going for his B.S. in electronic engineering and had maintained a 3.6 (A-) average for his two-and-a-half years. I readily assented. It seemed too good to be true--and it was."

"How was that?"

"The next year and a half of college were the happiest years of my life. Fred was true to his commitments. He barely looked at another girl. We had many great times together, and many serious and frank discussions. We seemed to share the same important values. When he found that I was a virgin and wanted to remain so until our wedding night, he agreed to respect my wishes, despite his almost overpowering urges. He had dreams of getting a master's degree and perhaps a Ph. D. degree, but he wanted to work for a few years first and get a better perspective of the electronics industry, its direction, its needs and the best opportunities for bright young engineers. He seemed so sensible and down-to-earth, despite his man-about-town image. He had a good job lined up months before we graduated, and we were married a month after graduation. All four parents got along well, and they seemed as delighted with the marriage as we were."

"What went wrong?"

"I'm coming to that. It wasn't long after the wedding that I began to see a side of Fred that wasn't at all evident during our courtship and engagement. It seemed as if he felt he owned me, now that I was his wife. When I accused him of it, he told me the story of the redneck who said, `I think women are great; every man ought to own one.' He thought it was hilarious. I didn't think it was very funny. His attitude toward our sexual relations became shocking: sort of sex-on-demand. When I suggested that some foreplay would make it more enjoyable for both of us, he said, 'To hell with foreplay' when I want it, I want it!' When I complied with his demands, I felt used. When I refused to comply, he would verbally abuse me. The language he used to debase me! I won't repeat it. Let's just say that it was incredibly disgusting. I couldn't believe my ears at first. Where was the courteous, considerate Fred I knew in college? It reminded me of Jekyll and Hyde. When I asked Fred where he got his ideas of how a wife should be treated, he told me how much he admired his father. His father had told him that was the way real men treated their wives and that any man who didn't keep his wife in control was a wimp. Then he asked me if I wanted to be married to a wimp, and I said it might be better than what I had. He flew into an abusive rage. When I realized what I had gotten myself into, I felt it was too late to have the marriage annulled. I was already pregnant with our first child, John. I didn't like the idea of abortion, and I thought the stigma of having a daughter who was a single mother would be more than my folks could bear; and I love them too much to hurt them that way."

Tim was shocked and utterly lost for words. How could *anyone* treat such a marvelous woman so cruelly? He wanted to find that SOB, Fred, and beat him within an inch of his life. Instead, he just shook his head sadly as Cynthia continued,

"After John was born, Fred was a doting father; but he seemed totally insensitive to my needs. When I suggested that we take turns getting up with John so that I could get some badly needed rest, he just shook his head and announced flatly that that was women's work.

Despite my pleas of total exhaustion, he still insisted on sex when he was in the mood. I finally decided to refuse, and he raped me! That's when Colleen was conceived. I went to a lawyer to see if I could file charges; but he advised me that the Minnesota courts didn't accept intercourse, forced by a husband on his wife, as rape because of what they called the `husband's rights'. They've become more enlightened since then. To avoid another rape, I put a dead bolt on the door in the spare bedroom where I slept for a few nights without fear of being molested. When he realized what I had done, he became insanely angry and kicked a big hole in the door. I became so frightened that I took a martial arts course. I was strong already because of the strenuous exercise regimen I use to keep my body in shape as a first class model. On the other hand, Fred had let himself get flabby and had lost a good share of the muscle tone he had as football player."

"Did you ever have to use your martial arts training?"

"Just once. Fred thought he would catch me by surprise one day and force sex on me. I yelled 'Let go of me or you'll be sorry.' But he kept right on trying. I managed to break free and gave him a karate chop to the throat that floored him. I'll never forget the look on his face: a combination of surprise, shock, pain, fear and total disbelief. He couldn't speak for three days--just a hoarse croak. I was scared stiff that I had maimed him for life, but about the time I had concluded we should see a doctor he recovered. He never tried to force his intentions on me again. Our wonderful marriage had degenerated into an armed truce. When Fred realized he couldn't get what he wanted by force, he tried his darnedest to tear down my self-esteem. He said that models were first cousins to whores, that I had sold my body to the fashion designers, that nobody would look at me twice in a very few years, and then I wouldn't be able to

feed myself. Then I'd have to do his bidding or starve.
I had read everything I could lay my hands on about
verbal abusers. There wasn't too much then, but I
realized he was trying desperately to regain control by
destroying my self-esteem. I vowed that I would never
let this happen."

She paused long enough for a deep, heavy sigh and
then went on,

"There's much more, but I'm sure you get the
picture. We don't really have a marriage, just an uneasy,
disagreeable co-existence under one roof."

Tim felt led to say, "I'm terribly sorry."

"Oh, my life isn't all bad. I feel a great sense of
fulfillment in having instilled good values in two wonderful children whom I love dearly; and I feel that love
returned. I've taught John everything I know about wife
abuse. I've urged him to love and respect his father for
his good qualities, but to realize that violence and abuse,
even verbal, is not an acceptable form of behavior in this
enlightened society. I fervently hope, for both his sake
and his future wife's that I've been successful. He had
promised me that, if he finds himself having these
tendencies, he'll seek professional help. I've tried for
years to get Fred to seek help, but his answer is always
the same: 'Me? There's nothing wrong with me; you just
don't understand how a good wife is supposed to behave.'
I've also cautioned Colleen: no matter how charming a
young man seems, don't ever commit to marriage until
you've talked to his mother confidentially and determined whether she is abused. It's probably not necessary
for me to advise her; she's learned plenty from observing
her parents' marriage. On the other hand, she didn't
know how her prospective mother-in-law would feel
about such a personal question. I told her I thought the
woman would respect her all the more for her wisdom,
regardless of what the answer was."

For over half an hour Tim had been having a hard time suppressing an impulse to say,

"Why don't you divorce the SOB?" but that didn't seem like what a good counselor would say. So he said, instead,

"So how can I be of help?"

"Now that the children are on their own, I feel as if I should break free from this marriage-that-isn't-a-marriage; but I'm having trouble with several issues. First is the effect on Fred. Except for his abusive nature, he really is a good person. He's been a good father; he loves the kids and treats them very generously. He tries to treat Colleen as if she were a child, but that doesn't seem to faze her. She seems able to kiss it off. He's a good provider. He's not been unfaithful; and I'm sure he doesn't want to lose me.Then there's the fact that I promised to stay with him `as long as we both shall live'. Last but not least, is the effect on my folks. As wonderful and loving as they are, they just don't understand verbal abuse. Whenever I say anything to them about my problems, which isn't very often, Dad'll say something like, `Can't you two just sit down and talk it over?' I have to bite my tongue to keep from saying, 'Dad, you just don't understand'. But that would hurt him, and I love him too much to do that. So I say something like, 'Dad, it just isn't that easy; Fred won't admit that he has to change in any way.' Then Mother will chime in with her `Dear, you have to remember that marriage is a two-way street, and you have to make compromises; Dad and I have had our differences, but we've always been able to work things out.' I'm sure, if I filed for divorce it would be a great blow to them. When they finally realized that things weren't getting any better, Dad suggested I call you."

For the first time she seemed about to lose her composure; her eyes became moist and she dabbed quickly at them with a handkerchief. Tim wanted to hold her hands in a gesture of sympathy, but, instead, he said,

"Cynthia, you've been an incredibly brave woman, a fabulous mother, a dutiful daughter and a loyal wife. I admire you greatly, and I'm going to do anything and everything I can to help you."

"Thank you," she said quietly.

"Now let's take the issues you've raised, one by one. It's a measure of your good upbringing and your outstanding values that you've kept your wedding vows. Fred also promised to `love, honor and cherish' *you*; he may think he loves you, but he has strange ways of showing it, and he surely hasn't honored and cherished you. So he hasn't kept the vows *he* made."

"I try to tell myself that, but I'd still feel guilty walking out on him."

"That's another measure of your outstanding values; but we both know that Fred *has* to stop his abusive ways before you could ever have a decent marriage."

"That's right; but he could only do that with counseling, and he isn't willing to seek counseling."

"Exactly! And therein lies the key to that issue. We both know that it's harder for an abuser to change than it is for an alcoholic to go dry. In fact, there are a lot of parallels."

"I--I--I'm not sure I understand the solution."

"Have you heard of the confrontation process to get alcoholics into treatment?"

"Yes, but I'm not sure I understand how it works."

"It's simple in principle but must be very carefully planned and executed. Someone who has the power to take away something he dearly cherishes must give him an unavoidable, either-or choice. I've done several confrontations with my chemically dependent employees, threatening them with the loss of their jobs."

"Does it work?"

"Nearly always. Employers have to be cautious with the laws that say you can't fire an employee for drinking because it's a disease. They have to be careful to show that termination is due to the employee's inability to perform on the job. It works even better when the wife confronts the alcoholic--or the abuser--and threatens to leave him if he doesn't go through treatment."

"But doesn't she take a great risk when she threatens him?"

"Oh yes, and it can't be an idle threat. She has to be prepared to move out immediately if he doesn't agree to go into treatment immediately. It takes a lot of courage. But you win either way."

"I'm--I'm not sure I understand."

"Either Fred agrees to go in for treatment, or he doesn't. If he does and if it's successful, you'll find yourself married to the same wonderful guy to whom you became engaged, and you'll fall in love with each other all over again."

"And...and if he doesn't?"

"You will have given him the opportunity to fulfill his marriage vows. If he refuses, he is the one who has broken the wedding vows; and you can leave him with a clear conscience."

She sat in thoughtful silence for a few moments before she spoke slowly,

"I think I can accept what you're saying; but I'm still concerned about my folks."

"First, I would suggest that you tell them, in as much detail as you can, everything we've said to each other today. The stark reality of what you've been through will be a great shock to them, but it will go a long way to help them see that your problems are different from theirs. In fact, you can make a point of the fact that your father has never abused your mother, nor has he forced attentions on her."

"But what if they still think we should be able to just talk it out?"

"I would give them the best book you've found on verbal abuse and mark the parts that show the necessity of treatment in order to save the marriage. When they've read it, you can talk to them again and enlist their support."

"How would they support me."

"There are several ways, Cynthia. First, even as emotionally strong as you are, you will still need all the emotional support you can get. Then, too, their physical presence at the confrontation would make a statement to Fred."

"Would you also be present?"

"I think I can be very helpful, but I'll come only if you want me to. In any event, it would be very important that some third party be present. You need a witness, and it would also keep Fred from doing anything you would both be sorry for."

"Oh, Mr. Hamilton, I definitely want you to be there!"

"I've been calling you Cynthia. I hope you'll feel comfortable in calling me Tim. After all, we're both adults; and we're not exactly strangers after the last two hours."

"Very well--Tim," she said tentatively.
Tim had honestly intended the invitation only to put her at ease, and his excitement had waned as he had focussed on the solution to her problem. But, as she spoke his first name softly, the excitement rose in him, stronger than ever. He suddenly found it hard to keep his mind strictly on her problem. It was almost two o'clock, and all of the other diners had left. He had a strong feeling of regret as he spoke,

"Well, Cynthia, I think we've done all we can for today, unless you have questions."

"What if my folks *still* think that Fred and I should be able to patch things up?"

"When you've done everything you can to make them understand, you will have to keep telling yourself that it's now their problem. You may suggest that they talk with me, and I would be glad to accept their invitation."

"Where do we go from there?"

"After you've done everything you can to gain your folks' understanding and support, we'll need to talk again. If you care to call me then, we can make another appointment."

"I'd like that," she said quietly.

As they rose from the table and started for the lobby, she put her arm through his and said,

"Oh Tim, you've been so understanding and so helpful. I don't know how I'm ever going to repay you."

They had reached the lobby, and she extended her hand. As he took it, he placed his left hand on top of her right hand. He had a hard time controlling his voice,

"You have already. I'll look for your call."

She looked at him quizzically, but he didn't offer to explain. As she turned to leave he saw a smile and a light in her eyes that made his heart leap. He had an almost overwhelming desire to walk her to her car. He forced himself not to follow her.

As he drove home, thoughts and questions whirled through his mind. What did that heavenly smile and that look in her eyes mean? Was it merely gratitude? Or something more? How would she interpret his remark that she had repaid him already? What was he getting himself into? After all, he was very happily married and really loved Becky. How would Becky react to all of this? Would she still be suspicious of Cynthia's intentions? He knew she would be burning with curiosity to know about the interview, especially since it took so long. What should he tell her? How much should he tell her? He decided on a bold course of action. He would enlist her help as a co-counselor. He would tell her about the interview in great detail; but he would skip the part about his mental--and physical--reactions.

His conversation with Becky was going better than he had dared hope. She, of course, agreed to keep all the information he gave her in strictest confidence. She listened in fascinated, sometimes horrified, silence as Tim unfolded the heart-wrenching story of Cynthia's marriage. She nodded her approval and agreement as Tim related the advice he had given her. Finally, it was her turn to speak,

"I do appreciate your sharing all this with me. I feel deeply sorry for that poor woman, as I know you do. But don't let your sympathy turn into anything more. You've both got a tiger by the tail, and she's going to need a lot of help and support. Just remember that you're married to a woman that loves you with all of her heart, and I intend to keep you all to myself."

They had risen from the table where they had finished their coffee. Becky took him in her arms kissed him warmly and hugged him firmly, and he responded. As he made his way upstairs he thought, "Wow, what a sharp lady!"

Tim had spent two mornings at the library, reading everything he could find about verbal abuse and the confrontation process. The days stretched into two weeks, still with no word from Cynthia. Tim couldn't get her out of his mind. He had given her his business number so as to increase the chance that he would answer the phone when she called. He had five business clients now, so he was getting accustomed to answering "Hamilton and Associates" when he heard the distinctive double ring. He was on the point of calling her when he heard the double ring. Eagerly, (perhaps *too* eagerly, he wondered) he picked up the phone:

"Good morning, Hamilton and Associates."

"Hello Tim, it's Cynthia. We need to talk again."

He suggested lunch tomorrow, but this time at the Decathlon Club, which is located about eight miles south of the downtown area and where he was less well known. She had done shows there and needed no instructions to find it. The time seemed to drag until noon the next day. Again he was early for their appointment. She arrived precisely on time. She was dressed simply and yet she looked so elegant Tim felt the excitement rising in him, stronger than ever, if that was possible. They were seated immediately after Tim had shown his membership card. This was the only club in town that took this precaution against deadbeats. As soon as they had ordered Cynthia began,

"I've had two sessions with my folks."

"How did it go?"

"Just fair. Mother says she understands, but she doesn't want any part of confronting Fred. She has always avoided conflict as much as possible."

"What about your dad?"

"He seemed real disappointed that you hadn't encouraged me to patch things up with Fred. I failed to make him understand that it wasn't that easy."

"You didn't fail, Cynthia. *He* failed to understand. Unfortunately, many of the best and wisest men don't appreciate the seriousness of verbal abuse, and how difficult it is to cure."

"What do I do now?"

"First, we must talk to your children, explain the confrontation process to them."

"Should they be at the confrontation."

"I don't think so. If Fred reacts badly, it would be very hard on them to see their father at his worst."

"They're already aware that he abuses me, and have encouraged me to leave him."

"That's good; but as the old saying goes, `they ain't' seen nuthin yet'. Fred doesn't want to lose you. His natural reaction to your ultimatum will be anger and more abuse and threats. We hope that Fred comes to his senses and realizes that the only way he can keep you is to go through treatment; but there is a very good chance that this won't happen. It could be a very ugly scene. As mature as they are, it would be difficult for your children. In fact, you need to be aware that this will be very hard for *you*."

"It's hard for me to imagine anything worse than I've already been through."

"Have you ever read a book called *The Games People Play* by Eric Byrne?"

"No."

"One of the psychological games he describes in that book is `See what you made me do'. It's a psychological ploy often used by verbal abusers in which they blame the other person for their own bad actions. They can be very successful in heaping a heavy load of guilt on their mate. You must prepare yourself mentally for a verbal onslaught intended to make you feel so guilty that you relent and back off the confrontation."

""Will you be with me at the confrontation?"

"Absolutely, for several reasons. First of all, I want to give you my moral support. You will need it. Then, you should have a witness. Finally, my presence should discourage Fred from any rash acts, and even tone down his language."

"What do we do now?"

"We must prepare your statement very carefully. I'd like you to draft it; then I'll review it and make suggestions."

"What should it say?"

"Say just how you feel about your marriage, that you're not going to take any more abuse, and that the only way for him to change is to go through treatment. There are several good programs right here in Minneapolis, and he can take his pick. He'll probably be very contrite at first and promise not to abuse you any more; and he'll insist that there's nothing really wrong with him, and that he doesn't need treatment."

"But I should insist on treatment?"

"You bet."

"You make it all sound so logical and straightforward."

"It will be up to that point; but we must be prepared for the fireworks when he realizes he can't talk you out of the treatment idea, he will look for ways to make you change your mind. He'll probably tell me to butt out."

"I hope you don't."

"I certainly won't."

"How long should my statement be?"

"Make it short and to the point. If I feel you've left anything out, I'll certainly let you know. There's another important issue."

"What's that."

"Fred will do his best to get you alone and work you over. You can't stay in the house after this confrontation. So, on the day of the confrontation, you must pack enough clothes and reading material to last you several weeks and have your bags in the trunk. Reserve a room in a suburban motel. Before the confrontation leave your car at my house and I will drive you back to your house for the confrontation. Before we leave my house, we'll transfer your bags to Becky's car. When we're through, I'll drive you to the Minneapolis Club and let you off at the front door, you'll walk through the club and Becky will be waiting at the back door. She'll take you to your motel, and we'll bring your car the next morning. Don't tell anyone where you're going. Change the message on your voice mail so that callers are referred to my business number."

"It all sounds so--so cloak and dagger like."

"It will be cloaked in secrecy in order to avoid the daggers."

"How long will I have to stay in the motel?"

"Only long enough for you to find a nice apartment. When you move to the apartment, you can pick a day and time when you're sure Fred isn't home and move all of your personal possessions out of your house."

"You mean I won't ever live there again?"

"If Fred elects treatment, you can go back to your house after he has entered treatment. Otherwise, you'll have to stay in your apartment until ownership of the house is determined by the divorce settlement. If you get the house, I would suggest that you sell it. Your kids are on their own already. You will be starting a new life, and it will be easier for you if you're living in new surroundings."

"How long before my friends and clients can call me direct?"

"Hopefully, it won't be too long before Fred realizes that your life together has ended. The divorce proceedings will be handled by the lawyers; and we'll see that Fred's lawyer makes it plain to him that he's not to try to contact you directly for any reason. Under no circumstances should you give him, or any of his friends, your address. If he bothers you by telephone, we'll warn him, through his attorney, that we'll get a court order to restrain him from doing so. He may leave messages to try to trick you into calling him. He'll ask what sound like innocent questions; for example, where can he find this or that. In that case, give Becky or me the answer and we'll relay it to him. You must not allow yourself to be tricked into talking to him. If you do, he'll lay a load of guilt on you like you wouldn't believe; and you don't need that. Be sure to caution your children not to call home for a few weeks and not to show up at the house. Fred will do his best to get to you through them. They should also screen their calls at school. You've asked all the questions; now I have one: This process won't be easy; do you feel up to going through with it?"

Cynthia was silent for a few moments before she said,

"Can I ask one more question?"

"Of course, as many as you want to."

"How long will you continue to help me."

"As long as you need help."

"Then I'll start right away on my statement for the confrontation."

"Good, you have my FAX number?"

"Yes."

She seemed to relax, and she smiled as she said,

"Oh Tim, you're so wonderfully helpful. How will I ever be able to repay you?"

As they left the dining room and headed for the parking lot, Tim replied,

"When I told you before that you had repaid me already, you looked quizzical, so I'll explain: I have a great urge to do good in this world, and doing so gives me a marvelous high. I can't imagine how I could do better than to help a wonderful woman like you through a difficult time in her life."

She put her arm through his and give it a surprisingly strong squeeze. Tim could hardly restrain himself from taking her in his arms. He felt a strong sensation of regret as they reached her car. He kissed her lightly on the cheek and said,

"Goodbye, Cynthia, I'll watch for your FAX."

As he drove home, his thoughts oscillated between reliving the excitement he had felt during lunch and questions: How would Becky feel about the commitments he had made? Would she be willing play her part in Cynthia's escape? He soon found out. Once again he told her the whole story, except for the even stronger feelings that had welled up in him. When he finished, she was smiling and shaking her head, as she spoke,

"Your tiger has grown into a big lion. But the poor woman certainly needs help, and I'll do my part--as long as you continue to remember that it's me you're married to--and I want *all* of your love."

Two days went by. Every time his FAX machine chirped and purred, Tim looked eagerly for Cynthia's statement. The two pages came that evening and he read them eagerly. It was well done, he thought, but he made notes of a few changes. He picked up the phone to call her, then realized Fred might be home, so he decided to wait until mid-morning. The following morning he gave her his suggestions, and they chose the following Thursday at eight o'clock in the evening for the confrontation.

It seemed as if Thursday would never come. As it drew closer, Tim's excitement rose. Thursday afternoon Cynthia called,

"Oh Tim, I'm scared."

"That's understandable. This is a very big step you're taking. Most likely it will change the whole future course of your life. But keep telling yourself that we've planned this carefully and that we're prepared for any outcome."

"All right--if you say so."

"I'll look for you at my house at seven-thirty. Call me before that if it doesn't look as if Fred is going to be home."

"I will--and thank you from the bottom of my heart."

The sound of her voice thrilled him more than ever. He tried to work at his desk, but thoughts of her-- and fantasies--filled his mind. He allowed himself to dwell on the fantasies and they surprised him with their vividness and with the pleasure and physical excitement he felt. Finally he willed himself to stop. Becky certainly understood him and the dangers of the relationship he had entered into; yet she seemed to trust him. Was he deserving of that trust? Then he remembered his mother's quotation from the bible: "As a man thinketh in his heart, so is he."

Driving to Cynthia's house that evening Tim felt a kind of excitement he hadn't felt since the first big game of college football. He was confident that Cynthia would do her part as long as he was there to support her; but how would Fred react? Would he get intensely angry? How would he show his anger? Would he get physical? How would Cynthia deal with that? In his heart, Tim hoped that Fred would refuse treatment. Why did he feel that way? He told himself that it was because there was some recidivism among abusers who went through treatment and Cynthia shouldn't have to suffer the consequences; but was there another reason for his feeling?

As Cynthia ushered him into the living room, she looked excited but confident. When Fred was introduced, he looked somewhat puzzled and apprehensive. Cynthia ushered Tim to one end of the davenport, and she sat down at the other end. Fred sat down in his favorite easy chair across the room from them. When they were seated, Cynthia pulled a folded paper from her purse and began reading in an even, cool voice. As she neared the end of her statement, Fred gripped the arms of his chair so hard that his knuckles went white and the colored drained from his face. Then the redness began from his neck and moved upward until his whole face became beet red. His mouth worked silently before he shouted,

"Why, you no-good bastard! You're no better than a cheap, lousy whore. In a very few years you'll be out on the street with the rest of them; and now *you* try to tell *me* that *I've* got a problem. *You've* got a hell of a lot of nerve telling *me I've* been a lousy husband. Why-why, I've got a good notion to give you what you deserve *right now*!"

While he was delivering his diatribe, Fred had stood up, fists clenched, arms flexed, mouth pulled into a hard line; and Tim and Cynthia had risen at the same time. As he started toward Cynthia, Fred seemed oblivious of Tim. Tim's instinct was to step between them; but before he could do so, Cynthia went into a defensive karate stance and spoke in a low, even voice,

"Be careful, Fred. Remember what happened the last time you attacked me. I wouldn't want to maim you permanently."

When Fred hesitated, Tim took Cynthia by the arm and quickly ushered her toward the front door. Before he closed the door he said quietly,

"Good-bye, Fred."

They began their drive to the Minneapolis Club. Tim spoke first,

"You were absolutely magnificent!"

She moved close to him as she replied,

"I don't feel very magnificent now. I feel weak and totally wrung out."

"That's understandable; that was a very difficult thing you did, and you carried it off superbly, all by yourself. Do you realize I never spoke a word after you began reading your statement?"

"I guess that's right, but I'm so glad you were there; I couldn't have done it without you. Oh Tim, I feel so good when I'm with you!"

The fireworks went off in his head. What did she mean by that? Was it a mere acknowledgment of his support--or something more? He struggled hard to remember that his only role was that of a counselor, before he spoke,

"It gives me a tremendously good feeling to be of help to such a wonderfully deserving woman as you. Becky will be waiting in the driveway at the back of the club. She drives a dark blue Lincoln. You can direct her to the motel. Here's a sleeping pill. Take it as soon as you get to your room."

"I've never used sleeping pills. I've never needed them."

"I think you'll need one tonight. Sleep well, darling, and call me tomorrow evening on my work number."

Before she moved to get out of the car, she put her left arm around him, hugged him tightly and kissed him warmly on the cheek,

"Good night, you wonderful man!"

"Good night, Cynthia, sleep well."

He restrained himself from saying what he was thinking, and he didn't trust himself to say anything more. Was she showing him anything more than profuse gratitude?

The next morning Tim was greeted by the now-familiar double ring of his phone.

"Good morning, Hamilton and Associates."

"You dirty, lecherous s-- of a b----, how dare you interfere with my marriage? I'll sue you for everything you've got!"

"Have you decided to seek treatment?"

"Of course, not, you silly bastard! I don't have a problem."

"Then I don't think we have anything more to talk about."

"Oh yes we do, you . . ."

Tim hung up the phone. What would this angry man do next? Did he now have *two* tigers by the tail? The phone sounded its double ring again. He let voice mail take the call. He waited until nine-thirty to call Cynthia. A sleepy voice answered,

"Hello?"

The voice aroused those feelings in him. He found himself thinking how exciting it would be if he were in that room.

"Good morning, did you sleep well?"

"Oh yes; that pill really knocked me out."

"I've heard from Fred already. He has no intention of seeking treatment."

"Oh Tim, I'm so mixed up! I feel so guilty and yet I feel a sense of relief."

"That's very understandable. Just keep telling yourself that you gave him a very clear message and a chance to save your marriage, and he refused. *He's* the one who decided to terminate the marriage."

"I suppose so. What do we do now?"

"Let's give him a week or so to cool off and find out how much he really misses you. Then I'll call him and see if he's changed his mind about seeking treatment. If he hasn't, I've already sought the advice of two of my lawyer friends. They both named the same divorce lawyer to whom they refer all of their clients who are seeking a divorce. He's the best in town."

"Won't he be expensive?"

"I understand that his fees are reasonable. What's more, it probably won't cost as much as a less experienced lawyer, because he'll work more effectively."

Tim gave her the lawyer's name, address and telephone number. He had a strong urge to offer to go with her, but there really was no reason why he should-- unless she asked him. He found himself hoping she would. She didn't.

Tim counted off the next seven days; that evening he called Fred and asked whether he had considered seeking treatment to change his behavior and attitude toward Cynthia. The reply was extremely rude, but succinct: "Go to Hell, you bastard!" It was followed by a loud bang as the handset was replaced forcibly. Tim relayed the message to Cynthia in a more polite form and invited he to call any time she felt she needed help or support.

Another two weeks went by without any word from Cynthia. Every time his business phone rang Tim hoped it was Cynthia. Finally, she called,

"Hello, Tim, I'd like to buy you lunch."

She suggested a small, quiet restaurant to which he had been only once; and they agreed on a date and time. When Tim arrived, she opened her arms and gave him a long, firm hug. As the fireworks went off in his head she murmured,

"Thanks, Tim, I needed that."

After they were seated and had ordered he asked,

"So how are things going with you?"

"*Cum si, cum sa,* as my friend, the Italian model would say. Your lawyer is wonderful. He's filed the papers already, but we haven't heard from Fred or his attorney. Oh Tim, I still have days when I wonder if I'm doing the right thing. I visit my folks frequently, and Dad always asked whether Fred and I have gotten back together yet. Fred is working on him to get me back. Dad says Fred is lonely. Fred tells him he can't imagine why I left. I hate even to think how Dad will feel when Fred tells him I've filed for divorce. Oh Tim, I don't know what to do."

"Cynthia darling, no one ever said this would be easy. There's nothing surprising about what you've told me. Fred has found a way to heap a load of guilt on you; and there's absolutely nothing more you can or should do about Fred's actions or your dad's feelings. They're both adults and you aren't, and can't be, responsible for what goes on between them. You are, however, responsible for your own actions and feelings."

"But what am I to do about them?"

"Nothing, absolutely nothing. You just need to keep reminding yourself that you gave Fred his chance to shape up and he refused it. My goodness, after all the miserable years Fred has put you through, you're more than entitled to a life of your own and the opportunity to make a fresh start."

Tim's heart went out to this wonderful woman, whose only fault was that she allowed a selfish, abusive man to make her feel like the guilty party. What could he do to help her out of her funk. Then he had an inspiration,

"You told me you and Fred played racquetball. So do I. How about a game?"

"Oh, I'd like that."

"How about tomorrow at two, at the Decathlon Club? Tell the locker room attendant you're my guest and I'll meet you in the corridor leading to the courts."

"That sounds wonderful! I look forward to it."

Tim took her in his arms in the parking lot and gave her another warm hug. She responded and kissed him on the cheek. On the drive home his thoughts alternated between anticipation of the following afternoon and questions about his own actions. Did Cynthia reciprocate his feelings? Was he getting in over his head? Was the racquetball date the justifiable actions of a counselor? Should he tell Becky about the racquetball date? He decided he would continue to tell her about his conversations with Cynthia, but not about the racquetball date.

Tim found the racquetball match both challenging and extremely enjoyable. She was in tremendous physical shape, expertly returned his toughest shots, and challenged him with multi-wall shots executed with the speed and precision of an expert player. Many of the points were settled only after long rallies, and the scores were close. The grace of her movements and her beautiful body, largely revealed by short shorts and a thin top, brought his physical feelings to a new high. They refreshed themselves afterward with soft drinks in the Discus lounge. He had not seen her so exhilarated before. It brought a new radiance that seemed to make her all the more beautiful. They talked animatedly about many things, and Tim enjoyed himself immensely. She seemed in no hurry to leave and this pleased him. They agreed to another match the following week. This one in mid-morning, to be followed by lunch. When they exchanged hugs in the parking lot, he brushed her lips lightly with his. Her only reaction was a smile, so radiant that the picture stayed with him all the way home and he could think of nothing else.

Fred used every trick in the book to contest the divorce and to drag out the settlement, meantime working through Cynthia's father to persuade her to drop her suit and "patch things up." She became resigned to this fact and was largely successful in avoiding the guilt feelings Fred tried so skillfully to heap on her.

The proceedings dragged on for many months and the weekly racquetball games continued, as did Cynthia's exhilaration and his excitement. What changed was his sexual fantasies. They became more intimate, creative and real, and many times they carried his excitement to a climax. They began to include a planned rendezvous in Chicago. He and Cynthia would be extremely discrete, traveing on separate flights, staying in separate rooms at different, small motels where there was little or no chance of being discovered by a chance encounter with some one who knew them.

Finally, Tim came to realize how dangerously close he was coming to acting out his fantasies. He had long ago learned the value of considering the consequences before he took action. He realized how close he was coming to ruining a wonderful marriage, spoiling his relationship with his children, tarnishing his reputation, hurting Cynthia, and ultimately destroying his own happiness. With deepest regret and sadness he concluded that the only sensible solution was to have the classic we've-got-to-stop-meeting-like-this lunch with her. After their regular weekly racquetball game he said,

"Cynthia, could we have lunch here the day after tomorrow? I have a special announcement to make."

"I would like that! Can you tell me now what it's about."

Her face brightened with excitement and curiosity. Tim sensed strongly that she had feelings about him similar to his own about her, but he couldn't be sure. He realized that had made his already difficult task all the harder by creating strong expectations in her. All he could say, lamely, was,

"I'd rather wait until we have lunch."

"OK, if you say so."

Tim had a hard time thinking about anything else for the next two days. Did her reactions mean that she loved him? If so, his announcement would come as a great blow to her. What had he done to this wonderful woman? If she didn't love him, would he make a fool of himself with a statement that assumed that she did? How could he word his statement if he didn't really know how she felt? He tried different approaches in his mind and rejected them. What *was* the right way to approach her? Or was there *any* right way?

After they had ordered lunch, Cynthia wasted no time in getting to the point,

"What is it that you have to tell me?"

He had rehearsed the words many time, but they still sounded awkward to him,

"Cynthia, it must be apparent to you that I've been developing an increasing affection for you over the last few months. I'm really afraid that, if we go on as we have, I'll fall head-over-heels in love with you and do something that we'll both be sorry for. We just can't go on like this."

The change in her countenance was like a sudden summer thunderstorm. Her face became dark and filled with anger. Her voice was icy and the words had the edge of cold steel,

"What do you propose to do about it?"

He had never seen her like this before. He was shocked by the power of her anger, and he had to struggle hard to keep his composure. He tried to choose his words carefully, but they sounded weak and inadequate to him,

"I'd like to continue as your friend and advisor. I hope you'll feel free to call me any time you have a problem."

He wanted to say more, but he was afraid he would only make a bad situation worse. They sat in silence for a moment, before she rose from the table, picked up her purse, and said,

"I think I'd better go before I say something I'll be sorry for."

Before she turned to leave, Tim saw tears in the corner of her eyes. After she left he sat at the table in total confusion. He felt the weakness and relief one might feel if he had narrowly escaped from being hit by a train. Waves of sadness swept over him with the realization that an extremely enjoyable episode in his life had ended. Could he feel gratified that he had exercised the willpower to avoid a scandal? Or had he been a fool for letting it go as far as it had? What had he done to Cynthia? Would she feel that he had led her on, only to let her down--the classic plight of the single woman in a love triangle?

The thoughts and emotions paraded through his mind in an endless procession. He had no idea how long he had been sitting alone when he heard the voice of the waitress,

"Mr. Hamilton, are you all right?"

Suddenly he realized that all of the diners had left and all the other tables had been cleared.

"Yes, thank you. I guess I became lost in my thoughts."

He rose from the table, embarrassed, and left quickly. When he arrived home, Becky greeted him warmly. She didn't ask, but the question was written all over her face. He felt compelled to say something,

"I don't think Cynthia will need any more help."

She hugged him tightly,

"Congratulations, darling, you had a narrow escape!"

Chapter Fourteen
Downfall

Several years had passed since Tim had left Cornerstone. He had sold all of his Cornerstone stock except a token amount, which he kept so that he would continue to receive their quarterly and annual reports. He continued to attend the annual stockholders' meetings. The company had grown by leaps and bounds, and it appeared to be flourishing in all respects, until the latest annual report. In that report the auditor had placed a note stating that 15% of the company's bonds were in arrears on interest payments, that another 12% had failed to meet one or more provisions of their covenants, and that 18% of its mortgages were in arrears on their payments.

Executive Life of California had already shocked the nation with news of investment losses so large that its ability to meet its obligations to its policyholders was in doubt. The Minnesota Department of Commerce had announced that it had created a watch list of almost one hundred life insurance companies with amounts of high-risk investments so large that they might be headed for similar problems. There was a rumor afloat that Cornerstone might be on that confidential list.

Some months before this development, Cornerstone had announced a number of changes in its top management, including the chairman of the board, the president, and the senior vice president in charge of investments. Tim recalled the nightmare he had experienced before leaving Cornerstone, in which this scene had been so vividly portrayed. His nightmare had become reality. He had mixed feelings: gratification that time had proved him totally justified in the position he had taken; but deep regrets about the worry and concern this development would cause the millions of policyholders who had placed their trust--even their life savings--in Cornerstone.

Not long after the annual meeting Tim had a telephone call that totally surprised him,

"Good morning, Mr Hamilton?"

"Yes ma'am."

"Please hold for Mr. Robert Thompson."

Tim thought: Bob Thompson was the new board chair at Cornerstone; what could he want of me?

"Good morning, Mr. Hamilton. My secretary has already told you who I am. The chairman of our executive committee, Sterling Carruthers, and I would like you to be our guest for lunch. Would you, by any chance, be available next Thursday?"

"I've other plans on Thursday, but Friday would work."

"Very well, then; we'll look for you at the Minneapolis Club."

"Thank you, I'll be there."

After he had hung up the phone, Tim's thoughts raced. Carruthers had been on the board a long time. He was the one board member who had supported Tim. Do they want me to come back to work and pull their chestnuts out of the fire? Or are they merely looking for advice? They certainly had a serious problem. Did he have an obligation to help them solve it? Would his pension be affected? If they wanted him back, the decision would be easy: *no way* could he walk away from the commitments he had to his clients and the organizations on whose boards he served. Besides, not even someone with the

wisdom of Solomon could make all of those soft investments go away without tremendous financial losses. On
top of all that, he had never felt as happy and fulfilled as
he did now; and he loved his flexible life style, even
though he was working harder than ever. Would Becky
want him to go back? Would she understand why he
didn't want to? He would listen to what they had to say,
but no way was he interested in going back to work for
Cornerstone.

Carruthers introduced Bob Thompson and escorted them toward the dining room. After they ordered
and exchanged a few pleasantries, Thompson got right to
the point:

"As you must know, Mr. Hamilton, we are experi-
encing some difficulties with our investments."

"Yes, I'm acutely aware of that, and I'm deeply
sorry, particularly for your policyholders."

Thompson continued,

"As I see it, we really have two problems. One is,
of course, the large percentage of soft investments. The
other is a crisis in confidence: Doubts have arisen, and
threaten to intensify, in the minds of both our shareholders and our policyholders as to our ability to weather this
crisis without serious financial losses to them. As you
well, know, a loss of confidence can cause both groups
to want out, in which case their concerns become a self-
filling prophecy."

"I can certainly understand the problem, but how
do you see me being of assistance to you?"

"We need a president with the wisdom, integrity
and stature to solve both of these problems. Our new
president's performance has been a disappointment. You
have all three qualities in spades. We would be willing
to offer you whatever it takes to have you come in as
president and CEO. We are confident that you are the
best person to lead us out of the woods. Would you be
willing to consider it?"

Tim's mind reeled. This was an offer far beyond his imagination. Their board must really be desperate to offer him a blank check. Could he really help them? Did he have an obligation to help them? Certainly he felt no obligation to the board that had given him an almost unanimous vote of no confidence. Would his refusal trigger another crisis with Becky? He had been silent for what seemed like a long time, when Thompson spoke again,

"You are obviously interested in our offer. Let me clarify that it would include not only cash, but a liberal deferred compensation plan, generous stock options at a strike price substantially below the present market value, and the usual perks: club memberships, a limousine and driver, and perhaps other things you might wish. What do you think?"

"Gentlemen, I was obviously in deep thought, but I wasn't holding out for a better offer. It's a very generous and flattering offer, but I believe it creates some ethical problems, which I was trying to weigh."

Thompson interrupted and seemed somewhat offended:

"There's nothing unethical or under-handed about our offer, and we think it's very generous."

"I'm sorry, I didn't make myself clear. I see nothing unethical or under-handed about your offer. Let me try to explain the issues that concern me. In the years since I left Cornerstone I have taken on a great many obligations: to several non-profit organizations on whose boards I serve, to a number of individuals to whom I give personal counsel and advice, to over a dozen individuals who have placed the management of their personal fortunes in my hands, and, last but not least, to my family, who see a father and a husband happier and more fulfilled then he has ever been."

Carruthers responded,

"Tim, I remember the strong obligation you used to feel toward our policyholders. Those policyholders still need you."

"Sterling, in all reality, what can I do for them? I appreciate the nice things Mr. Thompson has said about me, but I can't work miracles. Cornerstone is going to take a severe financial bath on its soft investments, whether it holds them or sells them for what it can get for them. It's just fortunate that the policyholders don't read all of the auditors' notes to the financial statement, or Cornerstone would have had a calamitous run on its cash reserves already."

It was Thompson's turn:

"What do you think we should do to get ourselves out of this mess?"

"I think the Minnesota Commerce Commissioner has the power to declare a moratorium under which you would be required to make only modest loans on cash values to policyholders who show real need."

"But that would damage our reputation and ruin our new business sales.," Thompson protested.

Carruthers spoke again:

"Bob, Tim told us this would happen before he left Cornerstone, but no one except me was willing to listen to him." Carruthers said, "Everyone else thought he was being too conservative."

Tim couldn't help but feel a sense of gratification to his old friend, Sterling, for voicing a thought which had been in Tim's mind, but which he was too polite to mention. And he had a similar feeling as he responded to Thompson's protest,

"Yes, a large portion of your agency force will leave you and be snapped up by other companies. A good share of the employees in your new business department will lose their jobs, since you won't need them for quite a long while."

"Some of our agents have left already. They heard rumors about us."

"You also need to retain the services of a top flight merger-and-acquisition specialist. He or she can help you find some wealthy investors who will buy Cornerstone and infuse enough cash to make Cornerstone solvent after they liquidate its soft assets."

"Where would they find investors willing to do that?"

"Probably on the other side of the Atlantic. As Sterling knows, European investors tend to take a longer view of things. They would buy Cornerstone for a song, assure its policyholders that their money was safe, cut policy dividends, trim management to the bone. With those substantial savings, and without the heavy costs of acquiring new business they will actually make a handsome return on their investment."

"You say these new investors will buy the company for a song. Why would the present shareholders sell for so little?"

"A majority of Cornerstone's stock is held by large investors. They're sophisticated enough to know that the alternative to selling their stock at 10 cents for each dollar they paid for it is bankruptcy, from which they would get nothing."

"Mr. Hamilton, the scenario you paint sounds awfully drastic. Isn't there a better alternative?"

"The only alternative I can see is to continue as you're doing. Without a large infusion of cash to cover the huge losses on your soft assets, you will go bankrupt. With the course I've suggested, you keep faith with your policyholders; the shareholders get something. Unfortunately there will be a lot of long service career officers, managers and employees who will be looking for other ways to make a living. They are the people I really feel sorry for. I don't envy you the job of breaking the news to them. At least you folks won't have the miserable task of deciding who goes and who stays, nor will your new president. That will be the job of a ruthless manager who will be brought in by the new owners."

Tim had found no pleasure in this conversation; but he did feel a certain satisfaction that he had planted the seed of salvation for Cornerstone's policyholders. Carruthers and Thompson were staring dejectedly at the table. Thompson began to shake his head slowly. Finally he spoke,

"I didn't realize I had accepted the leadership of this great company only to preside over its demise."

"Mr. Thompson, yours is not a very enviable position; but through the strength of your leadership can come the courageous action needed to keep faith with Cornerstone's policyholders, many of whom have entrusted their life savings to the company. I have friends on Wall Street who can put you in touch with a merger-and-acquisition firm well qualified to find qualified investors and help you negotiate with them. I would urge that you waste no time in contracting with such a firm. If you wish, I will be glad to talk with your executive committee at an emergency meeting. I believe I can help you to persuade them to give you the authority you need to retain such a firm. After the merger-and-acquisition consultants study Cornerstone thoroughly, they will present their findings to your full board. I suspect that, after they hear the presentation, your board will vote to go ahead with the sale, subject to the approval of the shareholders holding a majority of your stock. This firm will be eminently qualified to take you through the entire process. By helping you get this process started I will have performed a greater service for Cornerstone than I could as its president."

Thompson looked both disconsolate and thoughtful for some time before he spoke,

"Mr. Hamilton, this meeting has turned out quite differently from what I had expected; but I do believe you have pointed out the best, or shall I say the least bad course of action. I will ask my secretary to call you for some available dates and to set up an executive committee meeting at the earliest possible date. And I do want to thank you for opening our eyes to reality."

Tim went home with the satisfaction of knowing that he had what his mother would have called "both his meat and his manners." He had done what he felt was best for Cornerstone without having to change the new life style he cherished so highly, and to which he felt totally committed. He and Becky snuggled on the sofa while he related at length his lunchtime conversation with Thompson and Carruthers. When he had finished, she gave him a big hug and kissed him warmly before she spoke,

"How could I have ever doubted you when you made your decision to do what was right and left Cornerstone! When I think of how you stood against all those people and risked both your job and your marriage, it must have taken an incredible amount of courage. And I'm deeply sorry that I added to your difficulties at the time. I hope you can forgive me."

"Honey, there's nothing to forgive. It was a tough time for both of us, and the separation has only brought us closer together since then."

"What'll Thompson and Carruthers do now?"

"They don't have a lot of choice. Tough as it is, selling the company is far preferable to going bankrupt. I'll find them a good merger-and-acquisition specialist. Hopefully they will find a buyer before there's a run on the company's assets. The new owners will be ruthless in trimming costs, but the policyholders should come out all right."

"Does that mean our friends will lose their jobs?"

"Many of them will. The ones who stay will find out what work really means. The good life at Cornerstone is gone--at least for a long time."

"What about the shareholders?"

"The stock is already selling for less than half what it was a year ago, and the new owners will pay only a token amount to buy 51% of the stock. The New York Stock Exchange will discontinue listing the shares, and the holders who don't tender their shares to the new owner will have a hard time finding any other buyer for them. In other words, their shares will be practically worthless."

"What about our shares?"

"I sold almost all of our Cornerstone some time ago. I kept just a few shares so that I'd continue to know what was going on, and I sold them after the last annual meeting. I even thought of selling short; but I would have felt like a vulture, and we don't need the money."

"What's selling short?"

"You sell a large number of shares you don't own, betting that the stock is going to go down. Your broker lends you the shares to make good on your sale. At some future date when the stock has gone down, you can buy enough shares at a lower price to repay the broker."

"What if the stock goes up?"

"You lose the difference between what you sold it for and what you have to pay for the replacement shares."

"Sounds complicated and illegal."

"You're right on the first count, but there's nothing illegal about it. In fact, there are substantial short sales made every day the market is open."

"Couldn't a board member or an officer of the company, who knew about the bad news, make a lot of money that way?"

"Not unless he looks good in stripes and is willing to spend a lot of time in jail. On top of that he'd have to pay back what he made. It's called `insider trading' when an officer or director buys or sells stock in his own company on the basis of information that the public doesn't have. It's illegal and the penalties are heavy."

"Well, Tim, I'm very, very proud of you, and I love you more than ever, but I've got one problem."

"What's that?"

"I didn't think it was possible to love you more."

He took her in his arms and they held each other tightly for a long time. Then Tim headed for his office, where he called a good friend on Wall Street.

Just a few days later Tim had a call from Bob Thompson,

"Good morning, Tim. Gordon Longstreet of Longstreet and Withers in New York is going to be in my office next Tuesday morning at ten o'clock. Would you be willing and able to join us?"

Tim looked at his calendar before he answered:

"Yes, Bob. I can do that; and congratulations for getting in touch so promptly with a first class M&A firm."

"Thanks, could you come 15 minutes early? I've another matter I'd like to discuss with you."

"I'll do that."

Tim was curious about the "other matter", but decided it was better not to ask now. He wondered what it would be like to be in Cornerstone's offices again. When Tuesday morning arrived and he entered Cornerstone's building, he felt a strange mixture of excitement and deja vu. The executive floor looked different, but he couldn't identify the differences. At exactly 9:45 he was ushered into Bob Thompson's office, where both Thompson and Sterling Carruthers greeted him warmly. The three of them took seats at a round table at the end of the spacious, lavishly furnished office opposite from Thompson's huge, hand-carved mahogany desk. Two empty chairs remained at the table. After greetings were exchanged, Thompson opened the conversation,

"Tim, we're about to venture into uncharted waters and we need all the help we can get. Would you be willing to accept a retainer, say ten thousand dollars a month, to advise and counsel us through this critical period?"

Tim thought quickly: What would they expect him to do? He could certainly advise them in conferences like this, but he didn't want to get drawn into other duties, nor did he want to feel that he was at their beck and call. On the other hand, he wanted to help them, and he wanted to be cooperative. Thompson tried to read his thoughts,

"We could make the retainer larger, if necessary."

"No, no. That wasn't the reason for my hesitation. On the contrary, I really can't think of what I could do for you to earn that kind of money. My regular consulting fee is five hundred an hour. I would prefer just to bill you on an hourly basis. I would expect that most, if not all of my activities could be performed in Minneapolis."

Before he spoke, Thompson looked at Carruthers, who nodded affirmatively,

"That's wonderful! I hope you've started your meter already!"

Thompson pressed a button attached to the under side of the table as he continued to speak:

"I don't think you've met our president, Anthony Weisbach."

"No, I haven't."

A balding man in his late fifties, with heavy glasses and a worried look appeared, and Thompson gestured him toward an empty chair at the round table, as he said,

"Tony, this is Mr. Timothy Hamilton, a man of great wisdom who is going to advise us during our discussions and negotiations concerning the sale of the company."

They were still exchanging greetings and pleasantries when the intercom tone sounded softly. Thompson answered,

"Yes?"

"The other members of the executive committee and Mr. Jonathan Longstreet are here, sir."

"Show them into the board room, please. We'll meet them there."

Jonathan Longstreet carried his six-foot-five athletic frame with an easy dignity. Dressed impeccably in an oxford grey suit, white shirt and conservative blue tie, he wore heavy, horn-rimmed glasses and a smile on his rugged, handsome face, topped with a luxurious thatch of dark brown hair. Tim thought, this man would be equally at home in the executive offices of a large company like Cornerstone, or in the offices of wealthy prospective investors. All of the members of the executive committee shook hands with Longstreet as they introduced themselves. Thompson asked them all to take seats at the board table. After they were seated, Thompson inquired politely about the quality of Longstreet's trip, and identified Carruthers and Weisbach by their titles. When he came to Tim, he said,

"Mr. Hamilton is widely known in this city as a man of great wisdom and acumen. He has kindly agreed to counsel us through our discussions and negotiations regarding the sale of the company."

Longstreet smiled and nodded his understanding and approval, as Thompson continued,

"Mr. Longstreet, please tell us about your firm and what you believe you can do for us."

Longstreet handed each of them a very impressive brochure and directed their attention to the imposing qualifications of each of the key members of their firm, and a partial list of the prestigious clients the firm had assisted in being acquired on the most favorable basis possible. Longstreet had not only read the most recent auditor's report, he had sent an assistant to Albany to examine the voluminous statement that a life insurance company must furnish to the insurance department of every state in which it does business. He pointed out that the auditor could only show the percentage of assets that were already "soft." In addition to that there was another 20% of Cornerstone's assets that were in imminent danger of becoming "soft" because they had failed to meet one or more of their covenants. These covenants are the commitments the bond issuers had made to the purchasers of their bonds: the fine print that only the most sophisticated investors read, only a small percentage of whom follow up to determine whether the bond issuers continue to meet the covenants.

Longstreet went on to explain the steps his company would take if Cornerstone retained them. First their investment analysts would put a realistic market price on every asset Cornerstone owned. At the same time they would retain a consulting actuary to develop a schedule showing the net cash flow that could be expected to develop from Cornerstone's existing policies. This net cash flow would be discounted at a very high rate of interest to determine whether the present value of that cash flow, plus the market value of the assets was sufficient to meet the company's obligations to its policyholders. Even with the assurance of the new owners to the policyholders that they would all be paid in full, many of them would want to pull out their cash value immediately. Although this would require a large amount of cash, it actually represented a source of profit for the new owners, because the company's future obligations to its policyholders were valued at considerably more than the cash value they received, particularly during the first ten years after the policy was issued. Longstreet then stopped for questions. Thompson went first:

What will the shareholders get?"

"A dollar a share, perhaps a little more."

Thompson was shocked:

"Good God, man! Before our last annual report came out our stock was trading as high as $125 a share!"

"Yes, it will be quite a shock to them. But when we tell it like it is, the larger, more sophisticated shareholders will take their dollar a share."

"Why will they do that?"

"They'll recognize that the alternative is bankruptcy, in which case they would get nothing."

"But many of our officers and employees have a large portion of their assets in Cornerstone stock. They will be ruined! Can't they sell now?"

Longstreet wanted to tell them the board should have thought of that before they permitted their investment department to buy all those lousy bonds and mortgages. Instead he said,

"I'm sure your counsel has told you of the severe penalties for insider trading. If you tell any one else the condition of the company before you announce it publicly and they sell their stock, *both* you and they would face stiff fines and jail sentences, and they would have to pay back all of their proceeds, except for the dollar a share."

Thompson and Carruthers both shook their heads sadly. Thompson looked devastated and Carruthers put his head in his hands. Tim and Longstreet looked at each other, and they nodded slightly in silent understanding. No one spoke for what seemed a long time. Finally, Tim broke the silence,

"What is the fee for your company's services?"

Longstreet passed out a single sheet to each of the others who were present. It was printed neatly on their engraved parchment stationery. Below the subdued letterhead it read simply,

FEE SCHEDULE

Initial fee, payable quarterly
in advance, and credited
toward the final fee $1,000,000

Final fee, payable at closing, based on total
purchase price:

> 5% of the first $10,000,000
> 4% of the next $10,000,000
> 3% of the next $10,000,000
> 2% of the excess over $30,000,000

Thompson and Carruthers looked at their sheets
blankly. Both were still too stunned to react. Tim noted
the finesse with which Longstreet had dealt with the fee
question: The fee schedule was not in the brochure, so a
prospective client who scanned the brochure would not
be distracted from the presentation by thoughts about the
fees. Tim asked his next question,

"Can you give us an idea of how long this project
will take?"

"We realize that time is very much of the essence.
In the back of the brochure is an agreement form. We
will start our research within a week after we receive a
signed copy of the agreement. The research and preparation of a brochure will take about four months. We will
then do a road show for prospective investors in London,
Paris, Berlin, Vienna, Basil, Milan and Athens. That will
take another month. Normally, we would expect to be
negotiating with one or more prospective buyers shortly
after that. The buyer who offers the most favorable
terms will want another two months to perform due
diligence. Altogether, we are talking seven to nine
months. Are there other questions?"

It was Thompson's turn:

"What if we have a run on the company in the meantime?"

"As soon as you have signed our agreement, you can send a letter to all of your policyholders stating that arrangements are being made to assure that Cornerstone will continue to meet its obligations to its policyholders in full. Then you should have enough good assets to meet all of the surrenders during the next nine months, by which time we would expect to have a closing with the new owners."

The other men sat in shocked silence, until Thompson spoke again:

"Mr. Longstreet, we thank you for a very clear and thorough presentation. I also want to take this opportunity to thank Mr. Hamilton for putting us in touch with you. This is a duly called meeting of our executive committee, all members are present, and they have the power to act for the full board when urgent matters arise. If you care to have a cup of coffee in our reception area, you may be able to take a signed copy of the agreement with you."

Longstreet thanked them for their attention and left the room. A couple of committee members expressed shock at the dire straits in which the company found itself and asked whether there wasn't a better way to solve their problems without giving the company away to foreigners. Thompson turned to Tim who assured them that all reasonable possibilities had been explored, and that the only alternative was to let the company go into bankruptcy, in which case the shareholders would receive nothing and the policyholders would not be paid in full. After other members had expressed their regrets and dismay, the executive committee voted unanimously to go ahead with Longstreet, the meeting adjourned and the members left quietly, without the usual banter and good fellowship. Thompson asked Tim, Carruthers and

Weisbach to stay for a few minutes. When they were seated again, he said,

"I don't know where or how to begin to break this news to the officers, middle management, or the other employees. I need all the help and advice I can get."

Tim felt as if he could read their minds and their body English: Each of them wanted as little to do with that extremely distasteful task as possible. Should he offer to make the announcement for them? Or was it best to come from the people in authority? The others seemed to be waiting for him to speak, so he did,

"You folks have an unenviable task, but it has to be done. Moreover it must be done as quickly as possible. You won't win any popularity contests, but you do what you have to do; and if you do it properly, you can take some satisfaction out of having done a tough job well. The question uppermost in everyone's mind will be, 'How does this affect me'. We must focus all of our attention on that subject. We know that the new owners are going to lay off staff, and they will cut deeply. I think we'll actually be doing these employees a favor if we take the initiative."

All of the others looked shocked and astounded as Weisbach voiced their dismay and disbelief,

"Mr. Hamilton, are you suggesting that *we* do their dirty work *for* them?"

"At first glance it would seem that way, but let's look a little deeper. We will be much more compassionate than the new owners would be. We will be more generous in severance pay, we can provide more outplacement services. We can use our personal connections to help the officers and managers relocate. We can provide "sweeteners" to encourage and assist older employees to take early retirement."

It was Carruthers' turn,

"How are we going to carry on if we lay off a large number employees?"

"I suggest that you give serious consideration to discontinuing the issuance of all new policies. That will eliminate the need for almost half of your staff."
Thompson almost exploded,
"Mr. Hamilton, you *can't* be serious!"
"I'm quite serious. Cornerstone's assets are very deeply impaired. It will take several billion dollars to make the company solvent. All life insurance companies lose money on policies in the first policy year. The large commissions that are paid in the first year, the large number of employees in the sales department, the costs of underwriting and issuing policies, and the costs of setting up records all add up to much more than the first year premium. If you discontinue selling new policies, profits on the business already on the books are all immediately available to cover the losses on bad assets. I firmly believe that this is what the new owners will do."

Thompson, Carruthers and Weisbach sat silently shaking their heads in disbelief, and in contemplation of the terrible consequences on so many employees' lives. As Tim watched their reactions, he concluded that they were not going to act on his advice without a push; so he said,

"I see that Longstreet's stationery has an internet address. Why don't you send him an e-mail, asking him what he thinks of the idea of discontinuing the issuance of new policies?"

Tim saw relief on three faces and immediate nods of approval. They quickly agreed to follow this suggestion. The e-mail was dispatched, and they agreed that they would do nothing until they received Longstreet's reply.

Mid-morning of the next day Tim's phone rang it's now-familiar double ring.

"Good morning, Hamilton and Associates."

"Good morning. This is Bob Thompson, I have an e-mail from Longstreet."

Tim thought the voice didn't sound very happy.

"What does it say?"

"Congratulations on a bold, wise and courageous action. It will greatly increase our likelihood of finding a buyer. Let me know if I can be of help. Warmest regards and best wishes. J. Longstreet."

Tim tried to hide his elation at the thought that Longstreet had supported him in this bold suggestion,

"Good, I assume you will want to move as quickly as possible."

"Where's the hurry?" asked a reluctant Thompson.

"Rumors are already circulating about the financial condition of Cornerstone, and people tend to imagine things as being worse than they are; so the sooner you act, the better. Your bold, prompt action will minimize the likelihood of a run on the company."

Even as he spoke, Tim thought it would be hard for people to imagine things worse than what he had seen, and what Longstreet's initial research had confirmed.

"When do you think we'll be able to resume new business?"

"That's one decision we won't have to make. The new owners and their managers will decide that. Unless the American life insurance companies come to their senses, quit trying to eat each other's lunch, and stop putting themselves and each other out of business, the answer may be never."

"But," Thompson protested, "a company can't survive without selling new business!"

"You've got that right. The new owners will take the emerging profits from the business that's still in force, and the profits from the policies that are cashed in. They will continue to down-size the staff. When they reach a point where the remaining business cannot be operated profitably, they will sell it to another life insurance company, pocket their final profit, and congratulate themselves on having made such a wonderful investment."

Tim felt like adding that they would laugh at these stupid Americans who get themselves into this kind of situation, but he felt that Thompson didn't need that kind of gratuitous remark. Thompson was silent for a few moments before he asked,

"Can you come over for lunch and spend some time to help us plan our next steps?"

"I'm sorry, I have other commitments today; but I could do it tomorrow."

"Thank you, Tim; we'll look for you at noon."

Tim had not been in Cornerstone's executive dining room since it was remodeled. It occupied the entire top floor of the building. As he was ushered in by an obsequious host, he thought of the sharp contrast between the room's spacious, luxurious elegance and the company's current financial plight. The cuisine was exquisite, and the presentation and service was impeccable. Thompson, Carruthers and Weisbach greeted him warmly as they joined him; but they wore worried looks on their faces. After they had been served, Tim opened the conversation:

"Gentlemen, I've been thinking what a marvelous membership dining club this would make. For young executives who can't quite handle membership in the Minneapolis Club or the Athletic Club, this would be a most attractive place to entertain business guests, friends and relatives. There's only one place like it in the whole downtown area, and there's certainly a potential market for another. It would have a triple benefit: First, it would raise the morale of your staff when they see their executives making this sacrifice. Secondly, prospective new owners would be impressed; and finally, it would convert a cost center into a profit center."

The other three looked unenthusiastic; but they slowly nodded in agreement, since they couldn't escape the logic of Tim's suggestion. When they had finished eating, Tim pulled copies of a single sheet from his briefcase, and gave one to each of the other three.

"Here is a suggested news release announcing Cornerstone's decision to discontinue the issuance of new business in order to protect the interests of existing policyholders. I would call your administrative assistant right now and have her set up a tele-conference meeting of the executive committee for four o'clock today. Ask her to make a special effort to reach all of the members regardless of where in the world they are. After you make whatever changes you wish to make in the news release, I suggest that, at nine o'clock tomorrow morning, you place a copy on the desk of every member of the staff, FAX a copy to every salesperson, call a press conference for ten o'clock, then have it couriered to any of the news media not in attendance."

"But," Thompson protested, "Won't this raise more questions in the minds of the staff than it answers."

"This afternoon each department head will receive an envelope with strict instructions not to open the envelope until after he leaves the office today and to communicate the contents to NO ONE. The envelope will contain a copy of the press release, a memorandum directing him or her to prepare a list of the employees, supervisors, managers and officers whose services will no longer be required and a memorandum on pink paper with tomorrow's date. The pink memo will notify the employee that her or his services are no longer required, effective today. It will also contain the schedule of severance pay, temporary continuance of health insurance, out-placement services, career counseling, psychological counseling where needed."

"Isn't that terribly sudden?", Weisbach asked.

"The pink slips won't be received with joy no matter when they're delivered; but it's a lot better to do it this way than have everyone sitting around wondering who's going to get the axe. Fortunately, we live in an area with a shortage of skilled workers, so many of our departing workers will be snapped up relatively quickly."

"Will you be at the press conference tomorrow morning?" Carruthers asked.

Tim pulled one more sheet from his briefcase as he spoke,

"I don't think that's either necessary or advisable. Here is a list of questions you can expect. You will think of others. I know you will prepare your answers carefully. It might be a good idea to have the questions and answers on a second handout. It will greatly reduce the likelihood of your being misquoted. I'll be available by phone in my office if you have any more questions. One last thing: Your staff will be watching very closely to see if the cuts affect all levels of management, right up to the top. You can't cut a fraction of a person, but you can reduce salaries and directors' fees commensurate with the size of the job. That's not only business-like and fair, but it will make the medicine go down a lot easier."

The other three looked thoughtful and unhappy. They had all finished eating, and Tim rose from the table as he spoke,

"Well, gentlemen, you have a great deal of important work to do this afternoon, so I'll let you get started. Call me if you have questions."

The others had risen from the table, and they said their good-byes in a quiet and subdued tone.

As Tim drove home, he reflected on the meeting and the role he had played in it. Why had he carried the entire initiative? Was it because he was far enough removed to be objective, while the others were paralyzed by their subjectivity? Or was there a devil in him that wanted to give the tottering Cornerstone a final push to its downfall? Why did he feel so good about what he had done? Was it the satisfaction that comes from doing a difficult job well? Or was it a draconian form of retribution for the injustice that Cornerstone had dealt him years before? He decided he had done the right thing, particularly with the strong support that Longstreet had given him.

That evening at dinner, he and Becky dined alone. Tiffany had made other plans. Tim shared with her both the activities at lunch and his reflections on the way home. When he had finished, Becky looked at him with shining eyes and said,

"Oh, Tim, you don't have a spiteful bone in your body. I'm so proud of you for having both the wisdom and courage to do what you did. I just don't know anyone else who could have carried it off."

"From the looks on their faces I'm not sure they thought of me as being either wise or courageous, particularly when I declined to take part in the press conference."

"But you were absolutely right even there. Your presence at the news conference would have raised questions that would be difficult, even embarrassing, to answer."

"I guess that's so; but I sure don't envy those guys."

"You've given them the courage to do what they have to do, and you've made a great contribution to the solution of a very difficult situation. You should feel nothing but a great sense of satisfaction."

"Thanks, honey, I really needed that."

They had finished eating and Tim rose from the table. As he started toward Becky, she rose to meet him, and they slid into a tight embrace. They kissed deeply, and neither knew how long they stayed in their close, silent communion; but they shared the same strong feelings and thoughts: bedtime would come early tonight.

The following evening Tim eagerly turned on the six o'clock news. He didn't have long to wait. The anchor man led off with the Cornerstone story:

"In an announcement that shocked not only the business community, but the entire city, Cornerstone Life Insurance Company, one of the city's largest employers, announced the immediate layoff of almost 40% of its staff and the termination of the contracts of *all* of its sales people. These employees are no longer needed, because the company has decided to cease immediately the issuance of all new policies. Robert Thompson, chairman of the board, said, `This bold step is being taken to protect the interests of existing policyholders. It is no secret that Cornerstone has experienced losses on some of its higher yielding assets. It is not generally understood that life insurance companies invest a significant portion of their assets in putting new policies on the books. Discontinuing the sale of new policies will make these assets available to protect the interests of our existing policyholders.' Questioned about the plight of the employees and sale force, Thompson said, `The sales force will be quickly snapped up by other companies. We're fortunate to be in a job market where most of our terminated employees will find good jobs in a relatively short time. Moreover, we're providing generous severance pay, out-placement and a variety of other services to help these people make the transition.' Analysts have described the company's action as bold and courageous."

Tim could hardly contain his delight. This first public reaction to Cornerstone's move was everything he had hoped for. Now he would sleep soundly and arise eagerly to see how the press dealt with the story. His eagerness caused him to awaken half an our earlier than usual. He didn't have far to look: As he unfolded the morning paper, emblazoned across the top of page one he read,

HUGE LAYOFFS AT CORNERSTONE
Move called Bold, Courageous

Tim was pleased at the sub-head, and equally gratified at the rest of the article. The editor had made so few changes in the press release, Tim found it hard to spot them. It was also a pleasant surprise to find that the lead editorial concerned Cornerstone's announcement. After regretting the plight of the terminated staff, it went on to praise a courageous management for its bold action in protecting the interests of the policyholders against the consequences of poor investment decisions unfortunately shared by all too many life insurance companies in their eagerness to compete for the public's dollars. It also praised management for its generosity toward the terminated employees. Shortly after breakfast Tim's business phone rang. It was Bob Thompson,

"Tim, I can't thank you enough. When we left the lunch table two days ago, we weren't sure we were doing the right thing; but we decided to go ahead. We're very glad now that we did."

"How much hate mail have you gotten?"

"Oh yeah, we've had some calls and e-mail, and I suppose there'll be letters, but we expected that; and nobody has threatened to shoot us! On the whole, the reaction has been milder than we thought it would be. We're particularly pleased with the way the media and the analysts have treated us."

"Well, congratulations! You did what you had to do, and it took a lot of guts."

"Thanks again, Tim."

After they had hung up, Tim thought of the wisdom in the old adage: "It's amazing what can be accomplished if you don't care who gets the credit for it." But, after all, Thompson did deserve credit. It did take a lot of fortitude to act as he had done. And no one could predict the public reaction. And he had received his own reward a couple of nights ago, and the warm feelings he had enjoyed ever since.

About seven months later Thompson called to say that Longstreet was coming the following Tuesday with a couple of prospective investors. He hoped that Tim would be able to join them. He could.

The investors were very impressed with what they saw: a very effective job of downsizing, a physical re-arrangement of departments into a more compact area so that most of the un-needed space had already been rented out for offices. The crowning physical touch was the Summit, a top floor restaurant, beautifully furnished and with a fantastic view from its 650-foot vantage point of the surrounding city, the winding Mississippi and the beautiful countryside, cloaked in the usual fall display of brilliant reds, yellows and rich reddish browns, and punctuated with the deep greens of the conifers. They had a reserved table, otherwise they would not have gotten a place in this obviously popular, upper-class restaurant. Many diners took time before they left to stroll from window to window, feasting their eyes on this gorgeous pageant of nature.

What impressed the prospective buyers most of all was the statement of earnings for the first six months after Cornerstone had stopped issuing new policies. At Tim's suggestion this statement had been re-cast to show what the results would have been without the one-time costs of staff termination, remodeling and other non-recurring costs. Both versions were given to the visitors so that there was no suggestion of concealing anything. The emerging profits from existing business exceeded the "high" range estimates by consulting actuaries Longstreet had engaged. Everyone was delighted. Longstreet and his guests congratulated Thompson for what he and his staff had accomplished. Thompson accepted with pleasure and with no mention of Tim's significant part in the whole transaction. There was a glance exchanged between Tim and Longstreet, mutually acknowledging the human dynamics and their own indispensable roles in the process. Both of them recognized that neither could have done it without the other.

Both parties had done their homework, and it did not take much negotiating to reach an agreement in principle. This agreement would become binding when the buyers had done due diligence, and had acquired a majority of the stock through a tender offer. Tim knew the investors expected to make out like bandits, and he suggested that the buyers could substantially increase their likelihood of success by upping the price they would pay to existing shareholders on the tender offer. The buyers quickly agreed, and the deal was struck. Tim also described what he foresaw at the special shareholders' meeting: the larger shareholders, being more sophisticated investors, would appreciate that the buyers were being relatively generous in their offer. It would be the smaller shareholders who could think only of the money they were losing and who would express their anger in loud and angry shouting, throwing the meeting into chaos. He suggested that they invite the largest shareholders, who owned a majority of the stock, to a nice dinner, explain the situation to them, answer their questions, and get their informal acceptance on the spot. Weisbach suggested that they could get them to tender their stock on the spot, but Tim pointed out that it would be illegal to go any further than he had suggested, since all shareholders must be treated alike.

The deal went smoothly, the new owners took charge of operations within two months, and another chapter in Tim's life came to a close.

Chapter Fifteen
The Political Campaign

I t was near the end of the century. In almost every park you could find an evangelist or self-styled prophet predicting the end of the world and urging everyone to repent, dispose of their possessions, and prepare for the great cataclysm. Microsoft was talking merger with IBM, Apple was talking merger with Microsoft, the deficit was as large as ever, and Medicare was still being debated in congress. Tim's reputation for wisdom, tact and dedication to his clients and the community had spread far and wide. One day when he answered his business phone a strange voice said,

"Good morning, Mr. Hamilton, this is Jerry O'Connell. Could you arrange to have lunch with Magnus Erickson and me, let's say next Wednesday?" Tim recognized the first name as the state chair of one of the major political parties and the other name as their largest financial supporter and fund raiser. What could they possibly want of him? More out of curiosity and courtesy than anything else, he said,

"I don't know why not."

"Fine, let's meet at the Summit at 11:45. I'll have my administrative assistant reserve our usual table. That's a very popular place, you know."

"Yes, I know," said Tim with an inward smile.

The Summit had maintained its popularity ever since it opened, which was just before Cornerstone was sold. It was about the only place in the building where

Tim felt at home. The new owners had replaced most of the board and the top officers. A few of Tim's friends had managed to hang on to their jobs; but Tim and Becky saw them only socially and almost never discussed the company with them.

It was a beautiful late spring day. As Tim and his hosts were seated at a corner table, they all took time to look out both windows. One window overlooked the Mississippi as it wound its way toward St. Paul, and also afforded a birds-eye view of the sprawling University of Minnesota campus , which was based on the east side of the river, but extended across to the river's west banks, where its newer buildings housed the performing arts, the law school and the Carlson School of Management. The other window looked toward the international airport that served the greater Twin Cities and was the hub of Northwest Airlines, which had become one of the country's two largest airlines since acquiring its European, Russian and Asian links. Both views were elegantly accented by the many beautiful deciduous trees that had only recently acquired their gorgeously fresh spring foliage. After the group was seated, the small talk quickly led to the use of first names. They ordered and O'Connell came to the point:

"Tim we have searched this great state for our next governor, and your name keeps coming up, head and shoulders above the other possibilities. Our party executive committee was unanimously enthusiastic in their vote to ask you to run on our ticket. What do you say?"

Tim was totally taken aback. Could this be happening to him? Erickson was nodding his head in enthusiastic agreement as he added,

"Yes, Tim. We hope you'll give very serious consideration to this request. We'll provide all of the financial backing you need."

Tim smiled and shook his head,

"Gentlemen, this is very flattering, but I've absolutely no political experience. I've never been a councilman, or a school board member, or even a dog catcher!"

"We're quite aware of that, Tim." O'Connell responded, "The one thing the voters are unanimous on is their universal distrust of politicians. You have a marvelous set of credentials for this job. Your social outreach will appeal to the more liberal voters, while your impressive business record will attract the conservatives. Moreover, your impeccable reputation for wisdom and integrity will inspire a high level of confidence in all of the voters. Your vital role in leading Cornerstone out of the woods, and in seeing that its policyholders were made whole, is much better known in this community than you might think."

"Even if it all worked out as well as you think, I've many commitments to a great number of wonderful people. I can't just walk away from them."

"We're aware of that, Tim. But this is not a permanent career. We wouldn't even press you to run for a second term, if you didn't think you should. Surely you could find someone to serve your investment clients, and the many boards on which you serve would be delighted to give you a leave of absence."

Tim shook his head:

"I just don't see how it will all work out."

Then O'Connell shot his sharpest arrow:

"Tim, you have a stronger desire to do good in this world than any person I know; and we know how much good you've done and are doing. But think how much *more* good you can do as governor. Please give it some more thought."

Tim agreed that he would, and after an exchange of pleasantries and small talk, the lunch session ended.

When Tim told Becky what had happened, she responded quickly and vehemently,

"You're out of your mind, Tim, if you even consider it!"

"Why?"

"You're too honest to be a politician. Those spin doctors will tear you apart."

"But O'Connell and Erickson say that honesty is what the voters are looking for."

"That's what the voters *say* they're looking for; but when some wily politician promises them the world with a fence around it and says he'll cut their taxes at the same time by eliminating all that government waste, they'll knock the polls down rushing to vote for him."

"You really think the voters are that dumb, huh?"

"They're not dumb, just greedy. The majority of voters are not as idealistic as you are. Given a choice, a majority of 'em will put their own self-interest above the good of the state. They'll vote for the candidate who promises them the most."

"Becky, I didn't know you were that cynical."

Tim was getting a bit irritated at his wife's negative attitude. He broke off the discussion and retreated to his office with a mind full of questions. Who was right? Did O'Connell and Erickson really think he could win? If not, why would they ask him to run? Was this what his mother had in mind? How was he to decide? These questions paraded through his mind in an endless chain for a good share of the afternoon. Finally, he decided he needed to talk further with O'Connell and Erickson and raise Becky's concerns with them. He called O'Connell and got his administrative assistant, who volunteered to set up the lunch date. When Tim told Becky what he had done and why, she just smiled and shook her head.

When Tim told O'Connell and Erickson about Becky's misgivings, the former smiled, nodded his head, and said,

"Your wife is a smart woman. Left to your own devices, that's exactly what would happen. But we'll provide you with a campaign manager and speech writers who'll solve that problem."

"How will they solve the problem? I'm not going to let them misrepresent me to the voters."

O'Connell caught Tim's subconscious choice of verbs--the use of the future tense instead of the subjunctive--and realized that they'd been successful in their recruiting effort. He had hooked Tim with the vision of doing much more good in this powerful office. He mustn't overplay his hand; but he felt now that he knew how to keep up Tim's resolve. He felt confident in the ability of his candidate-handlers to take this idealistic man and represent him to the voters as the man they'd been looking for. So he said,

"Oh, they won't do that; but they can put together words that, as the old song says, accentuate the positive and eliminate the negative. Just as you are highly professional and skilled in your work, so are they. You will find yourself in good hands. Our challenge is to find a candidate with sufficient interest in the welfare of the people that he is willing to forego greater material gains temporarily and truly serve the public."

Tim was already thinking about how he could best deal with his present commitments. He didn't see too much difficulty in being excused from his board obligations. Placing his investment clients in good hands would be the challenge. His friend, Gordon Springborn, had just taken early retirement from his position as senior vice president and chief investment officer of a major bank with many billions in trust funds. Gordy had both the high integrity and the expertise that would allow Tim to feel that he was leaving his investment clients in good hands. But would Gordy be willing to take on Tim's clients?

"I need to find someone who can and will manage the investment portfolios of my clients before I can make a commitment. It may take a week or two to find such a person. Then it would take two or three months before I could be totally free from my present business and community obligations."

O'Connell felt a strong surge of elation from his success. This had really been easier than he thought. He tried not to appear too excited as he spoke,

"That should work out well, Tim, provided you can spend a few hours a week with us during the next two or three months. We will want to brief you on the party's position on the issues. You will want to get acquainted with the other members of the committee and help us select your campaign manager. The committee will be getting together for dinner a week from tomorrow evening. Would you be able to join us?"

Tim consulted his pocket organizer and allowed that he could. While they finished eating, Erickson and O'Connell talked enthusiastically about the upcoming campaign, how well Tim would be accepted by the party leaders and the voters alike. They even suggested that victory was virtually assured if they did their homework and carried out a well organized campaign. When they had said their goodbyes, Tim hurried home to tell Becky the great news. Becky shook her head sadly as she spoke:

"Oh Tim, I knew those guys would hook you! I'm not looking forward to this one bit. You're going to find yourself torn between your own good conscience and the impossible promises those politicians will insist that you make."

"But honey, I'm not going to compromise my principles. I'm going to tell it like it is, and I believe in the intelligence and goodness of enough people that they will see the logic of my position and vote the right way."

"Tim, I know you won't compromise your principles, and that's where the trouble begins. Those political hacks will insist on putting words in your mouth, and you won't let them. That'll lead to one donnybrook after another. They'll be extremely angry with you for being so stubborn."

"I've been through tough situations before, and I have a good track record in working out solutions."

Becky heaved a deep sigh:

"Your problem, lover, is very plain to see: You're letting your idealism blind you to the harsh realities of political life. It pains me deeply that I can't make you see that. Those hacks were smart enough to hook you through your idealism; but they're not smart enough to see that it won't work. They're convinced that you'll be realistic and be willing to let them bend you and mold you into their concept of a successful candidate. They've never encountered such a straight arrow, and they just assume that you'll think like they do."

Tim had a hard time containing his frustration and irritation with her. She could be so negative. Couldn't she see the great opportunities he saw for doing good in this powerful position? He decided to challenge her,

"How come your so politically smart? You've never been a politician."

"No, thank God, and I never want to be one. But I've lived with you for more than a quarter of a century, and I know you far better than they do. They see all of your assets, but they don't see your great political liability."

He was very close to being just plain angry with her as he mocked her words:

"So what's my great `political liability'?"

"Your honesty and absolute integrity."

"Are you saying there are no honest politicians?"

"There aren't by your standards. In your lexicon honesty is an absolute quality. In theirs it's a relative term. They believe it's OK to speak with enough ambiguity that the voters hear what they want to hear. They think the end justifies the means. It's even OK to lie if you don't get caught at it, and to put through pork barrel legislation in order to keep your voters loyal. You're an honest politician if you don't steal and you don't take bribes."

He knew she spoke the truth, and he retorted,

"Maybe it's time to start raising those standards."

"Good luck! The worst will be the outcome. You will lose gloriously, and your new political friends will blame it all on you for being so stubborn and refusing to accept the political realities. And they'll be right."

"Are you saying I *should* compromise my principles?" he goaded her.

"Oh, come off it Tim, you know better than that!"

"Then what *are* you saying?"

"That you shouldn't run. It will be the most frustrating, bitter experience you've ever had."

"I've got to try."

She knew that no amount of argument was going to dissuade him:

"All right, lover, you try, and I'll support you in every way I can. And when it's all over, I'll bind up your wounds and help you get on with your life."

They embraced warmly, both thankful that the argument hadn't degenerated into a fight.

Gordon Springborn couldn't believe his good fortune. He had dreamed of starting his own investment business, just as his friend, Tim Hamilton, had done so successfully, but he didn't know how to begin. And now Tim had just offered to turn a going business over to him. Granted, it might be only temporary, but it would be a great way to start. Tim was equally happy that his friend had accepted so enthusiastically. The chairs of the boards on which he served seemed excited about his candidacy and were more than willing to find ways to accommodate his absence. All were emphatic, however, that they wanted him back whenever he became available again.

The telephone call was from Jerry O'Connell:

"Hi Tim! I've got wonderful news. We've been lucky enough to hire Joe Pattinelli as your campaign manager. Joe is one of the best in the business; he has a number of highly successful campaigns under his belt. When can we get together for lunch?"

"I'm free the day after tomorrow."

"That's great! The Summit at 11:45?"

"OK."

Joseph Pattinelli was slight of build with a swarthy complexion and dark beard which he kept very neatly trimmed. He spoke with a Boston accent,

"Jerry has told me of your many virtues and your wonderful reputation. I'm really looking forward to working with you."

"Did Jerry also tell you that I've had absolutely no experience in the political arena?"

"Yes, he did, but in a way that's good. You won't have any bad habits to unlearn. What he didn't tell me is that you have a profile that will look terrific, not only on TV but in the still shots."

"Thank you, I think."

"Jerry also tells me that you speak clearly and with good diction and that it comes from the heart. I'm delighted to hear these things."

"What do you see as our biggest challenge?"

"If you're to win in the final election the greater Minnesota voters must know you much better than they do now. I hope you enjoy small planes and long car rides."

"I can't honestly say that either one is my favorite pastime, but I've no objection to them."

"You'll also have to become a household word with the working class. I'm gonna guess they don't know you as well as you're known in the business community."

"Probably so."

"There's a lot of work to be done. Jerry tells me you've got other obligations to take care of before you can give your full attention to the campaign. How long before we can really get down to work?"

"I'm in better shape there than I thought I'd be. I'd say another three weeks and I'll be able to devote almost full time. I have several young people with whom I'm doing career counseling; I'll need one or two more interviews with each of them."

"That'll work out well. Jerry and I can map out the campaign and clear major issues with the committee in the meantime. How will it be if we start, really start work, meeting regularly in the campaign headquarters three weeks from Monday?"

"I can do that, but I need the address."

On the way back to his office Tim reviewed the lunch table discussion. Pattinelli seemed highly intelligent and nice enough. These guys surely weren't the political hacks Becky had in mind. There'll be differences of opinion, but nothing they couldn't work out as intelligent adults. He felt glad that he had accepted the candidacy. This would be a new and exciting experience. O'Connell was right. He would have much more opportunity to do good.

While driving to campaign headquarters three weeks later, Tim found himself excitedly anticipating the opportunity to "really start to work", as Pattinelli had described it. He found O'Connell and Pattinelli chatting over coffee in the reception area. They greeted Tim warmly, took his coffee order and ushered him into a small conference room. On the table were folders each neatly labeled: INCOME TAXES, PROPERTY TAX RELIEF, EDUCATION, ROADS AND BRIDGES,

PUBLIC TRANSPORTATION, OPPONENTS, ABOR-
TION, POVERTY, CRIME, and so on. The one labeled
OPPONENTS intrigued Tim. Pattinelli opened the
conversation,

"I've been over each of these subjects with the
state committee and with the platform committee. My
first challenge was to get them to realize that their
personal views are not nearly as important as how the
majority of voters in their districts feel."

"That makes sense."

"Yeah, but the challenge is to get them to see that
without bruising their egos."

"Were you successful?"

"More or less. I don't think they realize yet how
much homework they have to do. They've got to get a lot
closer to their constituents, and that takes tons of hard
work. A lot of these people are allergic to work. I can't
do their jobs for them. I can only show them what needs
to be done and push them as hard as I dare to do it. I can
sure see why they lost the last election."

"What do I do first?"

"Each of these folders contain's notes, memos and
compilations that summarize, as best we can, how we
think the majority of voters feel on each of these issues.
Their views are a moving target and we must never lose
sight of the target. There are only two ways to win an
election. The first is to vilify your opponent until a
majority of the voters reject him. The other way is to
convince the voters that what they believe is what you
believe with all your heart."

"So the big problem is lack of communication?"

"I wish that were so, but it's not."

"So what is the big problem?"

"The voters are not realistic in their beliefs. They
want all the benefits, but they're not willing to pay for
them."

"So we have to persuade them to be more realistic?"

"It would be great if you could, but it doesn't work that way."

"Then how does it work?"

"We must build an image of you that makes them see you as just the guy they've been looking for to carry out their beliefs."

"But I'm not going to lie to them!"

"You don't have to."

"Then how do you do it?"

"Your job right now is to study these folders and make careful notes of the things you don't buy. Our job is to build your image, like I said. We've been very successful in doing this with other candidates. That's why we have such an outstanding track record for winning elections."

"I don't see how you do this."

"Trust us."

After a few moments of silence, Pattinelli announced that he had a number of phone calls to make and that he would leave Tim to study the folders. It was late afternoon by the time Tim finished reading all of the files. He looked up Joe in his office. Joe greeted him with a big smile,

"Have you finished reading all of the files?"

"Yes I have. I found them very interesting."

"I hope you found yourself in agreement with a number of our positions."

"Yes I did; but I do have some problems."

"What are they?"

"I think the biggest one is this. You propose to build more roads, improve public transportation, provide more money for education, provide more social services, property tax relief, and a host of other new benefits--but you're not going to raise the income taxes or the sales taxes! Where is the money going to come from?"

"We're going to close the tax loopholes that the wealthy have enjoyed, and we're going to eliminate waste in government."

"But it's wishful thinking that those measures will provide anywhere near the money needed."

"You've got it, Tim!"

"In other words, you're proposing to tell the voters what they want to hear, instead of telling them the truth."

"You've scored again, Tim! That's what wins elections."

"Wait just a minute, Joe. I'm just trying to understand where you're coming from. I'm not saying I buy it."

"What do *you* want to do?"

"We need to be honest with voters. Point out to them that there are some tough decisions ahead, and that there'll be pain, sacrifice and disappointment in whatever course of action we take; and I need their help and support to arrive at the best solutions."

"That may be the truth, but I can promise you that, if you tell the voters things like that, someone else will be Minnesota's next governor."

Joe decided not to press Tim any further on that subject--not now, anyway:

"What else bothers you?"

"The statement on abortion. It's has lots of nice words in it, but it doesn't say anything."

"What would you say on this subject that all the voters could agree with?"

"I would say that I will bring spokes people for both points of view together, see what we can agree on, announce our areas of agreement and celebrate those areas. Then we'll meet again, listen carefully to each other's point of view, and try to work out a basis of understanding and a plan of action that will stop the violence and the fighting. I'd let the legislature and the courts resolve the remaining areas of disagreement, have everyone agree to abide by the law, and live in love and peace."

Joe shook his head sadly and replied,

"Tim, I can see that you're really new to the world of politics. That's a wonderful dream you have; but I can assure you that you and I will be long since dead and buried before we see that dream come true."

"But we can try to bring it a little closer to reality."

"You're shutting your eyes to the truth, Tim. These people don't *want* to hear each others' viewpoints. They'd rather `fight for what's right'. Freely translated, that means they'll fight for what some silver tongued orator has told them to believe. And believe me, those fights can get incredibly ugly. People with high moral and religious principles can violate these principles drastically without a single pang of conscience or remorse."

"Then what's the answer?"

"The subject is too important to too many people for us to ignore it. But the less the statement says about the real issues the better. Our objective is to have the voters read our press releases and hear your speeches, and have them all come away feeling that you're going to support their cause."

"But that's dishonest."

"Call it what you like, that's what wins elections. Let me remind you once again, Tim. Our job is to get you elected. If we don't, you're not going to do any more good than you are doing now in your own private, cozy little environment."

Tim was silent. He looked both sad and perplexed. Was Joe telling it like it is, or was he taking the easy way out to win the election and add another successful campaign to his already long list? How was Tim to know? If the first answer was right, should he withdraw from the campaign now? What would his boards and his clients think if he withdrew this early? If the second answer was right, how was he going to deal with Joe and the committee that hired him? Tim would know in his heart he was right, but that would be little comfort. Was this going to be another Cornerstone situation?

By now, both men were weary, and both realized they weren't going to accomplish anything more today. Joe broke the silence,

"Tell you what I'm going to do. I'll share your thoughts with my best writer and have him come up with a position paper on each of these subjects. When he's done, I'll call you for another meeting."

Tim nodded his head wearily and left without even a goodbye. On the way home Tim's mind kept playing the day back to him in kind of a confused series of instant replays, with many repeats. When Tim opened the front door, the delightful aroma of dinner greeted him. He sighed a deep sigh. It was wonderful to be home. It had been a long, tough day, and he felt more spent, physically, mentally and emotionally, than he had since some of the final Cornerstone meetings. When Becky saw him, she kissed him fervently and hugged him tightly before she exclaimed,

"Sit down, lover boy, before you fall down. You need something to adjust your attitude, and it'll be a double."

They took their drinks to the sofa and assumed their favorite position. Tim told Becky about his whole day: meeting Pattinelli, reading all of the folders, and then the dreadful conversations. He told her he had expected long, tough days of campaigning and facing angry voters and perhaps even some hostile reporters. But he hadn't expected to have such an enervating day so early in the campaign, when he hadn't even stuck his nose out of campaign headquarters yet. When he had finished, she looked up at him and smiled as she said,

"Congratulations, Tim. You've just completed Politics 101."

"But what do you think I should do?"

"Tim, you know how I've felt from the start. I wish I could be wrong on this because I know how important it is to you. But as they say, you ain't seen nothin' yet. I agree with you that people would misunderstand if you withdrew this early. I also know you won't compromise your principles, even if they all disagree with you; and I'm proud of you for that."

"Where does that leave us?"

"I think you have no choice but to take each day as it comes. In the last analysis, you have to make up your own mind. You're the one who has to live with yourself."

"You're no help!"

"If I told you anything else, I'd being lying to you, and you don't like people who lie. I think dinner's about ready. Let's go eat."

Tim had hoped that she might shed some light on his dilemma. He had a feeling of disappointment. But then, what could he expect? She had told him in the beginning that it wouldn't work and he had ignored her advice. Thank God for their happy marriage, their wonderful kids and all of the other blessings in their life. His world hadn't really come apart. He would enjoy dinner and a quiet evening.

He spent most of the next day at his desk, answering phone messages, reading mail, the usual mixture of junk mail, invitations to receptions and open houses, requests for money from a variety of charities, and corporate reports. His mind kept going back to the campaign? What would Pattinelli's best writer come up with? He didn't have to wait very long for the answers. Late that afternoon his FAX machine began to purr. Tim watched eagerly as the first page took shape. The cover sheet bore the party logo. The message was from

Pattinelli saying that the following pages were his writer's draft on the issues and that he would like to meet with Tim at ten o'clock the following morning to discuss the draft. Tim kept up with the machine, reading each page as it emerged. It was in the form of a press release and was headed:

HAMILTON IS PREPARED TO DEAL WITH THE ISSUES

The first page reported how quickly Tim had recognized the critical issues went on to credit Tim with the very eloquent statement of the issues that followed. That "statement" (which was, in fact, a list of the issues with no hint of what Tim thought about them) was followed by a very flattering description of Tim's abilities and his reputation throughout Minnesota for his business acumen and his great wisdom. It included a brief reference to his coming up with a solution to Cornerstone's problems that assured the policyholders that all of their benefits would be paid in full, when everyone else thought a solution was impossible. And that was it!

The next morning ten o'clock came all too slowly. Tim was eager to confront Joe Pattinelli. He was early to their meeting and challenged Pattinelli the moment he appeared,

"Joe, I thought your writer was going to produce a paper on the issues."

"He did, didn't he? Pretty eloquent, isn't it?"

Tim held up the FAX and hit it with the back of his other hand:

"All these pages and they don't say a damn thing about my position on the issues."

"After listening to you the day before yesterday, the less said about your position on the issues the better."

Tim felt his anger rising:

"I thought you were hired to help me in this campaign."

"I was hired to get you elected, not to help you put your foot in your mouth."

"If this is your idea of helping me, I'll take vanilla."

"I didn't come all the way from Boston to this God-forsaken part of the world to be insulted by a guy who can't fight his way out of a political paper bag."

Jerry O'Connell had heard the voices rising and had come quickly into the room:

"Peace, gentlemen. We're not going to resolve anything this way. Let's go get some fresh coffee."

By the time they returned to the conference room tempers had cooled, and O'Connell said,

"Now, gentlemen, what's the problem?"

Pattinelli quietly explained the problem as he saw it,

"Jerry, you told me you had recruited an outstanding candidate for governor, and you retained me to get him elected. Mr. Hamilton may have an impeccable record in the business world, but unless he recognizes some of the basic facts of political life and plays ball with us, he's a sure loser. I'm not at all interested in working with a loser. It's just that simple."

It was Tim's turn:

"Jerry, when you recruited me, you didn't tell me I'd have to lie to get elected."

"You don't have to lie to anybody, Tim. But you learned in the business world that you can't succeed in any negotiation by putting the thick end of the wedge in first. That's even truer in politics. Most voters have a lot of fantasies about their government."

"Like what?" Tim challenged him.

"Their biggest one is that there's a lot of waste in government and that, if they elect the right man, he'll eliminate that waste and give them even more services for less money. You can't prick their bubble and expect them to vote for you. But you don't have to be dishonest in the process."

"But you're saying that we have to fool them into believing that, if they elect me, I'll make their fantasies come true. If that isn't lying to them it sure as hell is gross misrepresentation; and I can't be a party to that."

Pattinelli interrupted them, saying,

"Jerry, I've heard all I need to hear. My associates and I are outta here. We'll catch the first plane back to Boston. I'll bill you only for the hours we've spent so far and neither of us will have any further obligations under our contract. Good bye and good luck to both of you. You'll need it."

He shook hands with both of them and left the room.

Tim broke the silence that had followed Pattinelli's departure:

"Jerry, I guess maybe I'm not your man."

"Oh, come on, Tim. Don't let Pattinelli discourage you. He's pulled this stunt with others. He only wants the easy ones so as to keep his outstanding track record. Not to worry, we'll find a campaign manager who is easier to work with."

Tim sighed deeply before he answered,

"I surely hope so."

"I'll call you for an appointment when we find one. There's nothing more we can do today, so go and enjoy yourself."

Tim felt better. He wasn't sure how O'Connell would react when Pattinelli left. He seemed to take it all in stride. How would the next campaign manager approach things? How different would he be from Pattinelli?

It wasn't too many days before O'Connell called and asked him if he could come to headquarters the following morning to get acquainted with his new campaign manager. Tim said he could. When he arrived the following morning, O'Connell and a woman were already sitting in the conference room. Both of them rose to greet him as he entered the room, and O'Connell said,

" Sheila Corcoran, this is Mr. Timothy Hamilton, Minnesota's next governor."

Sheila and Tim exchanged greetings and they all sat down. She was a petite brunette with a thin face and dark, horn-rimmed glasses, and was dressed in dark blue suit. O'Connell began the conversation:

"Sheila will be your press agent. She's very highly regarded in her field. I've already told her how you and Joe differed on the way your positions on certain difficult issues should be presented. She and I both believe that you and she won't have that difficulty."

"That would be nice," Tim responded.

"Yes, Mr. Hamilton, where you have strong beliefs on an issue, and have the ability to articulate those beliefs, I believe in letting you express them in your own words. Then I merely polish the presentation and tailor it to the medium in which it will be delivered."

Tim liked what he was hearing,

"That sounds eminently sensible."

O'Connell nodded to express his concurrence as he rose to leave, Sheila started off with a question,

"Do you use a word processor program on your computer?"

"Oh yes."

"And do you have a modem?"

"Yes."

"Wonderful; I have software that allows my PC to be a host to your PC, so you can transmit your drafts on the controversial issues by telephone. That way we can get a lot more done in a short time and save wear and tear on our tires and our traffic nerves. Then, when I've edited your drafts, I can FAX you the finished product.

Here is my business card. My computer number is the same as my FAX number. I'll need a couple of minutes notice when you want to upload a file. Just call first on my voice line."

To Tim, this all sounded the like way life ought to be. Here was an efficient, business-like woman who would not try to tell him what to do. They were really going to let him tell it like it is. Then the voters would appreciate his honesty and sincerity. This campaign might go well after all. He was anxious to get home and start writing. Sheila interrupted his thoughts:

"Jerry tells me he would like our first release to make Thursday's paper. That means that I should have your drafts by Tuesday morning. I will FAX the rest of the release to you at the same time and you will have Tuesday to review it and make your comments. Do you have any questions you'd like to ask me?"

"I can't think of any."

Sheila rose and held out her hand,

"I'm going to enjoy working with you, Tim."

"Me, too."

After dinner that evening Tim told Becky about this wonderful person who had been assigned to work with him.

"You always did like the girls best," she teased.

"She's not nearly as good looking as you are," he responded.

She kissed him warmly, and he hurried up to his office, eager to get his views on taxes versus benefits into the computer. His thoughts on the subject seemed to flow easily: Education was important, particularly early childhood education; and you couldn't educate a hungry child. Now that the conservative congress had cut funds for Head Start and school lunches to a trickle, it was up to the state to see that these vital programs were not curtailed. He would do everything he could to see that they were maintained through private philanthropy; but it would be up to the good people of Minnesota to close the gap. Some of the money could be obtained through better investment of the state's reserve funds and by reducing the less essential services that the state was providing. He would work with the legislature to make sure that the additional burdens didn't fall too heavily on any individuals or groups, but all the people with discretionary income would be asked to make some small sacrifices. Their rewards would be the knowledge that they had invested their money in making better citizens out of today's children and that the returns would be immense.

He worked late into the night to get all of his thoughts down. In the morning he printed out his draft and eagerly showed it to Becky at breakfast. She nodded thoughtfully as she read. When she had finished, she looked up, shook her head and smiled at him, as she said,

"You don't really want to be governor, after all, do you."

"What do you mean?"

"How many successful candidates do you know of who ran on a platform of sacrifice and higher taxes?"

"Are you saying I shouldn't tell it like it is? That would be dishonest."

"I'm saying that I love you too much to see you get hurt. You couldn't be dishonest if you tried."

"I have to believe that there are enough good people in this state that they will elect a governor who is honest with them."

"Well, *I* have to believe that we've been through this discussion before and that it's not going to get us anywhere. So hang in there, lover."

She came around the table, kissed him and handed him the front section of the paper.

Just as she had promised, Sheila took his drafts, changed them only slightly and fit them into the rest of the release she had written. Tim liked the result.

Jerry O'Connell sighed when he came to the part of the press release about sacrifice and taxes. He sighed again when he came to Tim's thoughts about resolving the abortion issue. He thought briefly about trying to get Tim to soft pedal his positions on these tough issues, but he knew he wouldn't get far. Tim would learn soon enough. The paper planned to conduct a poll to see how people reacted to the first press release. If the reaction was positive, it would be wonderful. If it wasn't, Tim would learn his first lesson in practical politics. He didn't want to think too much about what would happen then.

Tim got up early Thursday to bring in the paper. He was pleased to see that it devoted most of a page to his statement of the issues. On the facing page was a similar statement by his principal opponent. It was eloquently and glowingly worded, but when he finished reading it, Tim had no idea where his opponent really stood on the controversial issues. And he didn't like the several pointed references to his own lack of experience in government. When he turned to the editorial page, he was delighted to see that the lead editorial praised him highly for his forthrightness and expressed the hope that the voters would react positively toward a candidate with this honest, open approach. Why wouldn't they?

Tim got his answer a week later when the paper printed the results of its poll. Tim lagged his opponent by almost 20 percent. He was incensed when he turned the page and saw a report on a newsletter that had been widely distributed by his opponent. The lead article in the newsletter had been captioned:

FAIR HAIRED BOY OR FAILURE?

The newsletter article stated that Tim had been fired from the only real job he had ever held, had tried to commit suicide in Hawaii, and that, questioning his sanity, his wife had left him and gone back to live with her mother. The article went on to speak derisively of his lack of political experience and to ask whether he was really the wise man his promoters had painted, or a failure. Tim was incensed. How unfair could they be? Where did they get all this stuff? Why had the paper reprinted it? Wasn't there a law against this kind of calumny? He could hardly wait to call his attorney. The attorney's answer was disappointing: It was almost impossible to win a suit for libel or slander against a public figure, and Tim had become a public figure when he threw his hat in the ring. Moreover, he could expect more of this kind of treatment, and the best thing he could do was ignore it.

Tim was still stewing about the outrageous news letter when Jerry O'Connell called,

"Good morning, Tim, how are you?"

"Boiling mad! Did you see the report on our opponent's newsletter in the morning paper?"

"I not only saw it; I've got a copy of the newsletter."

"Why in the world would the paper print such crap?"

"They did us a favor, Tim. Did you see their editorial about it?"

"No."

"Read it and you'll feel better. They deplore this kind of negative campaigning, and they go on to say that campaign managers stoop to that kind of slander only when they feel that their own candidate can't compete on the issues. Now let's get on to the important things. My staff has done a superb job on the monumental task of laying out the details of your campaign strategy. Could you come down about two o'clock this afternoon so that we could go over it together?"

Tim said he could. When he arrived in O'Connell's office, he could hardly talk about anything else than that calumnious newsletter:

""How in the world did they get hold of that stuff?" he asked.

"Do you remember one middle manager that Cornerstone laid off who was so angry with you?"

"Oh yeah, Wes Johnson. He called and read me out for about 45 minutes, how I cost him his job, ruined his career, destroyed his marriage and so on. He ended up telling me he would get even some day. If he's responsible, he ought to be punished in some way."

"His punishment has long since begun."

"How's that?"

"His bitterness is eating out his insides and destroying his soul. We should forgive him and pray for him."

"You certainly are charitable."

"Call it charity if you like. I think it's good, practical psychology."

"How are we going to respond to that crap?"

"You don't respond, Tim; you just ignore it. You want to run a clean, honest campaign, and that's what we're going to do. So far, your sleazy, mud-slinging opponent has seriously out-polled you. Hopefully, it's just lack of name recognition in greater Minnesota, and nothing that a good old-fashioned barn-storming tour around the state and some good TV ads won't cure. The latter costs money and the former takes a ton of sleeves-up traveling."

O'Connell handed Tim a note-book as he continued:

"This plan calls for six one-week tours, punctuated with a few days in between to rest and catch up on your mail. There are a couple of longer breaks to accommodate the prior commitments you told me about. We've chartered a luxury coach for the trip, so we'll travel in safety and comfort. I'll leave you alone in the conference room so that you can look at the book uninterrupted. My administrative assistant is checking final details as we speak, so if you see anything that won't work for you, please tell me right away. If you have any comments or questions, don't hesitate to interrupt me."

"O. K.", said Tim as he headed for the conference room.

As he perused the book, Tim couldn't help but think how much work had gone into its preparation. Little did the public know, from what they read in the papers, the mammoth effort that went into mounting a major political campaign. The book was divided into several sections: one covered coach times, hotels, and other travel details. Another had a page for every one of the 63 speaking engagements (better than two a day!) showing the name of the organization, speaking place, name of the MC or presiding officer, names and titles of distinguished guests, time allotment, special issues to be added to the standard talk, sensitive issues to be omitted, expected attendance with estimated mix by sex, race, religion, and predominant ethnic characteristics. Except for a one-hour siesta, the rest of each day was filled with plant visits, mall visits, park visits, museum visits, and so on. When Tim had finished reading, he stepped to the doorway of O'Connell's office.

"Come in and sit down, Tim. What do you think?"

"I'm impressed with the amount of hard work it takes to mount a political campaign."

"Wait until you're through the first day of the trip; you'll be even more impressed. I know you're in good health, and I hope you've tons of physical and emotional stamina."

"I think I do, but I guess we'll find out."

"Do you have any questions?"

"Yes. Is Becky expected to go with me?"

"Yes, to the fullest extent she can."

"I think she will; I'll ask her."

When Tim arrived home, he and Becky spent the next hour going over the book. When they came to the back cover, Becky said,

"Wow, someone sure has gone to a lot of work!"

"That's what I thought. You're expected to go with me."

"I wouldn't miss it for the world."

As they went to the table for dinner Tim was pleased with her enthusiasm. He was also pleased that she hadn't expressed any more negative thoughts about the campaign.

A few days later, as Tim was sitting at his desk, his FAX purred busily and produced a press release announcing his campaign trip. Although it contained nothing he didn't know already, he read it with interest. It all sounded good to him. Following the instructions in the note at the end, he called Sheila and expressed his approval. She told him it would be in Thursday's paper. He couldn't suppress his excitement as he eagerly opened Thursday's paper and looked for the article. There it was, at the top of page 3, under the headline:

HAMILTON ANNOUNCES AMBITIOUS STATEWIDE CAMPAIGN

When he sat down at the breakfast table, he laid the paper beside Becky's plate, already folded with the headline showing. The lead sentence began,

"In an effort to bolster his disappointing showing in the poll taken after his statement of the issues, Timothy Hamilton, the Democratic candidate for Governor. ."

She read it with interest, nodded and asked,

"Well, what do you think?"

"I wasn't particularly pleased with the lead sentence. What do they have to bring up that negative stuff for?"

"They're only telling it like it is, and that's their job. They've already shown an editorial preference for your forthrightness in stating the issues. I'm sure they're as hopeful as you are that your ratings will improve."

Their conversation was interrupted by the telephone,

"Good morning."

"Hi Tim, Jerry O'Connell here. Our research staff has been busy on issues we think have almost universal appeal and that you can support with enthusiasm. Sheila has turned them into speeches and is having them couriered to you this morning. I hope you can give them your immediate attention."

"What are the issues?"

"They're all on the theme of reducing the cost of government: eliminating non-vital services, increasing efficiency, using volunteers, contracting with private firms, and privatization."

"I'll be glad to look at them when they arrive."

"Good! Then you can work with Sheila on any changes or additions. We must work quickly; we don't have a lot of time until we go on the road."

Tim and Becky found their excitement increasing as the time for their departure approached. Neither of them had any experience in coach travel, and so they had many questions: what and how much should they pack? what should they wear? what would the weather be like? would there be any free time to read? and so on. Sheila had organized Tim's speeches into notebooks, small enough to be handled easily on a podium, but with print large enough to be followed easily, even in poor lighting.

Then there were briefing notebooks on each community they were to visit, and more briefing notebooks with suggested answers to the myriad questions that would be fired at him. He had spent endless days, it seemed, revising the suggested answers to questions. He thought many of the answers were evasive and tried to make them more forthright. He had expected more questions on what he saw as the broader issues, but so many of the questions were of the "what-are-you going to do for me" nature. Were people really this greedy and self-centered? The proposed answers to these greedy questions also disturbed him. They seemed to promise people everything they asked for. How could any government deliver all of those things and still keep costs in line? He had sharpened his red pencil several times before he finished working over these answers.

They would spend their first day in St. Cloud, a community of about 50,000 people located on the Mississippi River about 80 miles northwest of Minneapolis. Best known for the large state college located there, the city also served as a hub for the surrounding farm community and enjoyed a thriving tourist and resort industry. A taxi picked Tim and Becky up at 5:30 and took them to their coach. Large signs on both sides of the coach read,

TIM HAMILTON -- YOUR NEXT GOVERNOR

Jerry O'Connell, Sheila and a bubbly, blond-haired young woman they hadn't met were there already. O'Connell introduced Becky and Tim to Lori Rice and explained that Lori was in charge of all of the physical arrangements for the trip. Lori greeted them warmly and urged them,

"Don't hesitate to ask questions or mention anything you need. It's my job to see that you're just as comfortable and well cared for as possible, and I enjoy doing just that."

While the introductions were going on, the coach driver had loaded their luggage. A clear sun peeking out from a small, white cloud heralded a beautiful fall morning; and everyone agreed that this was a good omen for the start of their trip. O'Connell looked nervously at his watch and exclaimed,

"It's 6:22; we're due to leave at 6:30 and none of the press has shown up! Where in the devil are they?" As if in answer to his question, a small, red sports car tore into the parking lot and swung into an empty stall in one smooth motion. A dark-bearded young man jumped out, rescued his bag from the back seat and handed it to the coach driver. At the same time he announced,

"Hi guys, I'm Freddie Strangefellow from the Minneapolis *Star-Tribune!*"

"Welcome aboard!" responded O'Connell, "Are you planning to spend the week with us?"

"Maybe, but if you guys get boring, I'll jump ship."

While he was speaking, another small car wheeled into the adjacent stall. Out of it came a young, red-haired, bespectacled woman. She also handed her bag to the coach driver and stepped expectantly into the circle of people. O'Connell took his cue, extended his hand and said,

"Hi, I'm Jerry O'Connell, Democratic Party State Chairman."

"Hello, I'm Sharon Persoon, political reporter for the St. Paul *Pioneer Press*. My boss said you'd be glad to have me aboard."

"That's right" said Sheila as she introduced herself and then introduced Sharon to the rest of the group. She continued, "It's time to load up. Take seats wherever you like, except for the four marked `reserved'."

O'Connell was anxiously glancing at his watch when a mini-van marked "Channel 4" wheeled into the lot. A man and a woman hurriedly jumped out, opened the hatch and hauled out a variety of tripods, cameras, lights and other TV paraphernalia. Without a word they carried the equipment to the coach and handed each piece to the driver. O'Connell, poorly concealing his irritation at their tardiness, introduced himself and continued,

"Please climb aboard as quickly as you can so that we can be on our way. We'll make the rest of the introductions on the coach."

As soon as they were seated, Sheila gave each person a sheet which read,

ST. CLOUD
Monday, October 11th

6:30 AM	Assemble at Headquarters and board motor coach
6:45 AM	Depart for Sunrise Hotel, St. Cloud
9:15 AM	Depart for Farmers' Market
9:30 AM	Mingle with farmers and buyers
11:15 AM	Depart for Hotel
11:45 AM	Introductions in ballroom: luncheon open to public, jointly sponsored by Chamber of Commerce, Rotary, Lions and Kiwanis. Host: Lou Peterson, Chamber of Commerce President
12:00	Luncheon, followed by Hamilton address and questions
2:15 PM	Depart for St. Cloud Mall
2:30 PM	Mingle with shoppers and employees
4:45 PM	Depart for Hotel
6:00 PM	Depart for St. Cloud State College
6:15 PM	Introduction in Garvey Commons: dinner open to public, jointly sponsored by the Young Democrats, the Grange, the Farmer's Union Cooperative and the St. Cloud Allied Trade Unions

Tim had barely time to digest the schedule for the day when Sharon Persoon approached him,

"Mr. Hamilton, may I take a few minutes of your time?"

"Of course, Sharon, please sit down."

"My paper is impressed with your frank, open approach to the issues; but how will you be able to satisfy the diverse interests of the people in a community like St. Cloud where you have such diverse interests as business, professionals, labor, agriculture and education?"

"As articulately, intelligently and fairly as I can."

"That'll be refreshing after the kind of campaigning we've seen in recent years, but how will you satisfy the demands of all these different groups who seem only to want to know 'what're you going to do for us'?"

"I hope to make them see that the state can do only so much for the people with the limited resources that the taxpayers are willing to provide. We've seen in Russia and other middle European countries what happens to a nation when they become overly dependent on the government to meet too many of their needs."

"I read all of the letters to the editor after your frank statement on the issues in the papers. You certainly got mixed reviews. Were you disappointed?"

"Yes, I was, but I'm not discouraged. I think it takes a while for all of us to let reality sink in."

"How about your poor showing in the first state-wide poll?"

"I'm well known in the Twin Cities, but I lack name recognition in greater Minnesota. The purpose of this trip is to correct that problem."

"How did you feel about the very negative article in your opponent's newsletter?"

"I was angry when I first read it, but then various people helped me see that such negative campaigning is really a sign of weakness."

"But it does seem to sway the voters."

"I suppose some people are affected by that kind of trash; I just hope it's not too many."

"Thank you, Mr. Hamilton. We'll continue to watch your campaign with great interest, I certainly wish you the best of luck."

"Thank you, Sharon. I'm sure I'll need all I can get."

Becky had been listening to the interview with great interest and was quick to react:

"Congratulations, lover. I thought you handled your first interview well."

"She didn't sound too hopeful about the outcome."

"It's her job to ask questions, not to be a cheerleader."

"True."

The interviews with Freddie Strangefellow and the Channel 4 reporter seemed pretty much to be variations on the same theme. When they had finished, Tim remarked,

"I'm disappointed; they seemed much more interested in my direct approach to the issues than they did in the issues themselves."

"After all, your approach is newsworthy. And the week is young yet."

It was a beautiful time to travel in Minnesota. Nature had begun to work its beautiful chemical magic on the leaves of the hardwoods. The sugar maples had begun to display their brilliant reds and yellows. The deeper red of the oaks provided an enchanting contrast while yellow elms, birch, and cottonwood, punctuated by the deep greens of the pines, cedar, and spruce completed this magnificent chorus of color. Tim and Becky held hands in silent communion as they leaned back in their deep, comfortable seats and beheld this enthralling scene, lost in awe and wonder.

At lunch Tim shared his thoughts and beliefs on such issues as business development, education, roads, property tax relief and a balanced budget. The applause was polite, but not especially enthusiastic. Then came the questions: How much was he going to lower taxes in order to improve the business climate? Would he get them further relief from still-oppressive worker's comp premiums? What would he do to provide an adequate number of doctors in rural areas? Would he resist any attempts to raise the minimum wage? What would he do to encourage business development in the smaller cities? What would he do to provide some relief from the oppressive and unfair property tax structure? What was he planning to do to promote tourism more effectively? How much was he going to increase the funding for state colleges? There seemed to be no end to these myopic, self-interest questions.

In answer to the first of these questions Tim gave a reply that he had thought out carefully in the preceding days: In Minnesota there were dozens of diverse interest groups, all anxious for the government to do more for them, but none willing to have their taxes increased to cover these demands. He would work with both parties in the legislature to seek consensus on how the state's resources could be used to do the greatest good for the greatest number. He would also appoint a bi-partisan commission to study what non-essential government activities could be eliminated and how the cost of government could be reduced in other ways. He hoped there would be enough resources available to deal adequately with the questioners' concerns. To give a more specific answer to that question at this time would not be honest because it would imply a promise that he might not be able keep. As the other questions poured in, he referred them to his first answer. As he continued to field questions in this manner there were frowns and mumblings of dissatisfaction. One listener confronted him directly and somewhat belligerently,

"In other words, you're going to be evasive when we're looking for specific answers."

Tim looked somewhat non-plussed; and Gunder Erickson, the local party leader came to his rescue:

"Mr. Hamilton is giving you intelligent, honest answers, and you're not used to hearing that, particularly from his opposition."

There was a smattering of applause, and Tim took the opportunity to sit down. Lou Peterson, Chamber of Commerce Chairman, rose to the podium and said,

"Thank you, Mr. Hamilton, for coming to St. Cloud and sharing your thoughts with us. We hope you find the rest of your stay in the Greater St. Cloud area most enjoyable."

Again, the applause was polite, but not really enthusiastic. Exactly three people shook hands with Tim afterwards and told him how much they appreciated his honesty and forthrightness. It did little to remove Tim's sense of disappointment and devastation. Dinner that evening was no better. The questions were different, but they were just as narrow and self-centered. This time he was confronted by, not one, but two angry guests. One of them represented farm interests, the other labor. They both accused of him of being disloyal to the party that was supposed to look after their interests. Many of the other guests talked in unhappy tones with each other. Tim sat down, and the MC quickly stepped to the podium, thanked Tim for his presentation, expressed his appreciation to the other guests for coming, and adjourned the meeting. On the way back to the hotel O'Connell invited Becky and Tim to join him and Sheila for a night-cap in the lounge, and they accepted.

No sooner were they seated than Freddie Strangefellow pulled a chair up to their table,

"Mr. Hamilton, do you mind if I ask you a few questions?"

Tim was about to reply when O'Connell cut in,

"Freddie, I think it's a little early for questions. Why don't you talk to Mr. Hamilton on the coach tomorrow morning."

Freddie took his cue and left them to join his reporter friends at another table. The four of them sipped their drinks in silence, until O'Connell finally spoke:

"So much for honesty and forthrightness. I'm sorry you got such a cool reception today."

Tim stared at his glass in silence, but he finally felt obligated to speak, so he began,

"Jerry, I guess I'm just not cut out for politics. It's still over a year until the election; if you want to find another candidate, I would understand fully."

"One day doesn't make a campaign, Tim. Let's see how today plays on the evening TV news and in the morning papers, and tomorrow's another day. Sheila, I'd like to ask a favor of you. If it's all right with Becky and Tim, I'd like the four of us to caucus at breakfast at 6:30 and have Sheila present us with some other ways that Tim could answer these self-centered questions, ways that would give the questioners more hope without feeling that he's perjuring himself."

She replied,

"I'll give it a try, Jerry, but I don't really feel that I've got much wiggle room."

They finished their drinks with small talk. Becky expressed a wish to go to their room, and the brief session was ended. When they had secured their door for the night, Tim flopped into an upholstered chair and exclaimed,

"I didn't feel this tired and dispirited after my worst day at Cornerstone. I never dreamed that so many people could be so greedy and self-centered. They're not interested in the welfare of their community unless it lines their own pockets."

"And you haven't yet faced the folks in Hibbing and Eveleth where a good share of the people are unemployed or under-employed."

"Now I can see why most legislators lack the breadth of vision it would really take to solve this state's problems. In their pork-barrelling ways, they are truly representing the people who voted for them. What a travesty!"

Becky came over, settled herself comfortably in his lap and gave him a long warm hug before she spoke,

"You've learned a great deal in one day, lover."

"You know, Becky, it goes against my upbringing to be a quitter; but it seems like such an exercise in futility to go through with this campaign. I could endure the pain and the brickbats if I really thought we were winning votes; but if we could poll these people today, I really think I would get fewer votes than I did in that first poll."

"Some wise man once said, `discretion is the better part of valor'."

"Besides, it seems grossly unfair to O'Connell and his constituents to put them in the position of backing a loser. What would you think if I told O'Connell in the morning that I was withdrawing as a candidate?"

She kissed him warmly before she spoke,

"I would think I married a very wise man."

Becky looked at her watch, broke free from Tim's embrace, got quickly to her feet and exclaimed,

"Oh my goodness, it's time for the ten o'clock news! Do you really want to watch it?"

"Yes dear, I'm curious to see what they have to say."

They didn't have long to wait before the Channel 4 anchor woman got to the story of Tim's day,

"Timothy Hamilton, the Democratic gubernatorial candidate got a very cool reception in St. Cloud today. Speaking to a large luncheon group of business and professional men and women, Hamilton was forthright in saying that he doubts if Minnesota taxpayers are willing to provide resources to do all the things that the people demand of government. He indicated a strong interest in maintaining high standards in public education, keeping our roads and highways in good shape, promoting new business development, property tax reform, further reducting levels of crime, and helping able-bodied people on welfare to make themselves employable in living-wage jobs. He foresaw a stringent state budget as a result of shrinking federal funds. He promised to work closely with the legislature to eliminate services that no longer are essential to the state's welfare, and to encourage greater use of volunteers to stretch the state's resources. The audience responded politely but not enthusiastically. It was in the question period that Hamilton seemed to alienate his audience. They were not at all pleased with his non-specific answers to their specific questions about what he would do to help their particular interests. He felt he was being honest. His audience felt he was being evasive. When the audience became confrontational, the luncheon chairman closed off the question period and declared the meeting adjourned. Hamilton was obviously embarrassed and non-plussed. It was evident that he had lost more votes than he had gained."

Becky turned off the TV while Tim slumped in his chair looking disconsolate but thoughtful for quite a while before he spoke,

"I can't see this trip as anything other than a frustrating exercise in futility. Tough as this day has been, I would endure more of them, if I really thought anything positive would come of it. But this is not doing the party any good, and it's obvious that these people aren't going to vote for me. I'm going to call O'Connell and suggest he meet us 15 minutes earlier for breakfast.

If I don't feel any better about it by morning, I'll lay my withdrawal on him."

Becky brought him the telephone, climbed into his lap, and put her arm around him,

"Honey, this must be terribly tough. I'm really very, very sorry for you."

"Thank you. You have a right to say, `I told you so'."

She kissed him and said with a smile,

"I don't have to. You've said it for me."

Tim woke up before Becky. When she opened her eyes he said,

"I haven't changed my mind."

"That's good."

"I feel terrible about letting O'Connell and his constituents down."

"Don't worry about O'Connell. He recruited you; you didn't volunteer. Besides he hooked you with the thought that you could do more good for more people. Yesterday demonstrated that you can't do it by being governor. Even if you were elected, those legislators would tear you apart. Most of them are dedicated to getting re-elected. To do that they'll put the perceived interests of their own constituents a way ahead of what's good for the state."

A half hour later Tim met Jerry O'Connel in the hotel dining room. When they had ordered breakfast, Tim got right to the point:

"Jerry, I think it's best for everybody if I withdraw my candidacy. I'm sorry to leave you in a crack; but you shouldn't have to back an obvious loser."

O'Connell took a long slow sip of his coffee before he responded. He didn't look at all surprised. Indeed he looked as if a heavy weight had been lifted from his shoulders.

"I understand, Tim. I'm truly very sorry it didn't work out, but I really think you're doing the right thing.

It'll take my staff a couple of hours on the telephones to cancel the plans for the rest of this week. We'll be ready by ten o'clock to turn the coach around and head for home."

When Sheila joined the two men a few men a few minutes later, O'Connell greeted her,

"Good morning, Sheila. Mr. Hamilton has withdrawn from the campaign. I'm sorry if I sent you on a wild goose chase last night."

Sheila looked relieved when she said,

"That's OK, Jerry. I wasn't able to come up with anything that I thought would satisfy both Mr. Hamilton and the voters. Here are copies of the morning papers for both of you."

Tim didn't have to look very far in the local St. Cloud daily. The article was at the bottom of the front page. The headline read:

HAMILTON TREATED COOLLY IN ST. CLOUD

The wording of the article wasn't all that different from the TV story they had watched on the previous evening. Tim turned to the editorial page and quickly found what he was looking for. The editorial was short and to the point:

"Timothy Hamilton's cool treatment in St. Cloud yesterday is a sad commentary on the modern political scene. Apparently the voters aren't ready for his brand of honesty and forthrightness. We expect to see the Democratic leaders looking for a different candidate. This is a lamentable day for all Minnesotans."

The headline in the Minneapolis *Star-Tribune* was more abrupt:

HAMILTON BOMBS IN ST. CLOUD

The tone of Strangefellow's article which followed was also harsher:

"If Timothy Hamilton's speeches in St. Cloud yesterday had been a two-act Broadway play, it would have a very short run. Almost nobody but nobody liked what he had to say. The few who did seemed to feel overwhelmed by the tidal wave of negative sentiment, as did Mr. Hamilton. It was an extremely embarrassing experience for Hamilton and his sponsors."

The report went on to say where he had spoken and to whom, but had nothing to say about the content of his talks except that they were straight from the shoulder. Tim turned to the editorial page and found a short editorial that read:

"A man of Timothy Hamilton's stature and acumen deserves better treatment than he received yesterday at the hands of his listeners in the St. Cloud area. It wouldn't surprise us to see Mr. Hamilton withdraw from the race. That will be Minnesota's loss."

O'Connell saw no point in showing Tim and Becky the FAX he had received earlier that morning. It was printer's copy of a special, one-page news release from the opposing party:

DEMOCRATS LAY A BIG, FAT EGG IN ST. CLOUD

Tim Hamilton, the Democratic candidate for governor, went over like a lead balloon in St. Cloud yesterday. As we reported previously, Hamilton has failed in business and in his marriage. We don't understand why, without any political experience and with his previous record of failure, he thinks he can succeed in a contest for Minnesota's top political position. His bad judgement in deciding to run is just further evidence of his lack of political acumen.

The buggers will stoop to anything, thought O'Connell, including kicking a man when he's down. Tim said he'd like to finish the papers in his room.

"Fine," said O'Connell, "We'll meet you out in front at five minutes to ten."

As they settled into comfortable chairs in their room, Tim spoke,

"You know Becky, O'Connell seemed relieved when I told him I was withdrawing."

"I'm sure he was. He realized early last evening that he had made a mistake, but he hadn't figured out how to get out of it gracefully. You did him a favor by taking the lead."

"No doubt those reporters are going to want a statement from me. I'd better start thinking about what I want to say about this fiasco."

"That sounds like a good idea. I need some fresh air. I think I'll take a walk and leave you to concentrate on your withdrawal statement."

"OK, honey, but I hope you'll come back by nine-fifteen. I'd like you to read my statement and make suggestions."

"I'll do it, lover. Just remember that you've done the right thing and can be proud of your courageous action. It's take a strong man to admit he made a mistake."

"Thanks, dear. Have a nice walk; I wish I could go with you."

When he had kissed her good-bye and shut the door, Tim set up his notebook computer and plugged in the portable printer. He was still amazed at how small printers had become and at what high quality work they still turned out. It surely beat writing out a statement like this in long-hand. He also had a palm-top computer, but he preferred the notebook model because his fingers fit the larger keyboard better. Tim was in the middle of his draft when the phone rang. It was Freddie

Strangefellow wanting a statement about his reactions to his experiences yesterday. Tim told him he was not ready to make a statement yet but that he would hold a short press conference on the coach about 10:30. That seemed to satisfy Freddie, and Tim got back to work.

Becky came back in plenty of time to review his statement. She read it eagerly and pronounced it excellent. Tim printed a half-dozen copies of it. When they had finished packing, they went to the lobby and checked out. When Sheila and Jerry showed up, Tim gave them each a copy of his statement and told them of his date with the reporters at 10:30. Sheila gave him a short press release she had prepared. It gave the party's position briefly and Tim had no problem with it. It politely regretted Tim's withdrawal and made it plain that his decision had been his own. The reporters were given copies of both documents as they boarded the coach.

Promptly at ten-thirty the reporters gathered around Tim and Becky's double seat. Becky invited Sharon to sit beside her and Tim invited the Channel 4 reporter to sit with him. Freddie knelt in the aisle, and the cameraman wedged himself between Tim's seat and the one across the aisle. They had drawn lots for the order in which they would ask their initial questions. The Channel 4 reporter, who by this time had identified herself as Gretchen Wilson, would go first, then Sharon and then Freddie. When they were all settled, Gretchen signalled the cameraman to begin,

"We're aboard the luxurious motor coach chartered by the Democratic party for their initial campaign trip in the race for governor, a much shorter trip than any one expected. The coach is just south of St. Cloud and headed toward Minneapolis. I'm sitting with Mr. and Mrs. Tim Hamilton on the last leg of this very abbreviated campaign trip. Mr. Hamilton has just announced his withdrawal from the campaign. Mr. Hamilton, how do you feel about the very cool reception you received from your listeners in St. Cloud?"

"I was disappointed, of course; but on further reflection I believe they did a favor to both the party and me."

"How's that?"

"They gave me a very clear signal that most of the voters don't buy my straightforward approach to the issues."

"It's certainly not the reaction you had hoped for; why do you consider it a favor?"

"By getting such a clear signal this early, we're able to save a lot of time and money, and the next candidate still has time to campaign adequately."

"What will you do now?"

"Pick up my life where I left off six months ago. It's a good life, and I didn't burn any bridges behind me."

"Thank you, Mr. Hamilton."

"You're welcome."

It was Sharon Persoon's turn:

"Mr. Hamilton, I've read your statement carefully. I don't see any bitterness or resentment against the people who treated you so shabbily yesterday. Are you hiding your ill feelings toward them?"

"No Sharon, I honestly don't have any. I told it like I think it is, and they made it very plain how they feel. It was an honest exchange, and that's the best kind."

"Don't you have any negative feelings?"

"Of course I'm disappointed that so many individuals in all walks of life put their own interests ahead of the broader welfare of all of the people in the state. Until that changes, we're not going to have really good government."

"Aren't you expecting an awful lot of people?"

"Yes I am; but I believe our founding fathers expected no less of us."

"Are you saying democracy isn't working?"

"Sharon, I still believe we live in the greatest country in the world and that our system of government works better than any other that's been tried. But I don't think we should be satisfied until we make it come much closer to our ideals."

"How are we going to do that?"

"We must find some way to change the minds and the hearts of the majority of the voters so that our elected officials will feel a mandate to do what's best for the state and focus on finding meaningful solutions to real problems rather than appeasing special interests."

"And how are we going to do that?"

"I wish I knew."

Freddie Strangefellow had been waiting impatiently for his turn. He asked,

"Mr. Hamilton, how do you feel about all those nasty things your opponent and his party have been saying about you?"

"At first I was upset; but my wife and other good friends helped me see that it's really a sign of weakness."

"How do you feel now?"

"Now I feel the same as I do about the other negative campaigning: a deep sense of regret."

"Shouldn't the voters know the truth about the candidates?"

Tim wondered if Freddie was baiting him, but he chose to treat it as an honest question,

"Yes, but the typical negative campaign is based on distortions and half-truths that don't do anyone any good. What's more, it diverts attention from the real issues and discourages good prospective candidates from running."

"But it seems to get votes. Isn't that what counts?"

"At the polls, unfortunately yes; but in a broader sense, regrettably no."

"Can you explain that?"

"A wise man once said that people get the kind of government they deserve. I'm afraid that's all too true. So until we can find some way to get voters to listen only to candidates who stick to the issues, and to look beyond their own narrow interests, government will not be able to deal with the real issues."

"Aren't the people of this state going to think that you turned tail and ran away when the going got tough?"

"I believe and hope that my friends and others who know me will respect me for being true to myself. I hope that other fair-minded people would do the same; but at this point I guess that really isn't important."

"Do you think you'll run for office again?"

"Not until there's much more evidence that a majority of the voters are ready to vote for what is good for all the people of this state."

The reporters seemed satisfied with the interview. They thanked Tim and moved back to where Jerry O'Connell was sitting. Becky, who had watched the whole process with intense interest, said,

"Tim, I'm very proud of you. I thought you handled yourself superbly."

"Thanks, honey. I can't decide whether Freddie is a shallow reporter, or a good reporter with a challenging way of getting me to respond."

"But you gave him the benefit of the doubt, and that's more than many people would've done. What's more, you said some things that badly needed saying. I only hope they get published."

"It seems as if we've been gone a long time. I feel as if I've learned a great deal. It will be good to get home."

"Yes on all counts, lover. What'll you do when we get home."

"Oh, I suppose I'll read my mail and check my voice mail. And--and some things much too personal to be articulated in public on a motor coach."

She snuggled close to him, kissed him on the cheek, put her head on his shoulder and shut her eyes.

Chapter Sixteen
The Obsession and the Vision

Becky and Tim were both overjoyed to get back to their familiar, comfortable environment: the large, but cozy house on the big lot shaded with beautiful, old elms and oaks. It seemed as if they had been gone a long time, although it was only two days. They celebrated by curling up on their comfortable settee with a glass of wine. The fire Tim had built radiated cheer and just enough warmth to take the chill off a cool fall evening. It was a long time before Tim broke the serene silence,

"Honey, it feels so good to be free of that rat race. It reminds me of the old saw about how good it feels when you quit hitting yourself on the head with a hammer."

"I feel the same way, lover."

"You were right in the first place. Those spin doctors know how to win elections, but I sure couldn't be a party to the kind of deception they practice. I never should have let them talk me into running."

"Don't be too hard on yourself. They hooked you with the thought that you could do a lot more good as governor. You had to try, or you never again would have been content with your present life. But if half of the people each did a tenth as much good as you do now, our country's problems would be solved."

"You're very generous, but I do believe you've hit on the real issue. We need to change the hearts and minds of enough people so that the majority of voters put the well-being of others ahead of their own greed and selfish interests. But can that be done?"

"That's the big question, but let's not try to solve it tonight. It's time to relax and enjoy a quiet evening together. Let's drink a toast to all of our good fortune and wonderful blessings."

"I'll drink to that. For starters here's to my wonderful, wise, beautiful and lovable, loving wife, who does her best to keep me out of trouble, and is so consoling and forgiving when I do get into trouble anyway!"

Becky responded in kind and they continued in this vein for some time until they were interrupted by the opening of the kitchen door. Mrs. Schatz announced dinner. As they walked to the dining room, Tim stopped to select some dinner music and adjust the volume on the home's sophisticated, built-in sound system. As if by magic, beautiful, soft music emanating from large sound panels on the wall filled the dining room and seemed to envelop them. When Becky had lit a pair of candles and Mrs. Schatz had placed dinner on the beautifully set table, Tim pressed another key or two on the control console and the lights dimmed to a soft glow.

This was no ordinary dinner: It was a sumptuous meal of their favorite dishes that Mrs. Schatz had prepared in celebration of their homecoming. They ate slowly, enjoying every morsel, their whole environment and, most of all, each other as they conversed intimately during and after dinner until they had fallen in love all over again. Although neither was sleepy, they found ample reason to adjourn to the bedroom early. They made their way slowly up the broad stairway, arms around each other, and continued to the bedroom where they proceeded to savor immensely their most favorite of the many activities they enjoyed together.

The following morning, after they had eaten a leisurely breakfast and discussed the morning news, Tim announced,

"I'm anxious to get at my desk and pick up where I left off."

"That doesn't surprise me, lover. Be on your way, but not until I give you a big hug and a heartfelt thank-you for an incredibly marvelous evening--and night."

Tim made a list of all the important things he needed to do and tried to prioritize them. He found that latter task difficult because they all seemed urgent. He decided that he would make some important phone calls before he opened the mail. His first call was to Gordon Springborn, the wonderful man who had agreed to take care of his investment clients while he was gone. After they had greeted each other warmly, Tim announced,

"I'm back to stay."

"Oh, what happened?"

Springborn's voice showed a mixture of surprise and apprehension. Tim had anticipated this reaction and had carefully prepared his answer,

"Let's meet for lunch at the Minneapolis Club at 11:45, if you're free. I can explain my premature return, and we can discuss the possibilities of a partnership, or joint venture."

Springborn sounded relieved and eagerly agreed to have lunch. Both men arrived punctually. After they were seated and finished their small talk, Springborn got to the point,

"I'm curious, Tim. What happened to your campaign plans?"

Tim told him briefly how it took only one full day on the campaign trail to realize that he didn't have what it seemed to take to be a successful candidate: the willingness to allow, or even encourage people to believe that you were going to do what they wanted done, even when you knew in your heart that you couldn't, or wouldn't, do that."

"God bless you, Tim. You'd rather have your integrity than the governor's job. It makes me respect and admire you even more than I have--if that's possible."

"Thanks Gordy. Now let's talk about our great future together. I propose that we become equal partners in a joint venture agreement. It would be what the lawyers call *mutatis mutandis*."

"I'm not sure I understand the term, Tim."

"To me, it means the same as what our grandmothers used to say, 'What's sauce for the goose is sauce for the gander'. More specifically, the one who brings in an account will get 30% of the fees. The one who services the account will get the other 70%. We'll split our out-of-pocket expenses right down the middle. Do you think that would be fair?"

"Do I! Tim, I think you're being overly generous. After all, you're the one who's built this business. I've acquired only two new clients in the three months I've been running it. I was surprised when you offered me all of the fees servicing your clients while you were gone."

"That was only fair, Gordy. After all, you were doing me a great favor to take good care of my clients. And, since both of us thought it would be temporary, I felt you were entitled to all of the fees because you were building no equity. But this is a permanent arrangement; and if you think about it, I think you'll find that it's fair under any distribution of clients. We'll each receive 70% for servicing a client, no matter who brought her or him in. Each of us will receive 30% for bringing in a client, regardless of who services him or her. Now do you believe that's fair?"

"Oh yes, Tim. It's so fair I feel guilty."

"No reason to do that. Now let's talk about the operating arrangements. I'm probably better known in the greater Twin City area than you. On the other hand, you're at least as good or better than I as an investment manager. Besides I'm a community service junkie, so it's likely you'll quickly have all of the clients you want to handle."

"Tim, my wife will be a very happy lady. When she heard you were back to stay, she was terribly worried that I wouldn't have any work. She was even more concerned than I was--and frankly, that's saying something."

"Gordy, I'm really looking forward to a happy, profitable and lasting relationship."

"Me too, Tim. How are we going to divide up the clients?"

"Well, for starters, you should certainly take the two you brought in. They know and trust you, and I don't even know them. Then, I suggest that each of us write down a list of the remaining clients and take turns choosing our favorites. When we run out of favorites, you can have the rest."

"But I'll end up with more clients than you."

"That's the way I'd like it, Gordy. That'll give me more time for my community service work and to develop new clients."

"This is far better than I had hoped for."

"Good, now let's talk about the housekeeping tasks. I really enjoy the financial record keeping and reporting, including the check writing and bank reconciliations, and I already have a good system on my PC for handling that work. If you don't mind, you can see to the other office tasks: having someone to do the filing. I don't need a secretary. I handle all of my correspondence on my PC. My preference is internet e-mail where the other person has facilities, then FAX, and finally, 'snail mail.'"

"That sounds great to me, Tim."

"Gordy, I feel bad: I just realized that I've spelled things out just as *I'd* like to see them and you've gone along all the way. If you'd like to see something different, please feel comfortable in speaking out."

"Oh, I do, Tim; but what you've proposed is so generous and sensible there isn't a thing I'd like to change."

"Good, but any time you do, don't hesitate to yell out. For a while, why don't we keep track of the number of hours we spend on housekeeping. If it isn't working out fairly evenly, we should either change something, or compensate the one who's doing the most work."

"That's fine. How long should we keep track?"

"How about a month? There'll be a little extra work at the end of the year, but not much. I'll run all of the bookkeeping through my sub-S corporation and most of the tax work is stuff I have to do anyway. I will make a 1099 for you, but I make a couple of those now. By the way, you'll want to check with your tax attorney as to how to treat this income in your quarterly estimated payments so that you don't get hit with a penalty for underpayment when he files your final return."

"Thanks for the tip, Tim, I'll do that right away."

"We haven't yet talked about the transition and effective dates. I'll draw a first draft of the agreement today and FAX it to you. If you or your attorney wish any changes, please be sure to propose them. I'm sure we'll have no difficulty in resolving them. I propose that it be effective as soon as it's signed, and on an incurred basis."

"What does that mean, Tim?"

"Just that any work you've done, you will be your own account receivable. Conversely, any expenses you've incurred will be your own account payable."

"I'll look forward eagerly to seeing the agreement."

"That seems fair enough."

"Gordy, is there anything else you'd like to talk about?"

"Not that I can think of."

"Then let's retreat to our respective home offices, and I'll get going on our joint venture agreement."

"Fine, Tim. I'd like to say just one thing: I have to confess that, when I first heard you say this morning that you're back to stay, I had mixed feelings of joy, curiosity and apprehension. Now I feel unmitigated pleasure when I look forward to the future under this new joint venture agreement. You're still the same generous, creative friend I've known, seemingly forever."

"Thanks, Gordy. I think we're going to have a lot of fun working together, and we'll serve our clients better than ever. We can cover for each other in case of absence or illness, and we can assign clients with an eye on which of us can best meet their needs."

By the time he arrived home Tim had pretty well fixed in mind the provisions needed in their joint venture agreement. Becky wasn't home, so he got right to work on his word processor. Less than three hours later he had the two-page agreement drafted, edited to his satisfaction, and FAXed to Springborn, as he had promised. When he finished, he listened to his voice mail and made notes of the people who had called. The next priority on his list had been to call the chairs of the half-dozen boards on which he served and announce his readiness to resume his service. Two of them had already learned of his presence and had left calls for him. He called them first and found them overjoyed at the thought of his early return to their boards. After determining the date of their next meeting, he promised to attend. He had similar conversations with the other four board chairs. And so ended his first day "back on the job."

At dinner that evening, after Tim and Becky had shared the day's experiences, they ate in silence for a few minutes. Becky broke the silence:

"Lover, you seem pre-occupied. A penny for your thoughts."

"I'm reflecting on my experiences in the political arena and trying to draw a conclusion from what I learned."

"And what have you concluded?" she asked with great interest. She knew that, whatever it was, it would probably affect their future lives in some significant way.

"That no matter which party or candidate wins any election, our government will not be able to solve the major problems of this country until a majority of the voters will elect and re-elect the candidates with greatest ability and desire to solve those problems, instead of electing those who appeal to their own greed and self-interest."

"And how do you think that a majority can be persuaded to do that?"

"We must find a way to change the minds and hearts of enough voters so that such voters become a clear majority instead of the modest minority they represent today. The easiest way to do that would be to enlist the aid of some organization that already reaches a huge audience. AARP (American Association of Retired Persons) comes quickly to mind, but I doubt if they can do the job: They represent only a minor segment of the voters, and so they're a special interest group themselves."

"But doesn't every organization represent the special interests and political biases of its constituents?"

"That's true. That's why it's so difficult to find a suitable organization. The ones that occur to me are the state and national organizations that represent the local churches, synagogues and other congregations. Granted they may have sharply differing religious beliefs that lead them to differing political agendas, but I believe that they all share the really important beliefs needed to achieve our objective."

"I'll give you all the support and help that I can."

"Thank you, honey, from the bottom of my heart. I've learned from my experience on non-profit boards that you never try to sell any concept to anyone without first preparing a case statement. That statement must cover important issues: your mission, how you propose to accomplish it, how long it will take, what it will cost both in dollars and people's time, how often you will make interim reports, how you'll measure your success, and so on. But the over-riding principle is to speak to the agendas of the people you want to persuade. I can't wait to get started on this vital document. I hope you'll feel free to criticize it. I've learned to value your opinions very highly."

They finished meal while conversing about other interests and concerns, punctuated by frequent interjection of levity, humor and expressions of affection. When they had finished dinner and shared a leisurely after-dinner cordial, Tim excused himself and hurried up to his office to begin work on his case statement.

Chapter Seventeen
Selling an Idea
to Religious Organizations

By the time Tim had completed his case statement and edited it to his satisfaction, it was long past his bedtime, so he resolved to sleep in the next morning. He was particularly pleased with the way the document addressed the agendas of the religious organizations, showing how adopting his program would strengthen them, increasing their membership and the active participation of their members.

He also had given a great deal of attention to the mission statement (getting the majority of the voters to vote for candidates who put the national interest ahead of their constituents' self interest). As he committed the statement to paper, however, he realized that there were a couple of other things people had to do. In order to vote intelligently, citizens had to be better informed. To be better informed they had to devote more attention to the political scene and less to sports, crime, scandals and other sensational news. If enough people changed their reading and their TV viewing habits, they could send a powerful message to both the print and the broadcast media to change their priorities as well. Tim also realized that such a large number of committed people could also alter the behavior of other entities, such as major employers. These entities must be persuaded to be good citizens , I. e. to balance the interests of their owners against the interests of their employees, their environment, and the welfare of the community in general. To alter behavior of employers, their boards must be persuaded that good citizenship will redound to the benefit of their owners if they look beyond the effect of such actions on next quarter's earnings. In completing the case statement Tim had noted that there are outstanding examples, both locally and nationally, of businesses that increased their profitability when they became good citizens. When their actions became known, people bought more of their products and services. Even more importantly, their employee's loyalty had increased, their productivity shot up, costs went down, and their employees were more willing to accept sacrifices during the crises that are inevitable in any business. In fact, such results make it clear that the principle applies even to those businesses whose market is outside of the local community. After he printed the document, he slipped downstairs quietly and left it on the breakfast table where Becky would be sure to see it.

Next morning, when he came downstairs two hours late, Becky had finished her breakfast but was still at the breakfast table, pencil in hand, reviewing his document. She beamed at him broadly,

"Good afternoon, love; welcome back to the land of the living."

Except for a sheepish smile, he ignored her teasing greeting as he kissed her warmly before he took his place at the table and eagerly attacked the half grapefruit that was waiting for him. He then went on to fix and eat his modest breakfast of dry cereal, toast and coffee, and to read the morning paper at a leisurely rate, not wishing to interrupt Becky's editing activity. Before he had finished his second piece of toast and the last section of the paper, Becky put down her pencil, smiled and broke the silence:

"In my opinion, lover, you've done a great job. I have just a few minor corrections which I've marked with a red pencil. Most of them don't need an explanation; the others I've penciled in the margin."

"Thanks honey. I do appreciate your efforts and your confidence in my approach. Now, what do you think of my chances of succeeding?"

Becky was thoughtful for a few minutes. Finally, she spoke,

"I don't think it's like a football game, where you either win, lose or go into overtime. It's more like bowling, where you knock over some pins while the others elude your best efforts. In other words you'll get some genuine support, some outright turn-downs, and a lot more `I'll see what we can do's.' I think you've got a long, hard road ahead of you. It'll be much tougher and more time-consuming than either of us thinks, but I hope you'll keep trying and don't lose heart."

Tim walked around the table, lifted Becky from her chair, kissed her warmly, and held her in a close embrace for a long time before he said feelingly,

"How could I have been so lucky as to marry such a beautiful, loving, wise and supportive wife. Thank you from the bottom of my heart."

"You're not so bad yourself, lover."

When he finally released her, Tim headed upstairs to his office, eager to make the changes Becky had noted and to print his case statement in final form. When he had finished, he wrote and printed a brief cover letter. Then he turned his attention to developing a prospect list. The best source he could think of was the yellow pages of both the Minneapolis and St. Paul telephone directories. He had mixed feelings when he saw the large number of religious denominations and beliefs represented. He counted 374 of them: a fertile field to plow but also a lot of time-consuming work. Many of the denominations, didn't seem to list a state headquarters;

but, by calling a local church, he was able to get the name, address and telephone number for most of them. By the time he had completed his efforts he had a mailing list of almost 350 religious groups. He was ready to go on a shopping trip. In a couple of hours he was back in his office with bound copies of his case statements, copies of the cover letters,, and a supply of mailing envelopes and labels. He printed labels and enlisted Becky's assistance to complete the mailing.

Tim's mailing had asked the religious leaders to join together in their own communities to persuade a majority of the voters to recruit and vote for candidates who pledge to put the broader interests of their community, state or nation ahead of the voters' own self interests. Several weeks later, Tim printed out the analysis he had kept of the reactions of the religious leaders to his request. Of the 62 who responded:

2   gave an unqualified promise to implement his program. (They and Tim made up the first members of a committee to carry on the program.)

10   said they would take it under consideration and let Tim know within the next 30 days.

15   said they would have to consult their cabinet or other denominational representatives, some of which wouldn't have their next meeting for almost a year.

20   were noncommittal

15   gave a flat refusal for one reason or another, or for no reason.

At breakfast Tim showed the analysis to Becky and asked her for her reactions. Becky read the analysis carefully and thoughtfully before she replied,

"I think you have your work cut out for you, lover. By and large, you're going to have to take your case to the people."

"How do you see me doing that?"

"I think you're justified in going to individual congregations, regardless of what kind of reaction you got from their state leaders. But I don't know whether you'll get approval from too many of the local congregational leaders either. Many of them will feel threatened. Others will feel that your program isn't consistent with their policies or doctrines. Still others will turn off because you are too ecumenical. Of course, you'll still have the option of going to the community through other service organizations. If you don't get results that way, your last resort is to invite the voters to a mass meeting."

"I can see I need help; I'd never get this job done working alone."

"You speak great wisdom, lover."

"I can see that we'll need to spend money in order to go directly to the people. I think we have the money to do that, but perhaps I should ask my committee members to contribute."

"That makes sense, but I'd wait until you see the need. By that time your committee members will have built up a bigger head of steam about the program."

"A good idea, honey. Do you have any prospects to suggest for my committee?"

Becky suggested some names. By that time they realized that they had talked themselves through breakfast. Once again, Tim expressed his heartfelt appreciation for Becky's help and support; then he went quickly to his office to begin the process of recruiting a committee. He started with the lists of directors of the nonprofit organizations on whose boards he served. After going through them care fully, he was pleased to note that he had marked over 30 who he thought would make good members of his committee. His next task was to call these people and invite them to be his guest at a lunch at the Minneapolis Club on a date 10 days hence. He had already reserved a private dining room for the purpose. Two days later he was delighted to count twenty of these people who had accepted the invitation and another six who expressed interest but couldn't come to lunch. He was pleased that five of those readily accepted an invitation to lunch a few days later, and the sixth one agreed to have a one-on-one lunch on another date. One prospect graciously declined, saying he was badly over-committed, expressing his interest in the project and inviting Tim to keep him posted on his progress. He had been unable to talk to the other three, but he planned to continue his attempts. He then made labels for all 30 of these prospects and enlisted Becky's assistance in completing another mailing of the case statement.

In preparation for his luncheon presentation Tim made a one-page job description of committee members' duties and gave it to Becky for her comments. He also invited her to attend the luncheon and she readily accepted.

The ten days flew by. As the committee ate a delicious lunch, Tim was pleased to note that there weren't any no-shows. It wouldn't have surprised him if one or two out of such a busy group would miss lunch because of some last minute development. After thanking them all for coming he reiterated their mission, stated his hope that they all had read the case statement, and asked for questions regarding the statement. While Tim was conducting the question and answer session, Becky passed out the one-page job description. After allowing his guests time to read it, Tim asked for a show of hands as to the number who were willing to serve on the committee and was delighted to see 15 hands go up. He then invited the other five to express whatever reservations prevented them from joining the project. Four of them asked if they could be considered as provisional members until the process became clearer to them and they were able to determine whether they had the time to do justice to a full commitment. Tim quickly accepted them as provisional members. The other guest said that he was still very interested but felt that he was unable to commit the time needed right now; he requested that he be kept on the mailing list in the hopes that he might join the committee at a later time. Tim then opined that the committee members would need two three-hour training sessions, preferably close together, and then worked out mutually convenient times for the two sessions. He announced that the last half hour of the second training session would be spent in determining assignments of congregations to specific members of the committee. After answering a few questions, Tim thanked them all for their enthusiastic response and said he looked forward to seeing them at the first training session.

In preparation for the training sessions Tim realized that the committee members were going to need some tools. Visual aids, for example, could be quite helpful when they spoke to gatherings of as many members of a congregation as could be assembled. He decided to retain the services of a communications consultant to advise him on cost-effective tool(s) for this purpose. The result was the development of a slide show with a script to be played on a tape recorder, and signals to prompt the presenter when to change slides. This not only provided an inexpensive and highly effective audio-visual presentation, but took a considerable burden off the presenter and assured a uniform high quality of the presentation. The speaker's principal jobs, then were to get the leader to recruit a local committee on arrangements, make sure the arrangements were satisfactory, begin the meeting with a short greeting and introduction, do the audio-visual presentation, answer questions, and ask those present to sign a simple pledge card to become active participants in the movement.

The consultant also stressed the value of finding a meaningful name for the movement, preferably one that could be shortened to a catchy and meaningful acronym. Tim had no idea of what to call the movement, so he decided to get help from Becky and the consultant as well as from the members of the committee. In the meantime he set his mind to developing material for the slide presentation, which would be based on the case statement.

The first training session went extremely well. Tim started off by running the slide show. It looked and sounded truly professional. The committee members asked good questions on important issues that Tim had overlooked, despite his careful preparation. Most of the members seemed relieved that they didn't have to prepare a speech, or read a canned one. Tim distributed and reviewed two check lists: The first one covered all of the things that needed to be done in advance of a meeting; the second one covered all of the things that had to be done after a meeting. Finally he distributed a supply of commitment cards and self-addressed envelopes in which committee members could return completed commitment cards , a list of the names, addresses and telephone numbers of the attendees, and a brief report showing the size of the congregation and the willingness of the pastor, rabbi, priest or other leader to carry on the initiative as a congregational project.

The cards provided for several levels of commitment: (1) to commit personally to study the candidates and determine their stands on issues affecting the national interest, (2) to put issues affecting the good of the nation, or political district, ahead of their own personal interests in voting for a candidate, (3) too urge the candidates to do the same, and to avoid personal attacks and other negative campaigning, (4) to urge the media to carry more news on issues and to devote less space to the "horse race" aspects of the campaign, negative campaigning, crime and other sensational items, (5) to try to secure the same level of commitment from other adult members of their household, and (6) to try to obtain similar commitments from their friends and neighbors through coffee parties, cocktail parties and other informal means.

Tim instructed the members to follow up by telephoning the registrants who had not completed commitment cards to secure, where possible, additional commitments. Only after they finished their follow up were they to mail the returns. Tim had bought audiovisual equipment (a sympathetic dealer gave him a very good price), which he distributed along with a tape cassette and a set of slides to each committee member.

Next came a discussion of how to assign prospects. Some members thought it could be done on a denominational basis. Others wanted to work in their own neighborhoods. It was quickly agreed to split the Twin Cities and their surrounding suburbs into geographic areas and assign all of the prospective congregations in each area to one committee member. Members expressed first, second and third choices on cards, which they gave to Becky, and Tim promised to have prospect assignment lists ready at the next training meeting.

One member suggested that, if they would extend this meeting by an hour, they wouldn't need a second meeting. Tim and the others quickly agreed, and Tim said that in that case he would mail the prospect lists. Another member expressed the need for reviewing questions and objections that would arise. They spent most of the next hour doing just that. Becky took careful notes and said she would mail a summary of the questions and answers along with the prospect lists. They agreed on a date, three weeks hence, when all committee members could come to a progress report meeting. Tim closed the meeting with a short pep talk, and everyone left in an upbeat, enthusiastic mood.

As they drove home, Tim remarked,

"Well, honey, so far so good; we seem to be off to a good start."

"Yes, lover, you've done an outstanding job of preparation, your choice of committee members was tremendous, and your leadership is superb. You would make somebody a great sales manager."

As Tim thought back to his Cornerstone days and the tremendous pressures on the sales department to set higher and higher quotas and to make or exceed them, he said,

"Deliver me from the job of a sales manager."

When they had driven awhile in thoughtful silence, Tim remarked,

"You know, honey, those committee members are an outstanding group of people: They are smart, personable, dedicated, community-minded, and above all, they're 'givers' and not 'takers'. That's one of the great fringe benefits of serving on non-profit boards: the quality of the people you meet."

Three weeks later they held the report meeting; all but one of the committee members were there. They reported a lot of activity, but the results were not what Tim had hoped for. Becky tabulated all of the results into a neat summary, which looked like this:

**Participation of the churches,
temples and synagogues**

20% held meetings, of those
9% of the resident members attended, of those
60% made a full commitment
15% made a partial commitment
15% said they would think it over
6% didn't turn in a card
4% said they weren't interested
45% said they would have to take it up with their governing council.

26% said such activities could not be pursued because of their religious beliefs.

9% said their people were too busy to be bothered.

Tim looked crestfallen as he spoke:

"All that work to get commitments from just over 5% of the potential."

Becky was too tactful to say, "I told you so." Instead she said,

"But think of it this way, lover: that's a significant number of the people that are registered to vote. And besides, we may nearly double the successes before the committee finishes their follow up work. What's more, we knew before we started that the job wouldn't be easy, and that we'd have to go directly to the people before we were through."

Tim nodded sadly and said,

"I must confess that I'm disappointed; I had really hoped for more. But we've no reason to delay the planning of our community meetings. I think I'd like to do two or three ourselves before we get the rest of the committee involved. At any rate, I love the way you've started to use the first person plural pronouns in discussing 'our project'."

"Oh, lover, you've made me feel so much a part of it, and I love that feeling. What's more, I think it's a wonderful project and that it has the potential to accomplish more for our country than any other idea I can conceive of."

"That's just what I needed right now, and I thank you for it. It's bedtime and a hug isn't enough," he said as he took Becky by the hand and led her upstairs.

Chapter Eighteen
Selling an Idea to Communities

After much telephoning, Becky and Tim managed to find a lunch date that worked for all of the committee members. They met at their favorite spot and shared their experiences in speaking at churches, temples and synagogues. From his tabulations of the reports sent in after the meetings, Tim knew the results were spotty and disappointing. They quickly agreed that they would have to try community meetings, and all of them were eager to try, even though it would be more difficult and expensive to organize. They had to find a suitable meeting place, hopefully available without charge, and a suitable date. After some discussion they agreed unanimously that Monday was the best night of the week. People had fewer meetings and dates on Monday; and historically, Monday had been the traditional town hall meeting night, They chose a date several weeks away to give themselves time for publicity and advertising, and to let people put it on their calendars before the dates filled up.

The committee also agreed that they would all work together on one community meeting, so that they would all gain experience before they divided into smaller groups. Tim asked for four volunteers for each function: physical arrangements, publicity and advertising, program, and coordination. The coordinators would handle record keeping, finance, see that all of the functions were performed, be MC at the meeting, and be sure that "one hand knew what the other was doing." For their pilot operation they chose the community of Minnetonka, a western suburb of Minneapolis. Tim agreed to give the principal message and act as treasurer. He asked the committee members to send him checks for whatever amount they felt they could contribute toward the expense of the first meeting. They agreed that a free-will offering would be taken at each meeting to help defray the costs of the next meeting. Becky agreed to keep records of the entire operation and handle notices and correspondence. Before they adjourned, they chose a date for their next meeting; excitement and enthusiasm ran high as they all agreed that they had accomplished a great deal in getting organized to perform what had seemed to be a monumental task.

At the committee's next meeting, each team reported on its progress. The physical arrangements team had secured the use of the gymnasium of a large local high school for the payment only of the cost of having a janitor there; and they had arranged to have the local police force alerted to the need for crowd control and the removal of any disorderly guests. They had recruited ushers, a refreshments committee, and a clean-up crew.

The program team reported that they had per-suaded a local popular band and singer to donate their services and that one of its members had agreed to be MC. The team confirmed that, because of his political experience, Tim would present the main message. The program team also reported that they had recruited five women and five men from the people who had indicated the highest level of support at the previous meetings. These people would each give a one-minute talk in support of the program and urge everyone present to support it with their money and their time. One of the committee suggested they have an experienced song leader to induce the attendees to sing a patriotic song to open the meeting and another one to close it.

Members of the publicity and advertising team had taken ads in both the Minneapolis *Star Tribune* and the suburban newspapers, had written articles for these papers, and provided information for insertion in their community events columns. They had also taken the managing editors to lunch to explain the program's mission and to secure their commitment to provide a lead editorial supporting the program and urging all citizens to attend the meeting and pledge to support the program with their time and money. Ordinarily the *Star Tribune* would not do that much for a project that didn't exist yet, but Tim's reputation overcame any reluctance the managing editor might have had. The publicity team had developed approaches to local radio and TV. Finally, they had handbills printed and gave one hundred dollars to a local boy scout troop when the scoutmaster agreed to have the boys distribute them to every home in the community.

The coordinators gave Becky written reports on their activities and gave Tim bills for the money they had spent, a list of the financial commitments they had made, and an estimate of additional amounts needed to complete their functions.

As the committee listened to all these reports, they realized they had not covered some very important functions needed to make the whole process a success: providing registration/commitment cards to each attendee, making an electronic data base of the results, and providing suitable follow-up. Those committee members who had not previously volunteered agreed to constitute the commitments and follow up team. Meanwhile Tim quickly added up the expenses that had been submitted and reported that they exceeded the financial support already submitted by several thousand dollars. Various members passed notes to Tim in which they agreed to increase their financial commitments. When Tim had tallied these commitments, however, he announced that they were still significantly short; so he asked the committee to allow him to cover any cash deficits and to repay the ultimate deficit from funds contributed by the attendees at the meeting. The committee agreed unanimously.

They agreed to meet again a week before the community meeting to make sure that every base had been covered and to do anything else necessary to maximize the success of the meeting. Excitement and enthusiasm ran higher than ever as they adjourned and talked animatedly among themselves.

As Tim and Becky drove home, they shared their own elation at the momentum the committee had developed and at each member's unreserved support and at the high level of exhilaration that had become contagious and apparently unanimous. Becky said,

"Lover, I'm so proud of you. You've started what I believe will become a great national movement and go further toward solving the major problems of this country than any other program on the horizon."

"Thanks, honey," Tim replied, "I couldn't have gotten this far without your powerful encouragement, help and support. I certainly feel much more optimistic than I did when I tried to go the political route, even before my traumatic failure as a candidate."

"But you weren't a failure; you felt compelled to try, but you had the good judgement and fortitude to retreat as soon as you realized that a candidate with your very high standards of integrity and openness wouldn't be elected by today's voters. I'm proud of you for standing up to the spin doctors who havecorrupted too many otherwise honest candidates."

"Thanks again, hon. Your clear-eyed perspective is one of the things that makes me so hopeful. For all our optimism, though, I must confess to a nagging uneasiness. I have to pinch myself to make sure I'm not dreaming. Everything seems to be going so well. I can't help wondering if it's going too well. What are we missing? What's going to hit us where we least expect it?"

Becky frowned as she thought for a moment, then said,

"That's a good point. Rarely does a project of this magnitude go as smoothly as this seems to. As I think about it, we have talked only to people who strongly support our program. We need to talk with potential detractors and be prepared to deal with them."

"Who do you think those people are?" Tim asked.

"No one can object to motherhood and apple pie. How about organizations that feel they're already doing our mission and feel threatened by the competition?"

"But it's obvious that they're not getting the job done."

"Agreed, but that's not the point, love. They'll still feel threatened, and we've got to be able to remove the perceived threat and replace it with something that will make them feel good about themselves."

"What if we agree with their goals, congratulate them for what they've achieved and pledge to work with them, while we attempt to provide an avenue for the good citizens outside their reach who are not actively working toward our common goal."

At home that evening after dinner and a lively conversation, Becky excused herself, saying that she had important things she needed to take care of before bed time. She knew her husband well enough to know that he would not be offended. Rather he would be secretly relieved, because *he* had things he was itching to get done that night. She hoped only that he would feel he had accomplished enough by bedtime that he would be ready to come to bed on time...

Tim believed that every hour was precious and that he should use each of them to the fullest extent, whether it was for work, family time or whatever. Consequently it was not like him ever to wish time away, but he looked forward to the community meeting with the eager anticipation of a small boy whose father has promised to take him fishing, impatiently waiting for that great day to arrive. He found it hard to keep his mind on whatever he was doing and, despite his determined efforts to focus on the present, he would find himself going over and over the plans for the meeting, wondering what they might have overlooked.

He had followed through on Becky's suggestion and talked to several church leaders who had seemed most negative about his group's plans. They listened to him with polite interest, and he probed for the real reason for their refusal to participate actively in his program. He found that their reluctance to participate was based solely on their conclusion that, desirable as his program might be, their participation in it would distract them from the things they were doing already, which had a higher priority. He perceived no animosity either in their words or their body language, as he looked carefully for signs that they might feel threatened, looking particularly for the most common signs of fear or concern: the narrowing of the pupils or the arms akimbo (arms folded across the chest with one hand on top of the biceps and the other tucked under the biceps. But he saw neither of these signs in any of them. So he concluded with some confidence that he also had nothing to fear from these leaders or their congregations.

He sought out a couple of ministers who were reputed to be militant and unyielding in dealing with beliefs that were different from his own on such issues as abortion, school prayers, treatment of criminals, etc. There too, he found no evidence of animosity--either overt or otherwise--only a total disinterest. Still, he harbored a gnawing concern. If the movement gained the success and momentum he hoped for, would they become threatened and view him as they did the doctors who performed abortions? If so, might their preaching of militancy lead some misguided souls to acts of violence? Perhaps he was borrowing trouble where none existed...

As the day came for their community meeting approached, the committee gathered to consider any last minute details. The one significant thing they thought of was the possibility of an overflow crowd. They agreed that it was worth the additional expense and work to have closed circuit TV equipment and several hundred folding chairs on hand just in case this pleasant problem should occur. The team on physical arrangements agreed to do this and to check with the fire marshall to be sure that their plans didn't violate any codes. To Tim, the greatest value of this last committee meeting was finding that all of the members seemed to share his feeling of excitement and eager anticipation. This helped to relieve his concern that perhaps he was losing his ability to concentrate on important matters at hand. Once more, they adjourned amidst animated conversations among themselves and Tim and Becky went home in high spirits.

On the day of the public meeting Tim and Becky went to the gymnasium two hours early to make sure everything was in place. They were not too surprised to find that other committee members had done the same thing. They greeted each other warmly and chatted excitedly. This was the big moment for which they had planned so carefully and worked so hard. The coordinator of physical arrangements had been there most of the afternoon, and he proudly showed Becky and Tim what he had done: Under his direction the janitorial staff had set up all of the expansion bleachers and put hundreds of folding chairs across the gym floor to where a portable dais and podium had been placed. The coordinator showed Tim the overflow crowd arrangements and told

Tim they could seat an estimated 3,500 people in the gym and another 1,500 in the hallways with good sound and vision from every seat. 5,000 people! Tim wondered how many would show up. He couldn't even guess.

Tim was anxious to try the sound system. Before he could open his mouth the coordinator invited him to do just that. "Testing! testing!" Tim said several times at various voice levels. The system sounded wonderful except for a slightly annoying echo. The coordinator assured him this echo would disappear when the first few hundred people arrived. Tim had a horrible thought: What if that was the total number of people who came? He tried to put this thought out of his mind, but it kept recurring whenever he wasn't occupied with something else. By the time he was through testing the sound, the band had arrived and had started to set up on the portion of the dais to which the coordinator had directed them. The vocalist and the song leader showed up a short time later and conferred with the band leader. Tim was glad to see them all smiling and nodding affirmatively.

By then the program coordinator showed up and began introducing Tim to the people who were going to make their one-minute statements. Tim greeted them warmly, thanked them profusely for their willingness to do it, and made sure that they all knew their mission and what to cover. The coordinator had done a good job: They were all going to tell their name, how they became acquainted with the program, share their great enthusiasm about the program and urge the listeners to join them in this great crusade for good government. They would end up by repeating their name and adding their telephone number and inviting their friends, old and new to join them in this great crusade. Some of them offered to give their talk for Tim. He thanked them and told them that wouldn't be necessary. Tim asked each of them if they planned to use notes or read their talk.

"Heavens no!" they replied almost in chorus, "This will come right from the heart!"

"Wonderful!", Tim exclaimed, and he thanked them again for their enthusiastic willingness to participate and invited them to gather afterward in room 115 for refreshments and congratulations."

While they were talking several hundred people had filed in and taken their seats.

"This is wonderful!" Tim thought excitedly, "It's still 45 minutes before the program starts." He couldn't help wondering what the total would be: 1,000? 2,000?, 3.000? more?

The teams had all done their jobs superbly. The registration team was already set up to provide registration/commitment cards to people as they came in. The ushers were there--young women who obviously had been carefully selected, screened and trained to greet the public warmly with smiles that would melt a heart of stone. Becky wondered where they had found so many charming young women.

With precisely 15 minutes to go, the band struck up the chorus of an all-time favorite of all ages: "I'm Looking Over a Four Leaf Clover", then segued right into "Mr. Sandman, Bring Me a Dream." By this time the audience was clapping in unison, keeping time with the strong beat of the music. This was exactly what Tim had hoped for. The people were pouring in now, and most of them began clapping along with the earlier arrivals. The band continued to play lively music and the crowd continued to respond and grew larger every minute. By five minutes after the scheduled starting time the regular seating was full and Tim could see through the wide doors that the ushers had seated a number of people in the overflow area. He felt an almost overpowering sense of gratitude, admiration and gratification for the tremendous efforts his committee had expended to make this event happen.

Five minutes later Tim gave a hand signal to the MC, his good friend and committee member, Jake Evans. Jake signaled the band leader and the song leader. The former struck up America the Beautiful as the latter stepped to the podium. At the same time another program team member flashed the words on a large screen above and behind the podium. The buoyant, upbeat song leader got everyone to their feet and the crowd sang with him in this stirring, patriotic song which Tim, and many of his friends, felt should be our national anthem. Thousands of voices filled the huge gymnasium and reverberated in a tremendous roar; and Tim felt the thrilling shivers of excitement race up and down his back, as Becky took his hand and squeezed it firmly.

When the echoes of the singing had died away, the song leader thanked the crowd profusely and invited them to be seated. They did, but not until they had given the song leader--and themselves--spirited applause. After they were seated, Jake stepped to the podium and asked for their attention. He thanked them all for coming and proceeded to introduce Tim. He was brief, as Tim had requested, but took time to extol a few of Tim's virtues: a man of vision, impeccable integrity, business acumen, and a person who set a standard of service to his community that was hard to match.

And now it was Tim's turn to deliver the message to which all of the rest of this program had been only a prelude. (While Jake had been delivering the laudatory introduction, Tim had been thinking about the golden opportunity his splendid committee had presented to him. They had brought together thousands of people, nearly all of whom must be of the very type that Tim had hoped to reach: the movers and shakers in their community. He had bowed his head and offered a brief request to his Creator that he would be equal to this exceptional opportunity.)

He spoke without notes, with eloquence, enthusiasm, intensity, with fervor. and straight from the heart. After thanking everyone for being there, he began his message, which was clear and simple: Very few people were happy with our elected officials at any level because of their inability to deal with the real problems that our communities, our states and our nation faced. Most voters and financial contributors to campaign funds were putting their own greed and self interest ahead of the real issues that faced their community, state and nation. As a consequence, few candidates who faced those issues squarely and with integrity could get elected. Worse yet, people with the greatest potential to deal with the issues were too smart to even become candidates. Good citizens will support candidates for all public offices who will seek the good of the country, state, county, school district or other political jurisdiction, who will promise to confine their campaign to the issues and to avoid negative campaigning, and who will use the precious time in their meetings to deal with issues and not as a campaign platform for demagoguery or other politicking; those same good citizens will support only those media that confine their political reporting to the issues and avoid the tendency to report the political campaigns like a horse race and other viewpoints that distract from the only real issues.

Tim continued: The solution was clear but not easy to accomplish: We must create a majority of voters who are eager to have their elected officials deal with the broader issues and wage positive campaigns that deal with these issues and not with self interests and the flaws of foibles of their opponents. Moreover we must insist that our news media focus on these issues instead of the "horse-race" aspects of elections. He paid tribute to the many organizations that were already working toward this end; but he observed regretfully that their efforts were too disparate to achieve their purpose. "Our goal," he said, "must be to bring as many of these organizations as will into a coalition for good government, and to invite good citizens who were not members of any of the coalescing groups to become individual members of the coalition."

Then Tim had an inspiration that he felt he needed to act on immediately: He invited all of those who were willing to work in their own particular areas toward organizing this coalition to write the word Coalition in the blank space on their registration/ commitment cards. He promised that his committee would supply guidance, tools and instruction to those who did so. He ended by thanking them all fervently for their attention.

Two totally unexpected things happened before Tim had a chance to sit down: Becky rushed up and embraced him warmly as she exclaimed,

"You were *magnificent*, darling!"

Then the audience stood and broke out in thunderous applause amid whistles, whoops and shouts of "well done." Their reactions sent tears streaming down Tim's face and he let them flow as he silently thanked his creator for enabling him to inspire his audience.

Jake returned to the podium and announced that there were a few volunteers who wanted to add their own brief testimony to their belief in the cause Tim had so eloquently set forth. All of them did well though later, at the reception they told Tim that they found him a very hard act to follow. Jake then announced that the ushers would pass large paper cups among them into which the audience was invited to make a contribution to help defray the expenses of this event. He concluded the meeting by reminding them all to be sure to hand their registration/commitment cards to an usher on the way out, thanked them again for coming, and wished them a safe journey home. Before Jake left the podium, Becky button-holed both him and Tim and suggested that now was an ideal time to evaluate the meeting and decide on their next course of action. Tim liked the idea and asked Jake to announce it when he reminded them of the reception for committee members and other participants in the meeting

Many of the audience rushed up to Tim, fervently pumped his hand and said words to the effect that his coalition idea was the answer to their prayers for a solution to the problem of obtaining more effective elected officials, and promised to be part of a team to organize the coalition. Meanwhile Becky had taken two large canvas bank deposit bags to the table where the cups had been placed and emptied their contents into the bags. She then asked one of the policemen to accompany her to their car. After making sure that no one was watching she quickly put the bags in the trunk of their car and locked it. The policeman asked her if the car had a burglar alarm, and she assured him that it had. He then volunteered to keep an eye on their car until they were ready to go home. Her first impulse was to tell him he didn't have to do that; but she thanked him profusely instead and hurried back inside.

Becky was torn between a strong desire to be at Tim's side and the feeling that she had a duty to greet people at the reception and again thank them for their part in making the meeting such a howling success. Regretfully, she decided on the latter. She found many of the committee members excitedly chatting about the meeting and professing their own delight in being a part of it. Listening to their enthusiasm confirmed Becky in her suggestion that they hold a committee meeting tonight.

Half an hour passed before Tim could free himself from the crowd and make his way to the reception. The band leader told Tim that he and other members of the band had gotten such a thrill out of being part of the program that they had all volunteered to be a part of similar programs in the future. He also reported that the song leader couldn't stay but wanted Tim to know that he felt likewise. He also said that a band-leader friend of his might be interested in filling the dates where his own band had a conflict and volunteered to ask him. Tim accepted his gracious offer, thanked him profusely for his stirring performance this evening, and asked him to extend his thanks to all of the band members.

After everyone at the reception had partaken of the refreshments, Tim asked for their attention. After thanking them all fervently for their magnificent performance in making the evening such a success, he said that some of the volunteers had asked if they could join the committee. He assured them they would be most welcome and asked any who so chose to give their names to Becky before they left. He also invited them all to stay for the committee meeting, which he then proceeded to convene. The participants were quick to praise Tim for his outstanding performance. He, in turn, thanked them all for their participation in making the event an overwhelming success:

"To paraphrase an old expression", he declared, "Together we *did* make it happen!"

He asked them for suggestions on how they might improve future meetings. The leader of the publicity and advertising team said that he felt they should have had more media coverage of the event than the one public service cable station and the one reporter who was there, and added that next time he would get a major TV station and reporters from both the large St. Paul and Minneapolis daily papers to cover the event. Meanwhile he would try to rectify the situation at tonight's meeting by persuading the cable TV station to make its footage available to a major station, and get the Minneapolis *Star-Tribune* to share their report with the St. Paul *Pioneer Press*. No one else had any suggestions.

The committee discussed the optimum size of future teams, recognizing that the more teams they had the fewer meetings each team would need to run, thus shortening the daunting task of covering the scores of communities in the greater Twin Cities area. They quickly agreed that four concurrent events was all they could manage, and that even that number would require some augmentation of staff. The commitments and follow up team leader said he would have no difficulty augmenting his staff from the huge pile of commitment cards they had received. The other team leaders followed suit and asked to see some of the cards so that they could do likewise. Some of the ushers volunteered to join teams, and the team leaders were quick to accept them.

Someone asked about the date of the next community meetings. Tim said he thought it would save a lot of effort and expense in the publicity and advertising function if they could hold the next meetings on the same date, or at least within a week of each other. The coordinator of physical arrangements said he thought that he could get three other coordinators recruited and four teams in place in about a week. All of the team leaders agreed that the time they had allowed for preparation and promotion of the first meeting had been about right, so they quickly agreed on the optimum date for the next meeting. They also agreed to meet a week ahead of that time and share their progress and any concerns. After a brief discussion, they selected the four communities they would cover next.

Tim remarked on the lateness of the hour and suggested that they take another half hour for celebration and socializing and be on their way. Many participants approached Tim and to express their enthusiasm about the evening and to note that there were few times in their life when they had had such a mountain-top experience. Tim thanked them and said that he shared their feeling. The half hour went by quickly; they reluctantly said their good-byes and left, but not until they had gathered up all their materials, put them in the tote boxes and arranged to carry it to their cars and vans. After greeting their parents warmly and congratulating Tim on his outstanding presentation, Peter and Tiffany helped carry material. Tim and Becky stood at the door, thanked everyone there for their help and hugged as many of them as they could. After everyone else had left, Tim then thanked the patient custodians, while Becky gathered up their things, careful to make sure that she had saved the profuse notes she had made. Becky apologized to the patient policeman who was waiting outside.

"The time went quickly, Ma'am." he responded, "So many people shared their enthusiasm with me as they came out, that I got turned on by listening to them!"

He agreed to follow them to the night deposit window and watch them until they had put the two large canvas bags through the secure chute. Tim and Becky thanked him once more, and they went their separate ways. Becky was the first to speak:

"Oh lover!" she exclaimed, "I have to pinch myself to be sure I'm not dreaming. I just can't imagine how the meeting could have been more wonderful!"

"I feel the same way, honey; but still I have a vague foreboding that something quite disturbing, if not disastrous, may happen soon. I hope I'm wrong."

"I certainly hope you are, too, lover, but right now I want to savor this triumphant moment."

They drove the rest of the way home in silence. As they closed the front door behind them, Tim said,

"It's past bedtime, honey; and we've had our happy hour. I'm ready to turn in."

"I'll second that motion darling."

She put her arm tightly around his waist and proceeded upstairs to their bedroom.

The next morning, after their typically pleasant, leisurely breakfast, they went to the bank together, retrieved their previous night's deposit, and counted the money in a private room reserved for that purpose.

Becky sorted and counted the bills, entering the total of each denomination on a deposit slip as she went along. Tim took the coins out to the machine which sorted, counted and wrapped them. Tim copied the total on a slip of paper and gave it to Becky to complete the deposit slip. When she had arrived at the total, she exclaimed exultantly,

"Oh Tim, it comes to $17,352.46! Isn't that marvelous?"

"Yeah! That's much more than expected. Together with what the committee has already donated, that may cover all of our expenses; but I won't know 'til the team leaders turn in all of their bills. I'm thinking that, with the growth I foresee for this enterprise, we may want to incorporate as a non-profit and seek IRS' approval as a 501c(3); but I want to consult my attorney before I do anything. In the meantime, I'll deposit it in our personal account. I'll have no difficulty keeping track of the money. With that neat little ledger system I use for our own books on our PC, I can set up a separate account for each community. What do you think, honey?"

"Lover, as the waitress said, that's not my station. I think you're smart to consult your attorney."

When they arrived home, Becky wasted no time in getting to her word processor, where she involved herself busily in getting down the notes she had taken at the meeting. Tim hurried to his office to dig into the mail and phone messages that had accumulated; but first he wrote internet e-mail messages to all of his team leaders. He congratulated and thanked them once more for their outstanding jobs in making the previous evening such a howling success. Then he urged them to FAX him all of their bills within a week; if there were any significant items that hadn't been billed by then, they should FAX him estimates or quotes that the vendors had provided him. He also invited them to call him any time with problems or questions that arose in the preparations for the next four meetings. He thought about the additional work load he would be taking on, and whether it would be so heavy that he couldn't do justice to his other commitments, particularly the ones he felt toward his family. He remembered that once before he made a serious mistake in that area, and was reminded nicely by his Tiffany when she asked him, only half jokingly,

"Daddy do you love all of these people you help more than you love me? You've gotten so busy lately that I feel as if I had to stand in line and make an appointment to see you, like all those other people."

Her question had really hit him hard. He had apologized to her, thanked her for pointing out what should have been obvious and promised that it would never happen again. As he remembered that promise he resolved immediately to select and recruit four captains, one for each community project. As he went about his other work, the premonition, or foreboding hit him again. What would it be? Was there any way he could prepare for it? How could he, if he had no idea of the nature of it? He tried to concentrate totally on the work at hand, but these questions kept recurring and distracting him.

Chapter Nineteen
Pickets and Threats

Nine meetings had been conducted successfully and plans were well on the way for the next four. Of the meetings so far, all had been highly successful. Some had even matched or exceeded, if possible, the outstanding results of the first meeting. There had been a few minor glitches, of course, but nothing that skillful team leaders couldn't remedy, or at least minimize. Tim had been successful in recruiting meeting coordinators, and Becky had found people willing to takes notes at each meeting. They used her meticulous notes from the first meeting, and recorded only the things that were different. Tim began to wonder if he had experienced a false premonition; he had almost forgotten his earlier foreboding, except to wonder if it had been a needless worry. The answer came one Saturday morning: He and Becky looked out their front window and were surprised and shocked by what they saw: three pickets walking back and forth on the sidewalk in front of their house. Each carried a different sign; the first one read simply:
ANTI-CHRIST!
The second one read:
ENEMY OF GOD'S WORK!

And the third one was done with red spray paint; the last word had been sprayed heavily enough to run down the sign and look like blood:

CEASE OR KNOW GOD'S WRATH!

As Tim and Becky watched in bewilderment and horror, fear welled up in them like a rising storm cloud; and Tim exclaimed,

"This is crazy! I'm going to call 911!"

"They won't do anything!" Becky responded, "As long as these pickets are peaceful and don't hassle anyone, they're not doing anything illegal."

"You may be right, but I don't want them disturbing the neighbors and upsetting us!" he said as he rushed to the telephone.

When the 911 operator had listened to his report, she said politely, "I'm sorry Mr. Hamilton, but I'll have to refer you to the police sergeant on duty."

The latter gave Tim the same answer Becky had, so Tim called the City Attorney's office. An assistant attorney told him the same thing he had already heard twice. He hung up muttering,

"I still don't like it. I'm going to take their pictures."

He got out his zoom-lens camera that developed and printed out pictures immediately and took a number of shots. Some showed the entire scene, some showed one picketer at a time, some were close-ups of the individual signs, some were close-ups of the faces. After a quick breakfast, Tim put the best set in an envelope and hurried down to police headquarters with them. The sergeant on duty said he would have the pictures checked against police files and call him as soon as possible. He did point out that, since no crime had been committed, they would have to take care of any criminal cases first. Tim thanked him, but went away unhappy with everyone's apparent conclusion that it was lawful for people to threaten your life.

That evening Tim and Becky were jolted from a pleasant dinner by a thunderous crash followed by a dull thud and the sound of tinkling glass. They rushed into the living room to find their picture window shattered. Large shards of glass remained in place at the corners and around the edges of the frame, but the rest of the pane was strewn over their beautiful oriental rugs, chairs, tables and everything else within a range of ten feet of the window. Near the edge of the scattered glass fragments lay a large brick with a paper attached to it. Tim was about to pick it up when Becky spoke loudly,

"No Tim! Don't touch a thing until the police have had a chance to examine it."

"Of course, dear! What was I thinking of? I'll call 911."

Within minutes a special crime team arrived, and the fingerprint expert dusted the brick and took several close-ups with a special camera. In the meantime the detective asked Tim and Becky an exhaustive list of questions. Had they had any previous threats? Any known enemies? Anyone they suspected? And so the line of questioning continued. Tim and Becky answered all of the questions in the negative, except one: Tim told the detective about the picketing and about the pictures he had taken to police headquarters. He also showed the detective another set of the pictures and asked if they would be helpful. The detective replied,

"They may be, but most of these picketers probably don't have a record unless they've been picked up for obstructing traffic or hassling people."

Again, Tim had dark thoughts about things people could get away with under the First Amendment. While they were talking, the lab expert finished his work and handed the detective the paper that had been attached to the brick. The detective unfolded it and then showed Tim the message:

ANTI-CHRIST!
ENEMY OF GOD'S WORK!
CEASE OR KNOW GOD'S WRATH!

"That's exactly what the picket signs said!" Tim exclaimed, "We've found the perpetrators!"

"Not so fast!" the detective responded. "We don't know if we have IDs on any of these people, and we won't know for sure until our lab checks the fingerprints and gives us a report on them and the pictures. Even if we do, we can't bring 'em in 'til we find 'em. We've got lots of work to do yet, and it all takes time. The violent crimes involving human life come first, and we don't have nearly enough staff. We'll keep you posted."

The detective noticed that Tim looked crestfallen.

"Cheer up, Mr. Hamilton, these are probably just empty threats."

"But what if they aren't?"

"It wouldn't hurt to have a bodyguard 'til this blows over, and to watch for anything unusual. "

"Such as . . .?"

"Oh, if you see strangers in the neighborhood, particularly if they're walking or driving by slowly, call 911."

"I can't spend all my time being a watchdog."

"That's what the bodyguard is for. And keep your doors and windows and garage locked, and don't leave your cars in the street even for a few minutes. Have your house checked by a security expert. Here's a coupl'a good ones"

The detective handed Tim two business cards, and Tim studied them.

"Are these guys friends of yours?"

The detective grinned as he replied,

"Yeah, that's how I know they're good. I've got to run now. Good luck!"

A very unhappy Timothy Hamilton walked slowly into the kitchen, where he found Becky and invited her to have a cup of coffee with him. When he started to tell Becky about his conversation with the detective, she interrupted him,

"You'd better get a glass company to replace that window, and I'll call the cleaning lady and get that glass cleaned up."

When they had finished their phone calls and had gotten their coffee, Tim reported on his calls:

"The glass company is closed, but I reached my carpenter friend at home. He'll be over in a few minutes to board up the window. I don't like this at all, honey."

"Neither do I, lover, but I guess it's part of being a public figure; and you've certainly become that."

"But why would they be doing this to us?"

"Oh, they probably feel that you're a threat to their organized religion; and the militant ones are willing to go to extremes, including murder, to stop you."

"That's a happy thought!" Tim exclaimed sarcastically.

"But it's reality, lover; and the only way to stop it is to stop our crusade."

Tim called the private security firm the detective had recommended and asked if they could send a guard over as soon as possible. The dispatcher told him that they would have someone there within two hours. Tim thanked him, but added,

"The sooner he comes the better."

While Tim was still on the phone the carpenter came with a large piece of plywood, quickly cut it to the fit over the broken window, and put it in place with special fasteners that looked like a cross between a nail and a screw, which he drove/screwed into place with a special power tool. He assured Tim that this gave him the best security with the least damage to the house.

Becky and Tim slept only fitfully that night, and they were up very early the following morning. The guard had arrived as promised and had spent the night in the house, and as soon as he heard them stirring he called upstairs and asked them to come down as soon as they could. When they hurried down in dressing gowns and slippers, the guard asked them to follow him outside and pointed silently to the front of the house. What they saw sent chills up and down their spines, and Becky began to shiver with fright. Sprayed across the entire front of the house in red paint was the same three-line message that had appeared on the signs and with the brick:

ANTI-CHRIST!
ENEMY OF GOD'S WORK!
CEASE OR KNOW GOD'S WRATH!

As before the paint on the last line had been laid on so heavily that it ran in streaks. The impression of blood was gruesomely realistic. Tim asked the guard what he had seen or heard. The latter admitted with obvious embarrassment,

"I'm terribly sorry, Mr. Hamilton. I heard nuthin'. I saw nuthin'. I musta been watchin' out in back when them buggers done it."

Tim and Becky shook their heads in chorus, and Becky was the first to voice their thoughts,

"I just can't *believe* that none of us heard or saw them. Either they're incredibly clever or ..."

But Tim didn't hesitate to voice what he and Becky were thinking:

"Or we were *all* asleep." He said looking accusingly at the guard. The latter hunched his shoulders and turned his palms up in the classic gesture of helplessness as he spoke,

"I swear to *God* Mr. Hamilton, I wasn't asleep.'"
He lifted from the ground beside him, the largest thermos jug they had ever seen, uncorked it and turned it upside down. Nothing came out and he continued speaking,

"So help me, this wuz plumb full of strong black coffee when I come here las' night, an' I drunk every durn drop of it. *Please* don't turn me in fer sleepin' on the job, or the boss will fire me fer sure, an' then he'll blacklist me so I can't work fer no other agency, an' I dunno what I'd do 'cuz I dunno nuthin' else an' I need the money, an' we owe the landlord an' we owe the light people, an' the telephone's been cut off already, an' welfare won't pay when I'm workin' an' the wife's bin sick an' the drug man says he ain't gonna give us no more credit, an' we owe the doc more all the time, an' the kids shoes are all wore out, an I dunno what to do an' I dunno what'll become of us..." and then he broke down, slumped on the steps, put his head in his hands, and started to sob in great, wracking, convulsive spasms that shook his whole body.

Becky looked at Tim and was startled by what she saw. His body language described his state more eloquently than any words could: Never had she seen him so angry, so frustrated and so upset. She was desperately afraid of what he might say or do in this extreme state of agitation. She put her hand gently on Tim's arm and said to him quietly,

"Let's all go in the house before the neighbors see us out here in our robes. You come, too, Mr. ...?"

"Karonovich." He supplied the name with considerable difficulty between the sobs that continued to wrack his body.

"Thank you;" said Becky. "Come along both of you and I'll fix us all a little breakfast. What would you like for breakfast, Mr. Karonovich?"

"Anythin' you got," he responded. The thought of breakfast seemed to revive him a little, and he stood up slowly; though he was still wracked by an occasional convulsive sob. Tim removed his arm from under Becky's hand and announced stubbornly,

"I'm not hungry."

"Come on Tim. If you let these fanatics get you down, they've won, and that's not the man I married."

As those words sunk in, Tim walked slowly into the house behind Becky and the guard, and went quietly into the kitchen and sat down at the breakfast table. The guard hung back until Becky said to him,

"Why don't you sit right there, and I'll pour some juice for us."

As she did so and quickly made breakfast, neither man said a word. The guard had quit sobbing, but looked embarrassed and ashamed. Tim's anger had left him, and he was obviously deep in thought. When they had about finished breakfast, Becky was the first to speak,

"Those devils were incredibly skilled. Mr. Hamilton and I didn't sleep very soundly, and we never heard a sound. Since posting a guard didn't seem to protect us against these harassing and frightening threats, I suspect we'll want to make other arrangements, but I'm sure we won't give you a bad report, or give your boss any reason to fire you. After all, we have no way of knowing whether you were sleeping or not; and it would be grossly unfair to say anything that would cost you your job, and Mr. Hamilton is a very fair and considerate man."

"Oh, thank you, Mrs. Hamilton!" the guard exclaimed fervently, looking greatly relieved. Becky continued,

"Now that you've finished breakfast and your shift was over long ago, please feel free to go home to your family. I'm sure you'll be glad to see each other, and you need to get some sleep." Again, the guard thanked her profusely and took his leave quickly.

Tim didn't speak until he heard the guard close the door behind him,

"Becky you can't stay here. It's too dangerous."

"I agree, but neither should you. After all, it's really you they're after."

Tim pondered the frightening but obvious truth of Becky's statement before responding,

"Okay, let's do this. We'll take both cars. Pack everything you'll want for the next six weeks. Put as much stuff as you can in the trunk. You can lay your clothes across the back seat, but cover them with a blanket. I'll do the same. Take your time and try to think of everything you'll want. We should transfer whatever computer files we'll need to our notebooks. I'll also take that wonderful new lightweight printer, and we can both use it. When we get to our temporary home, we can talk about other precautions for our security. I've some calls I have to make before we leave: the glass company, a painter to take care of the graffiti, a new security company as well as the old one, my meeting coordinators and my business partner and other business associates."

"What're you going to tell all those people?"

"That we're being harassed by militant religious extremists who feel that our community meetings are a threat to their organized church, synagogue, temple or whatever, and that we won't be answering the telephone for at least a few weeks, but that we'll check our answering machine frequently."

"Will you tell them we're moving out temporarily?"

"Absolutely not! Only Peter, Tiffany and your mother will know that. They'll be sworn to strict secrecy, and not even they will know how to reach us except to leave a message."

"Won't anyone know how to reach us in an emergency?"

"Only the 911 office, and we'll tell our kids, your mother and the security company dispatcher to call 911, but only if it's a real emergency. I'll also ask my business partner to pick up a couple of wigs for each of us, and a false mustache for me, and drop them off at our house at three o'clock this afternoon."

"I've some calls to make on my own. I'll stop the papers and tell Mrs. Schatz we don't need her services until further notice."

"I hate to disagree with you, honey, because you're usually right; but in this case I'd like to suggest that we not stop the papers. Instead, how about having Mrs. Schatz come every day, bring in the papers, check for anything unusual, and change the three light timers in a random pattern."

"She won't know what random is."

"You're right. Have her imagine that we're home, but doing different things each evening. Don't let her use the same pattern more than once in 10 days."

"I feel like a spy, or an under-cover agent, or a fugitive."

"We are fugitives in a way, but I'd rather be a live fugitive than a dead crusader."

"Oh, Tim!. You really think it's *that* serious?"

"Absolutely, Honey. I truly believe these devils will stop at *nothing*, to achieve their purpose."

"Did you ever think of stopping the community meetings--at least temporarily?"

"Yes, but only as a fleeting thought. If we did that, we'd have allowed the devils to win, and we just *cannot* allow evil to prevail."

"I thought you'd say that. You're a true crusader and I'm proud of you. It may be a bit inconvenient for awhile, but I'm with you a thousand percent, all the way, lover." As she spoke she kissed him fervently and hugged him tightly.

"Oh honey! How was I ever lucky enough to marry such a marvelous wife!" Becky allowed as how this was a lot more fun than making phone calls and packing, but that they had a lot to do and they had better get started. Tim agreed on both counts, and they each headed for their own phones. When Becky had finished her telephoning, she went to Tim's office and asked how much longer he'd be. He estimated about 15 minutes. Becky announced,

"It's almost lunch time, you can come down for lunch whenever you're through. It's a cold lunch, so don't hurry."

As they ate their lunch, Tim filled Becky in on further plans he had made,

"When I spoke to Gordon, he suggested that someone might recognize our cars, so he'll rent two cars under our new names I made up. You're Rachel Bromfield and I'm Terry Erickson. Gordon and his wife will have to know what we're up to, but they've sworn themselves to secrecy, and I trust them as though they were family. Your wigs will have beautiful, raven-black, lustrous hair, one short and one long. Mine will be light blond, one long, wavy, and parted on the right, and the other will be short, straight and parted on the left. I will have two mustaches, one fairly short and the other long, with waxed tips."

"What color will our cloaks and daggers be?" asked Becky with an impish grin. Tim stuck his tongue out at her and grinned back,

"That's great! I'm glad this hasn't killed your sense of humor. But you've only heard half of it; was it the poet, Robert Browning, who wrote '...the best is yet to come'?"

"If the best is yet to come, I'm all ears."

"That's OK. Honey, nobody's perfect." It was Becky's turn to stick her tongue out. They both grinned, and Tim continued,

"When we're ready to leave, you will put the long -haired wig in your purse and drive to the Kelly Inn in St. Paul. That's the hotel just north of I-94 by the Sears store."

"I'm familiar with it. I've been there."

"Good! Park in the west parking lot in the row nearest the street, so Gordon's wife can find your car. Go to the ladies room, put on your wig, and wait inside until you see Gordon drive up in the car he has leased for you.

Get in the front seat quickly, move close to him and give
him a firm kiss on the cheek. He's looking forward to it,
so don't disappoint him! I'll call him when you leave.
He'll drive you to the Country Inn in White Bear Lake.
It's on U. S. 61 about 12 miles north of St. Paul. You'll
go in alone and tell them you're Rachel Bromfield and
that you have a reservation."

"What do I say when they ask about my luggage?"

"Tell them that your maid will be bringing it a
little later."

"What'll I do when they ask me how I'll be paying?"

"When the receptionist checks her screen, it
should show that Gordon has guaranteed your reservation
with his credit card. If not, you can tell her."

"She's going to have evil thoughts!"

"Yes, she will, particularly when she notices that
you have the nicest two-room suite in the inn. And she'll
be partly right: your all-night visitor will be me, not
Gordon and it won't be a one-night stand. You'll have an
all-night visitor *every* night for several weeks!" Tim
announced with obvious glee and a broad grin.

"Oh Lover, this is getting more romantic by the
minute. I'm getting positively excited!"

Tim didn't miss her double meaning and felt a
special excitement of his own welling up in him. What
a jewel he had married! How many other wives would
find romance and humor in this situation instead of
grumbling at the inconvenience or being terrified at the
dreadful risk he was doing his very best to avoid? He
continued,

"I'll leave shortly after you do and drive to the
Pine Point Lodge. That's a remote bed-and-breakfast
hidden back in the woods just a few miles North of White
Bear Lake. In the meantime Gordon's wife will take a cab
to the Kelly Inn, pick up your car, make sure she's not
being followed, go to the Pine Point Lodge, park, and

wait for Gordon and me to arrive separately. She and Gordon will have already left my rental care there and will have checked in for the night to avoid arousing suspicion about the extra cars in the lot. Gordon's wife now becomes your maid and, with the help of my long, flowing blond wig and handlebar moustache, I become Terry Erickson! We quickly transfer all of our belongings to our rental cars. Then Gordon and his wife go back to the Country Inn in your new car, and he helps his wife take your belongings to your room, explaining to the desk clerk that Gordon is her boy friend who came along to help her. I wait 20 minutes and then drive to the Country Inn in my new car. I pick up the Springborns, take them back to Pine Point Lodge, wish them pleasant dreams, return to the Country Inn and check into my room. In the morning they will drive our old cars to a storage place that Gordon has rented, and then resume their normal life. Do you see any flaws in it?"

"Have you considered becoming a spy or an under-cover agent in your next incarnation? I'll have to digest that whole thing and have you play it back a time or two before I can give you an intelligent answer. But isn't this an imposition on the Springborns?"

"Not really, Gordon is so happy with the business arrangement we have that he feels he owes me one. Besides they want to help us protect ourselves against those devils in every way they can. And they'll have a nice mini-vacation at Pine Point. Have you got any questions before we start out?"

"Boy I can't think of any; let me play back my part just to be sure I understand it."

"That's a good idea; but let's wait until we're ready to leave."

Except for a short time to eat a light supper, it took them all afternoon and until well after dark to finish packing and loading the cars. Then Tim pointed his finger at Becky like a film director cuing an actress,

"Now!"

Becky re-played her part with only one minor hesitation, and Tim quickly prompted her.

"You're wonderful! You can be my accomplice when we're reincarnated. If a question does come up, don't hesitate to call me. Leave your cellular on, and I'll do the same. But be sure to call me Terry and I'll call you Rachel, and don't refer to any thing, person or place by the right name. Gordon will be The Chauffeur, and his wife will be The Maid. The Kelly Inn will be the place where The Chauffeur is to pick you up, so forth. Cellular phones are anything but private, you know"

"This gets more exciting all the time, lover; are we on the National Security Agency payroll yet?"

"OK, Honey. On your way!"

They kissed fervently in a long, lingering embrace, and Becky drove off.

The plan went smoothly. Becky called only once with a simple timing question.

And so their new life began.

Chapter Twenty
Attacks, Hiding and Precautions

T he turn of the century was just a few months away. In almost every public park there was at least one bearded, long-haired evangelist, usually mounted atop a chair or a step ladder, fervently delivering an apocalyptic message:

"My dear friends, repent while yet ye may! The time is at hand when only the righteous will be caught up into heaven and walk the streets paved with gold. The earth shall open up in a great chasm, and those who remain mired in sin will be swallowed up by the eternal fires of Hell there to languish eternally in anguish and torment. Come forward now and give your hearts to the Lord before it's too late. Kneel down and receive God's blessing."

Typically, a few listeners came forward, and knelt while the evangelist put his hands on their heads and recited reverently,

"Bless you my son, bless you my daughter! Ye are saved from the eternal fires of Hell and damnation. But ye cannot take your riches with you. Throw your money and your jewels in this box before it's too late, and I will see that it's used in the Lord's work to save others from the eternal fires."

While a few usually did so quickly, many hesitated and looked dubious. Others departed furtively. And invariably several got up and strode away indignantly muttering "Scam," "Cheat," "Impostor," Fraud!" In some small, scattered churches the same message was being preached, and a goodly number of the congregation came forward.

Meanwhile the movement Tim had started continued to gain momentum. Meetings were held as scheduled despite the threats against Tim and Becky. In fact the next few meetings went smoothly except for three pickets, who marched peacefully on the sidewalk in front of the entrance to the meeting hall. They carried signs identical to the ones that had been used in front of Becky and Tim's house:

ANTI-CHRIST!
ENEMY OF GOD'S WORK!
CEASE OR KNOW GOD'S WRATH!

Rachel Bromfield and Terry Erickson arrived at separate times and made their entrances surreptitiously through a back door with the help of an accommodating janitor. Terry arrived in a friend's car just five minutes before he was scheduled to speak, made his way quickly to the employees' washroom, locked the door behind him, became Tim Hamilton and donned a bullet-proof vest, and walked quickly to the podium. Two highly experienced body guards with impeccable references had been hired to protect Tim. The guards carried side arms and were stationed at each side of the podium; they watched the crowd intently during the entire time Tim was on the platform. As soon as he was through speaking, Tim left the platform and hurried back to the same washroom, accompanied by the guards. There Tim proceeded to become Terry Erickson once more. When the transformation was complete, Terry knocked on the door. After making sure that no one was within sight of the door, the guard returned the knock on the door. Terry emerged from the washroom and walked casually back to the entrance he had come in, got into the same car in which he had arrived and disappeared down the road.

The plan worked well for three meetings. At each meeting TV cameras were set up on tripods in opposite corners at the back of the meeting room. They were located in the darkest areas so as to provide the least distraction to the audience and so that the camera operators could view their monitor screens most clearly. The recording engineer was in the habit of dismissing the camera operators for a brief break while Tim was speaking and no camera movement was necessary or even desirable. Because of the remoteness of the cameras from the podium and the dim lighting in those locations, neither guard noticed the quick and brief movement that had occurred next to one of the cameras. Then, as Tim was finishing his speech at the fourth meeting, it happened!

From one of the camera locations came a sudden flash accompanied by a loud, sharp crack that echoed through the meeting room. At the same time Tim, who had been standing beside the podium in order to feel closer to his audience, fell backwards to the floor while grasping at his chest with both hands. The guards snapped into action almost, it seemed, before the sound of the shot quit echoing. One guard bent over Tim to check the nature of his injuries. The other guard raced to where he had seen the flash and quickly asked members of the audience sitting near by whether they had seen anyone who might have been the assailant. They all said that they had been so intent on what Tim was saying that they were unaware of any suspicious movements. One man *thought* he had seen someone lurking in that vicinity, but he was vague about the suspect's appearance that the guard quickly moved on. When he had given up hope of apprehending the assailant, or getting any useful information he pursued a different tack. Carefully scanning the floor in that part of the room, he soon found what he was looking for: a shell casing from a large automatic pistol. Handling it deftly, he put it in a small plastic bag that he produced from his pocket.

In the meantime the other guard had joined him. He announced that Tim had not been seriously injured. The Kevlar jacket had saved his life; but the speed and the mass of the bullet had been sufficient to knock the wind out of Tim. A registered nurse had rushed up to the podium and administered skilled first aid. Tim was breathing normally in just a few minutes, and was able to report that he didn't think he had anything more serious than a badly bruised chest. In the meantime a physician had joined them, sized up the situation , and asked Tim's permission to check him for broken ribs and other apparent injuries. He found no serious damage and simply suggested that, for pain in the bruised area, Tim use a topical analgesic, like the ones the athletes use for sore muscles.   He also told Tim he was a very lucky man, but cautioned him to get to his doctor quickly if he developed any adverse symptoms, such as coughing up blood and/or an excessive amount of fluid. Tim addressed both the doctor and the nurse,

"You folks have been very kind, how can I repay you?"

"Repay us?" they exclaimed, almost in chorus, "How can we ever repay you for the wonderful thing you're doing for our community. Your name has become almost a household word throughout the greater Twin City area", the doctor added.

"Yes," Tim acknowledged regretfully, "and, unfortunately, with some very evil people as well."

As soon as the doctor and nurse left, the MC, who had been hovering just out of their way, bent down and asked,

"Tim, what do you want to do about the rest of the program?"

"As soon as you can get everyone's attention, assure them that I wasn't seriously hurt, and do your best to salvage the evening. You guys have invested so much of your time and energy to make this evening a success it would be a shame to let that all go down the drain. And besides, if we don't salvage the evening, the terrorists will have won; and we can't allow that to happen."

"I'll do that; and you go 'home', wherever that is, and try to get some rest."

Becky knelt down, kissed Tim fervently, and exclaimed,

"Oh lover, I'm so relieved that you're OK! I want *so badly* to stay by your side, but I suspect you won't let me."

"You're right. We can't take any risks at this time. That gunman may be lurking outside, just waiting to finish me off. I think we should both leave right now and follow our usual procedure. See you at 'home' in a little while. And you can be *darn* sure we'll tighten security much further before I speak again."

She kissed him again, and left the meeting room through a nearby exit. With a little help, Tim got to his feet and left via the planned exit with both guards very much on the alert. The senior guard apologized profusely,

"I'm *so* sorry, Mr. Hamilton, that we let this happen!"

"It wasn't your fault." Tim assured him, "But I'll call you at ten o'clock tomorrow morning so we can discuss ways to reduce my exposure on the podium. Is that a convenient time for you?"

The guard assured Tim that it was, and they proceeded with their usual departure strategy. Within ten minutes Tim was nowhere to be found, and Terry Erickson was getting into the car of a waiting friend. Similarly, Rachel Bromfeld was getting into her friend's car, and they were on their separate ways to the Country Inn.

It was a long time before either of them felt sleepy. They talked in low tones about the near-tragic event of the evening. Finally Becky said quietly,

"Lover, if you decided to give it up, I'd still love you and still think you were the most wonderful man in the world." His answer didn't surprise her:

"Thanks, honey; but no way are we going to let those devils have their way."

Tim assured her that he would increase security in any and every way that he, his guards, and other crime experts could conceive of. They wished each other pleasant dreams, but finding that possibility hard to imagine, they enfolded each other in a close embrace and lay there in silence . . .

They awoke early the next morning, not sure how much they had slept, but with little inclination to try to go back to sleep. Tim, as Terry Erickson, retreated quickly to his room, where he took care of his personal activities for the morning. Becky ordered a very generous breakfast for one in her room. When it had been delivered to Rachel Bromfield, she walked casually down to Tim's room. After making sure no one was in sight, she used the distinctive knock they had agreed on: four quick raps, followed by two quick raps ("Hi" in Morse International Code), and walked back to her room, where she hung out the "DO NOT DISTURB" sign and became Becky once again. In a very short time, the "Hi" knock was repeated at her door. She quickly let Terry Erickson in. He bolted the door behind him, latched the security chain, and quickly became Tim. Becky had carefully closed the blinds and set the table for two, using dishes and silverware that she had brought with her. They enjoyed a leisurely breakfast and read the papers that had been delivered to their door. When they came to the article about the attempted assassination, the spell was broken and Becky felt forced to ask,

"Tim, how are you going to protect yourself against these devils? I'm worried."

"I don't know yet, honey; but my first call this morning will be to the senior guard. I'll ask him to consult with the best personal security experts he has ever worked with and to report back to me by calling 911. They will alert me, I'll call him back and probably approve the arrangements."

"I sure hope they come up with something good, lover. I don't want to lose you!"

"Don't worry your pretty head about it. These guys have protected politicians and high-profile executives; they know their stuff."

"Yeah, but look what happened to Martin Luther King and the Kennedy's."

"They ignored some safeguards in order to get closer to the public. I intend to take every precaution available. I've got a lot of things that I want to do yet, and it'll take me many years to get them all done; so I want to be around a long time."

"I surely hope so. How do you feel this morning?"

"Much better, thank you, but I'm still plenty sore." They embraced long and lovingly, before Tim announced,

"I'd much rather stay here with you, Honey; but it's time for Terry to return to his room, and get this security process started. And I've a number of other calls to make. Terry would like to meet Rachel for lunch at the Dock, that beautiful riverfront restaurant in Stillwater. Do you know how to get there?"

"If I remember correctly, I head east toward the St. Croix River, turn south on Minnesota 95 when I get to the river, follow my nose right down Main Street, turn left on the road to the inter-state bridge and watch for the Dock on the right."

"You got it, see you there. I'll knock on your door when I leave, and you can leave ten minutes later. Just don't get picked up for speeding!" She stuck out her tongue at him as he started for the door, but she stopped him, grinned at him and said,

"Wait a minute lover, I don't want you to ruin my good name. Let me step out first and make sure the coast is clear." She stepped out into the hallway, leaving the door ajar; then she turned around abruptly and re-entered the room as if she had forgotten something and nodded to him. Terry left quickly and returned to his room. He called the senior guard. After assuring the guard that he was feeling much better, Tim said,

"Would you please call the best expert on security you know and get his suggestions for making my appearance on the rostrum just as secure as possible. Don't spare the cost; security is supreme. When you've got all the details, call 911 and tell them you need to reach me. They'll forward your message."

The guard acknowledged his request and said he would call back just as soon as he could. Then Tim called his meeting coordinators, assured them he was all right, and asked them to pass the word along to each of their team leaders. Each of them was relieved to hear from him and agreed to pass along the good word, along with Tim's thanks for the wonderful job the teams were doing on the meetings. Tim also assured them he had ordered maximum security measures for the remaining meetings.

After finishing those calls, Tim called Peter and Tiffany, assured them that he was alive and well, and asked how things were in their lives. Each of them expressed their relief and said about the same thing:

"We don't really think this will stop you, but please be very careful." To this Tiffany added, "Remember, Daddy, we love you very much!"

Tim responded, "Thanks Tif, that goes both ways," and gave her the same assurance he had given Becky earlier that morning. He had finished dressing for lunch and was starting to read the mail that his driver had given him the previous evening, when the phone rang. It was 911 asking him to call the guard. The latter answered immediately and said, "I've got good news, sir." (He had been instructed never to use Tim's name, except in the meeting rooms.)

"Go on."

"The best security expert in Washington, D. C. has suggested we use a bullet-proof enclosure, made of extremely clear plastic, in which you'll stand while making your appearance in the meeting hall. It has a door made of the same material, which you will close behind you as soon as you enter it. It even has its own miniature air conditioning system, which I've been assured is very quiet; it also has a mike which can be quickly converted, when necessary, from radio to even the almost obsolete wire transmission, which can be connected to the PA system through a receptacle in the base of the bubble. I've talked with the company that makes these bubbles, and they can air freight one in plenty of time for our next meeting."

"How awkward is this rig to handle?"

"It's light enough for two of us to handle, and I can store it in my house when we're not using it. The security expert also gave me the specifications for a canvas passageway in which you'll walk from the door into the hall right up to the back of your bubble. He also cautioned that you should walk slowly in the passageway so that you don't create a ripple along the side that would give away your whereabouts. I've given the specs to a local tent-maker, and he says he can make one up in plenty of time for our next meeting. We can either buy the bubble or lease it for your remaining eight talks. Your cost, all told is about 17 grand if you lease and 20 grand if you purchase the bubble."

"Go ahead and buy it. I think someone else may need it." Tim didn't offer to explain, and the guard didn't ask. "Thanks for another great job."

"You're very welcome, sir."

Terry Erickson left the room shortly after hanging up the phone. When he was sure no one was in sight, he knocked the "Hi" sign on Rachel's door, continued toward the stairway that led to the parking lot. He drove to their appointed rendevouz in Stillwater, secured a table in a quiet corner, and busied himself with the menu and the local paper until Rachel showed up. After they had enjoyed their usual, warm greeting and ordered lunch, Terry wasted no time in telling Rachel the morning's events:

"I had good talks with both Tiffany and Peter this morning. They both seem to be taking the incident in stride and keeping their concern in bounds."

"Yes lover, I called them both after you did. They're both deeply concerned; but then they wouldn't be the wonderful children we know and love if they weren't. I think they'll handle it OK. Now, what about the plans for your security?"

He told her that he'd had a good conversation with the senior guard, but he said,

"You wouldn't want to be bothered with all of the details."

"*Au contraire* lover, this is the most important thing in my life. I want to know every last detail."

After Terry had described the plan, he said,

"The only way those devils can touch me now is to put a bomb under the rostrum."

She shuddered involuntarily as she said,

"Please don't give them any ideas, lover. I wouldn't put it beyond them!"

About then their food arrived. They savored each mouthful for some time without saying a word, until Rachel broke the silence,

"You know something, lover? This food is terrific! How did you hear about this place?"

"A friend told me about it several months ago; but we've been so busy I've never felt we had the time to try it out."

"Isn't it strange? It took a terrifying event to jerk us out of our pleasant rut. It seems peculiar even to say this: In one way I miss our home and all of our friends, but in another way I've come almost to enjoy this life. I can't decide whether we're on an extended vacation, or if we're the leading characters in a spy story, full of excitement and intrigue!"

" Honey," he exclaimed, "You're one in a million! I've been having the same thoughts! In a strange way it's an exhilarating challenge to try to keep ahead of these clever devils."

Suddenly they became aware that the restaurant had become quiet. Tim looked around and then glanced at his watch:

"Oh my goodness, do you realize we've been here over two hours? There's only one other couple left in the restaurant, and I happened to notice that they came in quite late. We've got to blow this place before we become conspicuous."

"Blow this place!" she chuckled, "I haven't heard you use that slanguage since we were in college."

Tim paid the check and they sauntered outside as Becky spoke,

"It's such a beautiful Fall day; let's stroll down along the riverfront and feast our eyes on that gorgeous scenery."

"That's a great idea!"

As they walked slowly, hand in hand, they watched with all of the enjoyment and curiosity of small children, along with hundreds of other visitors who had taken time from their busy lives to look with awe and wonder at nature's incredibly beautiful spectacle. The trees across the river on the Wisconsin shore were arrayed in the height of their autumn splendor: The sugar maples had taken on their brilliant bright red color, and some of the oaks had begun to turn to a more subdued and darker red. the aspen and birch trees had acquired a bright golden yellow, and the sumac added an accent of intense vermillion. The various shades of green and blue-green that were displayed year-round added further excitement to this almost incomparable panoply of beauty. They watched with interest and curiosity the parade of beautiful yachts, both sail and power, that circled slowly waiting for the bridge to lift and allow them to pass. A beautiful new inter-state bridge had been built several miles downstream, but many autoists found this historic bridge more convenient and more fun, if they weren't in a hurry.

A couple of hours later both Rachel and Terry regretfully concluded that this beautiful afternoon, which both them had enjoyed immensely, must end.

"But let's not break the spell yet,"Terry said, "I know a nice restaurant in another town just a few miles north of here. It's called Crabtree Kitchen, and it's in a tiny community called Scandia. Let's have dinner there."

"Sounds great; let's go!"

Crabtree Kitchen was quite a contrast to the scene of their lunch, but it didn't disappoint them. The food was good, home-style cooking, the decor was bright and rustic, the service was friendly, and everyone seemed happy. Both of them enthusiastically agreed that they had had many enjoyable times together in their new, cloak-and-dagger life-style, but that this one had topped them all.

"Oh Terry, I hate to see it end."

"It's not over yet, Honey. In the words of an old song, 'The night is young and you're so beautiful'!"

She found the look in his eyes even more eloquent than his romantic words, and she returned the look with equal eloquence. As they left the restaurant, arm-in-arm, Terry said with a grin,

"You go ahead, Honey. I'll listen to the news on the car radio for a while so as to protect your good name at the Country Inn." She made a face at him before she got in her car and drove off.

The next eleven meetings went smoothly and safely. Some of the audience were startled, and a few were even frightened, by the implication of danger which they saw in the bubble and in the canvas runway. But the MC assured them they had nothing to fear: He explained that this arrangement had been set up to protect Mr. Hamilton from another attempt on his life, and that it had worked successfully and without incident for many meetings. Most of the audience sensed this already because of the wide publicity that had been given to the previous attack.

The last meeting was about to end, and from the seclusion of the private washroom Tim could hear the strains of the closing song. No matter how many times he had already heard it, he was always excited by the inspiring sound of this great audience, joining in a great mass chorus to sing this patriotic song with such enthusiasm. As he changed from Tim Hamilton to Terry Erickson, he congratulated himself for his survival and thanked a Gracious God for sparing him from any real harm. The thought came a moment too soon.

As he was reaching for the door, a deafening and incredibly powerful explosion seemed to lift the building off its foundation and hurled Terry Erickson to the floor. He lost consciousness as the wall collapsed around him and he was buried in a pile of rubble.

Chapter Twenty-One
Search and Recovery;
Did the Devils Win?

As Tim once again became aware of his spirit leaving his crushed body and rising perhaps 15 or 20 feet, he beheld a scene of incredible destruction. The entire back half of this large building had been reduced to a pile of rubble. The front of which half lay open and relatively intact, people were still pressing toward the exits. Some were bleeding and dazed. Perhaps a dozen lay inert around what had been the stage end of the auditorium. Among them were the MC, the song leader and members of the band. In a very few minutes ambulances, police cars, and other emergency vehicles converged on the street opposite the front end of the building. The area between the building and the street was filled with people who had already left the building, many in shock, a few already leading and helping others toward the ambulances. The paramedics made their way quickly through the crowd, doing a sort of rapid triage as they went, occasionally turning and helping someone back to an ambulance. The less seriously injured were being led to school buses by Becky and several others.

Then the scene was engulfed in darkness and total oblivion. Tim's spirit was being rapidly propelled through the now-familiar long, dark tunnel and into the brilliant but mellow golden light. In what seemed to be a very short time his mother greeted him warmly and lovingly. She sensed his curiosity about his father and his brother and became sad as she formed the thought,

"They were unable to stay here and have gone to a place of darkness, suffering and torment to spend the rest of eternity. They are lost from us forever." Then her countenance brightened again as she continued,

"But you, my beloved son, are earning your place in this land of eternal joy and happiness. You have already accomplished great good, but you have an even greater work left to do and must return shortly and continue that work. Goodbye for now; I'll be here to greet you when you return."

It was on the second day after the explosion that Tim's body was uncovered where he had been buried. It might have taken even longer if it hadn't been for the specially trained dogs that had located him, along with the badly charred bodies of the two guards. They had been in the long hallway that ran all the way from the back to the front of the building, where they were directly exposed to the tremendous blast of searing heat that had raced the entire length of the building like a gigantic blowtorch from Hell. It had even scorched the shrubbery and nearby trees at the front of the building. Tim's body had been miraculously sheltered by the same cinder blocks and concrete that had entombed him seconds later. Rescue workers carefully removed the blocks and picked out the pieces of mortar and concrete by hand to avoid doing further injury to the inert body that they suspected lay underneath. Since Tim had been missing, Becky had urged them to search this area of the rubble very carefully; and she now worked frantically along with the rescue workers hoping and praying that they would find him alive. Eventually a leg appeared; then with agonizing care other parts of the body were exposed in what seemed like hours to Becky as she continued to work frantically and pray desperately. Blood still oozed slowly from his head and body, and the paramedic in charge pronounced this to be a good sign. He carefully raised one eyelid and shone a flashlight into Tim's eye as Becky held her breath. The paramedic nodded his head as he pronounced his verdict,

"Yup, there's still life there, let's get him onto the stretcher."

Quickly but expertly and very carefully, the paramedics slid the body onto the stretcher. Becky asked them to take Tim to Abbott-Northwestern hospital and murmured,

"That's the best hospital in town, you know."

They all nodded. Becky wasn't sure whether they were just nodding their understanding of her request, or also agreeing with her appraisal of the hospital.

To Becky, the trip to the emergency room seemed to take forever. As she continued to pray fervently, she leaned over and kissed Tim gently and listened carefully for breath sounds. When she could hear or feel nothing, she shouted frantically,

"He's not breathing!"

A paramedic quickly produced a small mirror from his bag and held it under Tim's nostrils. In a moment the mirror began to cloud over with vapor, and the paramedic nodded his head as he said,

"There's still breath there, Ma'am, but none too much." He quickly took another blood pressure reading and announced, "78 over 40; that's up from 69 over 35 when we found him. Lucky thing his head was lower than the rest of his body or he'd be brain dead by now for sure. We'll give him another shot of adrenalin to keep the pressure up there. If you notice, we've still got his body tilted head down."

"How do you know he *isn't* brain dead?" Becky asked anxiously.

The paramedic shook his head: "Only God knows right now, but you keep on praying like you have been, Ma'am, and pretty soon we'll get the verdict from the ER doc."

Although her watch said only 15 minutes had elapsed since Tim's leg had been uncovered, it seemed like an age to Becky before the emergency room doctor began her examination. Because of the excellent radio contact between the paramedics in the ambulance and the ER supervisor, everything the doctor needed to assess and stabilize Tim's condition was already arrayed in the extra-large examination cubicle that had been prepared for Tim's arrival. The doctor gave rapid fire orders as the emergency team brought her the articles she requested; she had already scanned the clip-board that the chief paramedic had handed him and announced,

"Great job, guys! Thanks to you we've got a live body here instead of a DOA."

She quickly scanned the broad tape that had emerged only seconds before from the electro-encephalogram machine, and continued,

"You also kept his brain alive: With that very low initial blood pressure reading, his heart wasn't pumping enough blood to overcome the intercranial pressure, even in a prone position; but by tilting him head down you let gravity help his heart just enough to keep his brain supplied with oxygen. I see no signs of brain damage. You've given him two shots of adrenalin; I think he can stand one more." She motioned to the nurse as she spoke.

When Becky heard this, she heaved a great sigh of relief and breathed an ardent prayer of thanks. The doctor straightened up from her ministrations to Tim, wrote some findings and prescriptions in the chart the paramedics had started, handed it to the head ER nurse so that she could transfer her pages of notes from another clip-board. As she began to peel off her gloves, she motioned to Becky to follow her into a small conference room which was near by. When they were seated, she began speaking to Becky in soft, gentle tones:

"Mrs. Hamilton, your husband will be taken to the ICU (intensive care unit) and kept there until all of his vital signs have been normalized, including a BP reading of at least 115 over 55. I can't tell you exactly how long that will be--probably in the range of three to five days. From there he will go to special care for a week or two, then on to a standard nursing station until he's ready to go home. His regular doctor has already been notified; he said he would re-schedule his next two appointments so that he can see Tim immediately in ICU. He may even beat your husband there!

"Please excuse my use of your husband's first name. I mean no disrespect. It's just that I feel as if I know him. I heard him give his marvelously inspiring talk in New Brighton a couple of months ago. I've told my friends all about him and have already given two coffee parties to get as many people involved as I could."

"Bless your heart! Of course you may call him Tim, and I hope you'll feel comfortable in calling me Becky. Now I'm anxious to know how badly he's hurt and what your prognosis is."

"He has a moderately severe concussion and perhaps a minor skull fracture. It's a miracle that there were no internal injuries that required surgical repair--at least not that we could find. There was relatively little internal bleeding, and most of the blood you saw was coming from a few severe lacerations. Fortunately no large arteries were punctured, or the loss of blood over that prolonged period probably would have been fatal. We think some part of the structure must have fallen above the body in such a position as to form a sort of protective bridge over the body; otherwise the tons of rubble that were cleared away would have crushed the life out of him almost instantly. His own doctor will examine him thoroughly, prescribe any additional tests he feels necessary, and probably recommend consultation with a neurologist regarding the diagnosis and treatment of the head injuries. I understand that Tim and his doctor have been friends for several years, so the doctor probably knows already what neurologist Tim wishes to have called. I'd like to add another thought, perhaps unprofessional, but I still feel that I want to share it."

"Please go ahead."

"Most 62 -year-old bodies I see would be in the morgue now after the terrible beating that Tim's body experienced, but Tim is here and in relatively good shape, thanks to three things: the workings of a merciful Providence, his marvelous physical condition, and--", she hesitated. Becky nodded,

"Please go on..."

"The paramedic told me you held Tim's hand and prayed aloud fervently all the way over here in the ambulance. Not too many doctors agree with me yet, but I really believe that helps. I hope you will continue to do that as much as you can while he's in ICU."

She stood up and started for the door as Becky spoke,

"Thank you again, doctor, you've been wonderful! Could I ask your full name? I'd like to drop a note to the hospital president and tell him how marvelous you've been."

"I'm Sarah Harding," she said simply, but her expression showed that she was obviously pleased.

Almost instinctively, Becky stretched out her arms and they hugged briefly but warmly. Becky followed Sarah out of the room and hurried to the family waiting room where Peter and Tiffany were anxiously waiting for a report on their father. Becky gave them the good news and they all hugged and shared their tears of joy and relief. Peter had not yet learned that real men do cry and dabbed at his eyes with obvious embarrassment. Tiffany was the first to speak,

"Oh Mom, thank God for sparing Daddy! He's such a wonderful man and he's doing so much good. I love him so. I just wish that he didn't work quite so hard. I know he's trying to make time for me and Peter, but I still sometimes feel like we're just two among many competing priorities."

"He loves you dearly, sweetheart, and he'd do *anything* to make you happy. But I know how you feel. I've been trying to get your father to slow down, though I've been trying . He really seems to thrive on his very high level of activity, and hasn't been able to see why he should slow down. I hope you tell him just what you've told me, and give him the whole nine yards."

"Oh Mom, you think I *dare* do that?"

"I think it's just what he needs."

"Thanks, Mom. I'll really have to get up my nerve."

Becky noticed that Peter had recovered his composure and was listening to the conversation with great interest. Her next remarks were addressed to him:

"Peter, I'm sure you know your father loves you, even more than most fathers love their only son; but he's from the old school: His father never expressed any feeling of love toward his sons, so it's very hard for your dad to express *his* real feelings. You know that real men don't eat quiche."

Peter found himself laughing at that old saw, and Becky had broken the tension. She continued:

"There's something you can do to help us all while your Dad's in the hospital. You'll both want to hear frequently how he's doing. You have conference telephone facilities in your office. Why don't you call me at nine, one and five o'clock each day and hook Tiffany in on the call. That way it'll save me giving the same report twice. We can also share in each other's questions and have a greater feeling of togetherness."

"Yeah, Mom, I can do that, but where will I find you?"

"I plan to get a room or a small furnished apartment as close to the hospital as I can, since I'll be spending most of my waking hours here until your dad is out of the woods. I'll give you the telephone number just as soon as I get it"

"Better yet, Mom. You have my office number. Why don't *you* call *me* at the appointed times and I can hook Tiffany in. She's still living with Grandma."

"Good thinking, Peter! I like that idea. We'll go with it. And now I must hurry up to the ICU."

They all hugged, and Becky disappeared toward the nearest elevator. As she entered the ICU, Becky was greeted by a smiling woman in her early forties who stepped from behind the portion of the nurses' station. As she approached Becky she said,

"Good morning, Mrs. Hamilton, I'm Brenda Gilbertson, the ICU charge nurse. My friends call me Bren and I'd like to consider us to be friends. We're so pleased and relieved to see Tim in such good shape, considering the terrible ordeal he's been through. My family and I were glued to a TV or a radio for every word on the progress of the rescue workers after that monstrous truck bombing. Frankly, we had given up hope the evening before he was found. I'm available from seven in the morning until 3:30 in the afternoon Monday through Friday. If you want anything or have any questions, you'll have my undivided attention."

"Thank you so much, Bren; but how did you recognize me?"

"Oh, Mrs. Hamilton, you and Tim are celebrities-- in the Twin Cities and probably the whole state! The results of the work you've been doing are showing up already in various ways. In the campaigning that has begun for the state primaries, the candidates are speaking to the issues instead of lambasting each other about their personal sins. The news media are reporting on the issues instead of making the campaign sound like a horse race. It's so refreshing!" As she spoke, Brenda ushered them toward comfortable chairs and gestured for Becky to sit down. She seated herself beside Becky and continued, "Dr. Frederickson is in the middle of his examination. When he's through, our nursing team will hook up the plumbing and wiring. I hope you don't mind our use of these metaphors for all of the support and monitoring systems we use."

"You are so kind and thoughtful, Bren; I appreciate it greatly, and my friends call me Becky. I know you have important duties to attend to. Before you go back to them, let me ask one question. You look so familiar; have we met before?"

"Oh yes! I was on the arrangements team when Tim gave that unforgettably inspiring address in Golden Valley, and I attended the terrific reception afterwards. I haven't seen that much enthusiasm since our high school basketball team won their semi-final game in the state tournament. I was tremendously impressed with the prodigious amount of work that went into that one meeting; and it was all so well organized! Everything went so smoothly. And to think that you have repeated that whole effort almost two dozen times now! I can hardly comprehend the amount of work involved. You folks are saints and organizational geniuses!"

"Thanks, Bren; but it all happens because so many people really want more effective government and are willing to work their hearts out to achieve it. When they see a movement that provides hope of achieving it where other organizations, including the major political parties have failed, they rally to the cause. It's all these people who give the movement its tremendous momentum."

As Brenda rose from her chair, she gave Becky's hand a long, firm squeeze, and they both smiled warmly.

Becky was watching the activities going on in various areas of the ICU so intently that she was mildly startled when a male figure slipped into the chair beside her. She saw a lantern-jawed man with a graying, well-trimmed moustache, a kindly face and piercing blue eyes smiling warmly at her with evident amusement at her reaction to his arrival. He was first to speak:

"Good morning, Becky. I didn't mean to frighten you. I'm Frank Frederickson, Tim's internist. He is in miraculously good shape considering what he's been through. He owes his very life to the people who worked tirelessly for the two days it took to find him, and to the paramedics who did exactly the right things when the life of his body *and* his brain hung by a thread. This amazing ER facility and its staff did a great job. Tim has a moderately severe concussion and a mild fracture; but I can detect no signs of brain damage or loss of function. Just to make sure, I have asked Dr. Donald Evans, who's a well known neurologist and brain specialist to examine him. He'll come in after lunch. He's over at United in St. Paul this morning."

"Thank you, Dr. Frederickson. Tim speaks very highly of both your medical skills and your obviously caring manner, your diagnostic capabilities and your openness in communicating with him."

"He's a good judge of doctors." He chuckled as he continued,

" Of course, Tim gets credit for his superb physical condition and his strong will to live."

"But how can you talk about will to live when he's still in a coma?"

"A good question. We've come to believe that even comatose patients and patients under deep anaesthesia still have faculties we had thought existed only in a conscious state. They have some memory of events occurring, they're traumatized by severe pain, and they hear much of what's said in their presence. So we deal with their pain, and we're careful about what we say around them."

"That's fascinating."

"You get a lot of credit, too, young lady! News of your fervent, hands-on prayers in the ambulance has already made its way around the hospital; and many of us believe that those prayers and your obviously deep love for Tim contributed to his very survival and to his remarkable early progress to a stable condition."

"Thank you, Doctor. As I come to know you better, I agree with your opinion about Tim as a judge of doctors."

They shared a good laugh.

"You're a remarkable woman in other ways. Your strength and composure during your own ordeal are outstanding and the talk of all the people who've observed you. Many women I know would be popping Valium and still be almost hysterical. But back to Tim, I'll be constantly in communication with the charge nurse with this gadget." He patted the beeper clipped to his belt. "I'll look in on Tim later this afternoon. I hereby declare this meeting of the mutual admiration society adjourned, and I'll be on my way to see my other patients."

They both rose and he gave her a shy little hug. She walked slowly toward Tim's room. The ICU team was just emerging, and the team leader spoke to Becky quietly,

"Normally the spouse is allowed only brief visits to the ICU patients, because they need their rest. But Dr. Frederickson has instructed us to make an exception in your case. You may spend as much time in his room as you wish, as long as we're not working on him. The doctor believes that your hands-on prayers are therapeutic, and so do many of us."

"Thank you very much. May I go in now?"

"Yes. He's doing incredibly well and all his vital signs continue to move in the right direction. I'll go with you if you wish and explain what all that tubes and wires are about."

It took the nurse almost 10 minutes to complete her explanation. Although Becky had been in ICU rooms before, she was still surprised at the proliferation of tubes, wires, bags, instruments and other equipment that had been connected to Tim. She was delighted to see that the blood pressure numbers had continued to rise, his pulse and breathing were very steady and much stronger, and his skin had taken on a much healthier glow. His head was swathed in heavy bandages, and several gauze pads of various sizes decorated various areas of the skin that she could see. Becky leaned over and kissed Tim long and lovingly on the cheek. She had a strong desire to kiss him on the mouth, but she thought that it was unwise to share any germs she might be carrying. Then she placed both hands gently on his exposed arm and hand and began her prayer vigil.

When Becky paused after a time, she looked at the large clock on the wall and was startled to see that it was already five minutes before one o'clock. She straightened up quickly, hurried out of ICU and headed down the corridor toward the family lounge which she had seen earlier. She was relieved to find the telephone free and quickly dialed Peter's office number. When she heard his voice, she said with relief,

"I'm glad I've got you; can you get Tiffany on with us?"

"I'll have to put you on hold while I dial her number, but when you hear it ringing, you'll know we're all connected."

In just a few seconds, she heard the ringing sound. Tiffany must have been sitting by the phone, and she was the first to speak:

"Mom? Peter? Is he OK?"

"Yes, darling, he's doing amazingly well, considering the ordeal he's been through and what a close brush he had with death."

Becky made her report as brief as she could, but she told them the important highlights of what had happened since they saw him being transported from the ER to the ICU a few hours earlier. She paused a moment to think if there was anything significant she might have missed. She was about to ask if they had questions when Tiffany asked anxiously,

"Is he going to be all right? When can we see him?"

"He's already been examined by two doctors and neither one saw any signs of brain damage or loss of function; but Dr. Frederickson has called in a neurologist for another opinion. He should be here shortly. It's a mira0cle that no major organs were damaged. Apart from the staff, I'm the only one who is allowed to see him while he is in the ICU; but we hope and expect that it will be only a few days before he is transferred to a special care unit, and you'll be allowed to see him there."

Tiffany was sobbing quietly as she responded,

"Oh Mom, I hope he'll be OK. I love him so; I *need* him." The sobs became louder.

"Yes darling, we all need him. The whole world needs this wonderful man. You just keep on loving him and praying for him. It will help him a great deal."

Peter finally broke his long silence. He spoke with more feeling in his voice than Becky had heard in a long time,

"Mom, I love him too, but you know I don't believe in prayer. What can *I* do for him?"

"I know Peter, and some day I'm sure you will. But right now you can help, too."

"How's that?"

"You just keep thinking how much you love him, and how much you want him to get well. It will help both of you. Well, my darlings, I must go now and get some lunch. Then I'm going to see what I can do about finding a room of my own with a telephone in it. I'll call again a little before five so that we can have our five o'clock update. And remember, I love you both very much."

"Thanks, mom, and goodbye," they seemed to say in chorus.

Becky next called Gordon Springborn, reported on Tim and then asked,

"What can we do to get those devils off our backs and get back to a normal life?"

Before Gordon could answer, she continued,

"I've an idea! We've finished our meetings, but they don't know that. What if we released a story to the media, saying that Tim has decided to discontinue the public meetings out of concern for the safety of his family?"

"I think that's a great idea, Becky. Let the devils *think* they've won. But I wouldn't have the faintest idea of how to do this."

"That's easy, Gordon. All you have to do is make three phone calls and these wonderful people will take it from there. You can also give them the good news about Tim. In fact, if you don't mind, I'll give you a daily report you can pass along to them until Tim comes out of his coma. After that, I feel quite sure he'll want to call them himself ." She gave him the names and telephone numbers of their three meeting coordinators.

"Don't worry Becky, I'll be happy to do this and anything else I can to help you and that guy who's helped me to find myself again. He's been so generous and considerate in his dealings with me. I'm delighted at the chance to do something for him."

She thanked him and they said goodbye.

Three days after Tim had been rescued, when Dr. Frederickson had finished his morning examination, he came out of Tim's room beaming and announced to Becky,

"I've got great news, my dear. The neurologist has been in already. Dr. Evans says that Tim's latest EEG shows increased brain activity, closely approaching normal. He still sees no evidence of brain damage or loss of function. The fracture is healing well, and he expects Tim to regain consciousness some time today. I find Tim doing well in all other respects. He's had some pulmonary edema, but that's normal and will probably disappear on its own within the next day or so. I've ordered his transfer to the special care station this morning."

Impulsively, Becky threw her arms around the doctor and gave him a warm hug. A somewhat flustered doctor became even more embarrassed when he looked around the room and found three nurses smiling in friendly amusement.

"Oh, Dr. Frederickson! I'm so relieved and so grateful. You've been so marvelous!"

"Don't forget, my dear, that you've contributed to his recovery with your love and prayers. You may go in now and tell him how much you love him. I think he'll hear you."

Becky entered Tim's room and gently kissed him on the cheek and on the forehead, which was now exposed because the bulky bandage on his head had been replaced by a large gauze pad which revealed a significant area of closely shaved scalp.

"Oh Tim, I love you so much and can't wait 'til you come back to us; and thank you, gracious God, for sparing him so miraculously!"

She continued to stand close to the bed with her hands resting gently on his, watching his face closely.

After a while she thought she saw a slight movement of his eyeballs under the lids and the flicker of an eyelid. When she glanced at the clock, she could hardly believe it said 8:45. She kissed Tim once more and hurried out to the nursing station where Bren greeted her.

"Top o' the morning, Becky. I hear you've received good news. We'll really miss you folks, but were glad Tim's doing so well. He'll be in room 3424, and you should find him there by 10:30. Your children and a few close friends can visit him, but for not too long at a time. He'll need lots of rest."

"Gee Bren, you're a mind reader to anticipate all my questions. You've all been so wonderful and we're so grateful!" She gave Brenda a hug.

"Thanks Becky; we try to be good to all our patients and their loved ones, but you and Tim are special."

Becky looked at her watch.

"My goodness!" she exclaimed, "It's almost five to nine. I must get to a telephone and call my son before he tries to call me at my new digs."

She had barely finished keying the number when Peter answered,

"Mom?"

"Good morning, Peter, and it is a good one."

"Hang on and I'll get Tiffany on the line."

"Hi mom!" Tiffany said. "How's he doing?"

"Wonderfully, my darlings, I've nothing but good news. Dad's being moved to special care this morning, and the neurologist expects him to wake up some time today. I suggest you come to room 3424 about eleven; plan to stay a few hours, and we'll all be there when he becomes conscious. Peter, do you think you can get off work?"

"Yeah, Mom. I'm sure they'll understand..."

"Oh Mom, our prayers have been answered!" Tiffany exclaimed excitedly, unaware that she had interrupted her brother. "I'll get excused from my classes first thing this morning and come over by eleven."

"I'm glad you can both make it; but remember, there are no guarantees that he'll come to while you're here. Now I've got good news personally: This wonderful hospital has rented me one of the small furnished apartments they own just for this purpose. It's so handy: right across the street and connected by a tunnel in case the weather's bad."

She gave them her new telephone number, and continued:

"There's voice mail in case I don't answer. I have maid service every day, and the morning paper is there when I open the door. Have you seen the paper this morning?"

Neither of them had.

"Well, then, let me read you the headline that's on the front page of the first section in letters one inch high:

HAMILTON TEAM STOPS MEETINGS

She continued reading,

"Organizers of the community meetings at which Timothy Hamilton has been the featured speaker announced that no further meetings are being planned. They expressed their deep regret and sympathy to the families of the four people who had been killed in the truck bombing of the school where their last meeting was held and added that they don't believe it wise to risk the lives of any more people. They expressed pleasure that Mr. Hamilton was making rapid progress in his fight for survival from this monstrous act. They also expressed hope that the Hamilton family can come out from hiding and resume a normal life..."

"Oh Mom", Tiffany broke in, "The terrorists will think they've won!"

"Gordon and I discussed that, darling, and that's what we want to happen. It's a shame to give them the satisfaction, but the devils have shown that they'll stop at nothing. It's better than risking continued bloodshed. What's more, they didn't really accomplish anything, because we finished our work."

"I hope they find them and put them away for life." Tiffany said heatedly.

"I do too, darling so that they can't do damage to some other good cause; but we must pray for their misguided souls."

"Oh Mom, you're too soft." This came from Peter.

"I can understand how you feel, son; but I hope that you'll come to agree with me. When we hold anger and vengefulness in our hearts, we damage ourselves, not them. Well I must go down and have some breakfast now, so that I'll be ready to greet Dad when he arrives in his new home. See you in a bit."

When she had hung up, she called Gordon, told him the good news and thanked him for seeing that the article was published.

"Don't thank me. I was just the messenger."

"But it was an important message, and you carried it well."

Becky was waiting in a visitor's chair in 3424 when two transportation people wheeled Tim in. By the time they had placed his gurney beside the bed, two nurses appeared. Becky suspected they had been told to watch for his arrival. She never ceased to marvel at the skill and strength they applied to moving a body heavier than theirs quickly but gently from the gurney to the bed.

Not too long after they had come back from a quick lunch an excited and anxious Becky, Tiffany and Peter watched closely as Tim's eyelids fluttered a couple of times and opened slowly. Then his eyes focused slowly as he began to take in the scene. When he beheld his beaming family, a faint smile formed on his lips, and he managed a weak "Hi!" Becky leaned over and kissed his forehead and brushed his lips with hers.

"Oh Tim, darling!" she exclaimed, "thank God you've come back to us. You had a close call!" Tiffany kissed him on the forehead and expressed her own greeting and expression of love and thankfulness. Peter substituted a gentle handshake for the kiss, and he seemed lost for words. He stayed a little while longer and then announced that he had to get back to work.

"That's OK, Peter. I'm so happy you were here when he woke up. I'm sure it meant a lot to both of you."

Tiffany stayed for quite a while. She was reluctant to leave Tim's side, but finally she kissed him again, turned around, hugged Becky and exclaimed,

"Oh Mom, I love him so much!" Then she smiled impishly, and said "But I suppose you two lovebirds want to be alone." Becky made a face at Tiffany as she turned and left the room.

That evening Tim had a little soup and half a glass of milk as he sat up on the side of the bed. The following day he had a light breakfast and walked a short distance in front of his room with Becky at his side to steady him. After a light lunch they walked around the nursing station. By the second day Tim was eating regular food, and he and Becky were enjoying their walks all around that large floor of the hospital. On the morning of the third day Dr. Frederickson announced that Tim could go home. He congratulated them both, and he beamed as he said,

"I've never seen such a smooth and remarkable recovery. The good Lord must be very anxious for him to get back to work."

"Thanks, Frank. I've had your usual marvelous care, and I just can't imagine receiving any more tender loving care than I've received from every member of the staff here. I have a question: how long was I out cold?"

"Let's see," the doctor replied, "you were buried alive for two days and in the ICU for three--about five days altogether."

"And I've nothing to show for it but a few minor aches and pains and a mild headache? That's remarkable! What a contrast to that long, painful ordeal in Maui--and that excruciating, and seemingly never-ending PT! I'm sure glad I didn't have to go through that again!"

"So am I Tim." the doctor responded. "Your recovery has been nothing short of miraculous; but give a lot of credit to your loving, caring family and your host of friends. Some times I feel that half the people in the greater Twin Cities have been praying for you. You can resume your normal activities. Come and see me in about a week."

The doctor hadn't been gone long before Gordon arrived. He and Tim greeted each other warmly as Becky looked on.

"How wonderful to have you back with us!" Gordon exclaimed. "I went to police headquarters yesterday to find out if it was safe for you and Becky to go home. Bless their hearts, members of their crack security squad have been spending hours every day and night, surreptitiously watching your home and the neighborhood . They travel in plain clothes and un-marked cars. There are no guarantees in this world, but they believe it is safe for you and Becky to return home and to pick up where you left off many months ago. You guys certainly deserve that--and a whole lot more."

"You and your wife have helped us so much during these challenging months. We owe you a great deal--even our very lives." Tim gave him a firm hug.

"You don't owe me a thing, my friend. I've just paid the first instalment on what I owe you. Good luck, and we'll be in touch soon."

Chapter Twenty-Two
Going National

The drive home filled Tim with the thrill of a homecoming. The closer they got the more excitement and anticipation he felt. He sat close to Becky for the entire ride. A fresh, dry snowfall had been followed by a heavy white frost that had flocked all of the trees, the light poles and any other upright objects. The sun had just emerged to illuminate this mystical scene. Tim relaxed, drank in the unsurpassed elegance and sheer beauty, and breathed a prayer of thankfulness that he was alive to enjoy it.

It was the last day of the twentieth century. Preachers of the apocalypse and millennium held forth in parks and street corners, each with a little group of followers, some with small carry-on bags, others with only the clothes they wore. All were waiting expectantly to be snatched up to their eternal glory. The nearer Tim and Becky came to their house, the greater Tim's excitement grew. Finally he exclaimed,

"You know what honey, I've a strong vision of a celebration that I can't explain. I know it's New Year's Eve and a very special one at that, but that doesn't account for what I feel."

"You've every reason to feel happy and excited, lover. It *is* a great day, and we've got so much to celebrate."

Becky drove into the garage and suggested that Tim go ahead while she retrieved the small bag with the clothes and other belongings he had with him in the hospital. His vision quickly turned into reality as he saw balloons and streamers festooning every room. Each room had its own colored banner and a different message,

WELCOME HOME, TIM AND BECKY
CONGRATULATIONS!
WE LOVE YOU BOTH
HAIL, THE CONQUERING HERO COMES!

Gordon Springborn stood in the living room doorway and greeted Tim with an enthusiastic hug. His wife, Sylvia, did the same for Becky and added a kiss on each cheek. Mrs. Schatz emerged from the kitchen with a tray containing four glasses sparkling with champagne and quickly returned to the kitchen. Peter and a beaming Tiffany appeared from the dining room. Other guests appeared on the stairway from the second floor. The president and the chairman of the board of Abbott-Northwestern Hospital, accompanied by their wives, greeted and congratulated Tim and Becky. They were followed by the three meeting coordinators and many other leaders of the community meetings. Gordon had hired uniformed maids who passed trays of champagne and hors d'oeuvres and collected the empty glasses.

After recovering from his initial surprise, Tim graciously accepted a toast to his miraculous recovery and continued good health. Then he began to mingle with the many friends who had gathered to honor him. As the first guests left, others took their place in what seemed like an endless succession of dignitaries, including the mayors of many of the communities, the chairman and executive director of the Metropolitan Council, the president and executive director of the Citizens League, and many other civic organizations. Each briefly expressed his or her thanks and grateful appreciation to Tim and Becky for their dedicated efforts to improve the quality of elected officials, and to restore a tone of decency and meaning to the campaign process and its media coverage.

The celebration lasted all afternoon. Becky and Tim had lost all track of time and had given up trying to estimate the number of guests who had come and gone. They had both been buoyed by the spirit of celebration, but they quickly collapsed on the sofa when the last guest had departed. Shortly afterward, Mrs. Schatz set up TV trays in front of them and served them a light supper. They ate in thoughtful silence for a few minutes until Becky spoke:

"You know lover, there were times when I wondered whether the community really appreciated all of our efforts; but today they left no doubt."

"That's for sure, Honey; but I always had a feeling of satisfaction and fulfillment. I did wonder though, whether I was justified in exposing my family to the risk and hardship, particularly you."

"But you made even that into an exciting and romantic adventure. And never once did those terrorists have even a clue as to who Terry Erickson and Rachel Bromfeld really were."

"Well, I'm *very* thankful it's all behind us, and extremely grateful to a merciful Providence that we're all survivors--except for those four poor souls who lost their lives."

They snuggled close in loving silence, until Tim found himself nodding frequently and announced,

"Now honey, I'm ready to turn in before I fall on the floor."

"Me too, lover!"

At the top of the stairs Tim turned and kissed her ardently in a long, tight embrace,

"Happy New Year, honey!"

"And a Happy New Century to you, lover!"

When they had finished their preparations and climbed into bed, Tim pulled her close and murmured,

"Honey I've dreamed of this day so many times during our exile. It seems forever since we've been able to snuggle in our very own bed."

Before she could even reply, he was sound asleep.

The following morning, after a leisurely breakfast, Tim adjourned to his office to attack the mountain of mail that had accumulated. Becky had not had a chance to perform her usually efficient task of opening the mail and sorting it so that he could look at the most urgent items first; so he quickly did so. On top of the urgent pile he had placed an envelope from the office of the Mayor of Philadelphia. He opened it eagerly and read it. The text read:

My Dear Mr. Hamilton:

We have watched with close and admiring interest your inspiring meetings in St. Paul and Minneapolis and their suburbs. We are particularly impressed with the reports we have received from various government officials and other community leaders whom we have queried.

Our community leaders are eager to run a similar program in Philadelphia and its environs. If you have a manual or handbook that you use to organize and operate these meetings, would it be possible for you to send us a copy? The other community leaders will be grateful for anything you can do to help us start a program like the wonderful one you and your associates ran in Minnesota.

I remain yours very truly,

Willie Parsons
Mayor
City of Philadelphia

As soon as Tim had finished reading the letter, he ran excitedly downstairs to show it to Becky, exclaiming when he entered her office,

"We're going national! We're going national!" Becky read the letter quickly and exclaimed,

"That's great, darling! I thought this would happen, but not quite this quickly."

"Now, what are we going to send him? In my spare time at the Country Inn, I did get a lot of my thoughts onto diskettes, but I could hardly call it a manual or a handbook."

"And I have a ton of notes. I can say the same thing about them."

"Why don't we co-author a book on the subject? I think that could be a very worthwhile effort--and an exciting project."

"So do I, Lover. How do you want to go about it?"

"Give me a few hours and I'll draft a table of contents for you to improve on."

"What'll you tell the Mayor?"

"There's a FAX number on his stationery. I'll FAX him a note saying that we're in the process of writing a handbook, and that it'll be a few weeks before it'll be in shape for him to use. And now, before I get started, may I seal the deal with my co-author with a kiss?"

"You'd darn well better do that, mister editor-in-chief!" She held out her arms as she spoke.

Except for a phone call to Gordon Springborn, thanking him for organizing the celebration, and the FAX to the mayor, Tim left the rest of his telephoning and his mail so that he could get right to work on the table of contents. After a couple of hours he came downstairs for his usual ritual of "forcing fluids." This was a term Tim had picked up from his hospital experience. Every morning and afternoon he and Becky would take a short break from their activities to enjoy a refreshing glass of iced tea, lemonade, or some other cold drink. Tim's favorite was a fifty-fifty blend of the first two. Some times he would "spike" his with a little bit of lemon-flavored soda. While they were enjoying forcing fluids, Becky asked,

"How's the outline coming, lover?"

"Pretty good, honey. If you don't mind having a late lunch, I'd like to finish the outline before I eat. Then, if it fits your schedule, you can do your thing with it while I catch up on my phone calls and look at the rest of my mail."

"That sounds good to me, let's go for it!"

A little after one o'clock Tim came downstairs with a couple of pages in his hand and hurried into the kitchen.

"Here it is, Honey. It needs a lot of your TLC. Please feel free to pick it apart and make suggestions. Remember this is *our* book."

During lunch, they talked excitedly about the project.

"What are we going to name our new baby, lover?

"I've been thinking about that, but I haven't come up with any brilliant ideas. Unless you have a bright idea, why don't we just wait until one of us does. Now tell me, which chapters would *you* like to write?

She studied the outline and put a "B" in front of several of the chapters, and a "BT" in front of a few.

"You forgot the lettuce; that should be BLT!" he exclaimed with a grin.

She stuck her tongue out at him. "That's for the ones we'll both have to work on! Now tell me. How are you going to find a publisher?"

"I think we can publish the first copies of the book ourselves. I thought I'd call the mayor's office in Philadelphia and see how many copies they would like. Then I'll add a few dozen to that for samples. Then we can ask Kinko's to run the copies and spiral bind them. You've more DTP (desk top publishing) skills than I have. How would you like to use your wonderful new Word Perfect 9.0, design the cover for us, and make the camera-ready copy for the printer?"

"Flattery will get you somewhere. Keep talking."

It was Tim's turn to make a face.

"We can edit each other's copy. OK honey, let's get back to work. We've got lots to do." Whereupon they retired to their own offices.

Chapter Twenty-Three
Author and Publisher

At dinner that evening Becky said, with a challenging glint in her eye, "So you've become an author *and* a publisher in less than one full day. How much are you going to charge for our first opus?" Becky asked.

" What do you think of $50 a copy? Then we could offer quantity discounts, say 10% for two to five, 20% for six to ten, 30% for 11 to 50, and 40% for 51 or more."

"Say, you really have been thinking about this. How about another 10% for non-profits? What're you going to do with money?"

"What money? Timbeck Publishing will probably operate at a loss, so we'll incorporate it and elect Subchapter S. That way we have some protection from personal lawsuits and the losses help keep down our income taxes."

"Where in the world did that name come from?"

"As Tarzan said to Jane in the old movie I loved, 'Me Tim, you Beck.' We need a board of directors. I'd like it if you would be the Vice President, Tiffany the Secretary, and Peter another member of the board. "

"Is it worth going to the expense and trouble of incorporating for such a small operation?"

"Oh yes, there are many advantages in addition to the ones I've named already."

"Name five."

"Gee, you're a tough vice president! But here goes: Number one, much more favorable tax treatment of my car. Timbeck will own my new car, which I plan to buy in the next few weeks. It will pay all of the operating expenses and absorb the depreciation, which as you know, is a very sizable item."

"But most of the miles you put on the car are for all of the community service that you do, and not for the publishing business."

"Timbeck's board will encourage me to be a good community citizen and cover the car expense for that work, so I don't even have to keep track of that mileage separately."

"But you use the car for personal purposes, too."

"When we go somewhere together, we always take your car. For the first year, I will log the personal miles I put on my car and pay Timbeck for those miles at the same low rate the IRS allows for the use of your car for charitable purposes. After that, I will take the same number of miles annually as long as my life style doesn't change."

"Does IRS allow you to do that?"

"There's no specific provision for it in the code or the regs, but I believe it is fair."

"But they put people in jail for breaking the law!"

"We won't be breaking the law, honey. There's no specific provision prohibiting this approach."

"Won't it cause you a lot of trouble when you're audited?"

"Of all my friends who have Sub-S corporations, I don't know of a single one that's ever been audited. IRS has bigger fish to fry. Except for fraud, they can't go back more than three years. And if they do prevail, there would be no penalties, only interest on the deficiency amounts, and we would have had the use of that money."

"All right, what's number two?"

"All of my other community service expenses are reimbursable and deductible by Timbeck, making them a net tax deduction to us. The only exception is meals. In the early 90's they were only 20% deductible, but that has been restored to 50%. Number three, a Sub-S can establish a self-funded health insurance plan. (that was taken out of the code a couple of decades ago, but it was restored a few years ago. Timbeck's board will pass a resolution creating such a plan. It will cover 100% of all of our health care expenses not covered by any other plan of insurance. That way we have a deduction for the medical expense we incur without the large exclusion that now hits us on our 1040."

"Number four, by capitalizing Timbeck for a nominal amount, say $1,000, and loaning it the rest of the money needed to operate, it is continually indebted to us. That way, we can withdraw freely any excess cash it accumulates, say after a large book order is paid for. That way, I never get in the position of having imputed salary, on which I would incur all sorts of payroll taxes and have a lot more paper work than I would want to do. Number five, if I receive speaking fees or honoraria, they become related income to Timbeck and can be used to offset some of the losses and help to provide operating cash, when needed. Otherwise, I would have to take them directly on my 1040 and be subject to self-employment taxes, which can get pretty steep."

"OK lover, you've made your quota." [1]

---

[1] This is a novel. The reader should consult a tax adviser on these matters.

"But I'm not even to the most important ones yet. Number six, I can pass all of Timbeck's operating losses directly to our 1040 without limit. This is in contrast to capital losses from investments, which are limited to $3,000 a year. What's more, you can take those losses each year as they occur, as opposed to investment losses on our 1040 where we have to wait until the company goes broke, or you liquidate your holdings, before you can take *any* of your losses."

"That's an impressive list of advantages. Where'd you learn so much about the tax laws?"

"One of the many advantages of being on boards of major non-profits is that you rub elbows with some very erudite people. If you listen and ask the right questions, you can learn a great deal."

"Don't they feel that you're imposing on them?"

"*Au contraire*, they're flattered, just as you and I are, to feel that someone thinks highly enough of them to consult them. And remember, these are very giving people, or they wouldn't take their precious time to be on the board in the first place. Well honey, there's lots for both of us to do, and we must be at it. We don't want to keep the mayor waiting." He gave her a big hug before they adjourned to their offices.

Tim and Becky made the writing and publishing of the handbook their top priority until they delivered the "camera ready" copy to Kinko's for the printing and spiral binding of the first 100 copies. Instead of the three or four weeks Tim had hoped for, it had taken over six weeks to complete the process. Somewhere in the middle of their efforts, Becky remarked,

"You know, lover, we haven't named the baby yet. Why don't we simply call it Improving the Effectiveness of Elected Officials Through Community Meetings Underneath that put Handbook and Guidelines."

"There you go again Honey, showing your genius! I like it."

When Kinko's finished the printing and binding, Tim sent a complimentary copy to the mayor of Philadelphia, along with an order form that showed the prices for larger quantities and asked for full payment with the order. The order for 75 copies came back by return mail with a check in full payment. Becky packed them neatly in boxes and sent them by UPS the next day. About two years earlier, UPS had raised its prices significantly for packages going more than 400 miles but now sent them all by air, thus insuring two-day delivery.

After making a substantial dent in the paperwork that had accumulated on his desk, Tim wrote an article with the same title as the handbook (except, of course, for the words "Handbook and Guidelines"). When he gave it to Becky to edit, he asked,

"I plan to submit this to <u>Readers Digest</u>. What do you think?"

When she gave it back to him with her corrections and minor suggestions, she said,

"It's not too."

"It's *what*?"

"It's not too long and not too short. I think it's just right. I'll bet they accept it."

Thus encouraged, Tim sent it Priority Mail, hoping to get their prompt reaction. They were both right. It wasn't quite two weeks before Tim received a letter from a senior editor that read,

Dear Mr. Hamilton,

Your article is well written and should be of great interest to many community leaders. We propose to pay you $2,500 within 15 days after we receive your acceptance for all rights to the article, including the right to sell reprints. Please FAX us as soon as possible, telling us whether these terms are acceptable. If they are, we expect to publish the article in our June issue.

Thank you for your excellent submission.

Kindest regards,

Tim wasted no time in FAXing his reply and sharing the good news with Becky:

"Honey, I've dreamed of the day when this would happen. We couldn't buy the wonderful publicity that this article will bring us! I'd better get busy lining up a printer so that we'll have an adequate supply of handbooks to take care of the orders. Do you think Tiffany would like to provide fulfillment service?"

"Perhaps, lover. You would have to ask her. What does fulfillment mean in the publishing business?"

"In the usual sense it includes storage, order filling, packaging, mailing, billing and accounts receivable. I'll have our favorite carpenter partition off an area in the basement to store the books, and I was hoping you would do the billing and accounts receivable."

"I think I could handle that; but you'll have to kiss your billing and accounts receivable manager every morning."

"And I can handle that. In fact, if she does a good job I'll double her salary!"

The following morning he called the two largest book printers in the area and asked them for prices on 1,000, 3,000 and 5,000 copies of the handbook. He discovered that they wanted many answers to a lot of questions he hadn't thought about, such as how many pages (he estimated about 225); the dimensions of the book; what kind of cover (hard or soft, if hard did he want a dust jacket, if soft did he want it coated, black and white or four-color, would he furnish the color separations (a film for each primary color), what kind of binding, what quality of paper (acid-free or pulp), in what form would the text come (camera-ready copy preferred). He made a quick trip to the library and came home with a couple of books about publishing. He pored over these books until he felt he had all of the answers to the questions the printer had asked.

The days seemed to fly by as Tim immersed himself in the activities of an independent publisher. He joined the Midwest Independent Publishers Association (often called just MIPA), attended their meetings, listened intently to the informative speakers, picked brains before and after the meetings, and read all of their newsletters from front to back. He took a short course on publishing and bought a copy of the handbook that the speaker had written. He found it very encouraging that he brought more to the table as a new publisher than the instructor had when she had started out. She had been an English teacher with no background in business, and Tim realized how valuable his business experience was in his new venture.

Then came the great day when Becky practically ran up stairs breathless with excitement, waving the Readers Digest with his article in it.

"Oh Tim, you made it, complete with the requests for reprints!" she exclaimed.

He read it eagerly and was pleased to note that they had not changed very much. He jumped up from his chair, took Becky in his arms, and they did a little dance around the room together.

By the time the books were delivered by the printer, orders for almost a thousand copies had accumulated. Tim was glad he had ordered 5,000 copies, but he had been unable to appreciate fully what 100 cases of books would look like. When he realized that they weighed over a ton, he was glad that he had enlisted Peter and Gordon to help him and the truck driver unload the books and store them in their new "warehouse." (Tim had removed a basement window and placed a plank extending from the window ledge down to the basement floor. They then slid the cases down the board. It was almost dinner time when they finished. The driver hurried off, and Tim invited the others to dinner to thank them for their efforts. Gordon said he had other plans and left as soon as Tim had given him a warm hug and his profuse thanks. So the Hamilton family went to dinner and discussed their new venture excitedly. Even Peter seemed to be caught up in the fervor and proposed a toast to Tim's new business venture. They all retired early, Peter to his own apartment and the rest of the family to their own home, where Tiffany had agreed to stay over night.

The next morning, after a quick breakfast, Tim, Becky and Tiffany all worked eagerly at their fulfillment task, and they enjoyed their new activity immensely. It was late in the afternoon when Tiffany announced that she had filled the last order. Tim had been carrying the boxes and packages up to his minivan. Only when he slid into the driver's seat and headed for the UPS office did he realize how tired he was; but he was extremely happy at how well things had gone. His careful planning to have all the necessary packaging supplies on hand had paid off. He was glad he had discussed the planning with Becky and had taken most of her helpful suggestions.

In the weeks that followed Tim spent part of each day working on the manuscript of a book he had wanted to write ever since their community meetings had been so successful. The book covered the same subject as the Readers Digest article, but in much greater detail. Becky read each chapter eagerly as it came out of the laser printer; she found many mechanical errors and also had a number of helpful suggestions concerning the content. Tim had decided that he would need a professional editor to help him produce a book that was up to the high standards he wanted to achieve. He found the process of selecting a suitable editor to be quite challenging. How would he know a good editor from a bad one? He decided he would have to learn something about editing in order to answer that question. So once again he visited the library and came home with a couple of books about editing. By networking with his new friends in MIPA, he came up with the names and telephone numbers of over a dozen of them. He called each one to see if they had any interest. When he had accumulated six affirmative replies, he prepared an RFP (request for proposal) and mailed a copy to each of the six. When he had five replies, he picked what looked like the best three and arranged interviews with each of them. From these he picked two: one who had the depth and breadth of experience Tim felt would help him improve the literary quality of the book, and the other to catch grammar and composition errors. He gave them each a contract to do the first five chapters with the clear understanding that they might not be retained to do the rest of the book. When they had both finished their work, he was delighted to find that the one with the depth and breadth he wanted was also excellent at the mechanical aspects. The other one was so disappointed that she actually shed a few tears; and Tim felt sad at not feeling justified in retaining them both.

Tim had heard many war stories about authors becoming very angry with their editors, almost coming to blows in some cases. To his great delight, he became good friends with his editor and enjoyed their relationship immensely. Although he found writing to be much more work than he had realized, he continued to enjoy every minute he spent at it. And thus was his career as an author and a publisher launched.

Chapter Twenty-Four
Going International

The years went by quickly. Tim continued to grow and expand Timbeck, the independent publishing company that Becky and he had established originally to supply the demand for manuals on how to run a series of successful community meetings. He had written several novels, all with a common theme: changing the minds and hearts of enough voters so that good candidates would again run for office and, in most cases, prevail over those who were still being bought by the special interests and those who depended on pork barrel politics to hold office. Tim had succeeded beyond his fondest dreams in seeing the movement expand to almost every major community and population center in the country. As a result of these meetings that he had sparked, the national political scene had changed dramatically for the better.

Politics had reached its lowest ebb around the turn of the century. Many of the highly principled members of the congress had refused to run for re-election. Most were too polite to say that they were totally nauseated by the way so many members conducted themselves. Senators personally vilified each other and became so heated and intemperate that a few had come to blows right in their hallowed chambers. Dignity and personal respect were relics of the past and currently were used only as forms of sarcasm and derision. Good candidates could rarely be persuaded to run; when they did, they and their families were often ruined by the personal attacks of less principled candidates who had no qualms about spreading lies and half-truths that could ruin careers and mangle family relationships. The rare good candidates who survived such scurrilous attacks still usually lost to the candidates representing special interests who had expensive spin doctors to coach them in the hypocritical demagoguery designed to appeal to the selfish interests of the majority of voters. The cynical joke most frequently heard was that "we have the best congress money can buy."

The resulting effect was a nation rapidly heading toward disaster. Few elected officials felt any moral obligation to see that people placed in dire financial straits through no fault of their own received any financial aid, however temporary. As a result, these people took to begging in the streets with their tin cups and pencils, or to selling apples that no one was expected to take--just put a quarter in the cup. Their shelter at night was any public building to which they could gain entry. The police were ordered to move them into the streets; but they could not be totally successful because of the sheer masses of these people--also because some police were too soft-hearted to drive these lightly clothed people into the sub-zero night. Worse yet, the "get-tough on-crime philosophy flourished, even though that approach had failed miserably for years. Each year the masses of inner city youth burgeoned and the crime rate grew uncontrollably. Billions were spent every year on new prisons, while little or no money was appropriated for programs that might strike at the roots of inner city crime by giving these young people hope of making it in the establishment. The few congressmen who dared to suggest that these programs be strengthened were labeled as fuzzy-headed, spendthrift liberals, and lampooned derisively by their opponents, *despite the fact that more than three quarters of America's police chiefs had gone on record as believing that this approach was the best, if not the only, way to make serious inroads on the* problem. The movement that Tim had sparked had gone a long way toward replacing these vipers with good congressmen who voted their consciences. But it would be a few years yet before they gained enough seniority to pass legislation that would really deal with problems of our cities. And it would be a number of years after that before the results of these good policies would show significant results.

Tim was in tremendous demand as a public speaker, but he declined most of the invitations for two reasons, both of which grew out of his strong sense of obligation to his family. First, he had never forgotten the wake-up call Tiffany had given him so dramatically almost a decade before, which had sparked him to reduce his community service work load from 70 or more hours a week to not more than 50 hours a week. This assured his family that he did, in fact, have all the time they wanted to spend together, and that they were his first love and his first priority. The other reason was his family's concern for his safety. He had found two more bodyguards to replace the men who had tragically given their lives in defense of Tim's in that dreadful pipe bomb incident. Tim had vowed that he would never again place another human being in that precarious position. The new guards were happy to be retained as Tim's security consultants. Their only duty was to see that the physical arrangements for Tim's security met the standards that they and Tim had agreed on. Whenever he declined to speak, he always offered a copy of his notes so that an inspirational speaker in the requester's locality could take his place.

The handbooks had gone through repeated reprints. Tiffany's order-filling activities were no longer consonant with the rest of her life style, so Tim had replaced her services with those of Peter's 13-year-old son, Tommy. He was an eager boy and a quick learner; and he loved to help "Gramps" with this service. He had not lost that eclectic curiosity that develops at the age of four, and he wanted to know everything there was to know about the publishing business. Tim was delighted at his interest, and he answered each question patiently. On a typical Saturday morning the conversation might start with Tommy asking,

"Gramps what's that gadget in the corner?"

"Tommy, that's a scale that tells me how much it's going to cost to ship each package."

"I thought scales weighed in pounds. How come this scale weighs in dollars; how does it know how many dollars it takes to ship that package you've got in your hands? Huh, Gramps, how does it know? Are you kidding me?"

"No, Tommy, I'm not kidding you. Watch and I'll explain it. You see that map on the wall?"

"Yeah, I see it. What a funny map. It's got all sorts of circles on it; each circle has a smaller cycle , right smack inside it; an' Minneapolis is smack dab in the middle of the tiniest circle. What're they for, huh Gramps? Whatayado with that silly map?" Tommy broke into gales of laughter and Tim joined him. Just then Tommy's mother entered the room and said,

"Tommy, are you bothering Grandpa when he's trying to work? Can't you see he's busy?" Before Tommy could reply Tim answered,

"*Au contraire*, Glenda, he's helping me and learning all he can about the business. He's the best I could ever dream of. I never have to tell him anything twice. Give him another year or two and he'll be ready to take over the complete operation here. And, if he continues with anything like his present interest and enthusiasm, he'll own a flourishing publishing company some day." Tommy's chest expanded visibly with pride, as he looked defiantly at his mother.

"But he has to finish high school and go to college--"

"And continue until he has his MBA." Tim finished her sentence. No prob*lem*, Mon, as the Grand Cayman natives say, Timbeck publishing will still be going strong when he graduates." Tim watched Tommy closely as he spoke, and he liked the dreamy faraway look that appeared in Tommy's eyes. Tim had planted a seed and hoped that it would grow; but he would never urge Tommy into the business if he had his heart set on another career. Tim patiently continued his explanation of the various shipping zones, why Minneapolis was in the center of the circles, and how he keyed the zone into the scale, and how the scale had a little computer in it that showed dollars as well as pounds.

"That's cool, Gramps! Can I do one now? Please, Gramps let me do one, Will ya?" he urged, almost jumping up and down with excitement..

"Of course you can, Tommy. This one's going to Jacksonville, Florida. You know where that is on the map?"

"I can find Florida, that's the one that sticks down in the far right corner. Jacksonville's the capital; but I've forgotten where it is."

"Look in the northern part." Tim prompted. And so it went with each operation. In a very few months, he was putting meter slips on the packages; and, with a little prompting, he was using the computer to create the packing slip and the invoice.

"Gee, Gramps, this is fun! You have fun like this with all of your work?"

"I'm a very fortunate man, Tommy; I enjoy almost everything I do. Only about one in five people in this world are that fortunate."

"Why do the rest of them work if they don't have fun at it?"

"They work to buy food and clothing for them and their families, pay the light bill, the rent and all of the other expenses of running a home."

"Don't they have any fun in life?"

"Yeah, Tommy, they're able to set aside a little money to take the family to a movie once in a while, or take them fishing, or even go away for a vacation for a week, or even two weeks, once a year. The rest of the time they work for a living, and just look forward to quitting time."

"Why don't they enjoy their work like you do, Gramps?"

"That's a long story, son. I think you'd better save that question for a year or so, and I'll try to explain it. But don't forget to ask me again, Tommy, because that's a very good question.

Becky appeared on the scene and announced,

"OK you guys, it's time to knock off work. Grandpa needs to get dressed. We're celebrating his big seven-oh this noon in a special way. I'm taking him to lunch at the Turret.

"What's the Turret, Gram."

"That's the restaurant on the 58th floor of the new Radisson Hotel, the one down by the river, right on the very top of that tall building. It's perfectly round, and the whole floor revolves, inside and out. You can see all the way into Western Wisconsin and across Lake Minnetonka on a clear day, and we're having more of them now that the new super-clean air act is really being enforced."

"Gee, Gram. That's sounds really cool; can I go too?"

"Yes, Tommy, but not tonight. I've made reservations only for six."

"Who-all's goin' then?" His face fell.

"Just Gramps and I, your Mom and Dad and Tiffany and her friend."

"I sure wish I could go." Tommy looked as if he was going to cry.

"I'll tell you what, Tommy. You and I'll go there to celebrate your 14th birthday. That'll be our very own special occasion. How'd that be?

" Wow! That'll be neat, just you and me. I'll go right home and mark it with a big red circle on my calendar."

He rushed over and gave Becky a big, warm hug.

"OK, Tommy. Now Gramps and I have to hurry. Lunch is at one o'clock."

"You sound mysterious, honey. What's going on?"

"Don't ask questions, lover. You'll find out in due time." She had a merry twinkle in her eye. The years had been kind to Becky, who wasn't far from the big seven-oh herself. In Tim's eyes, especially, she was more beautiful than ever; and he told her so frequently.

After a gourmet lunch with all of Tim's favorite foods, Becky piled them all into her large sedan and drove to her favorite Cadillac dealer in St. Louis Park, where Sonia, the sales woman Becky always asked for, was waiting expectantly for them. She led them to a beautiful, sleek, metallic gold vehicle sitting just outside the showroom. It was shaped like a torpedo, but held six people in luxurious comfort inside. Sonia explained that the car was electrically powered by light-weight, deep-discharge batteries that were being recharged by the newly designed voltaic cells in the car's roof, which drew energy from the energy in the sky whenever the car was outside during daylight hours even though the sun wasn't shining. She opened the driver's door for Tim and announced,

"I'll sit next to Mr. Hamilton and explain the options to him. He'll open all of the windows so you can all hear what I'm saying."

After Tim slid into the driver's seat, Sonia got into the front passenger seat and said,

"Say 'all down'". Tim did so, and all of windows slid open quickly and noiselessly.

"But why didn't they open when you said it?"

"All of the controls answer only to your voice and Mrs. Hamilton's."

"But what if we want to let someone else drive?" Sonia handed Tim a small plastic box with two buttons on it: one red and the other green. She reached out of the window and handed another one to Becky.

"These are your keys. Press the green button and the car will respond to any voice. Press the red one and it'll respond only to yours and Mrs. Hamilton's."

"What if we lose our key?"

"The car will still respond to your voices. But you'll still need the keys to give to your serviceman or chauffeur, so that he or she can drive it. There's another option. Let's say your chauffeur's name is Fred. When he comes to work for you, you say 'New voice: Fred'. He recites the first verse of *Mary Had a Little Lamb* and he becomes an authorized driver."

"What if Fred leaves me?"

"You just say, 'Cancel Fred', and Fred can't drive your beautiful Auto-Electra any more."

Tim went to turn the small steering wheel and it spun freely in his hands.

"The steering wheel is broken!" He exclaimed.

"Not really. Just say 'steer'."

He did so and the wheel became firm with the usual feel of power steering.

"Now say 'auto-pilot.'"

He did so, and the wheel spun freely again.

"How does the auto-pilot work?"

"Are you familiar with GPS (global positioning system)?"

"Oh yes, I have it in my boat and its wonderful. But I don't see how it would work on land."

"Have you ever seen computerized precision mapping."

"I saw it on a friend's notebook computer; but how would that work in a car?"

"Just say 'computer'." Tim did so and a small computer popped out of the instrument panel.

"Now say 'show route to home'." As he did so, two maps appeared side-by-side on the screen. The one on the right was a small scale map that traced in red their route to the vicinity of their home. The one nearest Tim was a blow up with the street names. On their street was a red arrow pointing to their house with their street number displayed in large clear letters.

"That program will take you anywhere in the contiguous 48 states. You can buy additional CD's for Alaska, Hawaii and the more developed foreign countries."

"What happens when there's a change in the highways?"

"You get a new CD every two months with all the updates on it."

"What about road construction?" Tim was sure he had stumped Sonia, but she merely said,

"Before you start out, be sure your selected route for that day is on the screen. Then say, 'road construction.' Your car phone will connect you with the national mapping office; and in a few seconds your route will change to show the official detours. Where there are lane closings, the computer will ask you for your time of departure and estimated time off the road for lunch and rest stops. You might say, 'nine AM, one hour.' It will calculate your time of arrival in construction area and the extra time to get through it. If it's more delay than you care to tolerate, you say 'alternate', and it will show you an alternate route and say '30 minutes' or whatever the estimated additional time is on the best alternate route. Their files are updated by seven o'clock every morning by having their computer poll a special computer placed in the office of the construction supervisor in almost all the states, counties and cities with a population of 25,000 or more.

"That's a marvelous service, but it sounds prohibitively expensive. How much will I have to pay for this service?"

"Only 25 dollars a month."

"That's reasonable for me. I value my time at $250 an hour. This will certainly save me a lot more than six minutes a month. I can also see it being of value to oodles of sales reps and other business people. But who's subsidizing the real cost?"

"No one. The system is being built by a very wealthy, creative and foresighted capitalist who actually lives in the greater Twin Cities area. I'm told that the estimated cost of setting up this system is around 15 billion dollars; 14 billion of that is in computers placed in the thousands of government offices. But he believes that, by pricing it reasonably, he'll have over ten million subscribers within five years' time."

"But that won't pay back fifteen billion bucks."

"It doesn't have to. The government agencies agree to buy the computers and pay for them over 10 years at an interest rate much lower than their normal cost of borrowing."

"What motivates the government agencies to spend this money?"

"Cost studies show that the economic payback will exceed the cost of their debt service because of the increased efficiencies in road maintenance. The computer program makes the data base available to all foremen and sub-contractors, who must update their daily progress and their work plans for tomorrow before they leave the project each evening. This gives the top managers a much better handle on their projects than they've ever had. And, if any agency drags its feet, the department of tourism gets on their case. Well I see our guests are getting restless.

Let's have a driving lesson. One of you can sit in the front with our driver and me; the others can climb in back. We'll tool up to St. Cloud and back."

As they all climbed in, Tim protested,

"But, Sonia, that's 160 miles!"

"No sweat, that's less than half an hour each way on the new I-94 mag-track."

"I've heard about that, but I didn't pay much attention since my car couldn't use it."

She quickly gave Tim the necessary instructions to set up their route to St. Cloud, and display it on the screen. Then she exclaimed,

"It's a miracle! No road construction!"

"How do I get started?"

"Just say 'steer' and press the accelerator gently until we're out in the traffic lane." When they had moved into the traffic lane, Sonia said,

"Very good. Now just say 'auto-pilot', then say 'to St. Cloud', and sit back and enjoy the ride. The auto-pilot can deal with all of the city streets"

"How does it know how fast to go?"

"The speed limits are all in the data base."

"What if the car ahead of me is going slower than us?"

"There's radar input that won't let you get closer than two seconds of the car ahead. If the ABS detects slippery roads, the computer will increase that interval up to three seconds, or even four seconds in a glare ice condition."

"What if I see other conditions that makes me want to slow down?"

"We're still in a 30- mile-per-hour zone. If there are no cars behind us, just say '25." Tim did so and the car slowed down until the heads-up display on the windshield read 25 in large, clear numbers. Sonia continued,

"Now say 'slow'." Tim did so and the car began to slow down.

"Now say 'limit'." Tim did so and the car accelerated to 35. Tim thought something had gone wrong until he noticed a "speed limit 35" sign, and marveled silently at this high tech car. They were headed west on a frontage road that would take them to westbound I-394 on which they'd continue toward I-494, which would take them north to I-94. Sonia said,

"Now say 'compass'." When Tim said the words, the numbers 270 appeared above the 35.

"Now say 'points'." Tim did so and the a large W replaced the 270. As they approached the ramp onto I-394, Tim became tense,

"What do I do now?" He asked excitedly.

"Just sit back and relax." Tim found that difficult. Gradually, however, he did relax as the car slowed for the ramp, navigated perfectly, adjusted its speed in the acceleration lane until it found a safe interval to merge into the nearest traffic lane. Immediately it began to gather speed until the numbers read 55.

"How did that feel?" Sonia asked.

"I felt totally helpless and very apprehensive!"

"Just like you did when you turned on your first cruise control on a busy highway?"

"Yeah, only much more so!"

"But you soon became very comfortable. So will you while on autopilot in this car. What's more, this is much safer because of all of the interlocks that keep you from running into things."

"How about people running into me?"

"Believe it or not, it will prevent most of those collisions. When it senses another car on a collision course, it will do what any alert and competent driver would do: It will look at all the aspects and speed up or slow down until its input says the collision course no longer exists. And, begging your pardon, Mr. Hamilton, it does it much better than you could. It's computer brain reacts in microseconds--as compared to your relatively sluggish brain that takes tenths of a second to react, it never hesitates with uncertainty, and it never loses its concentration, day dreams, or falls asleep. You folks are in an incredibly safe car."

"What about being rear-ended.?"

When the computer senses a car approaching from the rear, it senses the traffic conditions, ahead and on each side. If they permit, it will actually jump out of the way: it will accelerate forward rapidly enough to prevent a collision. If your car is boxed in, it will set the brakes hard, and yell 'brace yourself'. If the impact is hard enough, your emergency PBPM will actuate from the impact."

"What's PBPM?"

"Personal body protection mechanism. It works like the old fashioned air bags, but it gives you a lot better protection. It completely envelopes all of your body that doesn't normally rest against the seat or the seat back. The large, soft inflated bladder protects you against impact and trauma from any direction, and deflates quickly as soon as the risk has passed."

They entered I-94, and Sonia said,

"All of you sit back in your seats, press your heads against the head rests, take a deep breath and hold it. OK, say 'mag-track'. As soon as Tim did so, the car , pulled into a special lane on the left. Then it began to accelerate at an incredible rate: five G's, close to the maximum the body can stand without blacking out or damaging internal organs. Tim felt his body pressed hard against the seat back; his vision blurred slightly, but he could still read the numbers as they changed rapidly: 55-75-100-125-150-175-200-210. In about one and half seconds the pressure stopped and everyone breathed a heavy sigh. Tiffany exclaimed,

"Wow, what a thrill. That beats anything in the amusement park!"

"It sure does!" the others chorused.

"Do we have many mag-tracks like this? They must be very expensive." Tim asked.

"This is the first one in the country to be completed, but others are being constructed. It cost almost half a billion for this 80-mile stretch, over six million dollars a mile."

"Who's paying for it?"

"The users. Before you could use this mag-track, you had to provide a valid credit card. Mrs. Hamilton took care of that, so you can settle with her. This ride is costing you fifty dollars each way. The kids won't go joy riding on it at that price. Traffic studies estimate that about one thousand cars a day will use the mag-way each way. That will pay off the 15 year bonds and allow quite a bit of room for error. Instead of reducing or eliminating the tolls after that , they will use the money to build new mag-ways."

Thanks, Sonia, for all that information. Now I have a question: How am I going to remember all of the commands?"

"You don't have to. Just say 'help'."

When Tim did so, a large alphabetic list of commands came up on the windshield.

It was just twenty minutes later that a commanding voice came out of the place where an instrument panel used to be in older cars,

"End of mag-way approaching; prepare to decelerate."

"This is only one G. It will take about 8 seconds ro decelerate to 55 miles an hour. Then we do a U turn and had back. When they had once again accelerated, Sonia said,

"Say 'St. Louis Park Cadillac' and the car will let me off in front of the showroom. When you let me off, you'll be on your own from there. Just say 'home' . The computer is programmed to take you home, open the garage door and drive right into your stall. Mrs. Hamilton and I have already tested it, so you shouldn't have any trouble."

The trip home was still exciting, but Tim felt a little more relaxed than he had on the way to St. Cloud. Tim felt some apprehension after they let Sonia off and again as the car turned into the driveway; but everything went very smoothly. The younger generation wished him many happy returns and took off in their own cars. Becky and Tim watched the evening news before they headed for bed.

"What a wonderful evening you've shown me, honey. I just don't know how it could have been more enjoyable. And that car! I'm as excited as any kid with a new toy."

He kissed her fervently.

"You deserve it, lover, and a whole lot more. You've done so much good for this world, and you continue to do so. You're a wonderful person, and I love you dearly."

A few days later, as Tim was looking at his mail, his excitement grew when he read a letter,

Most esteemed Monsieur Hamilton:

We have been watching your work in the United States very carefully in the last few years, and we have been most impressed with the incredible political reform you have accomplished. My assistant deputy and I would consider it an honor and a privilege to call on you.

If you will accord us this honor, it will be only necessary for you to call our consul in St. Paul, Madame Danielle Marceaux. Her telephone number is 291-8800. We shall eagerly await your response to Madame Marceaux.

May we extend our very best wishes for your continued good health and happiness.

I am yours most cordially and sincerely,

Renee LaValle
Deputy Minister of National Affairs
Republic of France

Tim ran excitedly down the stairs, yelling,

"Honey, we're going international! Can you believe it?"

"Yes lover, I read the letter when I opened your mail, but I wanted you to have the privilege of reading it for yourself. Congratulations, and it is exciting."

He hugged her tightly; they danced out of the kitchen, and he continued to dance with her until they were both

breathless and collapsed onto the sofa. As they rested on the sofa, Tim kissed her repeatedly and murmured,
       "Thanks for all of your wonderful help, Honey. It doesn't get any better than this."

Chapter Twenty-Five
Fulfillment

The meeting with the French Deputy and her assistant went very smoothly. Tim had started it out properly by hosting a lavish dinner in their honor at the Minneapolis Club where he had reserved a private dining room. Tim had included the mayors of both Minneapolis and St. Paul and their spouses, and the Governor and her husband. Complimentary toasts were drunk and the speeches were flowery, but thankfully brief. The next day they met in the consul's office. The discussions were pleasant and, by and large, agreeable with one exception. They wanted Tim to come and speak to a large assembly of provincial and city leaders. Tim graciously declined, saying,

"Ladies and gentlemen, you have conferred a great honor upon me with your invitation to come and speak. Unfortunately, I am still a target of extremists who somehow construe our movement as a threat to their religions. Out of consideration for my family , I have made it a policy to decline all requests for public appearances. Too many lives have been lost in these persistent devils' attempts on my life. Fortunately, I've been spared to continue with my mission, which I intend to carry on as long as I'm able. I know that you have superb security in your country, but these terrorists are incredibly clever. I will assist you in every way I possibly can, short of an actual visit to your country."

The Deputy Minister was very gracious about his refusal. She said that she understood and respected his position, and that she wished to do nothing that would compromise his safety or that of others. She went on to say that they were, of course, disappointed that he could not appear in person, but that they would gladly accept any help he could give them in initiating a movement similar to the one that had been so successful in the United States.

Becky and Tim agreed to transfer exclusive rights for the Republic of France and its protectorates only for the sum of ten million dollars, payable in US currency upon execution of the papers. The contract gave France the right to translate into French and print all of Tim's work. That evening the Governor gave the French officials a good send-off by hosting a reception in their honor to which she invited almost 200 dignitaries. The reception was followed by a dinner party for the same group that Tim had hosted the previous night.

Tim ask that the Republic of France pay the money directly into two donor advised accounts, one at the Minneapolis Foundation and the other at the St. Paul Foundation. He and Becky had decided to split the money, since they felt that they were citizens of the greater Twin Cities community. Under these donor advisory agreements, they could advise the foundations of good charities and other causes that they felt were worthy. The foundations always followed their advice, even though they had no contractual or legal obligation to do so.

The years flew by as Tim and Becky continued to see Timbeck Publishing flourish. The funds in the donor advisory accounts were greatly augmented by the proceeds of similar sales to the UK, Germany, Italy, Spain, Japan and several other countries.

Tom (he had ceased to be Tommy before he graduated from high school) had graduated from college, and he had gone on to earn a summa cum laude MBA. He was delighted to accept Tim's offer to become COO of Timbeck, and he was doing an outstanding job, much to Tim's gratification. As a way to increase Tom's compensation Tim gave him full time use of his new, torpedo-like voice-controlled Cadillac Auto-Electra. (Becky had replaced the 10-year-old car on his big eight-oh with the new model, which had improvements beyond Tim's wildest imagination). Becky, as Senior Vice President, handled all of the correspondence with the help of two secretaries; and Tim signed only the most important letters. They had a full time editor, a full time bookkeeper, a telephone receptionist, and a mail clerk and gopher in the person of Tiffany's 13-year-old son. One thing they didn't need was a marketing manager or a sales vice president. Tim was kept quite busy just responding to publishers who wanted to buy Timbeck. Tim turned many of them down flatly. With several others he negotiated non-exclusive rights to publish his books in both hard and soft covers, but strictly excepting other rights, including but not limited to movie rights, TV rights, serial rights, rights in other countries, rights to publish in electronic form, or using any other medium, and so on.

The rush from other countries to establish his program had subsided, but there were still one or two a year. Tim had pretty well followed the pattern that had been so successful with France. It had worked well with all of the countries except Korea, whose officials walked out in a huff, saying Tim had offended them and caused them to lose face by refusing their invitation to come to their beautiful land. The many millions had augmented their donor advisory accounts so that Becky and Tim had become the largest philanthropists in Minnesota and one of the ten largest in the nation. To carry on their philanthropy after their deaths, they had amended their contracts with the foundations to have their children succeed them as advisors after Tim and Becky died. The codicils to their wills also remembered over 50 of their favorite charities directly. This brought them celebrity status in most of these charities, which Becky and Tim allowed only when the organizations assured them that such action provided impetus for other wealthy people to follow suit.

Despite all of the delegation of duties, Tim's remaining duties at Timbeck consumed so much time that Tim, once again, had to find ways to reduce his burgeoning work load. Much to his regret, he felt required to resign from most of the boards on which he had been serving, despite his great love for, and devotion to these organizations. He resolved to increase several-fold his already very major contributions to these organizations. In his discussions of the subject with Becky he referred to it jokingly as "buying his way out."

Despite their preoccupation with Timbeck, Becky and Tim took time for frequent travel. They particularly enjoyed the new nuclear-powered air boats that glided over the roughest seas on a cushion of air at 80 to 90 knots. These sleek, streamlined thousand-foot leviathans were reserved for the longer cruises: such as, Los Angeles to Auckland, New Zealand in just a little over two days and two nights. For pleasure travel they were giving the jet planes a run for their money because of their cheaper fares and greater luxury and aura of romance. Life had not been without its losses. Despite many advances in medical science Tim was beginning to have TIA (a disease like a series of temporary strokes) symptoms. His internist put him on an anticoagulant. Instead of the massive doses of vitamins (Beta-Carotene, Vitamin C and vitamin E) and selenium that used to be prescribed as an anti-oxidant formula, his internist gave him a prescription that he said would do as well or better. The treatment was designed to prevent strokes, but Tim had already had a slight stroke that cost him the macular vision in the entire left half of both eyes. For several days he couldn't read, play tennis, count his cards at the bridge table, or do anything that required the use of his eyes. Happily, his brain seemed to compensate for this loss, to the point where he could function again. Gradually, he became so competent at using the good right half of each eye that he rarely even thought about the loss.

Becky and Tim still enjoyed tennis. They played 12 sets a week in the winter months when they couldn't ride their bicycle. In the warmer months they rode the bike, which was four-wheeled, with two semi-recumbent seats side by side. Called Just Two Bikes (JTB for short), this style had become popular before the turn of the century. Tim and the man who invented and manufactured this machine had become good friends the day Tim bought his first one. They and their wives rode many bike classics together, traveling across the state of Minnesota several times, as well as numerous shorter rides. The early models attracted a great deal of interest, but they were quite pricey and too heavy (over 100 pounds) to catch on very quickly. But stronger, lighter, and cheaper alloys, together with mass production methods had greatly reduced both price and weight . Their popularity had rapidly increased so that by the turn of the century they were more common than the older two wheelers. Good bike paths had proliferated, and with them the popularity of biking had burgeoned. It was now possible to ride almost anywhere in the country, and down town in most cities, without ever being exposed to the hazards of sharing traffic lanes with cars. Minnesota had led the nation in the development of bike paths. An early one connected the Twin Cities with Duluth, 150 miles to the north. Over a thousand of the state's beautiful lakes were circled with bike paths, many of which ringed the shoreline with an almost uninterrupted view of the water. Many had predicted that this could never happen; but as bicycling increased, the biker lobby became so powerful that many counties had changed their tax laws so that taxes on lake front property were almost confiscatory if the owners refused to grant an easement for a bike path along their shoreline. In return, heavy fines were imposed on bikers who trespassed, littered, made loud noises or committed any other nuisance on a bike path; and those paths that ringed lakes were strictly patrolled.

Just before his 85th birthday, Tim had a stroke that left his right leg completely paralyzed. The incident didn't seem to dampen his high spirits or spoil his sense of humor or hearty enjoyment of a good joke. While he was in the hospital he received a card from Tiffany that read:

Did you know that hospitals use water for drinking and alcohol for your bath. So git on home here as fast as you can.

Another one from Tom read:

Never give money to a nurse. They're all panhandlers, you know.

His leg resisted all his and the physical therapists' heroic attempts at rehabilitation. So Tim ordered a three-wheeled electric cart. He seemed to enjoy tooling around in it. He and Becky equipped their mini-van with an electric lift and special equipment for the driver's area so that he could actually drive himself. But he preferred to be driven; and he drove himself only in the neighborhood on occasional short errands. His tennis career was ended, but his biking career flourished. Becky became the "pilot" (she occupied the left seat, did the steering and handled both front wheel brakes, which were controlled with one lever). Tim became the "co-pilot", whose station was equipped with a hand crank option which the creative inventor had introduced almost three decades ago. When Becky was unable to function as the pilot, other family members and friends gladly filled in.

On his "big nine-oh" the governor hosted a grand open house in his honor with a guest list of over 500 notables from around the state and the country. The affair began at ten in the morning and lasted well into the afternoon. Tim still enjoyed seemingly boundless energy and was able to greet all of the guests from his sitting position. The governor's secretary had thoughtfully allowed for rest breaks throughout the day. Tim used these breaks to relieve himself and to switch from the electric cart to his special bike, which many of the guests found quite amusing. Many of the guests brought plaques, or framed certificates, honoring his accomplishments and recognizing his tremendous contributions to the cause of good government. Tim enjoyed a one-hour nap between the reception and dinner, which was a relatively private affair with only the governor and her husband, immediate family and a few close friends. He was home and in bed by eleven o'clock, tired but happy.

Shortly after his 96th birthday Tim suffered a massive stroke, which seemed to affect his entire body. His living will, which he had executed many years earlier, provided that in such eventuality no life support devices be used, that he remain at home, and that only such medical care be given as was needed to relieve pain and to allow him to die with dignity. He died peacefully, surrounded by his family. Tom opened an envelope that Tim had given him several years before for such an occasion. Tom read the note that it contained, stopping frequently to blow his nose and wipe his eyes:

My dearest loved ones:

Please do not grieve for me at my departure from this earth. Rather celebrate the marvelous fact that God, in infinite grace and wisdom gave me all these wonderful years to do the work that I'm convinced was God's will for me. I leave you all in a spirit of utmost love, peace, happiness and total fulfillment. You have caused my cup to run over so that is seems to flood the entire room. God bless you all; I love you beyond all bounds of measurement or description.

Tim

When Tom had finished reading, he gave way to wracking sobs that convulsed his whole body. Many other members of the family were doing likewise. But as they beheld Tim's peaceful countenance and the smile on his face, (some were sure that they had seen his right eye wink in his characteristically mischievous manner) they remembered the admonition in his note: They all joined hands, and Tiffany led them in the chorus of Tim's favorite hymn: *How Great Thou Art:*

Now sings my soul, my savior God to thee:
How great thou art; how great thou art.
Now sings my soul, my savior God to thee:
How great thou art; how great thou art.[2]

---

[2] Copyright Manna Music, Pacific City, OR. Used by permission.

NOTES

NOTES

ORDER FORM

Red Oak Press
Box 10614
White Bear Lake MN 55110-0614

Please send _____ copies of *Almost Immortal* to:

_____

_____

_____

Enclosed is our check for $ _____ ($12.95 per copy including tax, shipping and handling.

(You may also order in any of the following ways):

TEL: 612-426-5704

FAX: 612-426-7039   internet:72317.1206@compuserve.com